Praise for Shona Patel's debut novel *Teatime for the Firefly*

"Patel's remarkable debut effortlessly transports readers back to India on the brink of independence…fans of romantic women's fiction will be enchanted by [the] *Teatime for the Firefly*'s enthralling characters, exotic setting, and evocative writing style."

—*Booklist*, starred review

"The historical detail makes this debut novel a rich reading experience. Those who enjoy historical fiction and portraits of foreign cultures will surely love this book."

—*Library Journal*

"Debut author Patel offers a stunning, panoramic view of a virtually unknown time and place—the colonial British tea plantations of Assam—while bringing them to life through a unique character's perspective.… A lyrical novel that touches on themes both huge and intimate and, like Layla, is so quietly bold that we might miss its strength if we fail to pay attention."

—*Kirkus Book Reviews*

"A captivating tale of discovery, adventure, challenge, romance and triumph over difficult conditions that rings with authenticity."

—*Bookreporter*

"With lyrical prose and exquisite detail, Shona Patel's novel brings to life the rich and rugged landscape of India's tea plantation, harboring a sweet love story at its core."

—Shilpi Somaya Gowda,
New York Times bestselling author of *Secret Daughter*

"Patel takes readers on a vivid tour of 1940s India, exploring the attitudes of the day and the traditions of the tea-growing region of Assam. The story ebbs and flows gracefully, sure to keep readers actively engaged and fervently enticed. Simply stated, *Teatime for the Firefly* is a true treasure."

—*RT Book Reviews*

"A lush, rich love story combined with history and culture…this gem of a novel is a perfect read for anyone looking for a deep, engrossing tale."

—*All About Romance*

Also from Shona Patel and MIRA Books

Teatime for the Firefly

FLAME TREE ROAD

SHONA PATEL

MIRA

Recycling programs for this product may not exist in your area.

ISBN-13: 978-0-7783-1665-7

Flame Tree Road

For questions and comments about the quality of this book, please contact us at CustomerService@Harlequin.com.

www.MIRABooks.com

Printed in U.S.A.

First printing: July 2015
10 9 8 7 6 5 4 3 2 1

For Mothy, my sister,
the key to my authentic self

FLAME TREE ROAD

The traveler has to knock at every alien door
to come to his own,
and one has to wander
through all the outer worlds to reach
the innermost shrine at the end.

Rabindranath Tagore
From *Gitanjali*

Small villages cluster the waterways of East Bengal in India. Seen from above they must appear like berries along a stem, dense or sparse depending on the river traffic that flows through. Crescent-shaped fishing boats skim the waters with threadbare sails that catch the wind with the hollow flap of a heron's wing. Larger boats carry people or cargo: bamboo baskets, coconut and long sticks of sugarcane that curve on their weight down to the water's edge. There are landing ghats along the riverbank with bamboo jetties that stick out over the floating water hyacinth. Here the boats stop and people get on or off and take the meandering paths that lead through the rice fields and bamboo groves into the villages.

Once a week, the big world passes by in the form of a paddleboat steamer bound for important destinations: Narayanganj, Dhaka, Calcutta. It shows up on the horizon, first a tiny speck the size of a peppercorn, and grows to its full girth as it draws closer. The village boats scatter at the sound of its imperious hoot, and small boys in ragged shorts jump and wave at the lascar who moves easily along the deck with the swashbuckling sway of a true seafarer. His long black hair and white tunic whip in the river breeze as the steamer gushes by with a rhythmic swish of its side paddles, leaving the tiny boats bobbing like toothpicks in its wake.

Once a bridal party loaded with pots and garlands caught the powerful wake of the steamer as it passed. It bounced the boat and almost tossed the young bride into the river. The shy young husband instinctively grabbed his wife, drawing her into an awkward but intimate embrace. The veil slipped from the bride's head and he saw for the first time her bright young face and dark, mischievous eyes. He drew back, embarrassed. His male companions broke into wolf whistles and rousing cheers and his bride gave him a slant-eyed smile that made his emotions settle in unexpected places. During the remainder of the journey, their fingertips occasionally met and lingered under the long veil of her red and gold sari.

CHAPTER 1

Sylhet, Bengal, 1871

Shibani was the lighthearted one, with curly eyelashes and slightly crooked teeth, still girlish and carefree for a seventeen-year-old and hardly the demure and collected daughter-in-law of the Roy household she was expected to be. Having grown up with five brothers, she behaved like a tomboy despite her long hair, which she wore, braided and looped, on either side of her head twisted with jasmine and bright red ribbons.

Everything was so strict in her husband's house. The clothes had to be folded a certain way, the *brinjal* cut into perfect half-inch rounds, the potato slivered as thin as matchsticks. Then there were fasting Mondays, temple Tuesdays, vegetarian Thursdays. Mother-in-law was very particular about everything and she could be curt if things were not to her exacting standards. But Father-in-law was soft-hearted; Shibani was the daughter he had always wished for. She brought light into the house, especially after the older daughter-in-law, who walked around with her duck-footed gait and face gloomy as a cauldron's bottom. Perhaps being childless had made her so, but even as a young bride the older daughter-in-law had never smiled. What a contrast to young Shibani, whose veil hardly stayed up on her head, who ate chili tamarind, smacked her lips and broke into giggling fits that sometimes ended in a helpless snort.

During evening prayers Shibani puffed her cheeks and blew the conch horn with more gaiety than piety. She created dramatic sweeping arcs with the *diya* oil lamps, and her ululation was louder and more prolonged than necessary. Mother-in-law paused her chanting to give her a chastising look through half-closed eyes. Father-in-law smothered a smile while her husband, Shamol, looked sheepish, nervous and love struck all at the same time.

Every evening Shibani picked a handful of night jasmine to place in a brass bowl by her bedside so she and her husband could share the sweetness as they lay in the darkness together.

A year after they were married, the first son was born. They named him Biren: Lord of Warriors. Shamol carefully noted the significance of his birth date—29 February 1872—a leap year by the English calendar. Shamol worked for Victoria Jute Mills and owned one of the few English calendars in the village. Just to look at the dated squares made him feel as though he had moved ahead in the world, as the rest of the village followed the Bengali calendar, where the year was only 1279.

In truth, moving ahead in the world had been nipped in

the bud for Shamol Roy. He was studying to be a schoolteacher and was halfway through his degree but had been forced to give up his education and work in a jute mill to support the family. This was after his older brother had been gored by a Brahman bull near the fish market a few years earlier. His brother recovered but made a show of acting incapacitated, as he had lost the will to work after he developed an opium habit—the drug he had used initially to manage the pain. Only Shamol knew about his addiction, but he was too softhearted to complain. He did not tell anyone, not even his own wife, Shibani. He considered himself the lucky one after all. Life had showered on him more than his share of blessings: he had a beautiful wife, a healthy baby boy and a job that allowed him to provide for the family. Every morning Shamol woke to a feeling of immense gratitude. The first thing he did was to stand by the holy basil in the courtyard and lift his folded hands to the rising sun to thank the benevolent universe for his good fortune.

CHAPTER 2

Mother-in-law was mixing chickpea batter for eggplant fritters when she looked out of the kitchen window and saw Shibani and Apu, her friend from next door, gossiping and eating chili tamarind in the sunny courtyard. Baby Biren lay sleeping like a rag doll on the hammock of Shibani's lap. She jiggled her knee and his head rolled all over the place.

"Shibani!" yelled the mother-in-law. "Have you no sense? Do you want your son to have a flat head like the village idiot? Why are you not using the mustard seed pillow I told you to use under the baby's head?"

"*Eh maa!* I forgot," said Shibani, round eyed with innocence, a smudge of chili powder on her chin. She scrambled about looking as if she was going to get up, but as soon as her mother-in-law's back was turned she settled back down again.

"The mustard seed pillow is currently being used to round the cat's head," she said to Apu, giggling as she tickled Biren's cheek. "The cat is going to have a rounder head than this one." Biren opened his mouth and she let him suck on her fingers.

"Aye, careful!" cried Apu. "You have chili powder on your fingers."

Biren's little face puckered and his big black eyes flew open.

"*Eh maa*, look what you did," chided Apu. "You woke the poor thing up!"

"Just look at him smiling," said Shibani. "He's even smacking his lips. Here, pass me the tamarind. Let's give him another lick."

"The things you feed him, really," said Apu reproachfully. She never knew whether to admire Shibani's audacious mothering or to worry about the baby. "Remember the time you made him lick a *batasha*? He was only four months old!"

Shibani laughed, her crooked teeth showing. "You were my coconspirator, don't forget."

The two of them had smuggled *batasha* sugar drops from the prayer room and watched in awe as the baby's tiny pink tongue licked one down to half its size. Of course, the sugar had kept him wide-eyed and kicking all night.

"This child will learn to eat everything and sleep anywhere," said Shibani. "I don't care if he has a flat head, but it will be full of brains and he will be magnificently prepared to conquer the world."

At six months Biren had a perfectly round head full of bobbing curls, the limpid eyes of a baby otter and a calm, solid disposition. He hated being carried and kicked his tiny feet till he was set down, after which he took off crawling with his little bottom wagging. He babbled and cooed constantly and a prolonged silence usually meant trouble. Shibani caught him opening and closing a brass betel nut cutter that could have easily chopped off his tiny toes. Another time he emerged from the ash dump covered with potato peels and eggshells.

"This one will crawl all the way to England if he can," marveled the grandfather. There was a certain sad irony to his words. An Oxford or Cambridge education was, after all, the ultimate dream of many Sylhetis and, being poor, they often did have to scrape and crawl their way to get there. Even with surplus brains and a full merit scholarship, many fell short of the thirty-five-pound second-class sea fare to get to England. Sometimes the whole village pitched in, scraping together rupees and coins to send their brightest and their best into the world, hoping perhaps he would return someday to help those left behind. But most of them never did.

CHAPTER 3

Shibani slipped around to the pumpkin patch near the woodshed behind the house. She cupped her hands over her mouth and called like a rooster across the pond. Soon, there was an answering rooster call back from Apu: a single crow, which meant, *Wait, I am coming.* Shibani smiled and waited.

The two friends no longer saw each other as much as they used to. Both of them had two-year-olds now. Apu's daughter, Ratna, was born three days after Shibani's second son, Nitin, who was four years younger than Biren.

Nitin turned out to be a colicky infant who grew into a fretful toddler. He clung to his mother's legs, stretched out his hands and wanted to be carried all the time. He ate and slept poorly and forced Shibani to reconsider the charms of motherhood.

Shibani shifted her feet. Now, where was that Apu? Out of the corner of her eye, she caught a small movement in the taro patch. Shibani gave a tired sigh. It was that nosy son of hers again. Biren had lately started eavesdropping on their conversations. Apu and Shibani often discussed private matters relating to their mothers-in-law, husbands and what went on in the bedroom. Six-year-old Biren had already picked up on the furtive nature of their conversation. How long this had been going on and how much he had overheard already, Shibani dreaded to know, but this time she was going to teach him a lesson.

Apu ran out of her kitchen, wiping her hands on the end of her sari. Shibani watched her nimble figure jump over backyard scrub and race around the emerald-green pond. *She is still so lithe and supple, like a young sapling*, Shibani thought fondly of her friend, who was a trained Bharatnatyam dancer.

Apu huffed up to the fence and mopped her face with the end of her sari. "I have only five minutes. Ratna will wake up any minute. Quickly, tell me, what?"

Shibani rolled her eyes in the direction of the taro patch and silently mouthed, *Biren. He's listening.* Then she said loudly, "Have you heard the latest news about the small boy in the Tamarind Tree Village? The one whose ears fell off?"

"No, tell me," said Apu, suppressing a smile.

"He had these big-big ears and was always listening to grown-up things. Now I hear his ears have come off. Can you imagine? One day he woke up and his ears were lying on his pillow like two withered rose petals. Now he has only big holes through which bees and ants can get in and make nests in his brain. So tragic, don't you think?"

Apu clicked her tongue. "Terrible, terrible. The poor fellow. What will happen to him, I wonder?" The shuffling in the taro patch grew agitated. Apu began to feel a little sorry for Biren. "Are you sure his ears fell off?" she asked. "I mean, fell *right* off? I heard they *almost* fell off. They had begun to come a little loose but thank God he stopped listening to grown-up things. He had a very narrow escape, I heard."

"I hope so, for his sake." Shibani sighed. "I would feel very sad if I was his mother. Imagine having a son with no ears and a head full of bees and ants."

The taro leaves waved madly to indicate an animal scurrying away.

"Oof!" exploded Shibani. "That fellow is impossible. He listens to everything. Now I hope he will leave us in peace. I can't wait for him to start going to school."

"He starts next week, doesn't he?"

"Yes," said Shibani. They had waited all this time because Shamol wanted him to go to the big school in the Tamarind Tree Village near the jute mill. It was a better school because the jute mill funded it privately. Most of the mill workers' children studied there. "Thank God Biren is a quick learner. He's already far ahead in reading and math because Shamol tutors him every night. That reminds me, did you talk to your mother-in-law about Ruby's tuition?"

Apu sighed. "I asked her. Twice. Both times it was a big no. It is so frustrating. Your suggestion made so much sense. Shamol can easily tutor Ruby along with Biren in the evenings. But Mother-in-law won't have it. She says if you educate a girl nobody will want to marry her."

"What nonsense!" cried Shibani. "We both had private tutors and we got married, didn't we? Thank God our parents were not so narrow-minded. Let me tell you, sister, Shamol especially picked me *because* I was educated. He said he wanted a wife he could talk to, not a timid mouse to follow him around with her head covered."

"At least you two communicate. My husband doesn't talk

at all," grumbled Apu. "He is gone all week and when he comes home I can't get two words out of the man. Living with him is like living with a mango tree, I tell you. He gives shade, he bears fruit, but he does not talk."

"He's a good man," murmured Shibani. "He adores you and the girls. We were both lucky, really, to get good husbands."

"But just see my karma! Thanks to my mother-in-law I am going to end up with two illiterate daughters."

Shibani gave Apu a crooked smile "What is your problem, sister?" she said sweetly. "Your Ruby will marry my Biren and Ratna will marry Nitin. It's all settled between us, remember? We decided that the day they were born. Now, concerning my future daughter-in-law's education—has your husband spoken to his dear mother? He may be able to convince her to change her mind."

Apu shook her head. "Oh, he will never go against his mother's wishes, even if he disagrees with her. It's just as well I have you to talk to, sister. Otherwise, I would have surely gone mad."

Shibani gave a noisy huff. "How can anybody go through life without talking? I don't understand."

A loud wail came from the direction of Apu's house. Apu glanced hastily over her shoulder. "Did you hear that? I better run! Ratna has woken up. I think she is coming down with a fever."

"Can you come and oil my hair for me tomorrow?" Shibani called after her. "You give the best head massage!"

"I'll come after lunch!" Apu yelled back. "Around this time when Ratna takes a nap. Don't forget my chili tamarind."

Later that evening Shibani overheard Biren talking to his grandfather. "Grandfather, can you please check? Are my ears getting a little loose?"

"Why should your ears be getting loose? Did your mother box them for you?"

"No, no, please see, Grandfather. I think they are going to fall off. What should I do?" Biren wailed.

Grandfather twisted Biren's ear and pulled out a cowrie. "Look what I found," he said, handing it to Biren. "Your ears are not loose. They are full of loose *change*."

"Sometimes I think I hear buzzing inside. I think it may be a bee."

"They are buzzing because they are full of money," said Grandfather. "I wish my ears buzzed like yours. I'd be rich."

CHAPTER 4

Every morning, Shamol Roy took the passenger ferry to the jute mill dressed in a spotless dhoti and a starched cotton tunic, with a handkerchief perfumed with rose water folded in his pocket. At sundown he returned, wilted and worn, smelling like the rotting dahlias in a flower vase.

The stench of decomposing organic matter clinging to his clothes and hair came from the raw jute in the mill storage godown where he worked as a bookkeeper along with his assistant. For ten hours a day Shamol Roy sat in the windowless godown of Victoria Jute Mills as sweaty laborers went in and out of the single door to unload the bullock carts lined up outside. The laborers hoisted the heavy bales on the claw hook of the large industrial weighing scale; the assistant squinted at the scales and shouted the weight, which Shamol Roy noted in neat, precise rows on his red tombstone-shaped ledger. The floor of the godown was black and sticky with dirt, and vermin of all kinds—cockroaches, rats, even predatory snakes—squeaked and scrabbled in the dark corners.

A small, tidy man, fastidious by nature, Shamol Roy sat on an elevated wooden pallet with four bowls of water placed under each foot to discourage the creatures from crawling up. There was little he could do, however, about the rotting smell that pervaded the godown; it came from the jute stalks that had been submerged in stagnant water to ret so that the useful fibers could be pulled out and dried for use.

The sun was already deeply slanted in the sky when he caught the ferry home. A sweet river breeze caressed his face and a great flock of cranes crossed overhead to roost in the marsh. The boatman sang a soulful river ballad accompanied by the beat of the oar as it broke the water into pleats of gold. As the boat turned the fork in the river, the flame tree of Momati Ghat first appeared like a gash on the horizon and blazed into full glory as the boat pulled up to shore. The tea shop was closed and a mongoose scrabbled among the broken terra-cotta cups. It streaked off into the undergrowth at the sound of his approaching footfalls.

As Shamol Roy walked down the crooked path to his *basha*, his heart skipped to see his pretty wife dressed in a fresh sari with jasmine twisted in her hair. His two little boys, scrubbed and clean with their hair combed, ran up to meet him. They each held a hand and walked him back to the house. Biren was bright with chatter about his first fallen tooth, which he rattled in a matchbox, while little Nitin toddled along sucking his thumb.

Shibani went inside the house to prepare his tea. She never waited to greet him at close quarters, knowing well that Shamol was embarrassed by his disheveled appearance and the smell that came off his clothes. The boys didn't mind.

For them it was the smell of their father coming home. In the bedroom Shamol Roy found a set of clean home clothes laid out on the bed: a chequered *lungi*, cotton vest and his wooden clogs on the floor.

He picked up the brass lota from the kitchen steps and headed down to the well, where he washed down the smell of the workday from his skin and hair. Only after he had changed into fresh clothes did he begin to feel human again.

He sat in the courtyard, a tumbler of hot tea warming his hands, a happy man.

"So how was school today?" he asked Biren.

"We had English lessons, and the new boy spelled *elephant* starting with an *L*." Biren rolled his eyes as if to say, *What an idiot.*

Shamol Roy feigned ignorance. "Oh, *elephant* is spelled with an *L*, is it not?"

"Baba!"

"Then what is it?"

Biren mouthed *E* and his tongue poked through the gap in his teeth, reminding him of his recent toothless status. He opened the matchbox and looked momentarily stricken when he couldn't see his tooth, but there it was in the far corner.

"So what should I do with the tooth?" he asked his father.

Shamol Roy looked at the sweet, solemn face of his son. "Let me see, now," he said gently, pulling down Biren's bottom lip. "It's the bottom tooth, isn't it? Then you must throw it on the roof of the house and ask a sparrow to get you a new tooth."

"But how can I do that, Baba?" Biren cried. "I'm not tall enough. I can't throw it over the roof. Then the sparrow won't get me a new tooth."

"I'll lift you up. You'll throw it over the roof, don't worry."

Nitin plucked at Shamol's sleeve.

Shamol turned to address him. "Yes, what is it, Nitin *mia*?"

Nitin pulled down his lip to display his own pearly whites.

"Now, let me see. Good, good, you have all your teeth. No need to throw your tooth over the roof. You don't need any new teeth right now."

Shibani emerged from the kitchen with a ripe papaya on a brass plate. Next to it was a dark knife with a white sharpened edge.

"The first papaya of the season," she announced, setting it down. "Perfectly tree ripened. Will you cut it for us, please?"

"But of course, my queen."

The boys settled down to watch. They never got tired of watching their father cut a papaya because he did it with such ceremonial style. Shamol Roy held the papaya in both hands, turned it over and pressed down with his thumbs to examine its ripeness. He then picked up the knife, and with clean easy swipes peeled away the skin in even strips. The bright orange fruit was laid bare and the juice dripped onto the brass tray. Then came the sublime moment, the lengthwise cutting open of the papaya. The boys leaned over and gasped to see the translucent seeds nesting like shiny black pearls in the hollowed chamber. The seed and the fiber were scraped away and discarded on an old newspaper. Nitin amused himself by pressing down on the seeds and making them slip around like tadpoles. The peeled fruit was segmented into long, even slices. The boys were given a slice each and the rest disappeared into the kitchen.

No matter how wilted and crushed Shamol Roy looked at the end of the day in his foul-smelling clothes and the jute fibers trapped in his hair, he became God in the eyes of his sons when he peeled a papaya. They were convinced no other person in the world could peel a papaya as beautifully and expertly as their own father did.

CHAPTER 5

Eight-year-old Samir Deb came to the Tamarind Tree Village School wearing knife-edged pleated shorts, knee-length socks and real leather shoes. If that was not impressive enough, there were two brand-new pencils, one red and the other blue, sticking out in a flashy manner from his shirt pocket.

The pencils were immediately confiscated by the young schoolmaster, who probably fancied them as much as the other boys. Pencils and paper were a luxury, after all, erasers coveted and rare and a mechanical pencil sharpener considered a technological marvel. The boys were given slates and chalks to use in class that remained in the school. To take a piece of chalk home, they had to steal it. No wonder Samir Deb with his new pencils created such a sensation.

Samir said he was born in Calcutta. He also claimed he had been to London—twice—and seen Big Ben. Since nobody in the village school knew who this Big Ben was, the boys nicknamed him Big Beng. Big Frog. He was rather froggy looking, as well, with his flabby face and thin legs; Samir Deb was odd in every way. To begin with, he arrived in a tasseled palanquin carried by four burly men instead of by boat like the other village children. During recess he tried to join the boys in their rough play and pleaded with them in a high girlish voice. When he got pushed, he fell down, scuffed his knees and cried. Sammy's humiliation was complete when he received a sharp rap on his knuckles from the schoolmaster after he was caught passing a wooden top from one boy to another in class. By the time he had climbed into the palanquin and left for home, he was convulsing in hiccupping sobs, and his knee-length socks had collapsed around his ankles.

The next day there was pandemonium in school. A brood of belligerent women in shiny saris and oversize nose rings rushed into the schoolmaster's tiny office and cornered him against the wall.

"Why did you beat him so?" cried a pitcher-shaped woman with gold bracelets up to her elbow. She had a pale froggy face that looked like Samir's, and was most likely his mother. "The poor child is completely traumatized. He cried all night. He would not eat, he would not sleep. Today he was terrified of coming to school."

"My goodness." The schoolmaster stared from one angry face to the other. "I hardly beat him at all. I just gave him a small tap on his knuckles because he was misbehaving in class. How else is the child going to learn a lesson?"

"You *hit* him with a stick." The woman pointed to Samir's knees, which looked ghastly thanks to the red Mercurochrome that had been applied to the scrape. “Look at his knees. The poor child can hardly walk.”

“I did nothing to his knees, excuse me,” said the schoolmaster indignantly.

“In our family we believe in kindness and love,” said a gray-haired woman who was probably Samir’s grandmother. She glared at the young schoolmaster severely. “You had no business to beat the child.”

“I repeat, I did not beat the child,” said the schoolmaster in a tired voice.

“But you just admitted you took a ruler to his hands. I want to make sure this never happens again,” said the pitcher-shaped mother in a stern voice. “This darling boy has never heard a harsh word in his life. It is unthinkable that anybody should beat and punish him.”

“So how do you suppose he is going to learn what is right from wrong?” demanded the schoolmaster.

“He will learn by watching others,” said the grandmother. “By following their example. May I please make a suggestion?”

“Go ahead,” said the schoolmaster in a resigned voice. Through a gap in the wall of female forms he spied the curious faces of his students looking in through the window. He clapped his hands abruptly to disperse them, and Samir’s mother, interpreting his action as a sign of mockery, flew into a sudden rage.

“Do you know who my husband is?” she shrieked. “He is Dhiren Deb. My husband is supplier of all the goods in the Victoria Jute Mills co-op store. My husband will ask the jute mill owners to stop all funding to this school if you do not pay attention, do you understand?”

“I am listening,” said the schoolmaster, a little taken aback.

"All we are suggesting," the grandmother said in a soothing voice, "is the next time Samir needs to be disciplined, just take the ruler and beat the child next to him. If Samir sees the other child suffering, he will be frightened and behave himself."

The schoolmaster was incredulous. "Beat some other innocent child who has not done anything wrong instead of the real culprit? How does that even make any sense?"

"Just try it," said the granny, nodding wisely. "We know it works. Samir gets very frightened when he sees somebody else being punished. At home we just beat the servant boy and Samir immediately behaves himself. Now, don't get us wrong. We want the child to be disciplined and grow up to be a fine boy. Just don't beat our little darling is all we are saying."

Samir quickly figured out some friendships were negotiable. He could join in a game by giving the leader a pencil. But most games involved a lot of push and shove, and he was deathly afraid of getting hurt, so he just stood on the sidelines and cheered the players on in his high girlish voice. Sometimes he was generous for no reason at all. He played treasure hunt and left coveted items in secret places so that they could be "stolen." He even left his leather shoes under the tamarind tree and watched secretly to see who would steal them.

The one person Sammy wanted most to be friends with was the brilliant and smooth-talking Biren Roy. But Biren Roy avoided him. He and his three friends walked around with their hands in their pockets avoiding the riffraff. In class, Biren Roy asked such intelligent questions that he made the schoolmaster nervous.

Samir learned that Biren Roy lived in another village and went home every day in a small boat with a one-eyed boatman. He also came to grudgingly accept that there was no hope in the world of ever calling him a friend.

CHAPTER 6

Some days after school, Biren loitered at the tea shop on Momati Ghat. It would be around closing time in the early afternoon with a few fishermen smoking their last bidis. Sold as singles in the tea shop, the bidis were lit with a slow-burning coir rope hung from a bamboo pole. The fishermen who idled at the tea shop were the ones who had returned without a sizable catch. There was no fish to spoil in their baskets and no need to rush to the market. Those were also the ones who told the tallest stories.

Kanai, the one-eyed fisherman, waggled his foot and sucked the smoke from his bidi through a closed fist.

"I saw the *petni* again last night," he said, narrowing his single eye.

"Saw it or *heard* it?" asked Biren. He had heard fearful stories from the fisherman about the faceless ghost of Momati Ghat with backward-facing feet who wailed in the voice of a child.

Kanai glared at him. "I saw it. I may have one eye but I am not blind."

"What did the *petni* look like?" Biren asked.

"It was white," said Kanai. "Completely white from head to toe."

"Was it a boy or a girl?"

"What kind of question is that? A *petni* is a *petni*. It is neither a boy nor a girl."

"If you are talking about the creature that is hanging around the ghat late at night, that is no *petni*, Kanai," said the ancient fisherman they called Dadu. Grandfather. He had a foamy white beard and the skin on his face was cracked and creased like river mud. "That is one of the cursed ones."

"Who is cursed?" asked Biren. He tapped a dimple in the soft ground with a twig and watched a tiny sand beetle pop out and take a swipe before sliding back into a whirlpool of sand.

"Widows," said the old fisherman. "They are the most wretched creatures on earth. A widow is even more dangerous than a *petni* because it can appear in the daytime and spit on the happiness of others."

Biren shuddered. "I hope I never see one," he said.

"You've seen them, *mia*. They are everywhere," said Kanai. "There's one that begs under the banyan tree near the temple. Surely you've seen that one?"

"Oh, *that* one." Biren sighed with relief. "That is only Charulata. She is harmless. We talk to her all the time. Baba said she is a poor woman whose husband died when she was only thirteen. A mango tree fell and cut her husband in half, poor thing."

Kanai spit on the ground. "She must be badly cursed, then."

"That is not true," retorted Biren indignantly. He flung

his stick in a wide arc across the riverbed. "My *baba* says only ignorant people believe in curses and bad luck."

"Just listen to this pooty fish and his big-big talk!" scoffed a diminutive fisherman nicknamed Chickpea.

"Your father is a good man, *mia*, but too much education is his undoing," said Dadu, the old fisherman. "Education leads a man astray. He becomes bewildered and loses touch with his roots."

Kanai took a deep pull of his bidi and waggled his foot. "Because your father works with the *belaytis* in the jute mill he has too much big-big ideas." He turned to the others. "Do you know his father tried to tell me the earth is round? I told him I have rowed all the rivers, but I haven't fallen off the edge yet, have I?"

The others laughed.

Of course the earth is round, Biren thought indignantly. But he did not know how to convince the fishermen.

Tilok, the tea shop man, stuck his head out of the shack and banged a spoon on his brass kettle. "Who wants more tea?" he shouted. "Today is the last day for free tea! No more free tea from tomorrow. Tomorrow you pay."

Biren looked puzzled. "Why is he giving free tea?"

"Don't you know?" said Chickpea. "Tilok had twin baby boys yesterday. He should be giving everybody free tea for *two* weeks." He cupped his hand and yelled, "Do you hear that, Tilok? We demand free tea for two weeks."

"Trying to make me a pauper, are you?" Tilok laughed. He burst into song as he poured the tea in thin frothing streams into a line of terra-cotta cups.

"Just listen to him—he is such a happy man." Kanai chuckled. "Now, if he had twin daughters, he would be singing a dirge."

Biren pushed his toe into the sand, thinking. His mother envied Apu for having girls. She made cloth dolls for Ruby and Ratna. She dressed baby Ratna in tiny saris and put flowers in her hair. "I wish I had a little girl," she lamented to Apu. What puzzled him was Apu wanted boys and Shibani wanted girls. They each wanted what the other had. The fishermen on the other hand were unanimously in favor of boys. Daughters were viewed as a curse, it seemed.

Kanai flicked the butt of his bidi into the sand and sighed. "I go to the temple every morning to pray my wife has a son this time."

"I have three daughters!" grumbled Dadu. "I had to sell my cow to get the last one married off. Marrying off daughters will pick you clean, like a crow to a fishbone. I would be in the poorhouse if my son had not brought in a dowry. By God's mercy, all four children are married and settled now."

Biren shaded his eyes toward the far horizon and jumped to his feet. "Oh, look!" he cried. "The jute steamer is coming!"

As so it was. A black dot had just popped up on the horizon. Its square form distinguished it as a flatbed river barge designed to carry bales of jute, tea chests and other cargo.

Biren dusted off his shorts and took off flying down the crooked path toward the riverbank. A small brown mongrel with a curled-up tail chased after him, yipping excitedly.

As the steamer drew closer, Biren saw a pink-faced Englishman sitting on a chair bolted to the deck. The man had one knee crossed over the other and was smoking a curved pipe, looking as if he was relaxing in his own living room. He surveyed the tumbled countryside, the cracked and pitted riverbank and meek-eyed cows huddled in slices of shade. When the man turned his head, he caught sight of the magnificent flame tree by the tea shop and stood up to get a better view. He failed to notice the small boy who waved at him from the riverbank. The steamer passed by smoothly, leaving the water hyacinths swirling in its wake.

Kanai spat on the ground. "Go, go, *mia*, run, run, run," he muttered. "Chase after the *belayti*, wave to him, bow to him, lick his shoes. He will never acknowledge you. To him you do not even exist. The sooner you get that into your foolish head, the better it will be for you."

CHAPTER 7

The river breeze teased Shamol Roy awake one night. He propped up on his elbow to gaze tenderly at his sleeping wife. Shibani lay on her side, her hands tucked under her cheek. Her lips were parted, and in the yellow light of the moon her skin glowed a satiny gold. Shamol traced her nose and lips with his finger.

"Precious pearl, sweet beloved, queen of my heart," he murmured in her ear. "Do you hear the river calling?"

Shibani's eyes fluttered open. Her smile gleamed in the dark. "Oh," she gasped. "Shall we go?"

"If you wish, my beloved."

They tiptoed out of the *basha* in their old cotton night-clothes and house slippers. The front door closed softly behind them and they ran giggling down the road, holding hands. Free from the cares of parenthood and family, they were like children again.

Shamol and Shibani had little opportunity to demonstrate their affections for each other during the day. Trapped in their roles of husband and wife, father and mother, son and daughter-in-law, a certain decorum was expected of them. Even in their early married days, and despite their yearning, intimacy had not come easy. The door to their bedroom had to be left ajar to allow Grandfather access to the bathroom, and nature called often and at random for the old man. Shamol and Shibani took to slipping out of the house and going down to the river, where under the flame tree, and calmed by the sound of water, they'd discovered each other for the first time.

The river sky floated with a thousand stars and a lemony moon sailed in their midst. Sirius, the Dog Star, the brightest of them all, was a twinkling jewel on Orion's belt. People whispered the Dog Star had mysterious occult powers. It caused men to weaken and women to become aroused, they said.

Shamol took Shibani's face in his hands and kissed her until every star was pulled down from the sky. When he looked into her eyes they sparkled brighter than the heavens.

He led her to the flame tree and drew her down beside him. They leaned against the trunk, their arms around each other, and looked up at the sky.

"Oh, I forgot," said Shamol. He fumbled in his kurta pocket and drew out a small paper-wrapped object. He pushed it into her hand. "I have something for you."

"What is it?"

"Open it. It's butterscotch toffee from Scotland. Willis Duff, the new engineer at the jute mill, gave it to me."

Shibani unwrapped the toffee and took a tiny bite. "My, it is quite delicious. Here, try a bit."

"No, no, you eat it. I only had one so I kept it for you. Every time I get something, I give it to the boys. Sometimes I feel bad—I never bring anything for you."

She squeezed his hand. "You bring me fresh jasmine garlands wrapped with your heart. What more can a girl ask for?"

The caressing tone of her voice made his nerves tingle.

Overcome by bashfulness, he squinted at the glittering sky. "Look, there's Sirius, the Dog Star. Do you see it?"

"It's the brightest star in the sky," murmured Shibani. "See how it sparkles. Maybe it's winking."

"Everything pales beside you, my darling."

Shamol pushed Shibani's hair aside to kiss the nape of her neck. "Do you remember our first time?" he said softly. His tongue tasted the salt of her skin. "Here, under this tree?"

Shibani leaned her cheek against his hand. Of course she remembered, and wasn't Biren the result? Anything could happen on a night when the stars begged to be plucked from the sky.

The same thought must have crossed Shamol's mind. "Little wonder our Biren has a keen interest in astronomy," he said. "He was excited to learn that Sirius is used by mariners to navigate the Pacific. When I told him Sirius has a small companion star known as the 'pup,' Biren said, 'That's like me and Nitin. I am Sirius and Nitin is the pup. I will show him the way.' Then he asked me completely out of the blue, 'Is Sirius really very serious, Baba? Does he not talk very much?'"

Shibani erupted in a bubble of laughter. "He says the funniest things, really!"

"When I explained Sirius was named after the Egyptian god and has nothing to do with the English word, he listened carefully. He has an excellent memory, our son—he remembers everything." He sighed and was silent. Somewhere on the riverbank a night bird called. "You know, Shibani, if I had my way, I would send Biren to an English school. I have always believed a correct English education is the passport to the bigger world. The bigger world is where our sons belong."

"The English school must be very expensive, don't you think?" Shibani asked.

"Not necessarily. Some English missionary schools are free. It is not easy to get admission, that's all. I heard our jute mill is affiliated with a famous institution in Calcutta."

"Maybe you should talk to Owen McIntosh about it. Your boss likes you. There's no harm in asking him, is there?"

"That's true," Shamol agreed. "Tell me, beloved, would you feel very sad if the boys were sent away to a boarding school?"

Shibani shook her head. "I only want the best for them."

"I do, too." Shamol sighed. "But even if the boys got admission, my biggest hurdle will be to convince my family. They all firmly believe the only agenda of missionary schools is to convert Indian students to Christianity by offering them free education."

They were silent, each with their own thoughts, for a while.

On the far horizon, tiny pinpricks of light appeared on the river. The melancholy strains of the Bhatiyali fisherman's song slipped in and out of the breeze.

"Look!" Shibani cried, sitting up. "It's the otter fishermen!"

They watched as the night fishermen from the mangrove village floated by in their bamboo houseboats. The glow of their lamps threw a broken sparkle on the water, and the dark, shiny heads of their trained otters bobbed up and down, their wet, gleaming forms tumbling in the boat's wake. The otters herded the fish into the waiting nets and when the net was lifted into the boat it was full of flashing silver.

"How clever the fishermen are, don't you think?" mused Shibani. "They just float along singing songs and the otters do all the hard work for them."

"It is not as simple as it looks, beloved," said Shamol. "It has taken generations to perfect this technique. Otter fishing is an ancient tradition passed down from father to son. The otters are bred in captivity. They would never survive in the wild. It is a symbiotic relationship between man and beast. But all these old traditions are dying out, aren't they? More and more fishermen leave the village to find work in the city. Soon the memory of the otter fisherman will remain only in song. Then that, too, will be forgotten." He got to his feet and held out his hand to Shibani to help her up. "Come, my queen, we must go back."

They walked back to the *basha*, hand in hand, fingers entwined like teenagers.

"There is so much I wish for our two boys," said Shamol. "I want them to be curious and have faith in their own ideas. I want them to know the wonder of books but also learn from the river and the sky."

Shibani hugged his arm tightly. "The most important thing is they have you for their father," she said in her honeyed voice. "You have given them everything. Now it's up to them."

CHAPTER 8

Biren looked forward to Tuesday all week. It was market day—the only day he had time alone with Father. Since Nitin had come along, Biren was forced to share Shamol with his brother. Nitin demanded constant attention. If Father stood up, Nitin wanted to be carried. If Father sat down, Nitin climbed onto his lap. Nitin interrupted important conversations by touching Shamol's cheek and, once having got his father's attention, he smiled his foolish smile and went back to sucking his thumb. Father judiciously divided his time equally among family members, the same way he divided a papaya. Mother had an unfair advantage because she and Father shared the same bed and they could talk all night long. The last sound Biren heard as he drifted off to sleep was their whispered conversation.

Thank God for Tuesday. It made up for the shortfalls of the week. The fish market was too far for Nitin to walk, which was just as well, although leaving the house in his presence normally provoked a monstrous howl. The only option was to slip out undetected in the wee hours, a conspiracy that made Biren feel grown up and in league with the adults.

The bamboo grove was still dark and hushed as father and son made their way to the fish market. Shamol carried his umbrella looped over his arm and Biren skipped along swinging two empty jute bags, one in each hand.

"You don't need an umbrella today, Baba," Biren chirped. "Look—" he swung his bag in a big joyful arc at the sky "—there is not a single cloud in the sky."

"I know, *mia*," Shamol replied. "My umbrella is broken. I am taking it to the market to be repaired. I don't want to be caught without it when the rains come."

The road opened out to an expanse of the river-sky, above which a feeble sun struggled to rise. The tea shop was still shuttered. Underneath the flame tree a *baul* minstrel sat cross-legged on a carpet of fallen blossoms, lost in his meditation. In his bright orange robe, he looked like a fallen petal himself.

A herd of cows bumped and shuffled across the riverbed toward the grazing ground. They were rounded up by a ragged lad with a neem toothpick stuck between his teeth.

At the ghat, the river ferry had just pulled up to disgorge a crowd of villagers. Vendors with earthen pots on bamboo poles slung across their shoulders pushed past women with large baskets on their heads and tiny babies on their backs. They skirted around an old man who shuffled slowly, dragging a monstrous elephant-size foot, the skin over it knobbed and lumpy like a custard apple.

Biren was about to swivel around to take another look

when Shamol cleared his throat. "There's no need to stare at him, *mia*," he said softly.

"What wrong with his foot, Baba?" Biren asked, trotting to keep up with his father. "Why is it *so* big?"

"The man has elephantiasis, *mia*, as a result of an unfortunate disease known as filariasis. It is spread by a mosquito."

Biren looked at a puffed-up welt on his upper arm with alarm.

"Oh, Baba, I have a mosquito bite!"

Shamol glanced out of the corner of his eye and suppressed a smile. "Don't worry, *mia*, you won't get elephantiasis."

"How do you know, Baba?" Biren cried. He scratched the bite gingerly. It made the itch worse. His leg was also beginning to feel unusually heavy.

"Because elephantiasis is a rare disease. That is not to say it cannot happen to us. After all, it takes but a small misfortune, the size of a mosquito bite, to change someone's life, doesn't it? You must remember to be compassionate, *mia*, and to try to help others less fortunate than yourself."

"Like poor Charudi, who lives under the banyan tree?"

"Yes, like Charudi. Remind me to buy some bananas for her at the market. We can stop by the temple and see her on our way home."

While Father was getting the *hilsa* fish weighed and cleaned, Biren wandered over to the chicken man's stall to check on his favorite rooster. Week after week, the black rooster never got sold. The chicken man said it was a special-occasion bird, too big and too expensive for most people to afford. Biren was secretly thankful, because he had grown rather attached to the rooster. He admired the bird as it strutted around its wire cage cocky and bright eyed. It had shiny blue-black feathers and a bright red comb and wattles—the exact same shade of vermillion his mother wore in the part of her hair.

But today the rooster's cage was empty. In the next cage, six miserable hens with soiled feathers were crammed together looking half-dead.

"What happened to the black rooster?" Biren cried, pointing to the empty cage.

The chicken man made a chop-chop gesture with the edge of his palm. "Sold!" He waggled his toes and grinned widely with *paan*-stained teeth. "Goddess Laxmi smiled on me today. Tilok, the tea shop man, purchased the rooster to celebrate the birth of his twin boys."

Biren's eyes wandered over to the pile of shiny blue-black feathers and freshly gutted entrails cast to one side. A mangy pariah dog slunk around trying to take a lick. He suddenly felt nauseated.

"I have to go," he said hastily, and ran back to his father.

Shamol flipped through his notebook. "I think we have everything," he said. "Let me see—fish, vegetables, joss sticks, areca nut and betel leaves for your grandmother, soap nut and *shikakai* for your mother." He looked up. "Is the flower man here? Oh, there he is. Let's buy a fresh jasmine garland for your mother. She'll like that."

"And bananas for Charudi?" Biren reminded him.

"Oh, that's right, bananas for Charudi," said Shamol. "Also, there is something else I know I am forgetting."

"Your umbrella, Baba," Biren reminded him. He looked toward the umbrella man's stall, but it was empty. "The man is not there."

"Oh, that's all right," said Shamol, picking up his bags, "we'll get the umbrella next week. Hopefully it won't rain before then."

They made their way out of the fish market and walked toward the temple. Shamol carried both jute bags to balance the weight on either side. Leafy mustard greens and bottle gourds protruded over the top of one. There was fish in the other. Biren walked beside him carrying a bunch of bananas and a large brown coconut.

Charudi—whose full name was Charulata—lived under the banyan tree by the river just outside the village temple. A hollow inside the banyan tree trunk served as her storage compartment. Here she kept a small brass pot and books wrapped in a red cotton towel. Charulata shared the tree with a family of monkeys. The monkeys seemed to have accepted her as one of their own because they never tampered with her belongings and left her in peace. They didn't afford the same respect to the temple devotees, however. Monkeys ran off with slippers, snatched fruits out of hands, gnashed their teeth and made babies howl. The animals were a nuisance but enjoyed the sanctity of the temple, thanks to Hanuman, the Hindu monkey god.

As Shamol and Biren neared the temple, they saw Charulata sitting under the tree, gazing out at the river and fingering her prayer beads. She was a tiny bright-eyed woman who wore a piece of white cloth, darned and patched in several places, but clean. Her hair, cropped close to her head, was a snowy fizz. Destitute since her teenage years, Charulata had taught herself to read and write Sanskrit, a language far more difficult than Bengali.

"She is even more learned than the temple priest," Shamol

once remarked. He had great admiration for Charulata. "She has studied all the great scriptures but the poor woman can never enter the temple."

"Why cannot she enter the temple?" asked Biren, puzzled.

"Because Charulata is a widow, *mia*, and Hindu widows are not allowed inside holy places. It is a cruel and meaningless custom of our society since ancient times. The poor woman is banned for no fault of her own. But Charulata does not need to go to any temple because she knows that God is hidden in every human soul."

Charulata looked up and saw them. She motioned them over with a smile and lifted her hand to caress Biren's cheek. The skin on her fingers was rough but her touch was tender.

"This boy gets more handsome every day," she said softly.

Biren gave her the bananas.

"Bless you, dear child," she said. "Wait, I also have something for you." She turned around and, reaching inside the tree hollow, pulled out a flat object wrapped in newspaper. She handed it to Biren.

"What is it?" he asked curiously, setting the coconut down to accept it. He turned the packet over in his hands.

"A gift." Charulata looked at him with shining eyes. "Open it and you will see. I made it specially for you."

"How is your cough, Charulata?" Shamol asked, setting down his heavy bags. He took out a white handkerchief to mop his brow.

"Much better, much better," chirped Charulata. "My nephew, you know the one in Dhaka Medical College, gave me a herbal tonic. But more important he gave me a book of the Brahma sutras. I don't know if it was the book or the medicine that cured me."

"Baba, look!" cried Biren. He held up a slim oblong-shaped palm bark with beautiful patterning in white. He turned to Charulata, incredulous. "Did you make this?" The paisley designs were painted with delicate strokes and closely woven together like the border of an embroidered sari.

"Why, yes." Charulata laughed.

"But how?" asked Biren wonderingly. He fingered the bumpy pattern.

Charulata dismissed it with a wave. "Oh, it's just a design painted with a duck feather, some rice flour and gum arabic. You can use it as a bookmark if you like. Do you like it, *mia*?"

"It's beautiful," said Biren reverentially. "Very, very beautiful. I will use this bookmark for my most important book."

"Ah, that would be the Book of Life, *mia*. The one that's written by the universe. My book is nearing its end but yours has just begun."

Biren studied the design closely. "I can see a *B* entwined in the pattern. And here, another letter. Oh, I see my name!" He looked at his father with shining eyes. "Look, Baba, it's my name hidden in the design. It's like a puzzle."

"Yes, I see that," agreed Shamol. "That is indeed clever."

"I paint these palm leaf designs with the names of different gods hidden in the pattern. The devotees like that. The priest sells them in the temple and he gives me two paisa for each. But more than the money, painting the patterns feels like a kind of meditation to me. Now I am thinking of doing some colored designs using vegetable dyes. Turmeric, indigo, vermillion." She gave a mischievous laugh. "I may not be allowed to wear colors, but God gives me permission to paint in any hue I choose."

"You are an inspiration to me, Charudi," said Shamol. "They can take everything away from you but you still have all the essential things that feed the spirit and keep you joyful. I have much to learn from you." He picked up his bags. "I could spend all day talking to you, but we must rush home before our fish spoils. Come, Biren, we must go."

"Until next time, then," said Charulata. "God bless you both and thank you for the bananas."

"And thank you for the artistic gift," Biren said, wrapping up the palm bark in the newspaper. "I will put it on my study desk and look at it every day."

"I would keep it a secret," said Shamol when they were out of earshot. "Don't tell your grandmother Charudi gave you the bookmark. Otherwise, she will make you throw it away."

Biren was indignant. "I will never throw it away. It is a special gift with my name written on it. Why should I throw it away?"

"Then, don't tell Granny because she'll say it's bad luck to accept something from a widow's hand. That is, of course, not at all true."

They walked across the riverbed toward the bamboo grove and the road leading to the *basha.*

"Do you know it was Charudi who gave you your name?" said Shamol suddenly.

Biren stopped walking and looked at his father in surprise. "I thought it was Grandfather who named me Biren."

"That is what we led your grandmother to believe." Shamol chuckled. "Left to your grandmother you would have been named Bikramaditya. Your mother and I did not care for that name. Your mother, especially, was vehemently opposed to it so we had to do something. The Sanskrit letter associated with your lunar birth sign is *B*, so your name had to begin with *B*. We managed to convince your grandmother to name you Biren and we made Grandfather believe it was his idea. A child's name dictates his fate in life after all. Nobody in our family, besides your mother and me, know it was actually Charudi who suggested your name. You are the third person now to know this but you must keep it a secret for the reasons I explained to you earlier."

Biren absorbed this in silence. "My name means a soldier, does it not, Father?"

"*Biren* means *warrior.* There is a difference, *mia*. A soldier follows the orders of others. A warrior follows his own path. Sometimes a warrior has to act alone. You, Biren, are the Lord of Warriors. Never forget that."

"And Nitin? What does *Nitin* mean?"

"Nitin means Master of the Right Path."

"Did Charudi give Nitin his name, as well?"

"No, this time it really was your Grandfather's suggestion, but your mother and I both liked the name Nitin, so it worked out all right."

Biren skipped along and repeated softly, "Lord of Warriors and Master of the Right Path." More loudly, he said, "I am glad I am the warrior, Baba. One day I will become a lawyer and I will fight for Charudi so she can enter the temple."

"Oh, I don't think she's missing much," said Shamol drily. "I am not even sure she cares to enter the temple. She has found what she needs under the banyan tree."

"I will still fight for her. I think she wants me to. That is why she secretly wrote my name and pretended it was only a design."

"Just keep it to yourself, *mia*. Do you know the wise sages believe there is a great power in secrecy? If you talk loosely about your intentions this power will disappear. But if you keep your good intentions a secret, the universe will conspire to make it happen. This is one of the great spiritual truths, *mia*. Wise people never talk about their intentions. They let their actions speak for them."

CHAPTER 9

It was Shamol's day off. He sat on the kitchen steps in his pajamas with Nitin half dozing on his lap, a cup of tea and a sugared toast beside him. Shamol watched Biren play marbles in the courtyard. His aim was excellent; he rarely missed. But as soon as one marble clicked against the other, a tiger-striped calico cat hiding behind the holy basil shot out to pounce on the marble, spoiling Biren's game.

Biren stamped his foot. "Shoo!" he said sternly to the cat. He grabbed the marble out of its paws and placed it back on the spot where it had rolled. "The cat is not letting me play, Baba," he complained to Shamol.

Shamol took a sip of his tea. "Perhaps he wants to play, too."

"I want to play, too," said Nitin, taking his thumb out of his mouth. He clambered off Shamol's lap.

"Now you have two cats to play with you," said Shamol, smiling.

Biren sighed.

"Aye, Khoka!" Granny called to Shamol from the kitchen window. Granny always called Father by his boyhood name every time she wanted something done. "Plant the marigold seedlings in the pots for me, will you? I want to grow the flowers for my *puja*."

"Yes, Mother," Shamol called back. "I am just finishing my tea."

Biren glared indignantly at the retreating form of his grandmother. *Khoka, do this, Khoka, do that.* Never a moment of peace for poor Father. No time to even enjoy his cup of tea!

Shamol whistled a boatman's song and went into the kitchen to return his cup. He must have said something funny because Mother replied with a laugh—the girlish laugh she reserved especially for him. His parents had their own little secrets, Biren suspected. Where did they run off to in the middle of the night? And why was there sand on their bed in the morning?

Shamol emerged from the kitchen. "Is anybody going to help me plant the marigolds?" he asked.

"I want to play with marbles," said Nitin. "Dada, play marbles with me."

"You play with the cat," said Biren in an imperious voice.

"I don't want to play with the cat," Nitin pouted.

"Come along, then, wear your slippers," said Shamol, heading toward the woodshed. The two boys ran to catch up with him.

Shamol dug up the rich black soil, Biren broke up the

clumps and placed them in the terra-cotta pot and Nitin sat on his haunches and handed Biren the seedlings one by one.

"Careful, *mia*, you are pulling them up too roughly," Shamol said. He took the seedling from Nitin's hand and pointed to the roots. "See these small white hairs? If you break them, the plant will die. Use a stick and pull out the seedling very gently, like this, see?"

"Father, if you could be a tree—any tree in the world—what tree would you be?" Biren asked suddenly.

Shamol leaned on the worn-out handle of the shovel. "What tree would I like to be, now? What an interesting question. I will have to think about it."

He went back to digging, then stopped. "I know what tree I want to be. I want to be a bamboo, although technically it is not a tree. It belongs to the grass family. Does that count?"

Biren frowned. "I suppose so." He was disappointed in his father's choice. He had expected him to pick something more significant like, say, a mango tree or a banyan, even a papaya tree. But *bamboo*? Father must be joking.

"But why bamboo, Father? It's so…so ordinary."

"Your father is an ordinary man, son. But why a bamboo, I will tell you. A bamboo is strong and resilient. It has many uses. You can build a house with it, you can make a raft and float down a river with it. You can eat it as a shoot, and drink out of it as a cup. Most important, the bamboo is hollow and empty inside. If a person can be hollow and empty like the bamboo, all the goodness and wisdom of the universe will flow through him."

Biren was still not impressed. He did not want to be a bamboo. He saw himself as a magnificent and glorious flame tree, admired by all from near and far. He told his father that.

"The flame tree is an inspiring tree," Shamol conceded.

"It gives cooling shade and when it blooms it brings joy to all. But also know this. When the flame tree sheds, it loses everything. You see this in life, *mia*. Sometimes a person has to lose everything to renew and bloom again."

Biren twirled a marigold seedling between his fingers. "Why is there only one flame tree, Baba? I have not seen any other flame trees around here."

"Because it is an unusual tree for these parts. The natural habitat of the flame tree is in tiger country, hundreds of miles away."

Shamol smiled at Nitin, who was frowning at the ground. "So what do you think, Nitin? What tree would you like to be? Dada wants to be a flame tree and I want to be a bamboo."

"I…I…" Nitin faltered. He looked distressed, like he had been given a difficult piece of homework.

"Don't worry," Shamol said kindly. "You don't have to be a tree. You can be anything you want."

"I want to be an ant tree!" Nitin blurted out.

Shamol twitched his lips. "An ant tree!" he repeated. He leaned on his shovel and studied the round, earnest face of his younger son. "How marvelous! But tell me, *mia*, is it a tree where ants live or a tree that grows ants? I am curious to know."

Nitin brightened. "An ant tree is a tree that grows ants and when…when…the ants get ripe they all fall down… and…when they all fall down they all play together and go to school!"

"Is that so?" Shamol's eyes widened. "Be sure to warn me, *mia*, if you ever see an ant tree. I would be very much afraid to walk under one, with all the ripe ants falling on my head."

Biren rolled his eyes at their silly talk. He tried to give

Shamol a knowing look to say, *Nitin is such a baby*, but Shamol's face was deadpan as he struck his shovel into the ground and continued to dig.

CHAPTER 10

The schoolmaster told Biren to see him in his office. When Biren stood in front of his desk, he handed the boy a folded note.

"Give this to your father," he said, without looking up. "And don't forget to bring back the answer tomorrow."

Biren looked at the schoolmaster nervously. This was the first time he had written a note to his father—for that matter, to *anybody's* father. Disciplinary measures were taken care of in school with no interference from parents, except, of course, in Samir's case. Even that was most unusual. Most parents could not read or write anyway. Biren's father, who had attended college in Dhaka, was the most educated man in the village, even more educated than the schoolmaster himself. To send Biren home with a handwritten note for his father and expect an answer the following day was all very odd. Biren wondered what the note was about.

"Did I do something wrong, Mastermoshai?" he said anxiously. "Please do not report me to my father."

The weasel-faced schoolmaster looked mildly amused. "Why, *mia*? Do you have something to confess?"

Biren shook his head. He looked so worried the schoolmaster felt sorry for him.

"This is another matter," he said shortly. "It has nothing to do with you. Run along now and remember to bring back the answer from your father tomorrow. This is urgent."

Biren hopped from one foot to the other as he waited for Father to come home. He desperately wanted to go and meet his boat at the riverbank, but it was too far for Nitin to walk, so Biren had to be content to wait at their usual place down the road. Father was running late. Biren walked up and down while Nitin squatted by the side of the road and pushed ants around with a stick.

"One ant has died, Dada," Nitin lamented with a woebegone face. "Shall we bury it?" Biren ignored him and gave a small shout when he saw his father turn the corner of the bamboo grove. Now he could see why his father was running late. Shamol held a big bunch of pink and white lilies, the stems wrapped in the pages of an old ledger and tied with a piece of jute string.

"A present for your lovely mother," Shamol said. "I asked the boatman to stop at the backwaters today. Every day I pass these beautiful lilies and I always forget to bring a small knife to cut the stems. Today I made the boatman do a detour and take me there."

Biren was not interested in the lilies. "Baba, Mastermoshai sent an urgent note for you. Here it is." Biren waved the note under his father's nose. "He said you must read it at once. He needs an answer by tomorrow."

Shamol glanced briefly at the note. "I see," he said vaguely. "Hold on to it. I will read it after my tea."

Biren pulled at his shirtsleeve. "But this is most urgent, Baba. You have to read it now!"

Shamol gave him an amused look. "Is anything going to change between now and when I take my tea? I don't think so. In any case your mastermoshai needs the answer by tomorrow. So what's the hurry?" He stopped and turned to see Nitin trying to catch up. "Why have you left your brother behind? Why are his hands so dirty? Hold him by the hand. I can't because of these flowers."

Biren gave a noisy sigh, ran back and pulled Nitin by the hand.

"So what do you think the note is about?" he asked, sounding elaborately casual. He jerked Nitin's hand to hurry him along but it only made him stumble. Nitin gave an indignant howl.

"Careful," reprimanded his father. He lifted the lilies to his nose and inhaled deeply. "Smell these. They are heavenly."

"I want to smell!" cried little Nitin.

Shamol bent down and held the lilies under Nitin's nose. He grinned when Nitin closed his eyes, gave a dreamy sigh and went "aah" in a fitting imitation of Shibani.

Biren twisted a toe in the dirt. There was little he could do to hurry his father and Nitin along. He fingered the note in his pocket and the back of his neck prickled with impatience.

Finally on reaching home, the lily blossoms settled in a brass bowl and his father settled in the courtyard with a cup of tea, it was time to bring out the note again. Biren peered over his father's shoulder trying to decipher the schoolmaster's tiny, pristine Bengali script. The letter was full of big words.

"What is it, Baba?" he asked. "What is it? Tell me, quickly."

"I see. It appears the new boy is your school needs private tuition. Why, is there a new boy in your school who is struggling with his studies? His name is Samir Deb."

Biren shrugged. Samir Deb's academic challenges were of little interest to him.

"Who needs tuition?" said Shibani, coming out of the kitchen. She handed her husband a rice crepe with coconut filling. "Try this *patishapta*. I made them today."

"Samir Deb. The new boy in Biren's class. The child is falling behind in his studies. His family wants to send him to study in Calcutta. The schoolmaster has recommended me to give him private tuition. I wonder why your mastermoshai does not give the child private tuition himself?"

"Because he is afraid," Biren blurted out. He remembered how the belligerent ladies had cowed down the poor schoolmaster.

"Afraid?" said Shamol, puzzled. "Afraid of what? I don't understand."

"His mother is very…" Biren tried to think of the right word. "Ferocious."

"Well, I am not worried about his ferocious mother. The problem is I get home too late. I don't have the time to go to the child's house but I can tutor him if they send him to our *basha*."

Biren looked at his father in horror. "But he cannot come to our *basha*, Baba!" he cried.

"And why not?" said his father, mildly surprised.

Biren wanted to say, *Because he wears knee-length socks and cries like a girl. Because he is too rich and we are too poor, because my friends will laugh and everybody will think he is my friend.* But all he could say was, "Because he rides in a palanquin."

"Why, that's rather fine," said his father.

"Like a *girl*," Biren added, to drive home the point. "Only girls ride in palanquins."

"I wouldn't mind riding a palanquin," said Shibani.

"Someday, my darling," said his father, "and I will decorate it with sweet-scented lilies for you." He gave Shibani a long tender look that made her toss her hair back in a girlish way.

Biren tugged his father's hand. "Baba, what are you going to do?"

"I can offer to teach him at the same time I teach you two. They don't have to pay me any money for that."

"But they are rich," said Biren. "Very rich. He brings new pencils and erasers to school every day."

Shamol Roy looked at his son sadly. He wished he could buy his wife a palanquin, but she had to be content with a few lilies instead. Here was his boy hankering for a new pencil and all he could afford were the pencil stubs discarded at the office. Biren, dexterous for an eight-year-old, used a razor blade to pare both ends to get maximum usage out of them.

Biren was quick to catch his father's sadness. "But I like the small pencils much better," he said brightly. "They are easier to carry around in my pocket and if I lose one I don't feel so bad because I have many more. Also, you want to know one more thing? Carrying long sharpened pencils in your pocket is very dangerous. If you fall down and get poked in your eye you can become blind. Then you won't be able to go to school, or read, or…or…even fly a kite. So what's the use?"

Shamol Roy smiled at his son, the diplomat. Biren was wily with his words, but more important he was a thoughtful, compassionate child. "Bring me one of your pencils," he said. "Let me write a reply to your mastermoshai."

"They will pay you lots of good money for the tuition,

Baba." Biren jumped up, dizzy with the vision of new pencils and erasers. Why, they might even be able to afford one of those mechanical pencil sharpeners.

"They may offer to pay me," said his father. "But I don't need to accept it."

"But why not?" Biren was crestfallen. "Samir's family has lots of money."

"That is not the point," said his father. "Do you know the difference between opportunity and advantage, *mia*? An opportunity is something that is offered to you. An advantage is something you take. It would be foolish to miss an opportunity but it is sometimes wise to forgo an advantage."

"So why are you not taking the money?"

"Because I am not going out of my way to tutor the child. I am not doing anything extra. So why should I charge money for work I have not done? Never mind, don't worry about it. Go get me a pencil."

Shamol Roy scribbled a quick reply on the reverse of the schoolmaster's note and sent it back with Biren.

CHAPTER 11

It was all settled, and Biren was asked to bring Samir home with him. It soon dawned on Biren he would not be taking the boat back to the village with his friends. Instead—to his horror—he was expected to sit in the tasseled palanquin next to Sammy and be carried to his own house. The very thought of it made him wish he had never been born.

He loitered under the tamarind trees in the schoolyard and kicked dirt while furious thoughts raced through his mind.

Finally he approached the palanquin bearers. "My father has strictly forbidden me to ride the palanquin," he told them in an authoritative voice. "I can show you the way to my house but you will have to follow behind me."

"But how will you walk? It is too far," said one of the men. "It is much shorter by boat, we know, but Samir-baba gets nauseous in a boat, which is why we have to carry him everywhere."

Biren was tempted to say he got nauseous in a palanquin, but that would not work. "What do you think I am? A cripple?" he said loudly, hoping to shame Samir into sending the palanquin home. But Samir was already seated inside sipping sweet *bael* sherbet and eating stuffed dates.

"Just follow behind me," said Biren abruptly. He marched stoutly ahead and the palanquin bearers, habituated as they were to their own brisk pace, hobbled awkwardly behind him like a broken bullock cart.

After a while Samir got bored and got down from the palanquin and skipped up to Biren.

"Don't walk with me," Biren snapped, looking nervously around him. His plan was to pretend the palanquin had nothing to do with him, but to have Samir Deb in his pleated shorts and knee-length socks walk alongside was a dead giveaway.

"Why?" said Samir in a high-pitched whine. "Why don't you want to walk with me? Why don't you want to be my friend?"

Biren stopped in his tracks, almost causing the palanquin bearers to bump into him. "Because I don't," he said fiercely. "I don't want to walk with you. I want you to stay two boat lengths behind me, do you understand?"

One of the palanquin bearers gave a snort, which made Samir fly into a rage. He looked like a miniversion of his mother. "Shut up, stupid donkey!" he yelled, kicking a small puff of dust with his shiny black shoe. "And *you* donkeys stay two boat lengths behind me, do you understand?"

And so the strange procession continued, Biren marching briskly ahead, followed by Sammy, two boat lengths behind, rounded up by the miserable palanquin bearers, for whom the lethargic pace was sheer torture.

When they reached the house, Sammy was hobbling and in tears. He removed his shoes to reveal two small, round blisters sprouted like *batashas* on his heels.

Shibani shush-shushed sympathetically, sat him on her lap, wiped his tears with the end of her sari and made him soak his feet in cool rose water. Just to see Samir with his fat tears wobbling on his chin and being fussed over by Shibani filled Biren with intense disgust. Even three-year-old Nitin had grown past such infantile behavior.

Shibani went into the kitchen to prepare fresh limewater.

"Your mother is so beautiful," Samir said in a mellifluous voice. He twirled his pink toes in the basin. "I want to marry someone just like her."

Biren went insane. "Well, you *can't*!" he said fiercely. "She is already married to my father and she will be married to my father *for the rest of her life*!"

Nitin, who was splashing his hands in the foot basin, looked up with big, scared eyes. He had never seen his brother so angry.

Sammy tilted back his head to admire his toes. "I had an aunt once," he said conversationally. He splashed a little water at Nitin, who darted away with a shriek, then tiptoed back to be splashed some more. "She used to be so beautiful. She had long black hair like your mother. Then my uncle died and she became very ugly. Nobody goes near her or talks to her anymore. Now she lives with the goats in the back of the house."

"Who is it, Biren *mia*? Do we have a visitor?" Grandpa, woken up from his nap, called in a cracked sleepy voice from his room. "Bring him to me. Let me see who this is. Oh, my, my, what a fair and handsome fellow! What is your name, young man?"

Samir puffed out his chest. "My name is Samir Kumar Deb. I was born in Calcutta and I have been to London twice," he said loudly. His eyes drifted lazily across the room, taking in Granny's faded saris lumped over the clotheshorse and Grandpa's lopsided clogs, the toes facing in opposite directions.

"London!" cried Grandpa, clapping his hands. "Imagine that! Tell me, *mia*, was it terribly cold? Lots of ice and snow?"

Biren left Samir sitting on Grandpa's bed telling him all about Big Ben. Even Nitin fingered the fringe of the bedspread and listened with his mouth open. Biren was sick to his stomach. Samir enchanted the whole family. He made Shibani giggle by telling her she was beautiful like a goddess. Granny told them the story of Surparnarekha, the ugly shedemon with her sliced-off nose and used a candle flame to create shadow puppets. Grandpa, not to be outdone, pulled a cowrie out of Samir's ear and offered it to him.

"No, thank you," Samir declined politely.

"I'll take it!" chirped Nitin, holding out his small hand. But Grandpa's eyes wandered slyly and he put the cowrie away.

When Father came home, he cut a papaya and Biren was secretly pleased to see the wonder on Samir's face. When Shamol handed him a slice, he wolfed it down wordlessly even before the others had taken a bite of theirs.

"I want some more," he said, eyeing the remaining slices on the brass platter.

Biren opened his mouth to say everyone only got one piece

each, when Shamol quickly cut up his own slice into equal portions and offered it to the boys.

"Here's another small piece," he said. "Today everybody gets a little extra."

When it came time for homework, Shamol followed exactly the same routine as other days, not doing any more or any less than usual. Nitin stuck his tongue out and laboriously fashioned a capital *A*, only to be distracted by Samir making funny faces at him. Nitin broke into a squealy giggle and covered his mouth with his hands.

Shamol looked up from his book. "Boys," he admonished them gently.

"I don't need to do this sum," Sammy announced, throwing down his pencil. "This is too easy. I already know the answer."

"Is that so?" said Shamol mildly. "Perhaps you can show me how to do it, then." He turned to Biren, who was standing beside him with a smug look on his face. "What is it, Biren, are you finished? Let me see. All right, you may put your things away and leave the room. And you, too, Nitin. Very good. Now, Samir is going to help me solve this tricky sum."

Biren knew why Nitin and he were being sent out of the room. His father wanted to spare Samir the embarrassment of looking ignorant in front of others. Shamol Roy in his own quiet way instilled in his students a deep love of learning. He guarded their private struggles and brandished their victories to all. He was, after all, a born and gifted teacher.

The palanquin bearers slept peacefully under the mango tree. The shadows had lengthened in the bamboo grove and it was already time for evening *puja* by the time Samir was done. Shibani lovingly bandaged his feet in soft *mulmul* strips cut from her old saris and kissed the top of his head before sending him on his way. Biren sighed with relief to see the palanquin swing off at a brisk pace and disappear down the bend in the road. He had secretly begun to worry Samir would end up staying the night or, worse still, be adopted by the family and they would be stuck with him for the rest of their lives.

Six months later, Samir left for boarding school. Biren received a postcard with a beautiful photo of the marble domed Victoria Memorial of Calcutta.

Dear Biren Roy,
This is the Victoria Mangorial.
It is very fine.
I am very fine.
I hope you are fine, also.

Very truly yours,
Samir Kumar Deb

CHAPTER 12

It was Shibani's hair-washing day. Her jet-black hair, a whole yard and a half long, tumbled in tresses down to an old sari spread on the ground for the purpose. She sat on a footstool in the courtyard while Apu rubbed coconut oil into her scalp, parting her hair in sections with a wide bamboo toothcomb. Shibani's eyes were closed and her head bobbed willingly under her friend's massaging fingertips. She looked blissfully relaxed. Beside her stool was a brass bowl containing a solution of soap nuts and *shikakai* for her hair wash.

Shibani squinted up at the gathering clouds. "Looks like rain, don't you think? Maybe I should put off washing my hair today. It will never dry in this humidity. I always catch a head cold when I sleep with wet hair."

"Then, you will have to sleep with your oily hair tonight," said Apu. "This is your last oil massage for a while, sister. Remember I am leaving for my cousin's wedding on

Friday. I will be gone for a whole month. Tomorrow I have to prepare all the sweets to take to the groom's house. Coconut balls, rice cakes and palm fritters. I will send the maid over with some for you."

"Do you have enough saris for all the days? You are welcome to borrow some of mine, you know."

"Oh, no, no. Your saris are too expensive and fancy. You know what these family weddings are like. With hundreds of people coming and going, things get lost or stolen all the time. I would feel terrible if that happened."

"Don't be silly!" Shibani laughed. "Take my saris. I don't care if they get lost. I have too many. There will never be enough occasions to wear them all. I'll tell you what, when you have finished oiling my hair, we'll go and pick out some for you. I have a beautiful banana-leaf-green one that will suit you very well. Today I am free in the evening and I can do the hems for you."

That same morning on his way to work, Shamol Roy had noticed the clouds in the east had swallowed the sun. The river turned a dark and oily black against which the jute plants, eight feet tall, glowed an eerie and electric green.

Shamol fretted because he had not picked up his umbrella from the umbrella man. Now from the look of the sky they were heading for quite a downpour.

He arrived at the jute mill godown to find it still locked. Usually his assistant, who lived in the jute quarters nearby, came early to open it. The bullock carts laden with bales were already lined up outside. Shamol went to the main office to pick up the godown key and learned his assistant was sick and would not be coming in that day. Mr. Mallick, the mill manager, assured Shamol he would send help immediately.

By midday, no help had arrived and Shamol was finding it increasingly difficult to manage on his own. It was a brutally hot and humid day with no respite, not even a cup of tea. He had to run back and forth from the weighing scales outside to the ledger in the godown. The bullock cart lines grew longer and backed up all the way down the road to the bazaar. By early afternoon Shamol realized he would have to lock up the godown and drop off the keys at the main office at the end of the day. This meant he would most definitely miss the last ferry home. His only option was to stay overnight at a relative's house in the village, but before that he would have to send a message home through Kanai. Maybe Kanai could bring back a change of fresh clothes for him. If not, he would have to borrow something from his cousin to wear to office the following morning.

But despite the harried day, he did not forget his son's pencils. He had collected six stubs from the office, each two or three inches long. He wrapped the pencils in a piece of blotting paper and put them in the front pocket of his tunic.

Finally the last bale was weighed and the bullock cart ambled away, tinkling its bell. Shamol Roy made the last notations and closed his ledger. He sat down at his desk and felt the weight of the day slump on his shoulders. It was getting dark inside the godown. He knew there were candles and matches tucked around somewhere, but only the assistant knew where.

He was about to leave when the rain crashed down like a wall of glass. Shamol was trapped. There was nothing he could to do but wait it out, but he would have to find the candles before that.

He groped his way to the back of the godown. Squeaks and scrabbles emanated from the bales, and a small creature with scratchy claws ran over his feet, making him jump. To his relief he located the candles and a box of matches on a small bamboo shelf on the back wall. Shamol lit two candles and made his way back to the elevated platform of his desk. He considered shutting the door of the godown to keep out the rain but then it would get terribly stuffy. As it was, a thick vapor was rising off the floor and the smell of rot and decay from the bales was almost too much to bear.

He realized he had not eaten anything all day. The potato and fried flatbread Shibani packed for him that morning lay untouched in a cloth bag on his desk. He opened the bag and ate his cold food in the flickering candlelight while rain crashed and splattered outside. This kind of torrential rain usually did not last too long, he thought thankfully.

He missed Shibani and the boys. He was spending only one day away from his family and he was already homesick. He wondered what they were doing. Shibani was probably chatting with Apu. The boys would be out playing somewhere; there was no schoolwork after all.

His thoughts turned to Biren. The child was a dreamer. Biren saw the magic in the mundane. He imagined things bigger, better and more elaborate. When most children made a paper boat, Biren made a steamer ship with a chimney. When other children drew a duck, Biren drew a swan. He had natural showmanship and expressed himself with touching eloquence. His flashy good looks added to his charisma. Biren had curly hair, a straight nose and a wheat-colored complexion, but his most striking feature was his dark, expressive eyes.

Then there was, of course, little Nitin with his wandering smile and look of perpetual bafflement. No star quality there, Shamol thought tenderly of his younger son, but God had given the little fellow his own charm to get by in the world.

He wished he could do more for his boys. They deserved a better education, for one. He remembered what Shibani and he talked about a few nights ago by the river. She was right. Maybe he should broach the subject of the English boarding school with his boss, Owen McIntosh. There was no harm in asking after all.

The rain had almost stopped. In another ten or fifteen minutes he would be able to lock up the godown and leave. Shamol decided to use this time to write Owen McIntosh a letter and drop it off with the godown keys at the jute mill office on his way to his cousin's house.

He found a clean sheet of paper, uncapped his fountain pen and began to write.

Biren had just got back from school when Kanai brought news that Shamol was not coming home that evening. Biren's heart gave a little jump. That meant no homework. It was the perfect day to go fishing with Kanai.

After some persuasion, Kanai agreed to take him. It was a gloomy afternoon, and by the time they arrived at the backwaters, the clouds had deepened to purple-black like an angry bruise across the sky. A sly wind flicked the water and pushed the boat toward the reedy marsh, where it was difficult to cast the line because the wind blew it in the wrong direction. After an hour on the wobbling boat Kanai said they should go home. Biren was deeply disappointed.

Shibani was sitting on the bed, hemming the bottom border of a leaf-green sari. She wore an old turmeric-stained blouse and petticoat and her head, wrapped in a cotton towel, looked like a giant breadbasket. Biren had never seen his mother so slovenly. In the evenings she was usually dressed in fresh clothes with flowers in her hair. Then he remembered his father was not coming home that day.

Nitin hung upside down off the edge of the bed, swinging his hands. Shibani kept her foot firmly pressed on his bottom to make sure he did not slide off.

"I was worried about you," she said. "Today is not a good day to be out in the open water. Kanai should have more sense than to take you."

"We hardly got any time to fish," grumbled Biren. "There were many other boats still out in the river, but Kanai made me come home."

"Did you catch a big *chital* fish, Dada?" Nitin righted himself. His hair, long and straight, hung down like river reeds over his eyes.

Biren shook his head.

Shibani cut the thread with her teeth. "Go and wash your hands and face," she said. "I want you to take these saris to Apumashi's house before it starts raining. Come back immediately. Your grandmother is not feeling well. We are going to eat dinner and go to bed early tonight. I have to wash my hair in the morning."

That night Shibani dreamed of a snake.

She could not see it, but she felt it twisted around her throat in thick damp coils, choking her breath. When she tried to scream, the coils tightened. She woke up drenched in sweat to find her long oily hair freed from the towel wrapped around her neck. Her hand crept instinctively to Shamol's side of the bed and a small sadness fluttered in her heart when she touched his empty pillow. She lay in bed and thought of him. She hoped he would get some sleep that night. Shamol's cousins were a big noisy family with several ill-behaved children who ran rumpus over the house. Would he miss her? She smiled. Of course he would. Her husband was a deeply romantic and sentimental man.

Shibani's heart swelled with gratitude when she thought of him. He was such a caring husband and a good father. Shamol discerned unique qualities in each child and wove them into their self-confidence. She remembered a phase Nitin had gone through when he'd wanted to dress up in girl clothes and play with dolls all the time. Shamol had never once tried to dissuade him or make him feel it was wrong. "The child is only acting out his imagination," he'd explained to Shibani. "He will grow out of it." And sure enough, Nitin soon had.

Samir in the meantime had turned around and called Nitin a sissy. He'd done it in a mean-spirited way and Biren had been quick to lash out in defense of his young brother. "*You* are the sissy," Biren had shot back. "Imagine a grown-up boy like you riding in a palanquin!"

Shamol, who had overheard their quarrel, had quickly diffused it by telling the boys about the brave Scottish Highlanders in their wool-pleated kilts and Roman emperors who wore togas. He'd gone on to talk about Japanese emperors and brave Samurai warriors who were borne aloft on palanquins because of their exalted status. At the end Shamol had had all three boys keen to wear kilts and togas and ride in palanquins.

Shibani's fingers caressed her husband's pillow, remembering. She slipped her small supple hand under it and found a sprig of dried jasmine from the garland of her hair. Her sweet husband must have tucked it there. Breathing in the scent, she drifted off into a dreamless sleep.

An inky darkness had fallen outside by the time Shamol finished his letter. The rain had ceased and the candles, now reduced to shapeless gobs, spluttered in their pools of wax. Outside the door the jackals howled in a lonely chorus. Shamol quickly folded the letter, gathered together his things and picked up the ledger and keys from the table. Then he blew out the candles one by one. As he stepped off the platform, the keys slipped from his hand and fell with a clatter to the floor. He bent down and felt for them in the dark and bumped up against what he thought was the leg of the table. But it was hard and muscular and writhed against his upper arm. Too late, he realized it was a snake. He jerked back his hand and heard a loud spitting hiss followed by a needling stab on his right wrist. Shamol's knees buckled; he grabbed the table to steady himself and slowly crumpled to the floor. A milky film floated before his eyes, his tongue twisted to the roof of his mouth and ribbons of white froth dribbled down his chin. The last thing Shamol Roy felt was a tremendous crushing pain in his chest and the sensation of being sucked underwater.

Twenty minutes later, he lay dead in the jute godown, surrounded by the rats and the filth. His hand clutched his pocket that held the six pencil stubs wrapped in a blotting paper he had planned on taking home for his son.

CHAPTER 13

The disheveled man waiting for Biren in the headmaster's office looked vaguely familiar. His hair was uncombed and he was still in his night pajamas. It finally dawned on Biren he was their neighbor, Apu's husband, a man he had probably seen five times in his life and never spoken to even once.

"Mr. Bhowmik will take you home," said the headmaster, fiddling with a bunch of papers on his desk. He did not explain why. From the look on their faces, Biren knew something was wrong. It must be something to do with his granny, he thought. Maybe she had died. Old people died quickly and suddenly after all. Like Kanai's granny. Kanai said one day she was chewing betel nuts on the front steps and chatting with the neighbors and the next day she was gone.

On the boat ride back home the man turned his face away toward the jute fields and made no attempt at conversation. He was not one to talk much, from what Biren remembered.

If Granny had died, why hadn't his father come to get him? It was not like Father to send a stranger in his place.

Maybe he could trick Apu's husband into conversation.

"I wonder if it will rain tonight," Biren remarked, peering up at the clouds. "This changing weather is terrible. It is making us all sick. My granny had a high fever last night. She was terribly unwell."

The man coughed and gave a brief nod but did not say anything. The silence was getting sticky. The boat rowed past the backwaters.

"I went fishing out to the backwaters yesterday," Biren said brightly. "Kanai the fisherman caught a big *chital* fish a few days ago. Fifteen kilos, imagine!" Biren cast a sly glance to see if the man was impressed, but he just crossed his arms over his chest. "But it was hopeless for me," Biren continued. "I did not even catch a two-inch pooty fish! It is this rough weather, you know. When it gets too windy, the fish go down too deep and don't bite. It was a good thing we decided to come home..." His last few words dribbled off. His pitcher of conversation was running dry.

Finally, as the boat pulled up to Momati Ghat, the man cleared his throat. "You will stay at our house today," he said. Biren was startled to hear his voice. It was low and throaty. Something warned him not to ask further questions.

They entered Apu's house through the front door, which had a different street entrance from their own. Nitin was already there, behaving in a manner that would have earned him a sound paddling from Shibani. A half-packed trunk lay open on the floor. Nitin and Apu's two little girls, Ruby and Ratna, had pulled out an expensive silk sari from the trunk and ran shrieking through the house as they trailed the leaf-green silk behind them. Biren remembered it as the same sari he had delivered the day before.

A toothless granny with collapsed cheeks, her hair coiled into a walnut-size bun, sat on the bed with a string of prayer beads wrapped in her hand. She called after them in a wavery voice, “Careful, careful.”

“Ma!” yelled Apu’s husband loudly in the old woman’s ear. “I am going out. Keep an eye on the children, do you hear? Don’t let them out of the house.”

Biren tugged the man’s hand. “Can I go home?”

“Not now,” said the man. “Your Apumashi will come to get you both later.”

“Where is Apumashi?”

“She’s gone…out,” said the man. “You all stay here. You must not leave the house.”

He turned around and left.

Four-year-old Ruby came running up to Biren and hugged him tightly around the waist. “Oh, my husband! My sweet husband!” she cried. She grabbed his hand and kissed it feverishly.

“I am not your husband,” Biren said gruffly, snatching his hand away. He disengaged her arms from around his waist.

“But of course you are,” Ruby replied in a sugary voice. She gave him a sly, coquettish look. “You are, you are, my handsome husband.” She twirled her skirt and sang. “We are going to get married. I will wear a red sari and we will exchange garlands. Oh, I love my husband! We are getting married.”

“Getting married! Getting married!” shrieked the other two, flinging the folds of the sari up in the air.

“Careful, careful,” chirruped the granny.

It was strange, but there didn't seem to be another soul in the house.

"Granny!" yelled Biren in the old lady's ear. "Where is everybody?"

"Everybody?" pondered the granny. "Everybody must be doing *puja*."

The *puja* room was empty, the sandalwood joss sticks burned down to a bed of ash.

Biren grabbed Nitin as he ran by and shook him by the shoulder. "Nitin, who dropped you here? Where is Ma?"

Nitin shrugged off his brother. Reckless and out of control, he ran off screaming behind Ratna.

The kitchen looked as if it had been abandoned in a hurry. On the floor were several brass platters of grated coconut, sesame seeds, mounds of jaggery and a large basin of rice flour batter. Biren turned to the window, which faced the pumpkin patch, beyond which he could see the rooftop of his house in the distance. A small slice of their courtyard was visible. He saw several men in the courtyard but could not make out their faces.

Then he heard a strange sound. What was it? It was between a howl and a moan. Then came another and another. There were waves of them. It sounded like a dying animal in mortal pain. Maybe it was a wounded jackal in the taro patch. Biren made a note to himself to look for the poor creature when he got home.

CHAPTER 14

What a damned, wretched day, thought Owen McIntosh, the Scottish owner of Victoria Jute Mills. He sat on the veranda of his bungalow, the pipe in his mouth remained unlit, his cup of tea untouched. After the horrific events of the day before, he felt no desire for the small comforts he looked forward to every evening when he got home.

A dreary darkness had settled around the bungalow compound, and in the distance the jackals howled in chorus. It was around this time yesterday that Shamol Roy had suffered the fatal cobra bite in the jute godown and breathed his last. Owen was horrified to think of the poor man lying in his own vomit all night, surrounded by rats, cockroaches, the jackals wandering in and out of the open doorway. When the laborers found his body in the morning, the jackals had half dragged it out of the doorway and it was a gruesome sight. Owen McIntosh covered his eyes and felt the bile rise to his throat at the memory of what he had seen.

What a fine young man Shamol Roy had been. He'd had so much promise and was undoubtedly one of the best employees of Victoria Jute Mills. Owen believed Roy deserved better. He had been too educated and genteel for the rough work he did in that filthy godown, managing the common laborers, day in and day out. That man had a quiet presence about him, a dignity of carriage, speech and manners that belied his humble village upbringing. From what Owen knew, Shamol Roy had been the only earning member of his joint family. He had accepted the godown job because the pay was slightly higher than the administrative work at the mill office. Owen had had every good intention to promote him to a better paying position in the main office as soon as he could find someone to replace him. At one point, he had even toyed with the idea of grooming Roy as his personal assistant. Now it was too late.

More than just sadness and regret, Owen McIntosh was tortured with guilt. He knew in his heart he had delayed Shamol Roy's promotion because of his own self-interest. Raw-material management was a critical part of the jute mill business and Owen had yet to find someone as responsible and capable as Roy. Roy had had a gentle way of dealing with the rough laborers. He had known each laborer by name and often asked after their families. Shamol Roy had been meticulous about his job and never acted bossy or condescending toward his assistant. Because he'd managed the godown operation so faultlessly, Owen had let him run it. He had not tried hard enough to find a substitute, and the soft-spoken young man never once complained.

Shamol Roy had elected not to live in the jute mill quarters provided free to employees. Rather, each day, he traveled up and down by boat from his village to work. Most other workers went home only on weekends. A cluster of cheap wine shops and brothels had sprung up around the jute mill area to cater to these men. Many showed up to work red-eyed and hungover in the mornings, but Shamol Roy had always arrived impeccably dressed, never absent or late. He had to return home every night to tutor his children, he'd explained, to help them with their schoolwork, as he did not want them falling behind in their studies. Owen also knew he had collected the discarded pencil stubs from the office to take home to his son.

He had once met the older boy at the office of Saraswati Puja. Held in the jute mill compound during early spring, the *puja* was a joyous occasion celebrated with the beating of drums and blowing of conch horns. Employees brought their wives and children from the villages, dressed in bright new clothes to see the bedecked Goddess of Learning seated on her snow-white lotus, holding a stringed *vina* in her hands.

Owen had been in his office when Shamol Roy had walked in with his eight-year-old son. A bold and curious child, he was intelligent beyond his years. The boy had sat on the edge of his chair and knew more about jute manufacturing than most of the employees at the mill. Thoroughly charmed, Owen had, with mock gravity, offered the lad a job. To his surprise the young fellow piped up, "Thank you, sir, but I must complete my education first."

"And did you make a special wish to the goddess Saraswati today?" Owen had inquired gently. "What do you want to be when you grow up, young man?"

"I want to be a lawyer," the boy had replied without hesitation.

"Indeed! And why not a doctor, may I ask?"

"Because…" The boy's soulful eyes had deepened. "Because if I am a doctor, I can only make my living if people fall sick, but if I am a lawyer I can make my living by fighting for what is right."

Owen had been astounded by his sage-like answer. What was more remarkable, Shamol Roy had let his young son take center stage, never once chiding or belittling the boy in front of his boss. He had treated his son respectfully like an adult and as a result the boy stood tall and felt entitled to speak his mind.

Owen thought about his own two children. Alan, his son, was the same age as this boy, maybe a wee bit older, and his daughter, Margie, was six, but both his children seemed like toddlers compared to Shamol Roy's boy.

Owen's heart was filled with despair. What would become of Shamol Roy's young sons? Who would tutor them, who would give them the confidence to strive higher? Their education would be cut short and they would be sucked back into their village life. What a waste of potential. The more Owen thought about the two boys, the more wretched he felt. He blamed himself in part for Shamol Roy's death. How was he ever going to live with himself?

Another thing bothered him. A few years ago Roy had approached his office, stood shyly outside the door and asked to speak with him on a private matter. He had explained to Owen about his family situation. His brother was unable to work because of an injury sustained a few years ago, so the responsibility for his aging parents, his brother's family as well as his own, was on him. As Roy had talked, Owen McIntosh had begun to suspect he was going to ask for a loan, but he was wrong.

Roy had said he had been thinking about the future of his boys. To make sure there would be sufficient funds for their college education, he wanted to set aside a portion of his salary every month. Unfortunately, he would have to do this without the knowledge of his family. His older brother, who managed the funds of the family, was childless and did not put the same value on education as Shamol did. Shamol Roy himself had missed the opportunity to finish college. He did not want his sons to suffer the same fate. He had asked if Mr. McIntosh could deduct a small portion of his salary every month and put it aside in a separate fund for him.

Owen McIntosh had been deeply moved by his story. He said he would not only be glad to do that, but every month he would add a small bonus to compensate him for his hard work.

Shamol Roy was now dead at the age of thirty-four. The fund, meanwhile, had grown to a sizable amount. The question was, what to do with the money? If Owen handed the money over to Roy's joint family, chances were the boys would never see it. It became increasingly clear: he had a moral responsibility to protect the two boys.

Now there was Roy's final letter where he had asked, rather timidly, if Owen could help his sons get admission in an English missionary school. It had never occurred to Owen to do that for any employee, as it meant assuming full guardianship for the boys. But Roy was dead and Owen had his letter as proof. He decided he would do everything in his power to make Roy's last wishes come true.

Having come to that decision, Owen McIntosh felt better. He called for the bearer to make him a fresh pot of tea, and finally lit his pipe. He could only hope Shamol Roy's family would agree to his plans.

CHAPTER 15

Biren remembered very little of what happened in the next few days. He was told his father had died from a cobra bite in the jute mill. The house was full of strange people. They huddled in clusters; the women beat their breasts and wailed. Granny's potted marigolds all died because nobody watered them. Bunches of tuberose lay discolored and rotting, still wrapped in newspaper and string. Granny took to bed and cried day and night, Uncle disappeared and Grandpa retreated into a stony silence while the gloomy aunt did her best to manage the chaotic household. As for Shibani, she was nowhere to be seen.

Bewildered, Biren wandered around the house looking for his mother. He had seen her last on the morning before he left for school. She'd looked fine and had been getting ready to wash her hair. That night he and Nitin had fallen asleep in Apumashi's house. Somebody had carried them home late at night and they had woken up to find both their mother and father gone and the house full of crying people.

All he knew was his father had died and his mother had disappeared and nobody talked about her. There was a different bedspread on her bed. He looked for her sewing basket, which was full of needles, buttons and colored threads wrapped around bamboo spools. He often rummaged in this basket looking for tacking pins to bend into fishing hooks. Her basket was nowhere. Panic set in. He began to fear his mother had abandoned him and his brother. Maybe they were bad boys and she didn't want them anymore.

Everything that belonged to his mother was gone. Her trunk of saris, her comb, her bangles, the brass container of vermillion she used for the part of her hair. Oddly, his father's things remained exactly where they were before he had died. His *lungi* and vest were folded neatly over the clotheshorse. His books, English calendar, wooden clogs and even his comb with a few black hairs still stuck to them. It almost felt as if his mother had died and his father had gone away. Something was just not adding up, but Biren could not put a finger on it.

In the evenings Biren felt the urge to walk down the road to meet his father, only to realize with a stab of pain that his father would never come home again. He wished he could talk to Apumashi. She would explain everything. He wanted to go to her house, but Granny would not allow him. "We are in mourning," she said. "You don't visit other people in their homes for thirteen days." In desperation he imitated his mother and rooster called to Apu across the pumpkin patch but there was no answering call back.

Nitin behaved strangely. He walked around with his hair uncombed and sucked his thumb. He started to wet his bed and after a while he stopped talking entirely. One day Biren saw him put a blue marble inside his mouth. The next thing he knew, Nitin had gulped. Biren rushed over and forced Nitin's mouth open. He stuck his finger inside and moved it around but the marble was gone.

"Granny!" screamed Biren, dragging Nitin to Granny's room. "Nitin swallowed a marble!" To his shock, Granny did not seem to care.

Biren wandered around in a daze holding Nitin tightly by the hand. His father and mother had both disappeared; now Nitin had swallowed a marble and was surely going to die and nobody cared. What was going on?

Then out of the blue Nitin fell on the ground and threw a tantrum. He screamed and begged and promised never to play with his mother's sari again. Nobody, except Biren, knew what the hysteria was about. Biren knew for certain their mother had not gone away because Nitin had spoiled her expensive sari. Finally, he could stand it no longer.

"Where is my ma?" he asked his morose aunt.

"She will be here soon," said the aunt.

"Where is Ma's sewing basket?" he persisted. "Where are all her things?"

"They have been disposed of," said the aunt. "They are contaminated."

He heaved a sigh of relief. So *that* was the problem. His mother had caught an infectious disease and she was in quarantine, which is why nobody was allowed to see her. It was probably measles or chicken pox. Why didn't they just say so? She would soon recover, and Apumashi would come to wash her hair again and they would laugh and eat chili tamarind in the sun.

For now, he would have to take care of his younger brother.

Biren invented little games for them to play and tried to teach Nitin his ABCs. Nitin solemnly chanted in a singsong with his finger on each letter: "*A* for *pipra*, *B* for *cheley*," substituting the Bengali words for *ant* and *boy*, and Biren did not have the heart to correct him.

The next day he combed Nitin's hair, holding him firmly by the chin just as his mother used to do, and took him for a walk down the road.

"Is Baba coming home today?" Nitin's small face was bright with hope.

"Not today," said Biren. He wondered how much longer he would have to lie to his little brother. How could he explain anything when he was so baffled himself?

A neighbor they only vaguely knew hurried down the road on her way home from the fish market. She stopped to ask how they were doing, but made no mention of their mother.

"My mother is getting better," he called after her. "Come and see her soon." The neighbor just nodded and hurried along.

Three days passed in a blur. The house was sickly with the smell of incense and dying tuberoses. Most nights Biren dropped off to sleep from exhaustion. In his dreams he saw black twisted smoke, and smelled burning ghee. He started awake with a great choking sensation, unable to breathe, unable to cry. Every sound was amplified in the night. The soft wheezing snore from his grandfather's room, the rustle of a mouse scrambling on the thatch. One night, late, he heard a sound. It was same sound he had heard from Apu's house the day his father had died: the low, moaning sound of an animal in pain.

He crept out of bed, tiptoed out into the courtyard and stood beside the holy basil plant and listened. There it was again, louder this time. The sound came from the direction of the old woodshed next to the taro patch. He walked toward the shed and could see the flickering yellow glow of a *diya* lamp through the slatted wooden walls. There was somebody inside. The sound was a singsong moan, rising and falling, regular and monotonous, almost mechanical. Biren inched up to the papaya tree, not daring to go any farther. Someone was quarantined in the shed, and she was in a lot of pain.

Ma!

He ran across the undergrowth to the shed. The door was locked.

He rattled the lock. "Ma!" he whispered urgently. "Ma! It's me."

The moaning stopped. He peeped through the slats and froze in terror. It was not his mother at all but a bald old man dressed in a white cloth sitting on the floor with his back turned.

It was a ghost—the *petni* that Kanai spoke about!

Biren thought he would suffocate with fear. He was about to step backward when the man turned his head around and looked at him. The face was dull and white, flat as the moon with bloodshot eyes.

Biren stifled a scream, stumbled through the bushes and ran back toward the house. He flung himself down on his bed and lay there. His teeth chattered uncontrollably, his fingers dug into his palms; every muscle in his body was contorted with fear.

That pale, flat face with its red eyes kept floating into his mind. He had no doubt the creature in the woodshed was his mother. She had stretched out her hand and he'd recognized her plaintive voice as she called his name.

But what had happened to her?

★★★

He drifted off into a fitful sleep. Random choppy images swirled through his brain. He saw himself in a large field. The ground was strewn with damp white lilies and tiny pencils with broken points. There were so many broken pencils that they looked like scattered peanuts. Biren was bending down to examine the pencils when he heard something that sounded like the drone of bees in the distance. He looked up to see a crowd approaching. They were faceless, hairless people, neither men nor women, all dressed in white, moving toward him in a serpentine wave. As they drew closer, their hum turned into a mournful wail that looped over and over in a mounting crescendo. They trampled over the delicate lilies and left behind a brown, slimy waste. They headed toward the fish market and Biren followed them.

Next he found himself in the fish market with his father. Biren reached for his father's hand but came up with a fistful of coarse, white cloth. He panicked. Where was Baba? None of the people around him had any faces. To his relief, he saw the chicken man. Biren knew he could wait safely at the chicken stall and his father would surely find him. The chicken man acknowledged him with a friendly nod. He was in the middle of telling his customer the story of a man who contacted rabies after being bitten by a *chital* fish. Biren listened idly, thinking one did not get rabies from a fish bite. But he didn't want to spoil the chicken man's story. The chicken man stroked the beautiful black rooster on his lap as he spoke. The rooster's yellow eyes were closed and it looked like it would purr like a cat. Its blissful expression reminded Biren of his mother's face when Apu gave her a head massage.

The chicken man finished his story. He took a puff of his

bidi and, with the bidi still dangling between his lips, he placed both his hands around the rooster's neck and broke it with a single, sharp twist. Then he held the bird down until its wings stopped flailing. Biren felt bile rise in his throat as he watched the chicken man chop off the rooster's head, pluck the feathers, gut its entrails and tear out a small pink heart that was still pulsing. After splashing water from a bucket to wash off the blood, he shoved the heart, liver and gizzard back inside the chicken, trussed up the bird in a banana leaf and put it in the man's cloth shopping bag. Then the chicken man counted his money, shoved it under his mat, rocked back on his haunches and smoked the rest of his bidi. Every time he drew in the smoke, he narrowed his eyes.

Biren woke up clammy with sweat and lay in bed thinking. That was what had happened to his mother. In the same way the rooster was changed from a bright-eyed bird to three pounds of meat and bone in a banana leaf, his mother was stripped of her long hair, her colorful sari, her bright laugh and the kohl in her eyes. Dehumanized, she was just meat and bones wrapped in a white piece of cloth. She had become one of those cursed ones: a widow.

CHAPTER 16

Biren returned to the woodshed again that night. Shibani was expecting him. She pressed her cheek to the wall and touched a finger to his through a gap in the wooden slats.

"You came back, my son," she whispered. "I think of you and Nitin all the time."

"What happened to you, Ma?" Biren cried in a broken voice. "Who did this to you? What happened to your hair?"

Shibani touched her bald head. "Oh, I must look a sight, don't I?" she said ruefully. "I have not seen myself, which is just as well. This is what being a widow is all about, *mia*."

"Did they cut all your hair off?"

She nodded. "The priest shaved it."

"Why?"

Shibani gazed at her son's soft, troubled eyes. "It is the custom, *mia*. That is what they do to widows so they can never marry again."

"Why did they lock you here? Who gives you food?"

She sighed. "This is my mourning period. I must be kept in isolation. Even when that is over, things will be very different. I want you and Nitin to prepare yourselves. You will not see much of me after I come back into the house. I will no longer be a part of the family. I have to cook my own food now. Eat alone and only once a day. I can never touch meat or fish or eat spicy food or even drink a cup of tea."

"What about chili tamarind?" asked Biren. He had not meant it to be funny, but he was relieved to see her old crooked smile.

She looked away. "No chili tamarind," she said softly.

"When will Apumashi come to—" he was about to say "oil your hair" but stopped himself "—see you?"

She sighed. "I will not be allowed to socialize with anyone. A widow is a cursed being. Married women with children and happy families like your Apumashi are not allowed to come near us. They fear our bad luck may rub off on them. My friendship with Apu is over, I'm afraid."

It was inconceivable! They were best friends; they told each other all their secrets. Had they not promised to live next door to each other forever? They had even planned to get their children married to one another, so that they could live together as one big happy family.

Biren was beginning to feel desperate. His words came out in a rush. "What if...if I marry Ruby? What if Nitin marries Ratna? Then you will both be in-laws. You *have* to be friends."

Shibani regarded her son tenderly. His sweet, hopeful face, the feverish plea in his eyes. A tear coursed down his cheek. Biren dismissed it with a careless flick. Seeing this adultlike gesture broke her heart. Her sweet baby boy was growing up in front of her eyes.

Biren's chin trembled. "I will marry Ruby," he declared with manly determination.

Shibani was touched and amused at the same time. "Oh, you *really* want to marry Ruby, then?" She suppressed a smile. "So you think it is a good idea, after all, do you?"

"No, but…"

"I want you to listen to me, son," Shibani said firmly. "Your father…" Her eyes filled with tears, but she controlled herself. "Your father and I did not bring you up to do things against your will. Marrying Ruby is childish talk. That is not the answer and that is not going to solve the problem. You must take care of your brother. Only you can explain things to him. Just do the best you can. Be there for him. I cannot be there for you both any longer. My life is over. Yours has just begun."

Biren's thin veneer of adulthood cracked and he broke down with a cry. "Why do you say that, Ma?" He sobbed. "Why do you say your life is over? Are you going to die?"

"Shush, *mia*," she whispered, touching his cheek with the tip of her finger. How she wished she could cradle him in her arms and wipe those clumped eyelashes with the end of her sari. "Of course I am not going to die. This is no time to cry. I am just trying to prepare you for what lies ahead. I will be here, but I will no longer be a part of your life. A widow does not have a position in the family. I will remain in the background and you may not see much of me, but I want you both to remember me—not the way I have become, but the way I used to be. You can come and see me when you wish, but you must promise not to do so out of sorrow or guilt. Come and see me when you have good tidings and we will rejoice together. I may be cursed as a widow, but I have been blessed as a wife and mother, and nobody can take that from me."

Through the slit in the wood, all Biren could see were her eyes. They burned with the unnatural brightness of anger at the injustice of it all.

His mother may be trapped, Biren decided, but he was not. It would be up to him to set her free.

He did not go straight back to bed. Rather, he sat on the kitchen steps by the pot of holy basil and hugged his knees, thinking. A big moon sailed high in the sky, weaving in and out of the clouds, sometimes bright, other times clumped and patchy. Biren's thoughts churned deep and dark into his soul, trying to find glimmers of meaning through his sorrow. Surely there was something he could do.

His throat caught in a strangled sob. What would his father do if he saw what had become of Ma? Surely he would do something? But Baba was dead. He was no longer there to protect her. Biren sat up a little straighter. He had a young brother to take care of. Nitin would grow up and have his own life, but what would happen to his mother? Would she become destitute like Charulata and be forced to beg under the banyan tree?

He thought of Charulata. She had given him his name and painted it in the patterns of hopes and dreams. She must have seen in him the seed of a warrior. Baba said a warrior did not follow the dictates of others but his own conscience. Biren's conscience told him the treatment of widows was inhuman and unjust and it should be condemned. He would fight for them.

It was on that premonsoon night, in the moonlit courtyard of his village home, that eight-year-old Biren Roy watched the purpose of his life unfold. It came to him in the parting of the clouds and the full brilliant light of the moon, an uncommon zeal that would guide his journey forward.

CHAPTER 17

Owen J. McIntosh
Proprietor
Victoria Jute Mills
20th July 1880

Dear Mr. Anirban Roy,
Please accept my sincere condolences for the untimely and tragic death of your son Shamol Roy. Shamol Roy was an exemplary human being of great integrity and impeccable courtesy. He was also my most promising employee, and had the potential to go far in his career. I feel privileged to have known this young man. I saw him as a devoted husband and father and admired his honorable commitment to his family.

I would like to reassure you, Victoria Jute Mills is deeply committed to ensure your family is financially compensated in every way. To that effect, you will continue to receive Shamol Roy's full monthly salary for the next sixteen years—by which time he would have reached the retirement age of fifty—and this includes any bonuses he may be entitled to. After that, his widow will continue to receive a monthly pension until the time of her death.

Mr. Prabhu Mallick, our mill manager, will explain to you in detail the pension scheme and other compensations available to Shamol Roy's widow. You can also personally contact me if there is any other way I can be of further assistance.

Besides general compensation, I would like to put forward a separate proposal, which I hope you will take into serious consideration. This pertains to the education of Shamol Roy's sons. I am well aware how committed he was toward the education of his children. I have from him a letter expressing his wishes to admit them to an English school, and to that end I am willing to personally sponsor their schooling in Calcutta. Victoria Jute Mills is affiliated with one of the best schools for boys in India: the Saint John's Mission. The school offers full boarding, excellent teachers and is noted for its high scholastic record. Many of Saint John's students go on to study in Oxford and Cambridge on full merit scholarships. Since admission to Saint John's requires the signature of a British legal guardian, I am willing to offer my services to that effect.

It is my understanding that Shamol Roy would have wanted the best possible education for his sons. I would like to assuage any concerns you may have about the Christian/religious orientation of this institution. Although Catholic missionaries run Saint John's, it is not mandatory for students to convert to Christianity. I can get a written statement to that effect if you wish. I leave it to Prabhu Mallick to explain the details. One thing to keep in mind is the school session begins in September, which leaves us only six weeks. I will need your answer in the next few days to ensure the older boy's placement for this academic year. The younger child will have to wait until he is eight before he can be admitted.

I would appreciate your answer at the earliest.

Very truly yours,
Owen McIntosh

"It is completely out of the question," Biren's uncle exploded. "These Christian schools, all they care about is religious conversion. They bribe us poor Indians with education and the promise of opportunity and betterment. They are destroying our culture and killing our religion. These *belaytis* will do anything to control our country."

"But the letter said conversion to Christianity was not compulsory," said Grandpa. "Think of the opportunity. The boys will get a good education. It will give them a head start in life. Nobody gave us this chance."

"But it is an *English* education," argued the uncle. "English education gives Indian students false hopes. They will never be on the same rung as a white man. The *belaytis* dangle the carrot, then they take it away. What is wrong with the village school? Biren can continue to attend the school and pass his matriculation. After matriculation he will be old enough to go to work. He can easily get a job in the jute mill. As it is, he has already impressed McIntosh. Who knows, he may even give Biren an equal or better paying job than Shamol. After that it will be up to Biren to prove himself and move up the ladder."

"Shamol would not like that," said the grandma, wiping away a tear. "He always said he wanted his sons to get a better education, to go further than he did. He never wanted the boys to work in the jute mill. There is no future there.

Shamol was so brilliant in his studies, but he had to give everything up and go to work to support our family, because you…you…" She sighed. "You are ill."

"Ill, my left foot!" exploded Grandpa in a fit of rage. "You are bone lazy, that's what you are. Too high and mighty for any job. So many jobs have come your way but you turn them down because nothing is good enough for your highness. Even if you did a part-time job—which you know very well you are capable of doing—it would have eased Shamol's burden. He would have had time to pursue his own studies. Shamol was the brilliant one and look at the kind of job he did! Did he once complain? Now you are trying to deprive his children of an opportunity he has paid for with his life. What is wrong with you? Now, you stop all your *addabaaj* under the banyan and get some kind of a job. It's high time."

"Baba, please calm down," pleaded the older daughter-in-law. "We all want the best for Biren and Nitin. I just don't think Shamol would have wanted to send his children so far away from home, considering the current circumstances. We think the children should stay close to their mother and be a comfort…"

She froze and her hand crept up to her mouth.

Shibani stood in the doorway with her shaven head and her white borderless sari. Her face was waxen, her eyes cold and dead. She rarely showed herself in public and, when she did, her presence was chilling.

"You really think so?" Shibani said in a soft voice. "You really think my two sons are a comfort to me, sister-in-law?" she repeated, her voice turning hard and cold like marble. "Then, why are they kept away from me? Why are they never allowed to come close to me? Why can I not cook for my own boys, feed them with my hand, comb their hair like a mother should? Because my curse will contaminate their young lives, is it?"

Nobody said a word.

"My children have already been taken away from me," Shibani continued. "Do they even see me as the mother they once knew? Look at me!" She spat out the words. "Just look at me, will you? Is this the girl you brought into this house as your daughter-in-law? Is this the woman who gave birth to your two grandsons? Is this the way God wanted me to be, or is this your doing? You tell me." Her eyes, brittle with anger, snapped from one face to another. She exhaled sharply and, as she did, the flat look returned. It drifted over her eyes like scum, covering a splash in a pond. "I lost my beloved husband to snakebite, but I will not lose my sons to ignorance." Her voice was deadly. "I, as their mother, may not have a say in their future, but remember this—if you don't let my sons go, I will hang myself. The only reason I am keeping myself alive is to protect my sons, to see their future is not marred." She looked at her brother-in-law without blinking. "If you stop them from going to this school, you will have a widow's death on your hands, brother. And this family will be doubly cursed. Remember that."

With that, she turned around and vanished in a whisper of white, leaving her ominous words hanging like a shroud over the stunned family.

CHAPTER 18

Willis Duff, the twenty-two-year-old assistant engineer of Victoria Jute Mills, felt dreadfully inadequate about his wardrobe. After living three years in the small jute mill town, he had sacrificed fashion for the white ducks and bush shirt he wore to work every day. Now he was going to Calcutta on his furlough and his clothes looked hopelessly avuncular. Willis had looked forward to the Calcutta trip with feverish anticipation. He had saved up a nice bundle of pay and dreamed of cocktail luncheons at the Great Eastern with the pretty ladies of Calcutta who would hopefully grant him a kiss or two.

Any spare moment he could find, Willis sat at his office desk and browsed the mail-order catalog that had arrived from Cuthbarton and Fink, fine gentleman clothiers of Calcutta. He was just earmarking a page for white pique bow ties when his boss, Owen McIntosh, summoned him to his office.

"Duff, I have a job for you," he said.

Willis Duff's heart sank. Was his furlough going to be canceled?

"There is a young Bengali boy I want to send with you to Calcutta. Do you recall the godown clerk, Shamol Roy, who died from a cobra bite some months ago?"

Willis nodded. "Yes, sir."

He remembered the fine upright young man in his spotless white Indian clothes that looked out of place in that dank and filthy godown. Willis had felt sorry for the man and given him his last butterscotch toffee.

"This boy is Roy's son," Owen continued. "Your job is to take the lad and deliver him to the representative of Saint John's Mission. The priest will meet you both at the steamer docks. He will be carrying documents for the boy. You will need him to sign the documents when you release the boy."

Willis was so relieved to hear his furlough was not going to be canceled that his face broke into a grin. "That should be no problem at all, sir. No problem at all."

Owen McIntosh looked at him grimly. "I want you to take this assignment very seriously, Duff. I am entrusting this lad to your care. He is a plucky little fellow, very intelligent. I suspect he has never left the village before, so he is likely to be nervous and upset. Be gentle with him, will you? Don't leave him alone in the cabin and go off drinking with lascars on the riverboat. I am more than a little worried about the lad, to tell you the truth. He was very attached to his father. I want to make sure he is all right."

"Of course, sir. I fully understand. Please rest assured."

Owen's cryptic words had a sobering effect on Willis. He had indeed toyed with the idea of wild drinking and gambling on the riverboat with the captain and crew, but now he would have to be careful.

Willis Duff had only to take one look at Biren Roy to feel his heart melt. An orphan himself, he could well understand the terror and uncertainty he saw in the young boy's eyes as he stood clutching his uncle's hand at the steamer ghat. The wee lad looked small and lost in his new travel clothes—an oversize pair of matching sky-blue shorts and shirt that flopped on his skinny frame. His only luggage was a cloth bag worn on a long sling that hung past his knees.

"Traveling light, are we?" Willis joked. Seeing the blank look on both their faces, he tried again, speaking more slowly. "Is that all the luggage you have? Only one small bag?"

"Yes," said the uncle. "Biren is carrying two sets of clothes. The school said not to bring anything else. They will provide everything—uniform, books, toiletries, even pocket money."

"I dare say they'll throw in some whiskey, as well." Willis winked at Biren, who shied behind his uncle.

"No whiskey, no whiskey," said the uncle uneasily. "This is a strict Christian institution." The boy peeped out and gave Willis an impish smile. *Intelligent little fellow*, Willis thought. The uncle on the other hand looked as though he would not have understood a joke even if it jumped up and bit him you-know-where.

"Quite so, quite so," Willis agreed. He turned to Biren. "Say, Biren, do you know how to play fish?"

Biren's face brightened. "Can you catch fish from the steamer boat?" he said, momentarily forgetting his shyness.

"Not that kind of fish." Willis laughed, delighted to hear the boy speak English. He had worried how they were going to communicate. "This fish is a card game. I can teach you how to play it, if you like. But you know what? We may not even have time to play card games. Have you ever traveled by steamer down the big delta to the sea?"

Biren shook his head.

"Oh, you're in for an adventure, wee man! We will be sailing around the Bay of Bengal, then all the way up the Hoogly River to Calcutta." As he talked, Willis drew a map on the riverbank with the toe of his canvas boot. "There is so much to see! We will pass through mangrove forests. I am taking my binoculars so we can do some animal watching. You will see gharial crocodiles—you know, the small fish-eating variety with pointy teeth and a funny lump on their nose? Plenty of river otters and monkeys and, who knows, maybe even a Bengal tiger. We will have a cracking time, I guarantee you."

"What time will the steamer depart?" asked the uncle.

"Oh, I reckon it will be sundown by the time we set sail. We have to wait for the tide to come in. However, there is no need for you to wait here so long, Mr. Roy. Please do not worry about Biren. I will take good care of him. Also, I will be in Calcutta for the next six weeks and I will visit him in the school and make sure he's doing all right and bring back news for you."

"Shall I leave, then?" Uncle asked Biren in Bengali.

Biren nodded and turned his face away.

Willis held out his hand to Biren. "All right, wee mannie, let us go take a look at our cabin and settle you in. We can play a game of fish or two out on the deck, what do you say…aye?"

The riverboat captain was a tall bearded Serang dressed in an embroidered waistcoat and turban. He had under him a contracted crew of lascars who manned the decks. They were strong island people with dazzling teeth and a jaunty walk. Besides the lascars, there were the *mistris* who shoveled coal and worked in the dark bowels of the engine room as well as cooks, sweepers and other menials who stayed out of sight. The Serang and lascars were natural sailors with the river in their blood. They knew how to feel the pulse of the tide and maneuver the flat-bottomed hull of the steamer through narrow channels and waterways without grounding it on a shoal or sandbank.

Tired after a long and confusing day and lulled by the gently bobbing boat, Biren dropped off to sleep on a long chair on the deck. He woke up bewildered and disoriented when the steamer gave a sudden lurch and, with a great big hum of its engines, moved forward. Darkness had fallen all around. Biren peered over the railing. Everything looked very far down from the top deck. The riverbank slid by, past the blur of lighted tea shops and chickpea hawkers with their flaming torches. They moved into a dark patch of countryside dotted with swaying lanterns of villagers heading home. The river breeze, moist and balmy, whipped through the deck as the engine picked up speed. The steamer gave a steamy-sounding hoot that dissolved into the rhythmic *chug-swish, chug-swish* of paddles turning water.

"Ship ahoy!" Willis Duff shouted, pulling himself by the railing to the top deck. "We're off! Hurrah!"

Biren stood there silently. He held the railings of the deck tightly, his knuckles white, his face turned toward the shore.

"Are you all right, my wee man?" Willis asked kindly. He put an arm around the boy's shoulders and was surprised to find them shaking. He bent down to peer at boy's face and was aghast to see it streaked with tears.

"There, there," he said, squatting down, suddenly at a loss for words. He pulled out a white handkerchief from his pocket and handed it to Biren. "Wipe your face. There, there, you are a big boy now, aren't you? Going to boarding school, in Calcutta and all. Dinna cry, laddie. It will be all right, I promise. I know exactly how you feel, believe me."

Biren clung to the rails and continued to sob uncontrollably. He wailed with such heartbreaking sorrow that Willis began to worry. How was he going to manage the wee lad? He would fall sick at this rate. Not knowing what else to do, he held the boy and patted his back, but said nothing.

What Willis did not know was the steamer had just passed Momati Ghat. Biren could make out the dim outline of the tea shop and the shape of the flame tree against the darkened sky. Underneath the tree was a circle of small *diya* lamps and in the center was the figure of a woman dressed in white. She lifted a *diya* and held it up high in a blessing as the steamer sailed past.

That would be the last image of his mother Biren would carry in his mind as he embarked upon his brave journey into the unknown world.

CHAPTER 19

Located on the banks of the Hoogly River, Saint John's Mission covered one hundred and forty-five sprawling acres, enclosed by a moss-covered wall and tall iron gates with the letters *SJM* welded to the center in large metal cutouts. The Catholic school for boys, with five hundred students ranging in ages eight to sixteen, occupied the front end of the property. There was also a seminary for student priests that looked out toward the river next to a small, steepled church with a mossy bell tower. Several whitewashed buildings nestled in shaded mango groves interlinked by walkways lined with leafy neem trees that gave a dappled shade. Every now and then, a white-cassocked priest sailed out on a bicycle from one clump of trees to disappear into another.

Center stage were the administrative offices and a domed assembly hall built in a typical neoclassical style with a circular colonnade and a prominent cornice. Engraved on the frieze above, decorated with swags and ribbons of laurel, was the mission's motto: *Fungar Vice Cotis*. Be as a whetstone for others to be sharpened upon.

Biren was left to wait on a bench outside the principal's office on the second floor. On the facing wall was a framed picture of the Virgin Mary with melancholy eyes holding a strawberry-pink baby Jesus. The *clip-clip-clippity-clip* sound of a typewriter came through the open doorway of the next room, followed by a ratcheting slide and a *pling*. The sound stopped, a chair scraped and a young Indian priest came out of the room with a file in his hand. He had shiny, dark skin and wore open-toed sandals underneath his cassock. He lifted his eyebrows, smiled at Biren and glanced quickly inside the principal's empty office before swishing off down the corridor. A deathly quiet descended, broken only by the sound of a solitary sparrow chirping on the parapet.

A faint bell sounded far away. Biren peered over the top of the windowsill and saw a small boy with a hand bell run across the playground and disappear around the corner of a building. Seconds later a frightful din ensued. Chairs scraped, desks slammed and there were whoops and yells as hundreds of students poured out of several buildings at the same time. They were all dressed identically in gray-and-white uniforms, and Biren watched openmouthed as they pushed, shoved, loitered or hurried from one classroom to another. Three minutes later, they were all inside. Then, miraculously, abrupt silence. Again the only sound came from the same solitary sparrow chirping outside the window.

It was uncanny. How was it even possible for several hundred students to all become quiet at the same time? It sounded like the noisy transfer of glass marbles from one tin can to another: a sudden burst of noise, followed by pin-drop silence. How different it was from his village school. The schoolmaster would have to rap the edge of his desk with his ruler several times and scream, "Quiiiet! Quiiiet!" in a nasal shriek while the boys continued to chatter and misbehave. One or two of them would invariably get their ears twisted before they settled down.

Biren had yet to learn that discipline was an inner mechanism that grew out of a structured and regulated life. It could never be enforced from the outside.

The students of Saint John's consisted mostly of Anglo-Indian orphans, or the sons of clergy. There were only a handful of other Indian students, and they were the sons of progressive Bengali families of Calcutta with Anglophile leanings.

Student accommodations were organized in eight separate boardinghouses, each under the care of a housemaster and a matron. New students were required to undergo an orientation program to familiarize them with the rules of the school. There were twelve new students in Biren's class, aged eight to ten. None of them had ever lived away from home and they all had the same look of terrified kittens abandoned under a bridge.

Biren's house matron was a bosomy Anglo-Indian lady with shrewd eyes and sparse curls named Mrs. Clarks. The students called her Mrs. Clucks because she had a habit of clucking her tongue and saying, "Now-now-quickly-quickly," in a firm but kindly manner.

All students were given identical uniforms: gray pants, white shirts and an ash-and-navy-striped tie, which they had to learn to tie in a Windsor knot, like adult men. To remove some of the intimidation, Matron devised a tie-knotting game, and by the first week all the new students were tying Windsor knots in various sloppy lengths. The sloppy length was forgivable, but what was not forgivable was the untucked shirt, dirty shoes or uncombed hair. At first, the student got off with a warning but after that it was detention. Mrs. Clucks also made sure the boys made their beds correctly, with the sheet corners squared into envelope folds and tucked tightly into the mattress and the blue counterpane spread with the two hanging sides perfectly even.

Biren learned to say "thank you," "please" and "I beg your pardon." He was taught to use a fork and spoon and line them up on his dinner plate when he was done. The hostel food was spiritless but tolerable—mostly Anglo-Indian fare that consisted of watery porridge, rough bread with bits of rope from the flour mill baked in, gristly meat stew flavored with curry powder and gray wobbly blancmange for pudding.

Unlike the village school, where the entire focus was on studies, the education at Saint John's pushed all-round development. Physical education, swimming, elocution and drama—irrespective of a student's aptitude or inclination—were compulsory and a part of the curriculum, while music, metallurgy and woodworking could be picked according to interest. Every student was required to play at least one team sport. There was football, cricket, badminton and hockey to choose from. Competitions were fierce between the different houses. Sometimes the senior students challenged the seminary priests to a match. Once during a tug-of-war there was a great deal of hilarity when the rope went slack and all the priests fell backward in their white cassocks and flattened one another.

The hectic daily routine left Biren breathless. Even Sundays were busy. Attendance at church and Bible studies was optional, but that did not mean non-Christian students could idle around on Sundays. In lieu of church, they were put to work tending the vegetable garden or doing repairs around the school. What a monumental change from village life with its idle loitering and siestas!

Boarding school was also a great equalizer. Everybody dressed in the same clothes. You had the same amount of pocket money. You had to make the attempt to get along with others, work as a team and get things done. The most important lesson Biren learned in boarding school was that one kind of work was not more valuable or superior to another. Back in the village, he would never have had the opportunity to learn leatherwork, carpentry or metallurgy, as they were the occupations of the lower castes. In boarding school he was allowed to try his hand at different vocational activities, and because there was no pressure or expectations, he excelled at them all.

Every week letters came from home. Shibani's letters always felt like a soft embrace; Nitin sent him a drawing of two ants sailing on a boat. On the days the letters arrived, Biren was deeply homesick and he cried silently at night, stifling his sobs into his pillow. Mrs. Clucks must have known this because in the morning she knotted his tie and combed his hair for him. She told Biren to wait after class for a senior boy who would come to talk to him.

The senior boy turned out to be an Anglo-Indian with a pasty complexion and light brown hair, which he wore in a duck curl to one side of his head. His name was Harold D'Souza.

"I thought we could have a little chat," he said. "Let's go sit by the tennis court. So how are you liking school?"

"Fine," said Biren.

"Do you still miss home a lot?"

Biren hesitated, and then gave a slight nod.

"You know, I used to cry every night when I first came to Saint John's," said Harold. "But it won't always feel so bad after a while. Do you go to church?"

Biren shook his head.

"Everything changed for me the day I accepted Jesus Christ as my Lord." His eyes burned with feverish intensity. "Accepting the Lord as my savior is what changed my life. I have never felt lost or lonely again. I wish you could feel as comforted as I do. You can come to church with me next Sunday, if you like. Only if you want to, of course. Not everyone is called to the path. I am one of the chosen ones. Maybe you will be, too."

In church, they sang Latin hymns in great big waves of trembling sound that floated up to the high vaulted ceilings. It gave Biren goose bumps and brought tears to his eyes. The sun streamed in filtered ribbons through the stained-glass skylights and covered the congregation in a warm and wondrous glow. After the service when Biren emerged outside, the trees looked more vivid and the sky smiled a clear and friendly blue.

However, the ethereal feeling did not last.

Many years would go by before Biren would understand the reason why. He continued to attend church for six months. He did indeed feel a sense of belonging and wholeness; the feeling of loneliness went away. Then one Sunday, for no reason, he skipped church and went back to gardening. The next Sunday, he did the same. Nobody said anything or asked him why. The real reason why Biren stopped going to church was because he had unwittingly discovered he got the same spiritual comfort when he did gardening or for that matter any focused task—woodworking, metallurgy or even making his own bed—with a certain inner mindfulness. Performing simple physical tasks gave him a sense of joy that was no different, really, from singing a powerful hymn in church. It would only be many years later, after studying the *Bhagawad Gita*, that Biren would learn that he had accidentally stumbled upon the spiritual principles of karma yoga.

His father had once told him Charulata did not have to go to the temple to find God, because she had discovered her own inner shrine. The power of the universe was disguised in the patterns of daily life and somewhere, unconsciously, Biren had made that connection.

CHAPTER 20

Nitin suffered an attack of scarlet fever followed by two years of poor health. He was admitted to Saint John's Mission only when he turned eleven. By then Biren was a senior and well molded by the English school system. At fifteen, he was the tallest in his class, slim and strong with dark steady eyes. His hair grew out in disobedient curls, and just as disobedient was his voice, because no matter how hard he tried he could never tame it into submission. When it behaved, his voice was a rich and pleasing baritone, but with no warning it switched to a falsetto and often ended in an embarrassing squawk. Greatly alarmed by its unpredictability, he chose to speak little and cultivated instead a scholarly air in keeping with the image he wanted to present to the world.

Meanwhile eleven-year-old Nitin arrived at Saint John's thin and spindly legged, looking like a village cowherd. By then his classmates were already polished with their boarding school manners and established in their friendships. Biren worried Nitin's adjustment would be hard, and he kept a protective eye out for his young brother.

On Nitin's second day in school, Biren saw him at morning assembly with his hair neatly combed in a side parting and sporting a perfectly knotted tie. Assuming Mrs. Clucks had given him a hand, he was surprised to learn Nitin had groomed himself. Mrs. Clucks was so pleased, Nitin said, she gave him a piece of chocolate fudge. By the end of the second week he had made it into the junior football team. Nitin's sweet nature endeared him to all. He made the boys laugh by drawing funny cartoons of the teachers as ants with witty blurbs above their heads. Unlike Biren, who tended to be pensive and solitary, Nitin made friends easily. To Biren's intense relief, Nitin took to boarding school like a duckling to water. He never once looked back.

During the summer months the boys came home for seven weeks. Each year the gap between village and city life became more evident. Not a single twig changed in the village. The rusted tea shop on Momati Ghat still leaned on one side; the fishing boats sailed up and down with their ragged sails; the paddle steamer gushed past in the sleepy afternoon and the flame tree blazed a deep and torrid red.

At the *basha*, things had deteriorated. Grandpa developed cataracts in both eyes, Uncle got pyorrhea and lost all his teeth. Uncle lost his wife, as well. Following a big fight, the gloomy aunt had packed her trunks and went off to her father's house. This was two years ago, and it was unlikely she was ever coming back.

The most marked change was in Shibani. The part-time maid had been let go, and all the backbreaking household chores were thrust upon her. Shibani woke at dawn to light the fires and draw water from the well. All day long she cooked and cleaned, scrubbing heavy cast-iron pots with coconut husk and ash until her fingers bled. Her skin had turned a patchy gray; her nails were cracked. She looked like a beggar woman. When she embraced the boys, she reeked of lime and cow dung smoke, the unmistakable smell of the poor. For the boys, she was still their mother and they burned with a fierce love for her. They spent most of their time in the woodshed, which had been turned into her Spartan living quarters. They ate her bland vegetarian food, refusing the nice treats their Granny prepared for them. Careful all the while not to disrespect their grandmother, they slyly maneuvered their way out of her affections, proving that they had grown beyond her sphere of influence.

Biren and Nitin were no longer village boys. They walked and talked like *belaytis* and spoke to each other in boarding school slang that nobody in the *basha* could understand. Only Shibani looked on dotingly at her sons, her eyes soft with love. Her hand occasionally reached out to caress one's cheek or smooth back the other's hair. They stole chili tamarind, pickles and sour plums for her and acted as secret messengers between her and Apu. They were both big boys, bony and angular, but they still wanted to snuggle like little children under her patched quilts and listen to stories about their father and the things they used to do when they were young. To entertain her they told her stories about Mrs. Clucks and the senile priests in their boarding school.

"Father Lewis is so old he falls asleep during assembly," said Biren.

"And one time he fell—like this," said Nitin, and toppled

facedown on the bed. "The next day he had a big potato on his head."

All too quickly, vacation would come to an end. Shibani became matter-of-fact, almost brusque, as the time to leave drew near. She brushed them off like crumbs from her sari, acting as though she didn't care. There were no tears, sentimental words or lingering embraces. Yet when she kissed them on the forehead one last time they could tell by her trembling lips her heart was breaking like their own, but they also knew her greater joy came from setting them free.

CHAPTER 21

Father Anthony, the principal of Saint John's Mission, proudly displayed two beautiful handcrafted items on his big mahogany desk. One was a rosewood box, with the design of a Celtic trinity knot carved on the lid, which if you looked closely were actually the forms of cleverly braided fish. The second was a cast-iron bell with a clear sound and rich overtone. A gifted student named Biren Roy had made both items.

Father Anthony had picked them up at the annual charity auction to raise money for student scholarships. He had admired the box and the bell so much he'd ended up bidding well beyond his means for them. They were impeccably crafted, and every day he derived great pleasure just to look at them sitting on his desk.

Biren Roy was an exceptional student. He was meticulous, a perfectionist. His single-minded concentration and monk-like devotion to any given task was rather unusual for one so young. That child would make an excellent priest, thought Father Anthony. What a pity he had chosen not to embrace Christianity.

At first, Father Anthony was delighted to see him at church, but for some unknown reason the boy stopped coming. The child did not appear troubled in any way. He cheerfully did any chore he was given on Sundays; he just chose not go to church, for reasons of his own. Normally Father Anthony would have had a private conversation with a student to find out the reason for his change of heart, but he did not feel the need to do so this time because Biren was an exemplary student in every way. In fact, he was the very poster child of the same Christian values the school tried to instill in their students.

Father Anthony had already made up his mind, when the time came, to recommend Biren Roy for the Cambridge scholarship. The boy came from a poor village in Sylhet, he had lost his father at a tender age and nobody was more deserving than him. This fine young man would do Saint John's Mission proud, of that Father Anthony had no doubt.

London
2nd March 1889

Dear Biren,
It is a miracle to connect with you after all these years! I am very excited that you will be in England soon, and congratulations, dear friend, on your scholarship to Cambridge. Why am I not surprised?

I tried several times over the years to get in touch with you. My relatives in the village told me both you and your brother were studying in an English boarding school in Calcutta but they had no further details. I was very sorry to hear about your father's tragic death. The relative I wrote to ask about your whereabouts was reluctant to meet with your mother. Therefore, you can imagine my joy when you went to our village home and got my address and wrote to me. Now you are coming to England!

After completing my schooling in Harrow, I studied in Cambridge for a while. Now I am studying for my law degree in London. My older brother, Diju, and his English wife, Veronica, live in London and I stay with them. My mother and my immediate family are in Calcutta. A few of my relatives, including my grandmother, still live in our village home, the house with the big sour plum tree, do you remember?

Please let me know the details of your travel so I can meet your ship in London. You must spend a few days with me so I can show you around the city.

I will write more about myself in the next letter.

With best wishes,
Sammy (Samir Deb)

On August 15, 1889, Biren Roy, aged seventeen, boarded the P&O liner the *Britannica* and set sail for London. He carried sixteen shillings in his pocket, and inside his steel trunk packed lovingly by his mother were two hand-knitted mufflers and a three-year supply of dried ginger root to ward off the dreaded cough of England.

A feeling of desolation came over him as the ship pulled away from the Calcutta shoreline. Biren had lived away from home for most of his growing years, but he had never experienced the terrifying sense of disconnect he felt now. To be cut off from his birthplace by the endless sea seemed cruel and final—like a feather plucked from a wing. This separation would leave Biren forever stranded between two worlds with a finger stretched toward his homeland, almost touching, but never quite making the connection.

London
23rd September 1889

London is bewildering!

People rush in and out of buildings, step in and out of carriages, fold and unfold umbrellas—everything is in constant motion. What a contrast to village life in India, where boats, bullock carts and people flow, sway and amble along like they have all the time in the world.

The jittery haste of London has much to do with the inclement weather, I have concluded. One never knows what to expect. In a single day I watched a sparkling morning collapse with a thundery squall into a wet squelchy afternoon. The evening, surprisingly, was marvelously clear and enjoyable.

And the people!

Exquisitely gowned women with impossible waists and astonishing hats step in and out of carriages, their skirts lifted daintily in gloved hands. Their hats baffle me, as they can resemble anything from a plumbing fixture to a plumed creature of frightening proportions. Handkerchiefs are dropped strategically in front of select gentlemen to invite conversation. The Englishman carries himself with palpable pride. You can see it in the tilt of his chin, the swing of his cane, the cut and fashion of his clothing. They tip their hats and exchange polite nods. Even among acquaintances there is a level of formality and restraint. Watching them interact is like watching a courtly play of manners. How unlike the ways of my own countrymen with their loud cries of recognition and foot-waggling chatter over cups of tea.

The imperial prosperity of Britain is evident everywhere. Every wall in the city is plastered with advertisements of get-rich-quick investments, outrageous inventions and miracle health remedies. Small paperboys with chapped cheeks and the scheming eyes of grown men cry, "Payper! Payper! Speyshul." They zigzag across the tram track under the noses of thundering horses. Waiflike shopgirls stare out at the street with vacant eyes, and the grand old coachman in his long dark coat perched on top of his cab tips his hat and calls you "guvnor."

My old friend Samir Deb—who now calls himself Sammy—was at the port to meet me. He was hard to miss in his shiny blue suit with a pink carnation in the buttonhole. With his pomade-slicked hair, small tidy moustache and ivory tipped cane, he is quite the dandy. Sammy had an English girl on his arm whom he introduced as Dottie Dawson. Dottie has brass-colored hair and talks in an accent I can barely follow. She appears to be Sammy's latest love interest, although Sammy tells me—aside, in Bengali—his mother is looking for a girl for him to marry in India.

At the end of two exhausting days of sightseeing—and getting pickpocketed in Piccadilly—I will leave for Cambridge tomorrow where the most important chapter of my life is waiting to begin.

Cambridge
28th September 1889

This is my fourth day in Cambridge. Yesterday I walked around till I got a hole in my shoe. There is a substantial hole in my funds, as well. I am now reduced to six shillings and forty pence. Just as well, my food and board is paid for, but I will need to buy an umbrella, soap and candles, so I must look for part-time employment without further delay.

It is frightfully cold. The marshy lowlands surrounding Cambridge exude a crypt-like damp that gnaws at the bone. For accommodations I have been assigned a monk-like cell with moth-colored walls in a crumbling boardinghouse called Brockwell Lodge. It is right next to the university library and a ten-minute walk from King's College where I will be spending most of my time. The room is a double occupancy but I am told my roommate, a gentleman by the name of E. M. White, who was expected to arrive from Dublin, has taken ill and will not be joining this term, so for the moment I have the room to myself. The room is sparsely furnished with a desk and bed. The high ceilings make it rather drafty. Thank God for the coal fireplace. I may have to use my last penny to buy coal. Next on my list are stamps and candles. I will forgo the soap for now.

On the whole I feel a sense of elation. It is nothing short of a miracle that I am in Cambridge, England. There is a monastic stillness about this place. The pale stone architecture with its archways, turrets, spires, the great carved frescos and pillared halls, so richly steeped in history and legend, make me feel like I am on hallowed ground. To think of all the monumental discoveries, movements in science, art, literature and emerging political thought that have taken place within these walls, and to walk the same hallways and breathe the same air as Darwin, Newton, Tennyson and Donne, feels rather unreal. The enormity of it all is just beginning to sink in.

The hole in my shoe and my wet socks are a constant reminder I will need to earn money soon. I checked the help-wanted sections on the notice boards of different colleges. There is part-time work available at the bindery of the University Press. Also odd jobs such as gardening, cleanup, woodworking, painting, roof repairs, welding—all of which I am capa-

ble of doing thanks to my training at Saint John's Mission. I will be eternally grateful to them for that. Had I arrived here straight from the village I would have been completely useless. Tomorrow I will make inquiries and see which jobs are still available. First, I must find a cobbler in town to mend my shoe. I have stuffed a piece of cardboard inside for now. Also, I find an umbrella is not enough. I may have to invest in a secondhand raincoat.

Cambridge
30th September 1889

Yesterday I worked the night shift in the bindery. I came back to my room to find a note slipped under my door inviting me to an evening soiree to meet the Bengali student group of Cambridge. It was signed Samaresh Bannerjee, and the address is a boardinghouse in Kingsway, about a fifteen-minute walk from my hostel.

Samaresh Bannerjee is a brilliant philosophy student completing his doctorate in Cambridge. A genteel Bengali with a pampered moustache, he has a musical voice and dresses in silk pajamas and gold embroidered slippers. Samaresh hails from the famous Bannerjee family of Calcutta. They are high caste Brahmins who denounced orthodoxy to form the Bhramo Samaj, a reformist group who are pushing social change for women. The Bannerjee clan is very wealthy, having amassed vast fortunes through their family business in law, indigo, shipping and publishing. What I admire most is their commitment to philanthropy. Samaresh is older than the other students in this group. I would put his age around twenty-eight or twenty-nine. He is already married with a young wife in Calcutta.

As a postgraduate student he enjoys the privileges of a large pleasant room with a comfortable seating area, to which he has added brightly colored silk bolsters, a Kashmiri carpet and Madhubani paintings to create a cozy feeling of home. The windows of his room look out on a peaceful communal garden with stone benches dappled with the shade of plane trees. There is a kindly patriarchal air about Samaresh, and his room has become the gathering place for the Indian students of Cambridge.

Most Indian students, I find, do not socialize with the English. They stay glued to academics and rarely venture outside their rooms or study halls. The class and cultural differences create some awkwardness, as well. English students bond through sports and extracurricular activities. Cambridge attracts scholars of exceptional merit from around the world. It is also the wealthiest university in Europe and funded almost entirely by endowments. The majority of Cambridge students are sons of English aristocracy or landed gentry who take university education for granted. For them it is simply a rite of passage and not a life raft—like it is for some of us.

CHAPTER 22

Samaresh had a crackling log fire going and two braziers for added warmth. With plenty of sweet cardamom tea and arrowroot biscuits to go around, a nostalgic mood prevailed among the Bengali students gathered in his room. One of them pulled out the harmonium and started singing a popular song. Another accompanied him with a tabla beat drummed on a wooden desk. When several voices joined in a rousing chorus, there was hardly a dry eye left in the room. A sentimental song about rivers, heartbreak and monsoon skies never failed to stir up a deep longing for home.

Later the conversation turned, as it invariably did with Bengalis, to politics.

"The English people have a superiority complex," declared Ram, a third-year medical student. "They think they can rule the world just because they are white."

Samaresh thoughtfully stroked his well-tended moustache.

He sat in a half-lotus position, one arm draped over a raised knee like a maharaja. "It's more than being white," he said in his sonorous voice. "The English know how to manipulate minds."

"I think their secret is the power of organization," said Biren. "The British public school curriculum focuses on leadership training. In Indian schools we focus on bookish knowledge. We don't encourage critical or analytical thinking."

Ram frowned. "What do you mean?"

"What I mean is the British upper class is trained to think like leaders from a very early age. Look at the curriculum of English public schools—competitive sports encourage physical discipline and teamwork, subjects like logic, rhetoric and philosophy help to organize ideas and present arguments. The focus is on leadership. I think there's something to be learned there."

"Yet, if you think about it," said the sage-like Samaresh, "it is this same elitist education that divides British society and creates class barriers. English public school students go on to study in Oxbridge. They become members of Parliament and make laws that serve the interests of the upper class. Look at it this way—the caste system may divide India, but it is class that divides Britain. Every country finds a way to keep society divided into the haves and the have-nots. It's not so much about money as it is about entitlement."

Biren grew quiet as he thought about his mother. Society had found a way to keep her trapped as a widow. Irrespective of money or caste, the plight of all Hindu widows was the same. They had no voice; it was almost as if they did not exist.

It would take a new law to eradicate this social evil, thought Biren. Two other social evils—widow burning and child marriage—were both abolished by the British only after they enforced strict laws in India. This was the very reason why he was in Cambridge. To study law and effect change from the inside.

CHAPTER 23

Cambridge
7th February 1890

Dear brother Nitin,
I wonder how long my letter will take to reach you. Postage to India is dear, so my letters to you and Ma may not be as frequent as I would like, but I will try to fit in as much news as I can.

I am glad to know you are doing well in school. You seem to have better sporting abilities than me. Congratulations on being appointed captain of the football team. Sports and extracurricular are valued highly in English universities, and you will find it very easy to fit in. We are both lucky to have studied at Saint John's Mission.

I am still settling in. The student accommodation provided for me is very basic. I am thankful my room has a coal fireplace. I can heat a kettle for tea, make toast and boil an egg or two.

Some days I have to skip my evening meal as I am usually out doing some odd job or other. The nights are frightfully cold.

The beautiful row of poplars on the way to Grantchester is still bare of leaves. There is a lonesome beauty in their naked branches. England has the most beautiful trees you can imagine. Magnificent horse chestnuts, lindens and leafy willows along the Cam. I can't wait to see the meadows in spring. The purple crocuses have just started to bud behind Trinity College, and there is a wilderness area that runs riot with anemones and daffodils. Cambridge colleges are located in picturesque natural settings right out of an English storybook.

I work part-time at the bindery of the Cambridge University Press. I also do odd jobs—carpentry, painting and repairs. The drama club needs props, the rowing club needs boat painting and repairs before the annual Lent bumps, which is a boat race of sorts. To the untutored, the bumps would appear nothing more than a jostling and slamming of boats down the narrow Cam to get to first place. The victorious teams celebrate by decorating one another with willow branches followed by long sessions of feasting and drinking.

I spend a lot of time at the Cambridge Union Society. I am considering joining a private debating club, but membership to the best ones are by invitation only. The most interesting one is called the Erudites. They pick excellent thought-provoking topics but occasionally a completely inane one. I went to a debate where the topic was "Why laugh?" The speakers presented the most hair-splitting arguments on the whys and why-nots of laughter, all delivered in a formal parliamentary style, which made the whole debate unbearably funny. I've concluded the purpose of such insanity is not merely to amuse but to sharpen mental agility and develop nimble arguments.

The Indian scholars I have met here are some of the bright-

est and the best. If such groups of enlightened thinkers return to our homeland, India will break free of her narrow bonds and be transformed forever.

Not a single day goes by when I don't think of you and Ma. I have saved ten shillings, which I will send you. If Uncle is still managing the basha *funds, I wonder if poor Ma is given any money at all for her personal use. When you go home, please give her eight shillings and keep two for yourself.*

I remain your affectionate brother,
Dada

CHAPTER 24

There was always some news or other ringing the grapevines of Cambridge. First, there was Attila, the malevolent swan who hid in shadowy willows of the Cam and flapped out to bite innocent bystanders. Attila brought summer activities like punting and fishing along the river to a halt. The proctors, with the help of the townspeople, made several attempts to capture and relocate Attila, but ended up relocating two friendly black swans, while Attila still lurked darkly in the shadows.

The bigger news making the rounds was a scathing article that appeared in the *Archangel*, a magazine published by a feminist group at Girton, which, along with Newnham, were the two women's colleges of Cambridge. The article was an exposé on a recent debate held at the Cambridge Union Society, the controversial topic of which was that "Newnham and Girton are useless and dangerous and ought to be abolished."

Female education was still a contentious issue in Cambridge and the students attempting to earn degrees were jeered at and ridiculed. Cambridge had barred female students for centuries, and the male bastion was not going to give in easily. Biren had assumed the existence of two exclusive women's colleges would level the playing field, but clearly this was not the case. It was ironic that girls in India had no opportunity for education, while in England they had the opportunity, but that did not necessarily translate into equality.

This prejudice was clearly voiced in the *Archangel* article. The writer described Cambridge male students as a boorish, misogynistic bunch—nothing more than prehistoric creatures under their thin veneers of civility that viewed women only as useful ornaments. The article was signed E.L. Judging by the tone, the author had to be a woman, but there were no existing records of any females in the audience that day.

Biren scrutinized the article.

"It's brilliantly worded," he conceded. "I love the sarcasm of the writer. It must be a firsthand account because I was at the debate that day and every argument quoted here is almost verbatim. You can't write with this kind of detail unless you were present there and taking notes."

"Some students did notice a fellow taking notes," said Ram. "He was effeminate-looking, French, I believe, sitting in the second row on the right."

"Effeminate, you say? How interesting," mused Biren. "This article is written from a woman's perspective. What if that fellow was actually a woman disguised as a man?"

"Oh, that's impossible!" Ram laughed. "A disguise is not

an easy thing easy to pull off—onstage, yes, but not in real life. But think of the risk. Which woman would even dare to do it?"

"An interesting woman, for sure," said Biren. "One with a daredevil streak and a sense of fun. Man or woman, I would love to meet this E.L. person someday."

Cambridge
18th March 1890

I have been busy working on a stage set for the drama club's upcoming production of A Midsummer Night's Dream. *The painted tree cutouts and backdrops are taking a long time to dry, thanks to the inclement weather here. The carpentry workshop where I work is located behind the drama club. It is the meeting place for the theater types. All kinds of people drop by, to play Carrom, chat or borrow something.*

Yesterday a rather curious fellow came by. He is overweight with short legs and looks a little frayed about the gills. He introduced himself as Bertie McInnis and asked me if I was Indian. Bertie is a Cambridge dropout who has a passion for the theater. He is part owner of a private theater company called the People's Playhouse in town. They perform mostly Shakespeare and the occasional burlesque. Bertie is quite a talker. He has heard fascinating stories about India from his uncle, who was a famous surveyor for the British government. His uncle spent several years navigating the remote and dangerous jungles of northeast India, where he almost got scalped by a cannibal tribe! The famous tea-growing region of Assam was mapped out by his uncle's own hand.

Bertie's theater company is badly in need of backstage help. He asked me if I could help out on Tuesday evenings for two hours in return for free tickets. Their current production is a popular burlesque called The Runaway Shopgirl. *I agreed to meet him at the playhouse behind the stables of the Red Roof Inn next week.*

Cambridge
24th March 1890

Not only did I help backstage, I got roped into playing a minor role as a railway porter in The Runaway Shopgirl. *It was easy enough. All I did was wear a brass-buttoned blue uniform and carry bags behind a rather buxom female. Samaresh and a few other Bengali friends to whom I had given free tickets were highly amused to see me. I must admit I rather enjoyed my five seconds of fame. Later Bertie asked me if I would be interested in playing another minor role as a courtier in their upcoming production of* Twelfth Night. *I agreed for the fun of it. I admitted I had not done much acting. He convinced me that learning voice projection and other drama techniques would enhance my debating skills. I suppose he has a point. As long as I don't have to spend too much time in rehearsals, this could be interesting.*

CHAPTER 25

Following a freak storm in mid-April, Biren returned to his room in Brockwell Lodge to find his study desk covered with water from a roof leak. The damage was severe, and he had to vacate his room and look for temporary accommodation while the roof got repaired. His choices were limited. Many students lived in private boardinghouses around the university but the rents were much higher than he could afford.

It was Bertie McInnis who told him about the room for rent at Grantham Manor.

Biren learned that Grantham Manor had once been the stately country residence of the luckless Baron le Pomme, who had whittled away his family fortune. The baron still owned the manor but he was absconding somewhere in Europe to evade taxes. The manor meanwhile was falling apart for want of upkeep. The formal living room, the grand dining hall, boudoirs and private parlors were all closed off due to roof leaks and water damage. The only inhabitable section—the west wing—was rented out to the Lovelace family. They had lived in Grantham Manor for fifteen years.

"This is the same uncle I told you about, Samuel Lovelace, the surveyor in India," Bertie said. "After he came back from India he taught in Cambridge for a while. Now he has joined politics. He and my aunt Catherine live the summer in London when Parliament is in session and they come back to Grantham Manor during the fall. I spent many years of my childhood in Grantham Manor with my cousins."

"Do your cousins live there now?"

"Nobody lives there right now, as far as I know. James works in London and Estelle last I heard was gadding about in Paris. They come and go. I try to avoid Uncle Samuel. He was not too happy with me after I dropped out of Cambridge, especially after he paid for my tuition."

"I would imagine the rent at Grantham Manor would be quite dear," said Biren.

"The room for rent has nothing to do with my uncle—it's up to Mrs. Pickles. Mrs. Pickles is the old housekeeper of Grantham Manor. She ran the manor back in the grand old days when Baron le Pomme and his family lived here. Mrs. Pickles is very old and lives in the garret above the kitchen with all her disgusting cats. To support herself, she rents out a room in the old stables. The other day I went to Grantham Manor to pick up my uncle's mail and Mrs. Pickles mentioned the room had become available and asked me if I knew of anyone who would want to rent it. The rent should be reasonable, I would imagine. Go and meet Mrs. Pickles. Tell her you are my friend."

It was the perfect day for a river walk. The beautiful Cam flowed along the tall stony embankments of the colleges, ducking under the loops of tiny bridges and lingering over meadows bright with daffodils. On a rare sunny day, the English countryside was sheer poetry. The willows brightened to a deep frilly green and brushed the water like lacy petticoats. Biren watched a convoy of baby swans, still in their baby fluff, paddle behind elegant parents who looked as if they were dressed for the Queen's Ball.

He entered Grantham Manor through an apple orchard buzzing with bees, and passed an apiary with boxed beehives fallen into disrepair. There was an abandoned Gothic dairy next to a large kitchen garden growing a fine crop of turnips and leafy rhubarb on fleshy red stems.

Mrs. Pickles sat on a small stool in the kitchen shelling peas. She had a faded blue scarf tied around her head, and her tired old body slumped over a small stool like a sack of potatoes. She squinted at Biren through shortsighted eyes.

"Young man, you're late," she said. "Your note said you would be here at 10:00 a.m." She glanced up at the ancient wall clock. It was ten past. "I s'pose you want to see the room." She set the bowl down on the table and heaved herself to her feet, which were surprisingly tiny, and shuffled toward the larder. On the wall next to a wooden cross was a hook with several keys. She selected one hanging on a rope and handed it to Biren.

She pointed to the doorway. "If you go around to the front of the house, the stables will be on your left. It's the second room above the stables. Don't go to the first room. It is full of rubbish. Now, about the rent. It's fifteen shillings. Due on the first Monday of the month. I don't provide meals. I hope you know that. You can buy dry goods, tea, coffee, soap, candles and other things at the village grocers. The bakeshop sells meat pies and other cooked dishes." She squinted at Biren. "You probably don't eat beef like other Indians, do you? Now, wait a minute—or was it pork? Hindustanis don't eat one thing, Mohammedans don't eat the other. So which one are you?"

"I eat everything," said Biren.

"Just as well. You'll find plenty to eat in the village, then. You can also help yourself to coal from the coalhouse behind the kitchen if you want to make your own toast and tea. The stable room has a fireplace and, oh, yes, I must warn you about the peacocks. They will take some getting used to. I don't want you moving into the room and then wanting to move out and asking for your rent back. That's what happened with the last lodger."

"Did you say *peacocks*?"

"Yes, peacocks. Mr. Lovelace has a fondness for peacocks, having lived in India and such. The peacock cage is right next to the stables. Until a few years ago they were wandering all around the garden, but they tore up the plants and ate all the roses. Very destructive birds, them peacocks. Mrs. Lovelace had them all caged up. Now they make the most awful noise. The other student who used to rent the room left because he couldn't stand the screeching. Tore his brain out, he said, the peacocks did."

She walked back to the kitchen table and collapsed on the stool with a thump. "Young man, I may not be here when you get back. Put the key back on the hook and write me a note if you want the room. There's pencil and paper in the egg basket above the larder. I will need one month's rent. Fifteen shillings."

The room for rent above the stables was narrow and Spartan with rough stone floors. All it contained was a narrow bed against the wall, a grated fireplace and a porcelain basin on a wooden stand. The small window, set rather high off the ground, roughly at Biren's chin height, looked out at the ancient flowering trees of the apple orchard and a part of the crumbling rock wall separating the meadows. Biren watched a pale green caterpillar with white longitudinal stripes crawl in slow arching waves along the windowsill. He held out a finger and it crawled onto his hand. He carried it outside and set it onto the bark of an apple tree. His heart went out to the caterpillar—a small cheerful creature enjoying a spot of sun, blissfully unaware of the terrors beyond its leafy world.

After examining the room and finding it acceptable, Biren wandered around the grounds of the estate. Viewed from the front driveway, Grantham Manor was impressive. There were several wings in varying architectural styles that looked as if they had been added on at different times, and by different owners. The main hall was built of pale yellow Jurassic limestone—the same material as many of the colleges in Cambridge. The added-on wings all had different tints of stone, yet the mismatched pieces coalesced together in an oddly beautiful way. The graveled terrace and driveway extended out toward a pair of imposing gates flanked by great piers topped with urns. The boundary wall was ablaze with red ivy. The crescendo of color reminded Biren of the flame tree of his village in India.

Ancient oaks shaded the main lawn, and a serpentine path led to a mossy rockery and terraced garden with a beautiful climbing-rose wall. Next to a sweeping chestnut tree was a large netted enclosure that housed the family of peacocks. The male bird walked up and down with great pomp, his long tail feathers lifted delicately off the ground, while three homely females with mottled chests pecked earnestly in the dirt making small clucking noises.

It felt odd to see the sacred bird of Indian mythology strutting around in a formal English garden. The flamboyant bird with its tufted head and iridescent gold, turquoise and emerald feathers looked ostentatious and out of place. Back home, the peacock enjoyed the exalted status of a deity. Even a starving beggar in India would never dream of eating a peacock, whereas here in England the regal bird was roasted and served in a bed of his own tail feathers for special occasions. The meat was dry and gamey, he heard, not exactly delicious, which made even less sense why one would want to eat it at all. The English with their craving for exotic flesh were even known to eat larks. *Larks!* The poor little songbirds were baked into a pie to create a dainty dish for the king, Biren was told.

CHAPTER 26

Estelle Lovelace could hardly wait to get out of London.

It felt stifling, like being trapped in a corset, she imagined, not that Estelle had ever worn a corset in all her nineteen years, thanks to her carefree upbringing in India. Mummy was too busy with her gin luncheons and left the care of Estelle and her brother, James, to their ayah. As children they swam naked in rivers and ponds and their ayah, of ample bosom and little shame, swam right along with them. Estelle and James had seen more naked bodies during their childhood in India than in their entire adult lives in England. By the time the family was reinstated in England, Estelle had grown leggy and untrimmed like a wild rosebush. The English governess, Miss Smithers, with her crackling petticoats and herring breath, finally gave up and declared it too late to reshape her into any semblance of a lady.

Estelle made no bones about her disdain for London

society—the hatted ladies and their tea parties where the gossip was spread thicker than the clotted cream on their scones. Of course, Estelle had added the latest delectable morsel to their conversation after her broken engagement with Pierre Jolie, or the Jolly Pear as he was nicknamed by her brother, James. The Jolly Pear was half English and half French, which made him half acceptable for Mummy and half interesting for Estelle. She had drifted into the relationship from boredom, and suffered the occasional pinch of misgiving at the thought of surrendering her independence. Therefore it was a mixed blessing for her when the Jolly Pear turned out to be not so jolly when slapped with a court case for fraud involving railway stocks. The scandal, splashed all over the London papers, made Daddy furious because he had been roped in as the guarantor for Jolly Pear's nefarious scheme. Mummy collapsed while reaching for her sal volatile and Estelle was desperate to beat a hasty retreat out of London.

Grantham Manor called to her. Estelle longed for the quiet of the wooded glades and peaceful meadows. Maybe she would get the bicycle out and ride around the country a bit. She still had not worn the Turkish-style bloomer pants she had had tailored in Paris. They were the latest sporting fashion of the day, but Mummy would surely faint to see her in them. It was bad enough Estelle had cut off her waist-length hair, but to wear bloomer pants and cycle around in public would mean the ultimate demise of her matrimonial prospects.

Estelle had coerced Daddy into buying her the bicycle. It was only fair, she argued. James and cousin Bertie had bicycles, why not her? Mummy said too much time in the wind and sun would spoil Estelle's hair and complexion, but her concerns ran deeper.

The bicycle had become the new symbol of female emancipation. If a woman riding a bicycle was not shocking enough, a woman sitting astride the saddle wearing a pair of bifurcated bloomers instead of a skirt was certainly the height of scandal. Bloomers, viewed as a sexually provocative garment, elicited all kinds of lewd comments.

How utterly ridiculous, thought Estelle. Even as early as 400 BC, women in India had worn gathered pantaloons of thin, breathable cotton because it was practical for the tropical weather. Ironically, this was around the same time when Roman men ruled an empire in their effeminate flowing togas. Clothes, according to Estelle, should be designed for practicality and comfort, the frills and bows being secondary. Here in England it seemed to be the other way around.

Estelle's friends at Girton College were hardly the frills-and-bows variety. Estelle had a natural tendency to gravitate toward the rebels and the openly defiant. Most of her friends came from the privileged class but they were more drawn to social issues than to London fashion. By championing the rights of the motley and the maligned, they saw themselves as thinking women.

In open defiance, Estelle's friends had formed their own cycling club. The controversy surrounding bicycles was often the subject of discussion. Samantha Duncan, the president of the club, a bony, athletic woman—whom Estelle's mother once described as a hat rack—glanced through the latest newspaper report. She shook open the paper and gave a derisive snort.

"Just listen to this," she called out to the others, then read from the report. "The esteemed Dr. Osborn, orthopedic surgeon, is quoted here saying, 'Cycling poses a serious risk to women's health. The latest medical research concludes a woman's skeletal structure is too delicate and not designed for the vigorous pedaling motion. Such strenuous activity should be discouraged in females. It can cause irreparable damage to the kidneys, distort the pelvis and lead to infertility.'" Samantha threw the newspaper down on the desk. "This is utter rot!"

Isadora Burke, a spry, dark-haired woman, smoked her long-handled cigarette and blew two perfect smoke rings up at the ceiling. She was a member of a feminist group and often rallied outside Parliament for the rights of prostitutes and factory workers. "If the medical community is so concerned about women's health," she drawled in her gravelly voice, "why don't they ever talk about the conditions of female workers in the factories? What about the health risks of working long hours, without proper ventilation, in appalling, unhygienic conditions?"

"It's totally hypocritical," agreed Samantha.

"I was talking to my brother, James, the other day," said Estelle. "The bicycle, it seems, threatens men at a very deep level. Men fear that the pedaling motion will cause sexual arousal and lead women to promiscuity..."

The others burst out laughing.

"How utterly ridiculous!" said Isadora, wiping her eyes. "Surely you are not serious?"

"No, it's really true," insisted Estelle. "The fear is promiscuity will lead to women straying and break up marriages and our society will collapse like a deck of cards. Conclusion—women riding bicycles leads to collapse of society. End of the story."

Samantha rolled her eyes. "They make us sound like a flock of geese waiting to take off. Oh, for crying out loud!"

"But think about it seriously for a moment," said Isadora. "Every culture has its own way to keep a woman helpless and dependent on a man. In China, they have foot binding, in England we have corsets. It's all to the same end. Female bondage."

"That's an interesting topic," said Samantha. "Estelle, why don't you do a write-up for the *Archangel* on the female bondage theme? At least you won't have to go undercover for this one."

"You pulled off that one, you gutsy thing!" Isadora laughed. "There is no way I could have done it."

"I dare say I enjoyed it," Estelle said, twirling an imaginary moustache. "Maybe I should take up the job of a private eye. Bertie's makeup man is a genius. I hardly recognized myself. You should have seen Bertie at that debate. He was so jittery sitting next to me, his eyes kept darting all over the place. If I got caught that day it would have been his fault."

"You had no option but to go undercover," said Samantha. "Given the topic of the debate, any female in the audience would have stuck out like a sore thumb. You would have never been able to take notes, for one."

"There's another union debate coming up in August on the topic of women's suffrage," said Estelle. "Maybe we should go in a group. What do you say?"

"I'll go," said Isadora.

"Me, too," said Samantha.

"Very well, then," said Estelle. "We can decide on a time to meet outside the union building. Hopefully nobody will recognize me as the same Monsieur Jolie."

"Oh, I think you are perfectly safe," Isadora reassured her. "I don't think for a moment anybody imagined a woman would dare to enter the union disguised as a man. The idea is just too preposterous."

"Thank God," said Estelle, "we can all count on the gullibility of the male race. It doesn't take much to pull the wool over their eyes, does it?"

CHAPTER 27

As he prepared for the union debate, Biren discovered the empty meadow was a fine place to practice his voice inflections and think aloud his arguments. The topic of the debate was the opposition of suffrage rights for women in Britain, and Biren was speaking against the motion. He knew it would be an acrimonious debate. Legislation to advance female equality seemed to threaten the bedrock of any society, east or west. It was surprising to see Britain, for all its imperial glory, industrial advancements, its railway and ocean travel, still harbored a rather dim view of women. Biren decided he would have to appeal to human decency and challenge the motion on moral and ethical grounds.

And so it was among the buttercups and daisies that Biren practiced his arguments. His audience, bovine and kindly, chewed contemplatively, and occasionally twitched their ears in agreement. At times Biren imagined he saw rapt awe in their faces, and occasionally one would nod. Encouraged by their confidence, Biren marched up and down the meadow, brandished his arms and shouted at the sky. It was very liberating.

A small movement behind a clump of trees caught his attention. A fox cub was keenly watching him. Biren stopped talking to observe it, and the cub slunk away. On the second day Biren was back in the meadows and so was the fox in the same place. Biren noticed that if he talked loudly and acted preoccupied, the fox remained in its place, watching, its oversize ears rotating with every sound. Biren ventured closer and closer until he was barely four yards away. It was a beautiful creature, with a rich auburn pelt, tawny eyes and a plump bushy tail.

Biren clapped his hands. "Shoo!" he shouted. The fox gave a little scamper and crouched, acting as though it wanted to play. It was inexperienced youngster; it still did not know the meaning of fear.

So busy was Biren talking to the cows and befriending the baby fox, he was not aware of another red-haired creature watching him. She, like the fox, was intrigued by the sight of a madman marching up and down among the wildflowers and talking to the sky.

During summer months, the People's Playhouse held its performances on a jutting-out apron stage in a small meadow behind the stables of the Red Roof Inn. A carnival-like atmosphere sprang up around the playhouse. Pushcart vendors did brisk business with penny pies, and colorful stalls with streamers and buntings enticed people with games of lucky dip, coconut shy and hook-a-duck. The audience—farmers, shopkeepers and Cambridge students in various stages of inebriation—filled the ticketed, tiered seating, while the "groundlings," or freeloaders, packed the straw and nutshell-strewn dirt area in front.

Twelfth Night was playing to a full house and Estelle was running late. After stepping over several feet, she managed to find an empty seat just as the flamboyantly feathered Duke Orsino made his grand entrance surrounded by the lords of his court. A young courtier immediately caught Estelle's eye. He had an intelligent face and very dark eyes. The young man only had a few short lines to deliver, and when he spoke one of his eyebrows arched more than the other. Estelle found she was looking out for him and watched him intently whenever he appeared onstage.

The audience broke into a rousing cheer and drummed their feet when Bertie barreled out as the comic Sir Andrew Aguecheek in his loud striped bloomers, buttoned orange doublet and monstrous ruff. One of the loudest people cheering in the audience was a chubby-looking fellow who hooted and clapped for all he was worth. That pomade-slicked hair and shiny suit was unmistakable. *Goodness*, Estelle realized with a shudder, *it's that dreadful Sammy Deb.*

Sammy was a classmate of her brother James's at Harrow, and he once visited Grantham Manor. He obviously fancied himself a ladies' man and tried to impress Estelle with his family's wealth and connections in India. Sammy had courted her relentlessly for months, sending her gifts and writing flowery letters. He'd backed off only when she'd gotten engaged to the Jolly Pear. Just remembering Sammy's sweaty advances made Estelle shrink back in her seat. She prayed he would not see her.

She shifted her gaze back to the courtier onstage. A handsome fellow, he was, rather exotic looking with his dark eyes and curly hair—a foreigner, no doubt. He stood to the side, not doing much, really, but it was a pleasure just to watch him. Why did he look familiar? She had seen him somewhere. Estelle sat up with a start—of course, he was the same fellow she had seen in the meadows, talking to the cows. It had to be him! He must have been practicing for his part in the play. But that hardly made sense. For all the dramatics she had witnessed, he should have had a lead role in the play, but all he was doing was just standing around. How very odd. Now she was even more intrigued.

Biren walked Sammy to a cab before heading back to the theater. When he returned to the green room he saw Bertie standing outside still in his clownish breeches, the elastic suspenders unlooped off his shoulders. He was talking to a petite woman. She had strong cheekbones and a casual elegance in the way she wore her red hair pinned into soft curls framing her face. From the easy familiarity of their exchange, Biren could tell they knew each other well. He was about to slip past when Bertie saw him and called out his name. The girl turned to look at him. She had pale porcelain skin, and when Biren walked up he noticed a small sprinkling of freckles over her nose. She studied him with a bold and lively gaze.

"Here is the fellow I was talking about," Bertie said to her. "Biren, this furry creature is my cousin, Estelle Lovelace. Be careful—she bites. She's a rabid feminist." Bertie drew aside the curtain to the changing room, treating them to a peep show of unlovely male actors in various stages of undress. "I will leave you two to get acquainted while I get changed," he said, and slipped inside.

Left with the bright and shiny Estelle, Biren fidgeted. He was unused to making conversation with English girls.

"You are renting the room above the stables, I hear?" she said conversationally. "Daddy's peacocks make quite a racket. They are loud enough from the main house—I can't imagine how loud they must be for you."

"They have not bothered me much, to tell you the truth," Biren replied. She was standing so close that when she moved he caught a whiff of something fresh and lovely, like orange blossoms in the rain.

"Bertie tells me you are one of the speakers at the next union debate. Are you speaking for the motion or against?"

"I am speaking for the motion."

"Oh?" Estelle arched an eyebrow. "I am curious why an Indian man would be interested in the suffrage rights for women in Britain. Pardon me, but Bertie did mention you are from India. Your interest is purely academic, I gather?"

"It—it's…rather personal," stammered Biren, at a loss for words.

"I would love to attend the debate," said Estelle. "Of course, I will be an outcast sitting up in the gallery with others of my lowly sex." She made a woebegone face. "We females are not allowed in the main hall, you know, just in case we contaminate the Union."

"It's unfair, really," said Biren passionately. The Union's unfriendly attitude toward women no doubt fueled the resentment among female students, as evidenced from the stinging article in the *Archangel*. Then a surprising thought crossed his mind. E.L. Estelle Lovelace. Could she possibly be the author of the article? He tried to imagine her disguised as a man. With her hair tucked inside a hat, it was not entirely impossible. She'd make a very pretty man, for sure, but would she dare to sit through the entire debate in a disguise? Well, this woman wasn't shy, he could tell. She had an alert playfulness that reminded him of the young fox.

Estelle gave him a mischievous smile. "The next time you need a sounding board for your debate, you don't have to talk to the cows, you know. You can talk to me." Seeing his startled look, she laughed. "Yes, I was crossing the woods the other day and saw you in the meadows. At first I thought you were off your rocker. Now I realize you were practicing for the debate. The next time let me know if you need an audience."

Biren was flustered. "Thank you" was all he could say. "I will certainly keep that in mind."

CHAPTER 28

Estelle hated the gloom of an uninhabited house. She had not bothered to air out all the rooms. It was too much of an effort; besides, Mummy had her own elaborate system of getting the house up and running. The dust covers—and there were several dozen—had to be removed in a specific order, washed, folded and put away in a linen cupboard somewhere in the attic; all the windows had to be opened, the curtains aired and sprayed with lavender mist squeezed from a rubber ball attached to a scent bottle.

It was a relief to see all the furniture hidden from view. Under the bumps of their custom-fitted dust covers was Mummy's mishmash furniture collected over the years from Barrett Auctioneers. Mummy believed no room was properly furnished unless stuffed full of furniture and decorations. Estelle shuddered looking at the glass windows of curio cabinets crowded with knickknacks.

Her own bedroom and Daddy's study were the only two inhabitable rooms in the house, the latter looking out toward the peacock enclosure and the stables beyond.

It was mildly disconcerting to know the Indian man was living on the grounds now. She felt herself staring out of the study window more often. The chestnut tree obstructed the view of the stables, which felt like a relief and a frustration at the same time. She wished she could part the leaves just a little to peep through and catch a glimpse of him.

The man intrigued her. He was the first Indian man she had talked to in England, besides that obnoxious Sammy Deb. She had liked the sound of his voice. He spoke with a poetic lilt, the intonations curled softly around the edges of his words. She wished she had asked him more about himself. Biren spoke little and was content with silence, which made her jittery. He watched her with a soft indulgent look in his eyes. It was the same look Daddy had had when as a little girl she did a pirouette or some daredevil thing to impress him.

The mournful call of the peacock floated across the lawn. It sounded eerie, like a newborn infant. Estelle looked out of the window and saw the male bird give a shiver of its dorsal feathers and unfurl its tail into a fan of outrageous glory. Even though she had witnessed this marvel countless times, it never failed to evoke in her a feeling of awe. Daddy loved peacocks. Mummy hated them. "Too little in the head and too much in the tail," she said, and sniffed.

When she was a child in India, Estelle would collect the fallen tail feathers of the peacock, but her ayah had never let her bring them inside the house.

"It's bad luck, missybaba," Ayah had said.

"Why?" Estelle had wanted to know.

Ayah had pointed to the iridescent blue eye in the feather. "See the evil eye? Evil eye spoil missybaba happiness."

Ayah had braided Estelle's hair with colored ribbons and tied it with a bow at each end. "One day missybaba marry handsome prince," the ayah had crooned. "He come on a white horse and he wear peacock feather made of real emeralds and diamonds in his turban. That is only peacock feather you must bring into the house, missybaba."

Ayah had balled up the fallen strands of Estelle's hair from the hairbrush and spat on it before throwing it away. After all these years in England, Estelle still did the same. She never brought peacock feathers into the house, either. And unbeknownst to herself, she secretly waited for her Indian prince.

Sylhet
12th June 1891

Dear Dada,

You must have heard about the devastating floods in Bengal. We are in a dire situation. The water level has receded, but now Sylhet is in the grip of a terrible cholera epidemic that has spread from village to village. Our village has come under quarantine. A yellow flag now flies on Momati Ghat. No boats will stop here and every day people are dying like flies.

I have some very bad news. Our family is much diminished, Dada. What can I tell you? We have lost both our grandparents. Only Uncle, Mother and I remain. I was home for the summer holidays when the epidemic broke out. As a result I could not return to Calcutta. Kanai's village across the river is all but wiped out. Kanai lost his entire family. He packed everything in his boat and is leaving for Silchar. I am sending this letter through him in the hope he will be able to post it from there. Assam is still unaffected from what I know.

I am convinced Uncle and I are alive only because of Ma. As you know, Mother does not eat food from the main kitchen. Let me tell you, Dada, her widow's curse turned out to be a blessing. I had not been taking food from the main kitchen because I eat with Ma, which is why I was spared. Uncle miraculously escaped, as well, but within five days we lost both our grandparents one after the other. We are still in shock.

Uncle and I are eating Mother's vegetarian food now. Only boiled lentils and rice. But please do not worry. The worst is behind us. I have heard the quarantine has already been lifted in the Tamarind Tree Village. It will only be a matter of weeks before there is some semblance of normalcy here and I can return to Calcutta.

After having lived through this experience, I have made up my mind to pursue a medical degree and become a doctor. I think I can be of more use to our people that way.

Your brother,
Nitin

Cambridge
13th August 1891

Dear brother Nitin,
I am deeply troubled to get your letter. It took over two months to reach me. It is unimaginable both our grandparents are no more and it is by God's grace you and Ma have been spared.

Now it becomes clear to me why I have not received any letters from home. I feel very helpless being so far away. There is little I can do from here besides send you money. I had purchased some small gifts earlier for you. They seem paltry and meaningless after what you have gone through, but I am sending them to you in the hope that they will cheer you up. Ma once talked about a Scottish butterscotch toffee that reminded her of Baba. I have managed to find it. I am also sending her a vial of Floris Eau de Cologne, the fresh floral-citrus scent I am sure she will enjoy. The Pelikan fountain pen and folding pocketknife are for you.

Samir Deb will carry these back with him to India and deliver them to you. I am going to London to meet him today. He is leaving for India, permanently, to settle down. His mother has arranged for his marriage with a Bengali girl. Samir will take over the family business as his older brother, Diju, has settled in England and has no plans to return to India.

I must end this letter, as I have to leave for London shortly to meet with Samir.

More soon via post. My love to you all.

Your ever affectionate
Dada

For the next four days Estelle never caught a single glimpse of Biren. She wandered through the meadows and spent a long time hanging about the peacock enclosure. From under the chestnut tree she could see the small window of his room and the square of darkness beyond, but there was no movement within.

Finally, in a fit of brazenness she marched past the stables, through the orchard and into the meadows. She even coughed a little to attract attention. Nobody followed her or called out her name. On her way back she slipped behind the apiary and looked up toward the door of his room. Both the doors were padlocked but a small piece of white paper was attached to the second door. Estelle rushed up to read it.

13th August 1891

Dear Bertie,
I had to make an urgent trip to London.

The backdrops are inside my room. The paint is still drying. The keys are with Mrs. Pickles.

B.R.

So he was in London. Estelle walked back to the house feeling utterly foolish. To think she had spent so many hours imagining things when he was not even there.

"Pia-ow, pia-ow, pia-ow," screamed the peacock. He fanned his tail and pirouetted on fat, ugly legs, but Estelle marched past without giving him so much as a cursory glance. The peacock's tail deflated bit by bit. He cocked his head and gave a puzzled cluck at her retreating back.

CHAPTER 29

Estelle fingered the chipped rim of her bone-china teacup, the result of a small calamity that had occurred a minute ago. She turned the saucer over to read the back stamp and winced. It was the Spode Stafford White set. Mummy would not be pleased.

She was busy writing the article for the *Archangel* and had lifted the teacup absentmindedly without looking. The next thing she knew, it had bumped the rose-quartz elephant on Daddy's desk. *You naughty elephant.* Estelle tapped its trunk reproachfully with her pen. She regarded the whimsical elephant tenderly. It had a pink upturned trunk, ornate patterned back and sorrowful human eyes. Daddy's study was full of interesting memorabilia from India. The walls were decorated with survey maps, the edges curled and brown. There was a photograph of Daddy in his white jodhpurs and *sola* topee standing next to Naga tribal warriors in their full-feathered ceremonial dress. The corner cabinet displayed the tools of a surveyor's trade: a wooden box containing a vernier compass, a wye level and a small mounted optical telescope. There were hunting photographs, too: one of Daddy with his gun next to a dead royal Bengal tiger, surrounded by Indian villagers dressed in loincloths and turbans carrying long sticks.

Estelle's favorite section was what James called the "wall of horrors." There were tribal spears decorated with human hair and boar's teeth, head-taking baskets, a quill case embellished with a monkey skull and the infamous human shrunken head, which was the size of an orange and dangled at the end of a long shock of hair. It never failed to amuse Estelle that the room with the most morbid things in the house was in fact the liveliest. The south-facing window of Daddy's study invited a leafy green freshness from the lime tree outside, and made the wood-paneled walls glow a deep and friendly brown. In stark contrast, her mother's rooms, decorated with drapery and lace, smelled of dead roses and stale lavender—rather like a mortuary.

Estelle got up to pour herself another cup of tea. Wandering over to the window, she leaned against the lintel and glanced toward the old chestnut tree. She was about to take a sip when she almost dropped her cup. Biren Roy was standing by the peacock enclosure. He stuck his fingers through the netting, and it looked as if he was trying to feed the birds pieces of bread. The peahens gathered around, bobbing their heads, while the male luxuriated in the tree with his long tail cascading over the branch like a jeweled veil.

Estelle lifted her skirts and ran out of the study, down the stairs and across the garden path. She caught him just as he was disappearing around the corner into the orchard.

"I say!" she called out gaily. "You're back!"

He turned around and waited for her to catch up. His hands were thrust deep into his trouser pockets and there was a small notebook tucked under his arm. As Estelle drew closer she noticed he was growing a rather nice-looking moustache, which he obviously tended with loving care.

"How is the debate preparation going?" she gasped, stopping to catch her breath.

"It's coming along." His eyes were lively and warm and he had a quizzical, amused look on his face. He took his hand out of his pocket and twirled a pencil between his index and ring finger. A big droopy silence hung between them.

"My offer still stands. You can practice your arguments on me, if you like," she said. "I can pretend to be the opposition. I'll give you a good rebuttal."

"Of that, I have no doubt," he said, arching an eyebrow, the tiny smile wandering in.

"I was just going for a walk," she said impulsively. "It's such a jolly day. Perhaps you would care to join me?"

He fidgeted. "That's awfully kind of you, but unfortunately I have another engagement."

She was deeply disappointed but she did not show it.

"Very well," she said, giving an airy wave as she turned to go. "Some other time, then."

He cleared his throat. "Estelle?"

"Yes?"

"I can go for a walk tomorrow, if you like."

She gave a little hop of joy. "That would be lovely. I'll bring along a picnic."

"Oh, no, please, that would be too much trouble."

Estelle felt exasperated. *What was wrong with him?* Any other man would have jumped at the chance to go on a picnic with her.

"It's no trouble at all," she said firmly. "I will meet you here under the chestnut tree at eleven o'clock."

With that she ran back toward the house without giving him a chance to change his mind.

The day of the picnic turned out to be gray and miserable. A wolfish wind howled around the garden, and the peahens huddled under the chestnut tree, their beaks tucked into their wings. Biren pulled the coat collar of his tweed jacket up to his ears and waited at the appointed time. He fully expected the outing to be called off, but there she was rushing over in a pea-green coat, her red hair flying, a picnic basket looped through her arm. Estelle Lovelace, it seemed, was hell-bent on having a picnic, whether Mother Nature approved of it or not.

The tall grasses in the meadow whipped in frenzy and the daffodils were flattened to the ground. They found a grassy knoll, but the wind made it impossible to spread the tablecloth, so they ate ham sandwiches with frozen fingers and made attempts at teeth-chattering conversation that was quickly abandoned when two white napkins flapped off like wounded seagulls in the grass. Finally all semblance of a picnic came to a halt as big dollops of rain fell. They ran for cover to an abandoned mill, where, protected by a derelict wall, was a miraculously dry spot facing the pond. It was a sly and furtive hideaway, the kind lovers seek out. The hearts and initials scratched on the wall and the ashes of a burned-out fire hinted of forbidden intimacy. The same thought must have crossed both their minds because they were suddenly self-conscious. They spread the picnic tablecloth on the floor and sat side by side, their backs against the wall. The light rain dripped off the overhang with a soft *tippity-tip* sound.

The lull began to bother Estelle, so she talked. She told him about growing up in India. About the big thatched bungalow with the wraparound veranda around which she would gallop on her hobbyhorse. About her ayah, who'd told blood-curdling stories of she-demons and secretly fed her rice with her hand. Estelle asked Biren about his childhood and was surprised to learn he was poor and grew up in a small fishing village.

"My goodness!" she blurted out. "And here I thought you were a prince of royal blood."

It was Biren's turn to be surprised. "Where did you get that curious notion?" he asked. A furrow appeared on his brow.

"You have courtly manners and a princely way about you," she said. She waved her hands in a la-di-da gesture, which made him laugh.

"Are you disappointed?" He still smiled, but his eyes were serious, searching hers.

"Good heavens, not at all." She laughed, tossing back her hair. "On the contrary. I am fascinated!"

Estelle went on to describe the young men she had known, with their crushed suits and expensive accents who drank port and talked armchair politics and behaved like peasants at any given opportunity. "And here you are, a real-life peasant with the manners of a prince!"

Surprised by the compliment, Biren rested his chin on his knees and traced a pattern with his forefinger on the dusty floor.

Estelle's eyes followed his finger. He had nicely proportioned hands, she noticed. "What was life like growing up in the village?" she asked.

"It's a simple life," he said, dusting off his finger. "A little monotonous, but beautiful in a way." He told her about the rivers, the fishing boats, the bamboo groves and the jute mill.

"It sounds so romantic," she murmured. "And your parents, what are they like?"

He told her how his father died, his mother's widowhood, the great floods and the cholera epidemic that wiped out half his village. It was more than he had told anybody before. There was a deep sadness in his eyes when he spoke. "I have still not recovered from the news," he said. "I feel helpless being so far away."

Estelle fingered the soutache trim on her pea-green coat. "Oh, Biren," she said softly, "I had no idea." Her eyes welled with tears. She turned her face toward the millpond.

He hated to see her sad, so he talked instead about the upcoming debate and was able to stoke the old fire back. When Estelle was indignant, a high color rose to her cheeks and her eyes took on a wild look.

"Don't you think it's ironic we live in the most industrially advanced nation in the world and we are still so backward when it comes to social equality?" she said. "Women don't have the right to equal education, married women don't have the right to property and we don't have the right to vote. We need more people like you to rally for us in Parliament."

"There are plenty of people championing for the rights of women in Britain," Biren replied. "The women in India have no voice at all."

She scrutinized his face. "Surely you don't plan to go back to India?" She sounded incredulous. "What with all the floods, cholera and rampant diseases, life sounds very unpredictable."

He gazed into her round, innocent eyes. Estelle looked

like a small child worried about the she-demons in her ayah's stories.

"None of all this is new," he replied quietly. "In India we are not spared hardship or tragedy but, despite it all, I love my country. I plan to go back as soon as I get my law degree. I am here to study law because I want to effect change in my own country. All big social changes in India were the result of new laws approved by Parliament here in England."

"It seems our government is better at changing laws in other countries than in their own," Estelle said bitterly. "We English portray ourselves as the great liberators bringing the natives out of the Dark Ages, but look where we are. It is hypocritical. Our Royal Navy makes a show of intercepting ships and freeing slaves smuggled out of Africa, but the working conditions of our own factory workers is often worse than the plantation slaves. What a farce!"

What a pleasure it was to talk to her! Estelle was educated and well informed. She had a lively, questioning mind. Biren had never met anyone quite like her.

The sun did eventually come out later that afternoon to light up the meadow. The air smelled moist and rich after the rain. As they walked back to the house, Estelle bent down to pluck a daisy and weaved it into a posy with a sprig of wild grass as she walked. She stopped, turned around and threaded it into the buttonhole of Biren's jacket.

"There," she said, giving his chest a playful pat. "A boutonniere for Monsieur Biren."

Biren looked down at the lapel. "Why, thank you. That's really quite a professional job. Who taught you to make such a clever—what do you call it?—boutonniere?"

"Miss Smithers, my governess." Estelle made a face. She

slipped her hand easily into the crook of his arm. "That is the only useful thing I learned from her. She was awful."

As they walked toward the woods, Biren pointed to a thicket. "A friendly little fox lives over there."

"If it's friendly it won't survive," said Estelle matter-of-factly. "Foxes are by nature not friendly. I am not surprised it warmed up to you, though. Any creature would."

Her boldness constantly caught him off guard. Estelle did not cloak her feelings. She was playful and mischievous, a girl-child in a woman's body. He did not know what to make of her.

As they approached the orchard, the lightness of their chatter faltered. It was as if the ancient stonewall of Grantham Manor had come between them.

Biren climbed the four-rung stile into the orchard and held out his hand to help her over. With the playfulness of a child, Estelle gave a gleeful jump and he had no choice but to catch her in his arms. And there she was, flushed and laughing, her body against his own.

She lifted her face and gave him clumsy peck on the chin. Then, flustered by her own impertinence, she scampered through the orchard, fleet-footed as a ten-year-old, leaving Biren holding the picnic basket, his boutonniere on the ground.

They met a few days later, this time to go cycling.

Estelle was wearing some kind of new-fangled sporting outfit, the likes of which Biren had never seen. In her forest-green bloomers and fitted shirtwaist she looked wasp-waisted and exotic—like a harem girl out of *The Arabian Nights*.

Estelle confessed she was new to cycling and said she needed practice. She wobbled and teetered across the lawn and for a dreadful moment Biren thought she was heading straight for the old oak. He rushed up and caught her just as she fell. He was so relieved she was unhurt he missed the mischievous look in her eyes. It took several near disasters for Biren to realize he was being taken for a ride. The next time she headed for the wall, he stood his ground and watched. And he was right. Not only did Estelle know how to stop the bicycle in time, she had excellent control of it, as well. *Oh, you naughty, naughty girl*, Biren thought, grinning to himself.

A fine day it was to be out in the country. They cycled through the dim forest glade dazzling with bluebells and out on the open road to Wicken Fen. The wetland wildflowers were in bloom, rising from the deep peat—milk parsley, marsh pea and fen violet. The only sounds were the whirr of bicycle wheels and the trill of a lark rising from the tall grass.

When they returned to Grantham House they wheeled their bicycles back to the stables. She stopped suddenly, her hand on his arm. Her face was flushed, her eyes bright from the outdoors.

"I always wondered what the view of the main house was like from your window," she said innocently. "Do you mind if I take a look?"

Not knowing how to respond, he led her up the stairs and opened the door to his room. She went inside without hesitation.

"So this is where you live." Estelle swirled around, taking in Biren's neatly made bed, the washbasin, the melted tallow candle on a wooden ledge above the fireplace. On top of a notebook by his bed was the wilted posy she had given him. "You kept my boutonniere," she murmured, almost in a whisper.

She picked up Charulata's painted bookmark. "What is

this?" she asked, fingering the bumpy pattern. "What an exquisite design!"

"It's a bookmark," replied Biren. "Given to me by a special person. To remind me of my commitment…" He saw Estelle's face fall and added, smiling, "To an old widow in my village."

She flushed and tossed back her hair. "Oh!" she tittered. She ran over to the window and stood on her tiptoes to look out over the window ledge but it was just above her eye level.

She turned toward him, laughing. "I can't see a thing!" she said. "It's too high."

Without a word, he lifted her up by the waist. She felt buoyant in his arms, strong but delicate, like a bird. Estelle grabbed the windowsill and tried to hoist herself up for a better look.

"Careful," he chided her. After a few moments he relaxed his grip and let her slide down till her feet touched the floor. "So now you see what I see."

"The peacocks and Daddy's study window," she said breathlessly, turning to him. Her eyes were unnaturally bright. "Do you see me sometimes, standing by the window in Daddy's study?" Her voice was soft, wistful.

"Yes," he said.

She leaned her head against his chest. Her hair smelled of sunshine and wild grass. Through the thin fabric of her shirt he could feel the birdlike fluttering of her heart.

Then she lifted her face and pressed her lips against his. It was a long, winding river of a kiss. Her beauty blotted out everything. Through the madness of it all, something stirred in the dim recesses of Biren's memory. He drew his breath in sharply and pulled back.

"Please, Estelle," he murmured. His eyes were gentle. "I cannot do this."

She stared at him in disbelief. He watched the hurt spread in her eyes. She pushed him off with a choking sob and ran from the room.

"Estelle!"

He watched her fly past the chestnut tree and up the garden path toward the rockery. Sick with despair, he went looking for her. She was sitting on the stone bench by the old sundial, her face buried in her hands.

Biren sat down beside her.

"Please!" she cried in a strangled voice. "Please go away."

He stroked her hair softly. "Estelle, please try to understand."

"You don't have to explain anything," she sobbed. "Oh, I am such a fool!"

"Don't you understand? I have nothing to offer you."

She gave a broken sob and turned to face him. With her wild red hair and tear-clumped lashes, she was beautiful in her anger.

"Have I ever asked you for anything?" she demanded. "Anything at all?"

Seeing her so broken brought back memories of his mother's tearstained face in the flickering candlelight of the woodshed. It was more than he could bear.

He held her face in his hands and forced her look at him. His eyes were soft with tenderness. "I cannot bear to see you cry, Estelle. You must never cry. Please promise me that."

He rocked her gently like a child without saying a word. His heart chafed at the thought he would never be able to give her what she wanted. Biren's heart was locked away in an inaccessible place. It was not his to give, but Estelle would never understand that.

Grantham Manor
28th August 1891

She is the most unusual woman, more unfettered than anyone I know. She refuses to wear hats, she has freckles on her nose and the hairpins have surrendered their hold on her hair, which slips out in big, bright curls. She is bold and buoyant. A soap bubble floating through life, reflecting all the colors, unaware of its own fragility. Ma used to be that way when father was alive.

Estelle gives of herself without reserve. She slips her hand trustingly into mine and wants to skip through life by my side. How can I tell her I must travel alone? My wish for her is to remain free from sorrow. I grew up too quickly, but Estelle does not have to. Every person deserves to remain a child at heart: curious, playful and without fear. My wish for her is to stay like the young fox cub, bright eyed and eager for life.

I think of Ma. I think of Apu's daughters. I think of Charulata, who gave me my name. I think of all the stepping stones life laid in my path to bring me to this point. It points to a bigger purpose. I have chosen this path and I must walk it alone.

CHAPTER 30

The day of the Union debate dawned wet and sodden. What began as a sprinkle turned into long and stringy rain that spiked on the cobbled streets and ran down gutters that gurgled with overflow.

Estelle shook out her umbrella and waited at the entrance of the Cambridge Union for Samantha and Isadora. She wished she had chosen to wear her dark coat—the pea-green one made her feel too conspicuous standing there in the hallway crowded with male students. She studied them sardonically. They looked like crabs, she thought, the way they squared their shoulders, circled one another, all that manly shoulder bumping and hand thumping.

One student said loudly for her benefit, "Oh, don't get me wrong, old chap. I'm all for women's emancipation, just keep it below the waist, I say!" They jabbed one another in the ribs and laughed like hyenas.

Estelle was so enraged she wanted to hit them on the head with her umbrella, but all she could do was dig her fingernails into her glove and bite her lip. She fumed, thinking about the cowardice of the male race. When encountered alone, these same students would pass her by looking frosty and studious, but put them in a herd and they became crass and mindless. Something had happened a week ago to exacerbate this behavior. A crude effigy of a woman riding a bicycle and wearing bloomers had been found suspended above the Braxton and Beele bookshop in the middle of the town square. It was a student prank aimed to degrade the feminists and it created quite a ripple. The effigy was taken down by the college authorities but not before obscene jokes floated up and down the corridors.

"Why, good evening, Miss Lovelace!"

Estelle turned at the sound of the baritone voice and saw Professor Burton shaking out the raindrops from his umbrella. He was the visiting professor of philosophy at Girton—a delightful bespectacled man, with very bushy eyebrows, and an old friend of her father's.

"You are here to attend the debate, I see," he said. "Are you alone?"

"Well," said Estelle, glancing around. "My friends were supposed to be here. They are running late, it seems."

Professor Burton pulled out his gold chain watch. "You have another five minutes. I would go inside, if I were you. You are sitting up in the gallery, I presume?"

"That's right." Estelle sighed. "I better go in. I don't suppose my friends are going to make it."

"May I have the pleasure of sitting with you?" asked Professor Burton with a gallant little bow. "That is, if you don't mind my crusty old company."

"But of course," said Estelle, warmed by his kindness. He was doing this for her protection, she could tell, knowing well that if she sat by herself the male students would heckle her.

They climbed the stairs together and took their seats in the gallery. Estelle leaned forward on the railing, chin on her hands. From where she sat, she had a clear view of the front of the chamber and the speakers. The hall was packed. There were at least three hundred in the audience. She scanned the gallery and counted five other women, and felt deeply grateful to Professor Burton. None of the male students in the gallery would dare to pass a single comment with him sitting beside her.

The bell rang and the debate officers and speakers filed in to take their seats. Estelle caught her breath and her belly gave a flutter when she spotted Biren. He looked tall and elegant in a dark frock coat. He had a distinct courtly manner about him, Estelle thought, an old-fashioned baroque style. She admired his fine nose, the dark arch of his eyebrows. He looked so different from the shy, tender man who walked with her in the meadows. She missed him. They had not met since he had returned to his old student lodgings at Brockwell Lodge a fortnight ago. The tripos was coming up and he was busy studying for the exams, he said.

The speakers took their seats. The president stood up from his high-backed chair on the platform. He welcomed the audience, explained the rules and debating procedure and announced the topic: "This house condemns the principle of women's suffrage, and views with regret the advancement in that direction." He then introduced the speakers. Biren was to be the first speaker against the motion.

"This is going to be interesting," whispered Professor Burton. "That Indian speaker, Ben Roy, is very good, I hear."

"Biren," Estelle corrected him. "His name is Biren Roy. Yes, I know him. He's excellent." She turned back to watch him.

Biren leaned forward, his fingers steepled together. He looked attentive but not tense. He is so handsome, Estelle thought dreamily. She was so busy watching him she paid scant attention to the first speaker, an anemic-looking man with a high raspy voice who was speaking for the proposition.

Next it was Biren's turn. When he stood up he looked very relaxed. Gone was the shy reserve. Biren was a gifted speaker. He picked his words carefully, like perfect cherries from a basket, and used his hands in an elegant way to express himself. His tone shifted from seductive persuasion to forceful arguments, and Estelle was tempted to close her eyes, like she often did at a music concert, content to let the sound wash over her.

"Mr. Speaker, I am certain this house agrees that if the British Empire upholds justice, fairness and decency as the cornerstones of a civilized society we must extend the same rights to women. Women must be allowed to vote and they should also sit as members of Parliament." His brazen suggestion caused a titter in the audience. Biren waited for them to quiet before he continued, "And one day, who knows, we may even have a female prime minister." The audience broke into an uproar. The president banged his gavel for order and gestured at Biren to carry on. "The general argument is that women cannot make serious decisions because they are incapable of logical or intelligent thought. Today I am here to prove those critics wrong."

Someone in the audience called for a point of information, which Biren Roy accepted.

"It is an indisputable fact that the dominance of the British Empire today is unrivaled in the world," he continued. "The sun never sets on the empire, they say. Today at the height of Britain's imperial glory, we have at the helm Her Majesty—a woman, I might add. A woman not just capable of logical and intelligent thought but a woman who has led Britain to become the leading nation of the world. This demolishes my opposition's argument that women are incapable of sound judgment and making serious decisions. Women therefore should be allowed to vote."

He sat down to a rousing applause. The other speakers went one by one, and when it came time for the vote, Estelle's cynicism proved to be true. Despite all the strong arguments put forward by Biren and his team, the proposition won by overwhelmingly majority—199 to 65.

One thing became increasingly clear to Estelle that day at the Union debate. She realized that, despite whatever misogynistic biases existed in the real world, the Cambridge Union Society was an indispensable platform for honest and fearless discourse. Here within the four walls of the debating chamber, speakers could voice their opinions and, through an impassioned interchange of ideas, attempt to reshape public opinion. No matter which side won, there was still a respect for intellectual honesty. This gave Estelle hope.

The summer was gone and the wildflowers remained pressed in the pages of Estelle's diary, under different names—cowslip, bluebell, daisy, thistle. They were memories of her summer days spent with Biren. More difficult to name were the emotions she felt inside.

The Bramley apples had turned their rosy cheeks toward the sun. It was fruit-harvesting season and soon her parents would arrive in Grantham Manor for the fall. Estelle was keen for her father to meet Biren. She would invite Biren to tea one day, she decided. She hoped Daddy would see what she saw in him. What was it that made Biren so unusual? she wondered. More than his boyish good looks, gentle personality and intelligence—it was his courage in the face of opposition that set him apart. Biren's beliefs were really no different from her own. Both of them were fighting for fairness, equality and human decency. The difference was in who stood to gain. Estelle was fighting for something that would directly impact her own life, whereas Biren was fighting for something above and beyond himself. That was what set him apart as a true hero.

CHAPTER 31

The summery peace of Grantham Manor came to a halt with the arrival of Samuel and Catherine Lovelace. Overnight the house was teeming with maids flapping curtains, folding dust covers, dusting, cleaning and polishing. Male servants pushed furniture across the stone floor with earsplitting screeches. Catherine Lovelace spent sleepless nights configuring different arrangements for the drawing room furniture in her head. A new acquisition from Barrett—a blue-green Empire chair with winged armrests and gilded legs—had caused the latest unrest. The chair deserved pride of place, and arranging the existing furniture around it was proving to be a challenge. The peacocks, meanwhile, excited no doubt by what sounded like a rollicking jamboree inside the house, marched up and down their cage and added screeches of their own.

Trapped between the screech of furniture and the screech of the peacocks, Samuel Lovelace tried to immerse himself in the sonnets of Keats, to no avail. He finally shut the book, pushed it back in its empty slot on the bookshelf and walked over to the window. The sun winked through the scent-laden blossoms of the lime tree, and the garden glowed in patches of golden green.

What a beautiful day for a walk, Samuel thought. He had not ventured outdoors since his return. The old wound in his leg had been playing up. He missed Josie, his cocker spaniel of sixteen years, who had died the year before. Walks in the country were just not the same without her.

And where was Estelle these days? She used to be keen to go on walks and always entertained him with her chatter about all the things wrong with the world and the quick fixes to set them right. Oh, the sweet confidence of youth! As one grew older the needle wavered between the wide arc of truth and doubt where nothing was sharply defined.

He saw less and less of Estelle these days. She seemed moody and self-absorbed, wandering off in the garden by herself. Once he found her sitting on the steps of the old stable house, writing a letter. To that Indian fellow, Biren Roy, he imagined.

Estelle had invited him to tea one time and Samuel had observed the young man with a critical eye. He had to admit, there was something rather fine about young Roy. Samuel was rarely wrong when it came to judging people. His surveyor's work in the dangerous and unpredictable jungles of India had honed his instincts sharp as a wolf. He could size up a situation, man or beast in a matter of seconds. It was the same instinct that led him to speculate in oil shares and India stocks. When the risky investments had paid off, Samuel had quickly became a wealthy man.

Biren Roy had spoken sparingly and behaved older than

his twenty-one years. He'd mentioned the premature death of his father. That was what had made him grow up so quickly, Samuel thought. He knew what that was like. His own father, a coal miner from Durham, had died in a mining accident when Samuel was only ten. Samuel had been lucky to get an education thanks to a kindly vicar who ran a school for boys out of his vicarage. He'd gone to study mathematics in Cambridge and worked at the Royal Greenwich Observatory as an assistant astronomer before getting the job as a surveyor in India.

Samuel had vowed to spare Catherine and his children the poverty that he had known. Catherine was the daughter of a Scottish investor with plantations in the West Indies, and an heiress at eighteen when he met her. Samuel was home on furlough from India. At thirty-one he was a lean, hard man with eyes of ocean blue on a face tanned by the colonial sun. After they married, Catherine and the children went back and forth between India and England and things had worked out well. It all changed when they'd relocated permanently to England after his leg injury. Catherine became increasingly dissatisfied. Her constant fretting over furniture and the excessive need to accumulate things was something Samuel had not foreseen.

At the breakfast table that morning, there was a furor over a broken teacup. Samuel calmly sipped his coffee and observed the two women over the top of his newspaper. They were complete opposites. Estelle with her wild hair and excessive gestures; Catherine cool and statuesque with hardly a flicker on her thin, aristocratic countenance.

Estelle pushed back her chair and without so much as an "excuse me" marched out of the room. Samuel sighed and folded his newspaper. "I am off for a walk," he called out to

Catherine, who was at the Buhl writing desk flipping furiously through a Barrett's catalog. He pursed his lips to whistle for Josie, then remembered. Sweet Josie. If only the two women in his life were as sweet and uncomplicated as she had been, how peaceful life would be.

Samuel Lovelace walked along the river thinking of Estelle.

She had been six months old when he had seen her for the first time in England, and she'd owned his heart from the time her brown, shining eyes met his over the top of her ruffled pink bassinet. She was quick to take advantage of his weakness. He had no defense against those imploring eyes, her soft pleadings of "please, Daddy" and the occasional tear. When he returned to India she wrote him childish letters from England, which he'd carried in the pocket of his bush shirt and read on the muddy trail.

dear papa,
I dont like miss smithers she smels bad. Berti is a horid boy.
Ples come home.
Estelle

At nineteen she was a beautiful woman, willful, restless and outspoken. Men fawned over her, but she kept them at arm's length, claiming her independence over marriage. Her brief involvement with Pierre Jolie could hardly be called a love affair. For all her bookish knowledge and brazen talk, Estelle was naive and unworldly.

After meeting Biren Roy, she had changed. Estelle, who had never given much thought to beautification, now wore a dress of jade silk with a low neckline and a creamy lace trim. With her hair pinned in soft curls and her shining brown eyes, she had never looked more radiant. She had even applied a touch of salve to her lips, Samuel noted.

As for the object of her affections, he was suave and conducted himself with restraint. His jacket was tasteful but shabby, obviously purchased secondhand; his shoes were scuffed, but despite his shortcomings in dress, he was a self-possessed young man. Samuel could see he cared for Estelle from his attentive eyes and the way his head bent forward when he talked to her, but it was clear he was the one in control.

It was disconcerting to notice that Estelle and Biren seemed to talk at cross-purposes. They each had their own agenda, it seemed. Biren clearly wished to return to India. He was part of a society of Cambridge Indians, he explained, who were formulating a plan to promote education for women in India. Estelle meanwhile tried to convince him that in order to influence Parliament, it was more advantageous for him to remain in England.

"Don't you agree, Daddy?" she implored Samuel, her eyes pleading. "You have good connections in Parliament, don't you?"

Samuel made reassuring sounds.

He could see what Estelle wanted, but he was unclear about Biren. It sounded like Biren had no plans to remain in Britain after completing his education. Where would that leave Estelle? She had obviously taken a shine to the young man. It was one thing to marry an Englishman and live the colonial life in India, but would it be the same if Estelle married an Indian? Samuel knew from having lived in India, a certain prejudice still existed. Even educated Indians were considered outsiders in British circles.

Samuel could not bear to see Estelle brokenhearted. Maybe

this was a good time to send her and Catherine on an extended vacation to Europe. The change of scenery would get Estelle's mind off Biren and, who knows, now that she was looking so charming, she might even attract a suitor or two. She would need some fine clothes, he decided, and made a note to increase her allowance.

I won't always be around to take care of my baby girl, Samuel thought, getting a little teary eyed. *I just want to see her happy. Nothing else matters to me at this stage of my life.*

CHAPTER 32

Grantham Manor
30th October 1891

Dear Biren,
Daddy greatly enjoyed meeting you. He was pleased to hear you have been called to the bar at Lincoln Inn. You have impressed him greatly, Biren. He can be very critical of the young men of my generation. He says they have everything handed to them on a silver plate. Daddy was a coal miner's son in Northumberland and he had to work his way up. I think he admires the same grit and determination in you.

I am not surprised you find living in London expensive. I told Daddy you were looking for a part-time job and he said he would be glad to recommend you for an underwriter's position to Lloyd's. He will be writing to you separately regarding this.

Very fondly yours,
Estelle

A few days later, Estelle danced into Samuel's study flourishing a letter.

"Daddy!"

She did a little twirl, ran over and kissed the top of his head.

"Thank you, thank you! You are the best, most lovely father in the world!"

Samuel gave her a puzzled look. "And what has your old father done to deserve such rapturous praise?"

"Biren got the job at Lloyd's. Oh, thank you, Daddy, for putting in a good word for him." She read from the letter. "'I am greatly indebted to your father for recommending me for this job. I will be writing to him shortly.'"

Estelle turned to her father with shining eyes. She frowned slightly, seeing the odd look on Samuel's face. "What is the matter, Daddy? Are you not happy for me…I mean, Biren?"

Samuel quickly composed himself. "Why, of course, darling, I am pleased. He is a fine young man and he will do very well in life."

Estelle smiled. "If he gets a good job, I know he will change his mind about going back to India. He may go for a visit to see his mother, but he'll come back. I miss him so much, Daddy! I wish he did not have to live in London." She touched the letter to her cheek. "Oh, I must write at once and congratulate him." She whisked around and ran out of the study.

Samuel felt a twinge of concern. *She is so vulnerable in love*, he thought. The news of Biren's job had indeed taken him by surprise. In fact, he had almost given himself away! It had been on the tip of his tongue to tell Estelle that he had played no role in getting Biren his job.

It was true Samuel had dropped by the Lloyd's head office in Chancery Lane to speak to his college friend David

Furst, the senior partner, about Biren, only to be told Furst had gone to the West Indies and would return after six weeks. He'd left the office intending to follow up.

Meanwhile it seemed Biren had applied for and got the job on his own steam. Getting a job at Lloyd's without a recommendation was almost unheard of, and it spoke volumes for the young man.

Estelle could be right. The Lloyd's job might change young Roy's plans to resettle in India, but she would be foolish to pin all her hopes on him. Samuel still believed it would be in Estelle's best interest to travel the world, broaden her horizons and meet other young men. She had once mentioned doing a language course at a private school in Switzerland. It was beginning to sound like a good idea. Samuel made a note to add Switzerland to their vacation itinerary.

CHAPTER 33

Calcutta
12th November 1893

Dear Biren,
I am now finally resettled in the homeland. Seven years in England is a long time and it has taken me a while to adjust to life in India.

You will be interested to know I have taken over the family publishing business and I am now the appointed editor of the Bengal Star, *an English weekly newspaper. The paper struggled due to a lack of readership but I am happy to say it is picking up. My hope is to use the* Bengal Star *as a vehicle to influence public opinion. I was pleased to learn the paper found its way into British government circles. A few days ago I received a letter from George McCauley, the secretary of education, who praised the* Bengal Star *as reflecting the "intel-*

ligent and constructive opinion of educated Indians." As you can see, our words are reaching the right ears.

I am eagerly looking forward to your return to India. These are exciting times in our country. The political climate is changing and many of us now dare to dream of a free India. Forging a new identity for our beloved nation is the topic of much discussion within our group. You will meet them all when you are here.

I understand your first concern is to find gainful employment. I have spoken to my uncle, the judge, and he is keen to talk to you about a barrister's position with his law firm. I also imagine you must be anxious to see your mother after all these years. I have been in touch with your brother, Nitin, as you know. The medical college is very close to my house and Nitin often drops by. I was happy to learn from him your mother is doing well. It is always nice to see Nitin. He is a fine young man and turning out to be an excellent doctor.

Yours ever affectionately,
Samaresh Bannerjee

Calcutta
7th December 1893

Dear Biren,
From the dates you have given, I see your ship docks in Calcutta on a Thursday, the steamboat for Sylhet leaves on the following Wednesday, which will give us a little under a week together. Please consider staying an extra week. I am keen for you to meet several people and to finalize our proposal to the education secretary, George McCauley.

Your article on female education was much discussed within our group. It was reprinted in the Bengal Star, *and many readers have written back with their comments. The members of our association have conceded to your idea of using English as the medium for education. The proposal has a much better chance of gaining government approval this way, especially since you put forward your arguments so eloquently. You may be interested to know the government has substantial funds earmarked for educational programs in India, which makes me hopeful our proposal will pass.*

I will be honored if you stay as our guest at our family home in North Calcutta. This is really the most pleasant time of the year in the city.

Best wishes,
Samaresh Bannerjee

CHAPTER 34

Estelle went on an extended vacation to Europe. Biren received postcards from Rome, Milan, Brussels and Geneva. She was briefly in England for three weeks before she left to study at a private school in Switzerland. They kept in touch intermittently through letters. Whenever Estelle was in London, they made plans to meet but somehow the plans fell through. It was mostly Biren's fault. Between his work at Lloyd's and Lincoln Inn, he barely had enough hours in a day to eat and sleep. A few weeks earlier he had written to tell her he had finalized his plans to go back to India. After a prolonged silence, Estelle wrote back expressing her regret. Her letter was cryptic but Biren could sense the dark holes between her words.

He wanted to talk to her in person and explain things. When Estelle returned from Geneva he invited her to dinner at the Lamb and Castle, a well-known pub of Central

London. It had rained all day. The streets were filthy from the splatter of carriage wheels. Darkness had fallen early and the pollarded planes lining the streets looked ghostly in the yellow glow of the gas lamps.

Biren hardly recognized Estelle. She swept in wearing a steel-gray ensemble with a silver ribbed trim; her hat looked like a tin can trailing ostrich feathers. She seemed sharper, more brittle, than he remembered her. Biren must have looked different, too, in his formal work suit and his newly trimmed beard. There they were, two strangers meeting after almost a year in a crowded London pub, seated next to table of loud drunks. The old connection between them was lost, and their conversation lapsed into uneasy small talk. The subject of Biren leaving for India sat between them like a moat while they each waited for the other to let the drawbridge of communication down.

"I really don't understand you, Biren," Estelle blurted out finally. "Why would you want go back to India—when you have a future in England?"

"It has always been my plan to return," he said slowly, watching her. "Surely you knew that?"

She turned to him with angry eyes. "I hope you realize you put Daddy in a false position after he went out of his way to recommend you for the job at Lloyd's. Not many people get that chance, and you go toss it out like a cherry pit."

He looked at her, startled. "I was only looking for temporary work to pay for my living expenses in London. I thought I made that clear."

She ignored him. "I know the real reason you are going back to India." She bit her lip and looked away.

"What do you mean?" he said, puzzled. "The real reason

is what I have been telling you all along. We are forming an organization, Samaresh and…"

"The real reason is you are going to have an arranged marriage, like Sammy."

"Estelle!" Biren cried sharply. "That is simply not true!"

He could tell from her eyes she did not believe him.

"I am not Sammy, Estelle," he said tersely. "Sammy comes from a business family. He has certain obligations to fulfill."

Estelle opened her mouth to reply and cringed when the drunks at the next table broke into a ribald song. Biren wished they had gone for a walk to Hyde Park instead, and then he remembered it was raining.

He looked at her helplessly as she sat across from him with her wounded-child eyes, her small hunched shoulders in the stiff battleship dress. Where was the laughing, bright-eyed Estelle he once knew? It saddened him to see the distrust and cynicism creeping in. In a rush of tenderness he reached across the table to take her hand. It was trembling.

"Dear Estelle," he said gently. "You must believe me when I tell you, I am doing this only for myself, and marriage is not in my plans."

Biren felt her fingers relax slightly.

"You are my dearest friend," he continued. "We share so many thoughts and ideas, don't we? You challenge me with your insights, you make me think—you make me laugh. I don't ever want to lose our friendship."

She was silent but her face looked small and hurt like a child who has suffered a fall.

Biren released her hand and sighed. "My life in India is not going to be easy, Estelle. I was counting on your letters to sustain me. I was hoping you would write to me."

She took a small sip of her sherry and fingered the stem of her wineglass as the color slowly crept back into her cheeks.

Biren sought her eyes. "Will you write to me? Please?"

Estelle hesitated, then gave an almost imperceptible nod.

Biren looked around the table and realized both their dinners had remained untouched.

"Please," he said, indicating her plate. "You must eat something."

Estelle unfolded her white napkin slowly. "I had hoped..." she began in a small voice, and paused to blot her eyes with the edge of the napkin before she placed it on her lap. "I had hoped—rather foolishly, I suppose—that you would change your mind. But I know you must return." She looked up and gave him a trembling smile. "No matter what you do, Biren, you must know I wish you well."

Dear Estelle. She was so honest and brave. Biren felt a lump in his throat and his dinner plate blurred before his eyes. Her good wishes meant the world, because he knew when Estelle Lovelace said something it came straight from her heart.

CHAPTER 35

On a wicked, blustery day in February 1894, Biren Roy boarded the steamer ship *Imperial Saga* and set sail for India. The sky was sludge gray, and seagulls floated like shreds of paper over the rusted grime of the Southampton docks. A foghorn sounded from the bowels of a distant ship, and Biren Roy, dressed in his fine tailored suit of cheviot wool, leaned against the brass rails of the deck and scanned the crowds for his last glimpse of Estelle. He had not expected her to come to see him off, but there she was in her pea-green coat with the fur-trimmed collar buttoned at the throat, the corner of a lace handkerchief clutched in her hand. It may have been the sea breeze, or perhaps tears that pricked his eyes, but his heart felt like a leaden anchor unable to lift free. The ship was already moving away and Estelle grew smaller and smaller until she was no more than a dot of green in a sea of waving hands. The shores of Southampton receded in a torpid haze, leaving the chimneys stark and gaunt on the industrial horizon as the *Imperial Saga* plowed through the frigid gray-blue water toward India.

He landed in Calcutta on Bengali New Year's Day. Instead of Nitin, Samaresh was there to meet him at the port. Nitin had to leave unexpectedly for Madras a few days ago to work at a medical camp associated with his college, Samaresh said.

For Biren, this should have been an early indication that life in India rarely went according to plan. The next few days were caught up in a whirlwind of introductions and meetings and it slowly began to dawn on him that the genteel Bengalis of Calcutta, known for their legendary hospitality, were in no real hurry to get things done.

The Albert Hall Coffee Shop was the meeting place for the intellectuals of Calcutta. There were foreign scholars among them, as well—writers and artists from Germany, Japan and France. It was at this coffee shop that Biren met Boris Ivanov, a burly Russian writer, and Ren Yamasaki, a Japanese architect with a peaceful face and pale, tapered fingers. Here, around the marble-topped tables and over strong dark coffee, great minds gathered to discuss the political and social issues of the day. Many, like Biren, had been educated abroad. There was a general agreement that education was a priority and the key to social change in India.

"It's not just a shortage of schools, there is a shortage of teachers, as well," said Samaresh. "It is perfectly acceptable for an Anglo-Indian spinster or widow to take up a job as a teacher or secretary. They are encouraged to be self-reliant and lead a productive life because they are Christians. Think of all our Hindu widows, some so young, in their twenties and thirties. A woman loses her status in the family the day her husband dies. She cannot remarry and is expected to live a life of penance. If our widows were educated and trained as teachers, they could become the educational backbone of our society. Yet every time we make any effort at their rehabilitation, our efforts get thwarted."

"The opposition comes mostly from their own families," added Ram.

"Ram, tell them about the widows at Bhowanipore," Samaresh urged him.

"While researching mental illness, I spent a lot of time at the European Lunatic Asylum in Bhowanipore," said Ram. "Most of the inmates there are permanent residents, many soldiers among them. Recently I discovered a secret ward of about two hundred Indian women. They are perfectly normal—not mentally ill in any way. I was shocked to learn that they are all Hindu widows of prominent families who have been locked away—hidden from society—using the pretext of insanity. You should see their pathetic state. They live like beggars. People don't even know they exist."

Biren was outraged. Two hundred women locked against their will, mistreated, their lives ticking away, and here they were in a coffee shop calmly talking about it. How could anyone remain indifferent? One of those two hundred women could have easily been his mother. The only reason his mother had not been abandoned by their family was because her signature was needed to collect their father's salary every month. Who knows what would have happened to her otherwise? Nitin and he would have been too young to do anything about it.

Here he was, a grown man with a law degree from one of the best universities in the world, but where did one even begin? Samaresh and his peers came from wealthy established families of Calcutta. None of them had a need to earn a living. They were content to write articles and have intellectual discussions while they waited for change to happen.

This is where I am different, thought Biren. *I can't just sit around waiting. I need to do something. I have to see tangible results.*

Two weeks later Biren was on the creaky river barge sailing for his village home in Sylhet. His new friends loaded him with boxes of sweetmeats and waved him off cheerfully, but Biren left Calcutta with no job offer. Samaresh's uncle, the judge, had fallen gravely ill, and he was in no condition to meet with Biren. Biren put in several other job applications before he left, but unlike England where jobs were secured over a single interview and a handshake, the approval process in India was excruciatingly slow. There was really nothing for Biren to do but return home. Besides, he was anxious to see his mother.

Floating down the turgid waters of the river delta, he was seized by a sudden desperation—he wanted to push, to part the waves and move past quickly, but the steamboat swished along, giving a sleepy hoot every now and then as if to remind itself to stay awake. The coconut shells and dead fish left in its wake bobbed in exactly the same place when they passed. A slow malaise was creeping into his soul. After all the strides he had taken to forge ahead in the world, he now felt as though he was slipping back. For the first time since his return, Biren began to dread he was making a terrible mistake. But when he remembered the state of the widows languishing away in the Bhowanipore asylum he knew he had done the right thing by coming back.

A low hammock of rain clouds hung over the riverbank at Momati Ghat. The flame tree blazed in lonely splendor. The only sign of life was a scrawny goat scavenging among a pile of discarded coconut shells around the shuttered tea shop, the bell around its neck making a hollow sound. There was nobody there to meet him, but Biren was not surprised. The postal service from Calcutta was unreliable, and chances were his letter would probably reach home after he did.

The steamer docked among the floating purple hyacinths and the lascar lowered the gangplank and deposited Biren, his bedroll and his steel trunk on the riverbank before it chugged away. Biren dragged his luggage over to the abandoned tea stall and pegged his jacket on a bamboo pole. Overcome with desolation, he sat on his trunk and stared at the brown river. There was nothing to do but wait for the village to wake up from its siesta, another couple of hours at least, after which he could hopefully send word through someone to his family or find a bullock cart to take him home.

His unexpected arrival in the back of a bullock cart created quite a stir in the village. Small boys ran ahead to alert the family and an excited crowd followed the cart up to the doorstep of his *basha*. Biren's uncle, now only skin and bones, was sitting under the banyan tree. "Who is it?" he said in a thin, faltering voice. "Biren, *mia*, is it really you?"

"Yes, Uncle," he said, bending down to touch his feet.

"Why, I thought you were a *belayti*!" Uncle exclaimed.

Sunless England had indeed turned Biren's skin pale. He felt like an albino among his dark-skinned countrymen. He was a curiosity in his Western-style clothes, and half the village crowded into the house to stare at him while the rest peeped in through every available door and window.

Shibani had moved back into her old bedroom and was sitting on her bed cutting areca nuts. Her short hair had turned a premature gray, and Biren was surprised to see her quite round and plump.

"Ma!" he called out to her from the doorway.

Shibani turned at the sound of his voice and gasped. The brass cutter fell with a clatter onto the floor as she scrambled off the bed. Her fierce embrace left him gasping. She kissed his forehead, his cheeks and his ears as tears streamed down her face.

"My son! My son," she repeated over and over. "Is it really you?" She led him over to the bed and pushed the hair out of his eyes as if he was a little boy, trailing her fingers all over his face. "You are a grown man. I thought you were never coming back. Oh…" She choked, breaking into a sob. "If only your *baba* could see you. How very proud he would be."

"Don't cry, Ma," he said softly. "I'm home now."

Home. The word had a hollow sound. Biren felt out of place in the thatched *basha* with its chalky blue-gray walls, the doorway so small he had had to duck his head to pass through. But seeing his mother looking so well made it all worthwhile.

"You are very handsome, I can tell. I am losing my eyesight, *mia*." Shibani sighed. "That is why I did not see you."

Biren grabbed her face in both his hands and examined her eyes. She stared back sightlessly.

"What are you saying, Ma?" he cried anxiously. "Since when? Why didn't Nitin say anything in his letters to me?"

"Oh, he doesn't know, *mia*. I hide it quite well. I don't tell him because he will worry." Shibani scrambled off the bed. "But I am not too blind to make tea."

He followed her into the kitchen and sat on a footstool and watched her fill the kettle and put it on the stove. The kitchen was exactly the same as he remembered it, with its soot-stained walls, the round-shouldered mud stove and hammered-tin chimney.

"Your uncle saw your old friend Samir a few days ago," Shibani said. "His wife is a very nice Sylheti girl from a good family. She even speaks English, I am told."

"So I heard," Biren said. "I met Samir's brother, Diju, in London before I left. I heard Samir has moved back into the old family *basha*, the one with the sour plum tree."

"Now he has built his own house. With a wife and two children…"

"He has *two* children—already?"

"What do you expect? He has been married three years. We must ask him to look for a nice girl for you. Maybe his wife has a nice sister or cousin." Shibani shot him a sly smile. "Otherwise, there is always Ruby next door, you know."

"Please, Ma," Biren protested feebly. He suddenly felt claustrophobic. "I don't want to talk about marriage."

She patted his hand. "I know, I know. It is just your old mother rambling. Don't pay me any mind, son. I am happy you are home, that's all. I have waited for this day."

Despite her reassurance, Biren felt an unseen pressure tighten in his chest.

Shibani handed him a tumbler of tea. "Try these palm fritters. Your Apumashi made them."

"How is Apumashi?" he asked. "Do you see her at all?"

"Oh, yes, all the time. She comes here almost every day. Even though I have short hair, she still comes to oil it and give me a head massage," said Shibani.

"So there are no restrictions with Apumashi coming over to see you now?"

"Not after her mother-in-law died. It was always our mothers-in-law who put the restrictions on us. I have never understood why one woman would want to put down another. But that is the way our society is. After both our mothers-in-law died we were free. I have even started to eat some fish now. Food-wise, I have no restrictions."

"What about chili tamarind?"

"You remember the chili tamarind!" Shibani laughed with her crooked teeth. "It's funny, but both Apu and I lost our taste for chili tamarind. It was our girlish craving for sour things at that time, I think. Now we just drink a lot of tea."

"This tea is very good," said Biren. He took a sip. "Better than I remembered." The tea at the *basha* always had a hint of pleasant wood smoke boiled into the water.

"This is a very special tea your friend Samir sent through his servant. You cannot buy it in the market. Samir's family now handles the transportation for all the British tea companies of Calcutta, and Samir gets a nice quota for himself. You must go and see him immediately. He is impatiently waiting for you. His servant came here several times to find out if you had arrived." Shibani gave him a naughty smile. "They want to know when to send the palanquin for you."

"I wonder if he still rides a palanquin!" Biren laughed. "It wouldn't surprise me. I also want to go and say hello to Mr. Owen McIntosh at the jute mill sometime."

"Mr. Owen is no longer there, *mia*. He retired a year ago. There is a young man by the name of Willis Duff in his place. He knows you. Last year when they sent me your baba's bonus money, Willis Duff wrote a nice note and asked about you."

"Yes, I remember him well. Duff was the young officer who accompanied me to boarding school on my first journey by steamer. He was very good to me," said Biren, thinking about young Willis with his kind blue eyes and curly red hair. Their acquaintance seemed like such a long time ago.

Shibani had taken charge of her life. She managed the money for the household and ran the kitchen. Uncle was sober only for a few hours in a day, it seemed. Biren was greatly heartened to see traces of the old mother he remembered from his early childhood with her easy laugh and teasing ways. Despite her gray hair and failing eyesight, Shibani's skin and eyes were clear and she seemed to be in excellent health.

He looked at his mother fondly and thought she was like a tree sprouting its first tender buds after a long hard winter.

CHAPTER 36

Sammy Deb's family *basha* was where his joint family had lived for several generations. There were so many members in his household that Biren never quite figured out how they were all related. What was once a single-unit house had grown wings in every direction until it had become a sprawling mess of an establishment with several courtyards and wells—almost a minivillage in itself, all under one roof. The dominant feature was a sour plum tree, so unwieldy and overburdened with fruit that it had collapsed like a benign and overweight matriarch on the roof of the kitchen, and threatened to bring everything down. There were no plans to cut down the tree because it was a blessed tree, planted by a benevolent ancestor, and the good fortunes of the Deb family were attributed to it. However, to be on the safe side, the family constructed a new kitchen, and the old kitchen with its dangerously sagging roof became a relic of old times.

Biren arrived at Sammy's house to find the tree still standing. However, acid from the sour plums had eaten through the thatch until the bare bones of the rafters showed, yet the roof structure, miraculously, was still holding. A few goats now occupied the old kitchen, munching happily on vegetable peelings, oblivious to their impending doom.

As usual, the house was pell-mell with people, all of them looking vaguely alike with their pale faces and soft stomachs. A miscellaneous relative directed Biren to Sammy's new house. It was a pukka house with a neglected English-style rose garden full of anthills. Biren found Sammy in the living room, reclining on two sausage-shaped bolsters, smoking a hookah and getting his toes tweaked by a minion.

"Goodness gracious, Biren!" he cried, the hookah dropping from his mouth. He struggled to his feet, ruddy and obese. "When did you get here, old chap? You look marvelous!" He slapped him on the back, grinning widely with *paan*-stained teeth.

"Quickly, get *boudi*," he ordered the minion, "and tell her my best friend from England has come." The man scurried off and Sammy cupped his hand and yelled behind his retreating back, "And bring tea. *Tea!*"

"So, you old so-and-so. Come to get married, have we? Always following in my footsteps, eh?" He laughed uproariously, holding his wobbling stomach.

Before Biren could answer, a plump woman with a sweet face rushed in. She covered her hair with her sari and bent down to touch Biren's feet.

"Please, no," he said hastily, taking a step back.

"This is Uma," Sammy said, then turned to her. "My friend Biren Roy from England. Where are the children? Bring the children. Make sure their faces are clean." Facing

Biren once again, he said, "So tell me, how's the Old Country? How's our femme fatale Estelle Lovelace?"

"She's well," Biren said.

"Find yourself a nice country girl, I say, and settle down, for God's sake. All the village belles will be lining up to marry you now."

A tiny girl toddled into the room wearing a new dress, followed by Uma carrying a male infant who, seeing Sammy, immediately stretched out two chubby arms toward him. The baby's eyes were lined with kohl, and there was a black dot marked on the side of his head to ward off the evil eye.

Sammy took the baby in his arms. "One, two, buckle my shoe!" he cried, tossing the child in the air, making him break into a cackling laugh. The little girl pulled at the silk tassels on the bolster and stared at Biren with big eyes. Seeing her father distracted, her hands crept toward the hookah while Uma watched her husband with a soft, dimpled smile.

"Here, go to your uncle Biren," Sammy said, thrusting the baby into Biren's arms. The smile on the baby's face faded. He looked at Biren bewildered, and his face began to pucker as he mustered his forces for a colossal howl.

Biren jiggled him awkwardly. The howl became an earpiercing shriek, and he hastily handed the baby back to his mother.

"Gouri! Where did you go?" Sammy swiveled around. "No, no, don't touch the hookah." He gave her an encouraging prod. "Gouri can sing 'Twinkle, Twinkle Little Star.' And she will sing for Uncle Biren. Ready? One. Two. Three. Twin-kle, twin-kle lit-tle… Now, what's the matter?"

The girl scrunched her face and sniffled. She, too, looked as if she was about to break into a howl like her baby brother.

"Oh-hoh," said Sammy, exasperated. "Take them both away, Uma. Let me talk to my friend. Now, where is the tea?"

Uma whispered something.

"Send him for the sweets, but you can bring them later. For now tea will do. We will need several rounds. I am seeing my friend after a very long time." He turned to Biren. "Stay for lunch. Uma is an excellent cook." Without waiting for his reply, he called after Uma, "He is staying for lunch. Make something special, will you?" He settled himself back on the settee. "Care for some hookah?"

"I have my cigarettes," Biren said. He looked around and located a brass frog ashtray on the windowsill. A child's beaded necklace was stuffed inside it.

"Old habits die hard," said Sammy as he watched Biren roll his cigarette. "I switched to hookah. I have other bad habits, I'm afraid—*paan* and the occasional pinch of snuff. In England you pick up good habits, in India you lose them." He waved the mouthpiece of his hookah. "Vice and virtue, all the same. But you were the eloquent one. How I envied you. So what are your plans?"

"First thing is I need a job," said Biren. "I made some inquiries into civil service positions while I was in Calcutta but it may take a while."

"If it was just a question of a job, you know you can always work for our family. But I know you are quite ambitious. You may want to check out Silchar besides Calcutta. There are plenty of good jobs there with the British government, thanks to the growth of the tea industry. Did you try the tea I sent you?"

"Yes, it was very good. The best tea I've had, really."

"Remind me to give you some more," said Sammy. "The tea industry in Assam is booming. There is a big British population settled in Silchar and they have beautiful colonial-style bungalows, gymkhana clubs and a nice leisurely lifestyle. So unlike the hurry-scurry of Calcutta, if you ask me."

"Ma was saying your family now has something to do with the tea industry, is that right?" asked Biren.

"That's our main business now. We have our head office in Silchar. Our family handles the transportation requirements of all the tea gardens in the Surma Valley. We own several flatbed barges and we move tea, machinery and supplies between Silchar and Calcutta. If it had not been for my Uma and the children, I would live in Silchar. Uma wants to be close to her parents, and the children are happier in a joint family, so here we are."

"You seemed to happily settle down."

"Oh, yes, oh, yes, it a good life. My brother Diju was a fool to stay back in England. Who wants to live in that cold morbid country? At least you did not make the same mistake."

Sylhet
17th April 1894

Uncle disappears for long stretches. I suspect he goes to the opium den. When he is around he is dazed and incommunicado. He is thin as a rake. Ma has taken charge. She is doing exceptionally well. Nobody really needs me here. I should be in Calcutta looking for a job. This listless waiting is causing a great deal of angst in me. Every morning I wake up filled with a toxic dread that spreads through my body. I lie in bed and ask myself, what am I doing here? I feel as if I have one foot stretched forward and the other one stuck in the mud. The monotony of village life is enough to drive me mad.

The morning hours creep intolerably. Lunch takes up one half of the afternoon, siesta the other. Evenings are spent drink-

ing tea and in idle chitchat. Come dusk, conch horns sound deep and hollow, prayer bells tinkle in every house and the air smells of sandalwood incense. This time of the day brings back memories of Baba coming home from work. Even after all these years his memory is painfully sharp and clear.

Sylhet
19th April 1894

It has become the sacrosanct duty of every woman in the village to get me married. The fact that I am jobless is inconsequential. I am considered highly eligible because I am foreign educated and I have bright prospects. The fact that the bright prospects have not materialized is again inconsequential. Marriage proposals are flooding in. Invariably I come home to find a stranger waiting to meet me with an overeager smile and a box of sweets, and I know right away why he is here. It makes me want to turn around and run back to England.

Letters from Estelle arrived like a breath of fresh air. Even the paper she wrote on felt cool and crisp and carried the delicate scent of her citrus perfume. Once she enclosed a kingfisher feather of periwinkle blue, another time a pressed yellow burnet rose.

Daddy has a new puppy, she wrote. *Her name is Annie. She is a cocker spaniel, the same as Josie but with none of Josie's ladylike ways. Annie soiled the Persian carpet, broke the porcelain milkmaid figurine on the coffee table and chewed a hole in Mummy's silk cushion all in a single day.*

Dear Estelle! The joy and mischief in her voice made Biren smile.

Bertie gave up the theater and left for South Africa to work in a rubber plantation. Why, how or where, nobody knows or seems to care. How very typical of Bertie, don't you think?

I now spend most of my time in London. I joined my friend Isadora to volunteer at the House of Mercy, a charitable institution patronized by our prime minister dedicated to the rescue and rehabilitation of fallen women. The choice of my cause makes Mummy cringe, but Daddy is supportive as always.

Estelle at least was putting her energy toward meaningful work, Biren thought, which was more that he could say for himself.

Sylhet
20th April 1894

I went to the temple hoping to see Charulata. The priest told me she died a year ago. At first people thought she was peacefully asleep under the banyan tree, and only when the monkeys started making a curious howling sound did they realize she was dead. "Lying there like a small brown leaf," the priest said. Charulata was given a pauper's funeral and nobody attended her cremation. Her bundle of books, feather brushes and packets of rice paste were burned along with her body. The ground under the banyan tree had to be purified with holy water.

I came away from the temple deeply saddened. What a waste of human life. Charulata was so pure, so timeless in her wisdom, like the old banyan tree. Surely she deserved to be remembered. I felt the urge to write about her. I sat and penned a three-part essay called "The Banyan Tree Widow." I will send this onward to Samaresh for the Bengal Star.

Sylhet
21st April 1894

I have not heard from Samaresh ever since he wrote to say his uncle, the judge, had passed away. Samaresh's cousins have taken over the family law firm and it seems he does not get along with them. This has dealt me a blow on the job front. I need a job. Any job. My choices are limited because doing any job is not an option in India. I wonder what people would say if they only knew of the different kinds of menial work I did back in England? Most of what I did would be classified low-caste work. I even dug graves for a while! In India that alone would put me in the class of the untouchables. I would be disowned.

I took a boat ride to the jute mill to meet Willis Duff but again I was in for a disappointment. He has gone to Scotland on furlough. I did not leave my name because I did not want to draw attention to myself as the son of Shamol Roy. The office staff thought I was a foreigner and treated me as such. On the boat ride back home I remembered Baba. How many times he must have taken the same journey. I felt saddened to think he had to sacrifice his own dreams just to put rice in our stomachs. He died so we could have the opportunity he never had, but now it feels like I am wasting precious time.

I have taken up meditation. The old baul *sitting under the flame tree guided me in the practice. I found it very hard to concentrate at first but slowly the restlessness is coming under control.*

The tea shop now has a new owner. Tilok, the old owner, perished in the cholera epidemic, as did most others in his village. I learned Tilok's wife and one of the twin boys died, as well. Many of the fishermen of my childhood, including Chickpea and the ancient one they called Dadu, are all gone. Kanai became half-crazed with grief and wandered away in his boat, and has not been seen since. Most of the fishermen who gather at the tea shop now are unknown to me.

When the fishing boats come in I watch the fishermen unload their catch. Most days it is paltry pickings: bony fish, a crab or two. I find it hard to believe these same fishermen traverse the vast waterways leading out to the open sea but they have no yearning to venture beyond. They do not challenge their fate; there is no restlessness of spirit, no hunger of the soul. Is unquestioning acceptance the secret to contentment? I wonder.

CHAPTER 37

Sammy's generosity knew no bounds, and invitations arrived back-to-back. Every second day the manservant would show up at Biren's house with an invitation to lunch, tea or dinner—it hardly mattered which. Breakfast, thankfully, was exempt because Sammy was a notoriously late riser. After a slothful morning of drinking tea and mindless ambling around the anthill-ridden rose garden in his pajamas, Sammy indulged in a leisurely oil bath and head massage, by which time lunch was served. There was always some delicacy on the menu: sweet river prawns stewed in coconut milk, fish steamed with stone ground mustard or *elo-jhelo*, a sticky teatime snack made of twisted sugar dough. Sammy ordered Uma to pile up Biren's plate and watched Biren eat while a manservant stood and fanned them with a palm frond.

Despite the smothering love, or perhaps because of it, Biren began to feel claustrophobic. To avoid Sammy's endless invitations he started staying away from home, especially around mealtimes. He took long solitary walks by the river and sat on the bank and watched the brown mass of water push forward like a great, sluggish beast. The river never stood still. It was always going somewhere, carrying clumps of vegetation, floating driftwood and often curious objects all bumping and bobbing along. If he watched closely, he sometimes saw a muscular surge of water that hinted of a hidden force below. India was like the river, he thought. It looked as though things were not moving but an invisible current was directing the flow. Yet Biren felt as if he was trapped in an eddy, swirling in circles, cut off from the main stream.

Biren's river walks took him farther and farther from home. One day he found himself in a village of potters. Here nobody knew who he was and Biren gratefully accepted his anonymity. They called him the Belayti. Even though Biren dressed in Indian clothes, he still looked like a foreigner.

He watched, mesmerized, as the potters shaped mounds of river clay on hand-operated wheels into elegant vessels with scalloped rims. After being sun dried, the pots were loaded in a hay-covered pit and fired after a *puja* blessing ceremony conducted by the village priest. A single bad firing could ruin a whole week's work after all. After being fired, the pots were hand burnished to rich terra-cotta gold. Twice a month they were packed in straw and loaded on a flatbed river barge that came laden with cargoes of pineapple and coconut from other villages, and shipped off to be sold in the markets of Dhaka.

Every member of the potter's family had a specific role. Women and children gathered the clay from the riverbank in baskets and brought them to the village. The clay was dried, then pounded with sticks and sifted through a bamboo sieve into fine dust, which was then soaked in a clay pit. Younger able-bodied men used their muscle power to knead it to a soft doughlike consistency. Finally, the senior male potters operated the wheel and shaped the pots.

Biren was at the potter's village watching Hori, a seventy-five-year-old potter, take a mound of clay and transform it into a large round-bottomed pitcher. Working with effortless grace, he squatted on the ground and spun the wheel. The walls of the clay first rose as a triangular form. It was then widened and finally rounded out into a perfect pitcher shape, using just the dexterity of his dampened fingertips.

"How long did it take you to learn how to do this?" asked Biren, fascinated.

"All my life," said the old potter, "and all my father's life and my forefathers' before him. We come from generations of potters, *mia*. We are born into it. Everything I am today is because of the blessings of my ancestors. They guide the turning of the wheel. My fingers are their fingers. I learned how to throw a pot by first learning about the nature of the clay. Clay is very temperamental. It has a mind of its own. To shape it into something useful you have to know how it will behave under the pressure of your fingers. Every child in the village learns about the nature of clay from the day he is born."

Biren pondered what he said. This was what caste was all about. The collective skills of a community passed down from generation to generation, not easily picked up by an individual. Many of the pottery techniques were closely guarded community secrets.

"Didn't you ever want to do anything different?" Biren asked. "Like being a carpenter or a blacksmith?"

The old potter stopped his wheel, looked at Biren and laughed.

"What kind of question is that, *mia*?" he said. "Does a woodpecker ever want to be a kingfisher? Of course not! They are a different caste. We are born with different skills. Even if I worked very hard and learned the skills of a carpenter, could I ever be one? You are talking as if a man can be whatever he chooses. It is not so simple, *mia*, not so simple."

"Why not?" asked Biren, puzzled. "If you have the talent and skills to be a carpenter, you can change your profession. There's nothing wrong with that."

"Just listen to yourself talk! It is not skills that make a profession, *mia*, it is community. Would I ever be accepted into the carpenters' community? Do I know their customs? What would happen to my family? Where would we live? We would belong nowhere. We would become people without roots, like the water gypsies and the *bauls*, wandering from place to place."

"What is wrong with that?" muttered Biren, almost to himself.

"Be careful, *mia*. This is dangerous thinking. Without the blessings of your ancestors and the roots of your community, a man can lose himself."

"Or he can break free and find himself," Biren argued.

The old potter just smiled, shook his head and started turning his wheel again to shape his pot.

Strange, Biren thought. *You can take a lump of clay and mold it into anything you want, but why is it not possible to remold a human?* It would be interesting to see how far he could reshape his own destiny. He had been given every opportunity; now it was up to him.

★★★

Biren heard a shout and looked up to see a small boy in ragged shorts with clay-caked hands come running down the crooked path from the river.

The boy huffed up to them. He pointed at Biren. "The fisherman told me to find this *belaytidada* and bring him to the river. They are waiting for him."

"Who is waiting?" asked Biren.

"The real *belaytis.* The pink ones. They want to talk to you," said the boy.

"Pink *belaytis.* What do they want?" said Biren, puzzled. Englishmen normally did not come to a potters' village.

The boy just pulled Biren's shirtsleeve. "Come, come," he said. "The *belaytis* are in trouble. They sent me to get you because nobody can understand what they are saying."

On the way to the river, Biren gathered from the small boy that a steamer had broken down at the ghat and on board were two *belaytis.* The *belaytis* had rattled off in "eenglees" to the fishermen and nobody could understand a word. The steamer crew meanwhile had gone off toward the jute mill to get help.

Biren arrived at the ghat to find the steamer docked and two Englishmen in the tea shop. The older of the two, a disgruntled gentleman dressed in khakis and a *sola* topee, sat by himself on the battered old bench outside smoking a pipe. He glanced impatiently at his pocket watch and had about him the bristling stiffness of an army man. The other fellow was inside the shop smoking a bidi, communicating with wide animated gestures with the fishermen, who were trying not to laugh.

Seeing Biren, the fishermen all started talking at once and pointing at the two men.

"Is there some way I can help you gentlemen?" Biren asked.

The two Englishmen looked startled to hear him speak the Queen's English. Coming from a man dressed like a local in a blue-and-white-checkered *lungi* and cotton shirt, it did sound rather odd.

"My good fellow," said the older gentleman, getting to his feet. He spoke in a clipped manner. "Our steamer has broken down in this godforsaken village, as you can see. We are trying to get to Silchar. I am Reginald Thompson, district commissioner, and this here—" he pointed his pipe at the other gentleman "—is Griffiths, my assistant."

"How do you do," Biren said, shaking hands.

"You don't look like a potter, old chap," said Griffiths, looking at him curiously. "What are you doing here? You speak bloody good English, I daresay."

Biren told them briefly about his education in England. It seemed Griffiths had studied at Oxford and the two of them were just getting into a conversation when Reginald Thompson cut them short.

"Excuse me, dear fellows, this is no time for chitchat. We have a crisis on our hands," he said brusquely. He turned to Biren. "The steamer fellows say they have to send for an engine part. This is not a simple repair. It may take another day, maybe two. They have gone to the jute mill to see if they can send word to Dhaka. Now, it is absolutely crucial I get back to Silchar tonight, no matter how late. I have an important matter to attend to in the morning. We wanted to ask the fishermen if they could take us by boat to Silchar. I understand it is three hours from here by these small boats."

"Yes, approximately," Biren replied. "Do you have a lot of luggage? These small dinghies don't hold much."

"We have three trunks and a couple of bags. But we decided we can take a few essentials and wait for our main luggage to come by the steamer a few days later."

"Let me talk to these fellows," Biren said.

At first, none of the fishermen were interested. One fisherman said it was his child's rice-eating ceremony the following day, and the other one did not have a rowing partner and refused to make the journey back alone late at night for fear of river ghosts. Finally, two fishermen agreed, but first they would have to go back to the village and tell their families. And as it was already close to lunchtime, they would have lunch, then siesta. In other words, it would mean a delay of another three hours before they could start out.

"Three hours!" exclaimed Thompson. "What do they need three bloody hours for? We are willing to pay good money."

The fishermen shook their heads.

"It's not about the money," Biren said, and tried to explain about the rice-eating ceremony, ghosts, lunch and siesta, none of which made any sense.

"That's quite understandable," Griffiths said affably.

"Don't talk nonsense, Griffiths," snapped Reginald Thompson. "This is completely unacceptable." He clamped the pipe back into his mouth and glowered.

"Well, we might as well do some sightseeing while we wait," said Griffiths. "This is a potters' village. Maybe Roy can show us around."

"I will be glad to," Biren replied. "The village is a short walk from here."

"I will stay right here, thank you," said Thompson stiffly. "I don't care to visit the village in this heat. And—" he waved his pipe in a threatening manner at Griffiths "—if you are late, I will just leave without you."

"That's unlikely," replied Griffiths calmly. "The fishermen won't leave before Roy here talks to them. Besides, what will you do here by yourself? Looks as if this tea shop is shutting down."

"I can very well take care of myself, thank you," growled Thompson.

"Well, cheerio, then." Griffiths waved.

As Biren and he walked off together, Griffiths said, "Thompson is not a bad sort, really. He comes off a little gruff. He sprained his foot in Calcutta and it's causing him a great deal of discomfort."

"I just hope the fishermen show up like they promised," said Biren. "I won't be surprised if they go home and change their minds. I don't really know these fellows. This is not my village. I live farther downstream."

"Oh, I'm not too worried. Thompson is the one in a big hurry to get back. I wouldn't mind staying the night in these parts. The steamer people were saying the jute mill has a rather nice guesthouse by the river where we could spend the night. I am very much tempted by the idea."

"My father used to work in that jute mill before he died."

"Did he, now? So tell me again, what are you doing here? You had just started to tell me about it."

"I got my law degree in England and passed my civil-service exams. I came back to the village to see my mother. Now I am looking for a job in Calcutta," said Biren. "I am also working with an organization to get government funding to set up schools for girls in Calcutta. This is a long-term project."

"That's marvelous," said Griffiths. "Thompson is a big supporter of education. You should talk to him. Our office organizes fund-raising events for local schools in Silchar.

Thompson is also on the board of the education council in Calcutta. Once a year he goes to attend their annual general meeting."

That piqued Biren's attention. "Is that a part of his job as the district commissioner?"

"I would say that is more to do with his personal interest. But in his position he is able to influence decisions. Thompson has two daughters. He is very particular about their schooling. His own mother was a highly educated woman—a famous philanthropist. She was well ahead of her time, I believe."

"I wish I could talk to him more about it," said Biren. "But he's not too chatty at the moment, I suppose."

"You're right," agreed Griffiths. "He's too worried about getting home. But do drop him a letter and tell him about your plans for starting a school for girls. I think he will be most interested."

"I may just do that," said Biren. "But my first job is to get you both safely back to Silchar. I am just keeping my fingers crossed those fishermen show up."

They were standing next to the clay-mixing pit, which still had wooden poles stuck into the mounds. The workers were gone for lunch. "Now, what are we looking at?" asked Griffiths. "Tell me about the potters. From what I have gathered about India, a potter will naturally belong to a potter caste, am I correct? I believe they also marry among themselves and live in the same village generation after generation. I find India fascinating. We have a weavers' village near Silchar and it's the same thing."

"If you are born into a caste, you are automatically born into a trade at the same time," explained Biren. "The tailor is of a higher caste than, say, the cobbler. A tailor's daughter can never marry a cobbler's son, as she would be marrying beneath her caste."

"So are you going to marry the tailor's daughter or the cobbler's daughter?" quipped Griffiths.

Biren laughed. "I am afraid I am in no position to choose. I am casteless and jobless. In other words, completely ineligible."

As promised, the fishermen showed up later that afternoon, and the Englishmen were sent on their way. That very evening Biren wrote Thompson a letter and mentioned the proposal for the education program. He also enclosed newspaper clippings of articles he had written for the *Bengal Star*. Little did Biren realize a broken-down steamer and his meeting with Reginald Thompson would play a pivotal role in shaping his own destiny.

CHAPTER 38

Nitin, who was now in his second year of medical college, wrote to say he would be coming home for a visit. The last time Biren had last seen him was five years ago, before he left for Cambridge.

Biren could hardly recognize the strapping young man who waved back at him from the steamer deck. Dressed in a handloom cotton kurta and horn-rimmed glasses, Nitin looked distinguished and scholarly.

"Dada!" he cried as the steamer neared the bank. He leaped onto the shore without waiting for the gangplank to be lowered, and they embraced each other.

"I would have never recognized you," Biren said, stepping back to appraise him.

Nitin laughed. "You sent us a photograph from England but I had none to send you. So yes, I suppose you did not know what to expect."

"Would you like some tea before we start back for home?" Biren asked, still trying to recover from the fact that this young man was his baby brother. He remembered Nitin as the small boy with a pensive face and hair falling over his eyes who liked to play with ants.

"I would love some tea," Nitin said. "You have no idea how I miss the fisherman's tea of home. In Calcutta, they flavor the tea with cardamom. I can't stand it."

They walked together to the tea stall. Nitin's luggage consisted of only a cloth bag slung across his shoulder.

"I didn't realize you would not have any luggage," said Biren. "I got the bullock cart to take us home."

"Forget the bullock cart, Dada. Should we send it back?" suggested Nitin. "I could do with the walk, if that's all right. I need to stretch my legs. Besides, it will give us time to talk. There's something I want to tell you before I see Ma and Uncle."

They lit their cigarettes with the burning end of the hanging rope in the tea stall and carried their cups of steaming tea out to a log on the water's edge.

"I got married," said Nitin abruptly. "I don't know how to break the news to Ma and Uncle. You must help me, Dada."

Biren's first thought was Nitin had got a girl into trouble. But that was not the case. Her name was Bela, he learned, and she was the sister of his friend from medical college. Bela came from a conservative business family of Calcutta. Her father owned several sari shops. Nitin and Bela had been meeting in secret for two years with her brother acting as the accomplice between them.

"I had plans to propose to her family after I finished college and got a job," said Nitin. "Not that her parents would have approved of me—a village boy from Sylhet. No matter how educated I am, I will always be beneath their status. But still, I was prepared to propose formally when the time came. In the meantime Bela's parents arranged her marriage to another." He paused, crushing his cigarette into the mud cup.

"Then what happened?"

Nitin threw the mud cup into the river, startling a heron hiding in the rushes to take flight.

"We eloped. We went to the Kalighat Temple and got married by the priest," he said.

"Where is Bela now? Did her parents find out?" Biren asked anxiously.

"Yes, her brother told them. They have disowned her. I arranged for Bela to live with an Anglo-Indian spinster as a paying guest, but I can't afford it for long. I stay in the college hostel, as you know, so Bela can't stay with me. I came home to tell Ma about all this. I want to bring Bela to the *basha* to stay with the family till I finish college and get a job. Then I will take her back to Calcutta."

Nitin looked at Biren askance. "I don't know how Ma is going to take this, Dada. You yourself are not married. A younger son should not get married before the older son. That, too, I did without the permission and blessings of the families."

"First of all, I am really happy for you," Biren said. "You married someone you love. It's refreshing for a change." He got to his feet. "Let's walk back, shall we? I don't think Ma will be displeased. She keeps moaning there is no daughter-in-law in the house and everybody has been after me to get married. I think you will help to take the attention off me. Do you know Ma is losing her eyesight? I am worried about her, brother."

Nitin frowned. "I suspected that but she keeps denying

it." He walked with long, easy strides, his beautifully proportioned feet clad in a pair of open-toed Kolhapuri sandals. "So you have no plans to settle down soon, then?"

"I will have to find someone to elope with first, don't you think?" Biren joked.

Nitin grew serious. "I didn't have a choice, Dada. My intention was not to behave like a coward. I have lost the respect of my in-laws, and I don't know if I will ever get it back. Eloping should be the very last resort. If you only knew Bela's family you would realize I had little choice, after her hand was promised to another. She would have been married off within a month."

Biren put his arm around Nitin's shoulders. They were both almost the same height now.

"I am joking, of course, brother," he said. "You were forced to do what you did. I am sure Bela is a very nice girl. As for my plans, I have applied for jobs in the civil service and I am also involved with an education project. Has Samaresh told you anything about it? We are trying to get funding from the British government to start a girls' school. This venture is going to take up all my time, so marriage for me is probably not a good idea. But let's first talk about you and how we can best break the news to the family."

CHAPTER 39

Silchar
1st June 1894

Dear Mr. Roy,
It has been several months since our fateful meeting the day our steamer broke down near your village and you so kindly made arrangements with the locals to bring us to Silchar. The boat ride with the fishermen was harrowing to say the least and Griffiths will attest to that. But we managed to get back home safely, thanks to you putting us in the care of the trusted locals known to you.

I am writing this letter because I have a proposition to make. It is a job offer. I am hoping you will consider it. If I recall, you are a Cambridge-educated barrister. The Central Government in Silchar is looking to hire law professionals such as you. The burgeoning tea industry in Assam has put a lot of pressure on the local government in Silchar. There are laws and charters constantly being formulated and revised, pertaining largely to the river transportation and local governance. The salary and perks I think will meet your approval. I can tell you more about the job after I hear back from you indicating your interest. I am hoping you can come to Silchar to meet with my colleagues and me to discuss this further. It will be my pleasure to host you as our guest for a few days. Please do send me your reply at the earliest.

With very best wishes,
Reginald Thompson
District Commissioner

The port town of Silchar, girdled by the Surma River, was located in the Barak Valley of Assam. Surrounded by the undulating hills of the tea-growing areas, it had grown into a prosperous town with a sizable European population, garrisons of military and a river port built on a bed of stones to dock incoming ships.

While the British population lived quiet lives in carefully guarded bungalows along tree-lined enclaves, the rest of Silchar thrived with the disobedient randomness typical of small towns. The farther one got from town, the more the bamboo thickets unraveled, the roads lost their purpose and became skinny paths that disappeared into the rice fields and villages.

Far from the fishy port and tucked deep inside an enclave lined with stately eucalyptus trees was the private residence of the district commissioner. Reginald Thompson lived in a gracious white-pillared bungalow with a perfectly manicured lawn bordered by a tall box-clipped hedge of flowering hibiscus.

The front gate was unmanned, and when Biren clicked open the latch two blond Labradors set up a frightful din and raced toward him. They turned out to be surprisingly friendly, and with no further concern that Biren might be an intruder, they escorted him happily to the house, running around in circles, their tails thumping against his legs.

A uniformed man met him at the front veranda and went inside to announce his arrival while Biren studied the row of mounted deer antlers on the walls.

Reginald Thompson, dressed in jodhpurs and riding boots, entered the veranda. "Roy! Splendid to see you!" He shook his hand and led him over to a cane seating area surrounded by flowering wisteria vines. "Did you have a good journey? I trust you took the steamer, not a fishing boat?"

"I did indeed," Biren replied, sitting down. One of the dogs laid his chin on his knee and looked at him with beseeching brown eyes.

"Perhaps you would care for some tea? Some of the best teas, as you know, come from the neighboring Cacher tea-growing district."

"Thank you, I would like that very much."

"Let me tell you a little about the job and our requirements," said Thompson. "The candidate I am looking for has to be bilingual. I think you are well qualified in every respect. The second thing is certainly not essential, but it would be a big plus if you know how to ride."

Biren was a little puzzled. "I did take some riding lessons in England. I may be a little rusty in the saddle but I should be able to manage," he said.

"Jolly good," said Thompson, sounding relieved. "You see, we have transportation challenges out here. The roads are often bad during the rains and sometimes we are required to go into villages. The only means of getting there is by boat or on horseback."

"What kind of work do you do in the villages?" Biren asked.

"Well, we don't do any work there, as such, but we have to go into the villages sometimes to investigate if there is trouble. As you know, different communities live side by side, peacefully most of the time, but every now and then there are disturbances. Typically, the villagers sort it out among themselves, but sometimes things get out of hand and the trouble starts to spread into town. Then the police are called in to manage the situation, but we can never figure out what the problem is or who started the trouble in the first place.

"For one," he continued, "we have a communications issue. The villagers speak in several dialects. It sounds very similar to what you were speaking with the boatman when we first met. What is it? Bengali or Assamese?"

"It's the Sylheti dialect—a mixture of Bengali and Assamese."

"See, this is why I think you will be an asset."

"Daddy!" A dainty little girl ran out of a room wearing a pink flowery frock, her hair done up in ringlets. A Siamese cat galloped behind her and twisted its tail between her legs.

"Why, hello there, Enid. Are you all done with your lessons? Where are you going all dressed up, darling?"

"Birthday party," said the little girl, looking curiously at Biren.

"Would you like to say hello to Mr. Biren Roy?"

"Hello," said the girl shyly. She tugged her father's hand. "Do you like my new dress, Daddy? Oh, dear, I will be late for my birthday party! Goodbye!" She ran back inside with the cat chasing behind her.

Thompson smiled and his eyes softened. "They grow up so quickly, don't they? Before you know it, she will be off to boarding school in England." He stroked his chin pensively. "I read with great interest your proposal to set up an English school for girls. I have been entertaining the same idea for a long time."

Education, Thompson explained, had become an important priority for the local government. A large population of Sylheti Bengalis had settled in Silchar. They were the Bengali *babus* who fulfilled the bulk of clerical duties in government offices. The Bengali *babus* were diligent paper pushers but more important they were English educated. Without them the central government in Silchar would cease to exist.

"I find the Sylheti Bengalis as a community have a strong leaning toward English," Thompson said. "If we want to attract and retain our clerical staff we must provide English education for their children here in Silchar."

"My father was a strong believer in English education," admitted Biren. "He saw English as a window to the bigger world. He said otherwise we would remain frogs in a well, seeing only a small patch of the sky."

"Your father must be very proud of you."

Biren took a deep breath. "Unfortunately, my father did not live to see me fulfill his dream."

"I am sorry to hear that."

The Siamese had wandered back into the veranda and taken a lively interest in Biren's shoelaces.

Biren tucked his feet under the chair. "So you have plans of setting up an English school in Silchar, then?"

"That was my idea, but I have not had the time to develop it. There are already a few schools for boys in Silchar but none for girls. So my plan was to set up an English school for girls to begin with. If I had someone like you—young and energetic, with an interest in education—we can take this plan further. Initially this will be in addition to your regular office duties, of course."

Over a cup of tea, Thompson laid out the details of the job. It was an attractive offer. Biren's job designation would be that of a junior assistant to the commissioner. Griffiths was the senior assistant, and there was another fellow as well who was away on a six-month furlough to England. The salary was generous, and Biren's perks included his own private residence, which he was free to design and build on an open budget. His work would involve a fair amount of travel to Calcutta and possibly England. While his residence was being built he would be accommodated at the government guesthouse with the riding stables within walking distance.

"I would like to show you the office," said Thompson. "It's a five-minute walk from here. My colleague Davis is expecting us. After our meeting he will take you to our guesthouse. It's located on the banks of the river. A marvelous spot. I am sure you will enjoy the view." He got to his feet. "The bearer will show you to the guest room if you would like to freshen up, and I can meet you back here in the veranda in, say, fifteen minutes? Jolly good."

CHAPTER 40

Biren Roy was given a fine office on the ground floor of the big whitewashed government building with a grand view of the Surma River. He could not help but note all the chambers occupied by the Europeans were on the floor above. But overall he was pleased with his spacious office and his brand-new desk that still smelled of teakwood sap. From where he sat, he could glance over the top of the hibiscus hedge and see the fishing boats and river barges ply up and down the waterway. From his perspective they looked as if they were skimming over a bed of leaves.

The first week at work was confusing and dull. A four-day polo tournament had just started at the Silchar Polo Club, and the bosses were gone all day. They did not delegate any specific work and Biren was left with a pile of files to study, none of which made any sense.

Down the hallway was a buzzing hive of dhoti-clad Bengali *babus*, buried in their motley ledgers, and typists who clattered on steel typewriters with carbon-stained fingers.

On the third day, Biren found a sickly looking fellow in khaki shorts with a boat-shaped cap on his head perched on a three-legged stool outside his office. The man jumped to his feet with an elaborate salaam. He introduced himself as Biren's personal peon boy. His job was to bring Biren his tea, tidy the desk, ferry papers back and forth to the typists and other offices and doze on his stool trying not to fall off.

The next morning, Biren found the four yellow pencils on his desk sharpened to murderous points, lined neatly beside his writing pad. His water glass, freshly replenished, sat under a lace doily with a beaded edge to keep out flies. The finger-moistening pad, inkwell and squares of sky-blue blotting paper were lined with military precision at the top of his desk, looking like soldiers awaiting orders. Biren twirled the three rubber stamps in their merry-go-round holder and wondered what he was supposed to use them for. The bumpy orange lettering on one rubber stamp read REVIEWED, the second read APPROVED and he was trying to decipher the third when a loud commotion ensued outside his office.

A pompous ball of a human rolled in, tailed by the distraught peon boy wringing his hands. The man had introduced himself as Ganesh Pain, the town's sweetshop owner. Pushing the peon boy aside, Ganesh Pain announced he had come to report the "blatant thievery of his nuisance-making neighbor, Nimai Das, who had pilfered and consumed his bamboo cabbage." Biren, who was in the middle of admiring his nicely sharpened pencils and twirling the rubber stamps, was deeply perplexed.

"A stolen cabbage, did you say?"

"*Bamboo* cabbage," Ganesh Pain corrected him sternly.

"Why, sir, you have become too-much English to have forgotten your own native Sylheti delicacies?"

Bamboo cabbage, Ganesh Pain reminded Biren, was a rare and coveted delicacy—a man-made vegetable, ingeniously grown by crowding the tender shoots of a bamboo plant inside an upturned clay pot.

"I see," said Biren vaguely, wondering where this lesson in cabbage farming was leading.

"Four months," said Ganesh Pain, "*four months* it takes to grow a bamboo cabbage. So can you imagine my distress, sir, when I saw all my pots broken and my cabbage vanished?"

Biren tapped his pencil, wondering if this nature of crime came under his jurisdiction. He wrote *cabbage*, *theft* and *Nimai*, with a question mark on one corner of his new pad.

"Do you have any proof that this Nimai is the culprit?" he asked finally.

Before Ganesh Pain could answer, there were more loud voices, and soon several Sylhetis crowded into Biren's office. The typewriters down the hallway stopped and a few nosy *babus* peeped around the fringes of the crowd, tittering. A hush fell as clipped footsteps came down the corridor and a swath cleared hastily for Reginald Thompson, who marched with big strides into the room.

Biren jumped to his feet.

"What is the matter, Roy?" Thomson's voice was frosty. "What is all this commotion about?"

Biren indicated Ganesh Pain. "This sweetshop owner has come to report a theft, sir," he said, hoping to God his boss wouldn't ask, "The theft of what?" But of course he did.

"Cabbage? *Cabbage!*" Reginald Thompson thundered. "What kind of damn tomfoolery is this?"

Reginald Thomson snapped his fingers. "Everybody out,

please. And, Roy, report immediately to my office." With that he turned on his heels and thundered up the wooden staircase, his hobnail boots hitting each step like a gunshot. Biren followed, embarrassed, past the stares of the *babus* who craned their necks over their typewriters to see him pass.

Reginald Thompson's office was the last room at the end of the hallway. The doorway was flanked by two slit-eyed Manipuri guards in khaki uniforms with crimson hats shaped like inverted flowerpots on their heads. They snapped to attention when they saw their boss, and a mask clipped over their features. Thompson crossed over to his desk and pulled out his chair with a screech while Biren hesitated in the doorway.

"Take a seat, for God's sake," snapped Thompson.

Stung by his curtness, Biren sat down.

Thompson smacked a small brass desk bell on his desk with the palm of his hand. The shrill *trring* brought one of the foot guards scurrying.

"Call Griffiths, sahib," he commanded without lifting his eyes.

Griffiths, pink faced, rushed in straightening his tie. His ruddy appearance, which Biren at first mistook to be boisterous good health, was in fact a terrible attack of prickly heat.

"Good morning, good morning," huffed Griffiths. "What was that dreadful racket downstairs?"

"That is what we are here to talk about," said Thomson grimly. He pinned Biren with a stern eye. "You need to be briefed on protocol, Roy. This office does not deal with the cabbage problems of the masses. I do not care who these people are, but they cannot rush into this office and turn it into a fish market. Is that clear?"

He turned to Griffiths. "Have you briefed Roy on the

water gypsy problem? You have sat on this case for months and made zero progress."

"I..." began Griffiths, only to be silenced by another brassy *trring* of Thompson's desk bell.

He waved them both away. "Kindly take Roy to your office and give him the files. I don't wish to discuss this any further."

Perplexed, Biren followed Griffiths out of the office. What shocked him was the military-like hierarchy in the office. Rank was everything. The senior officers were all ex-army men, which explained their bossy behavior. Still, this would take some getting used to.

"Sorry, old chap," muttered Griffiths. "I should have warned you. Thompson is always in a rotten mood when he gets back from Calcutta. His has a terrible time dealing with the politics in head office. He is a good sort, really. Just stay out of his way when he's in a bad mood."

"What is this water gypsy problem he was talking about?" Biren asked.

"Ah." Griffiths grinned. "That's the albatross hanging around my neck. Now we're handing it to you because we don't know how to deal with it."

"What makes you think I am more capable than you are?"

"Thompson seems to think so. That is why he hired you in the first place. Let's just say, you are Indian and you have a much better chance of gauging situations and eliciting information than we have. We both noticed how comfortable you were talking to the boatmen, and then you were comfortable talking to us, as well. That is rare. The locals clam up around us. Just think about it—if they trust you with their cabbage problems, chances are they will tell you other things." He pointed to a door with *A. W. Wells* engraved on a brass plaque. "Here is my office. It still has the name of my predecessor. Fellow died from malaria two years ago."

Griffiths's office had lumpy files sitting on both chairs across from his desk. "Throw those on the floor, will you? Have a seat."

Biren lifted the files. "Hold on," Griffiths said, "pass me that one—the one with the blue paper sticking out. That's right, that's the one I need. All right, let's see. Water gypsy problem."

Biren glanced at the file as he handed it to Griffiths. *Bede/ Water Gypsy* was written on the spine.

"The *bedes* are boat people. Nomads," said Biren. "I guess you can call them water gypsies."

"Oh, so you know about them?"

"Yes, they are common around these parts. They dabble in herbal medicine and magic healing. I have never known the *bedes* to cause any problem. They usually keep to themselves."

"Wait a moment, I'm trying to find the details." Griffiths tipped his chair back and seesawed against the wall. Biren noticed the lime had chipped away where the chair bumped against it. Griffiths flipped quickly through the pages of the file. He grimaced, stretching out his chin, and stuck a pencil down the inside of his shirt collar to scratch his neck. "Damn prickly heat is killing me," he grumbled. "I could hardly sleep last night."

"Try a neem paste," suggested Biren. "It's a home remedy."

Griffiths peered over the top of the file. "What is neem paste? I've never heard of it."

"Neem is the *margosa* plant. It's very common." Biren pointed at the feathery branches outside the window behind him. "That's a neem tree. It grows everywhere. My mother used to make a paste with water and apply it to the prickly heat. You will get instant relief."

"Really? I must remember to ask the office peon to pick me some leaves." He turned his attention back to the file and tapped a kettledrum beat on the page with his pencil. "All right, here we are. Like you say, we have never had a problem with the water gypsies, but lately there have been several altercations between them and the weavers' village. We need to find out exactly what is going on. Which is where you come in."

"Have you asked around the weavers' village?"

Griffiths snorted. "You think they are going to tell us? They don't want government interference. When the police show up, both sides clam up. As soon as the police leave we have another flare-up."

Griffiths snapped the file shut, swung his chair upright and handed the file to Biren. "All yours with my blessings. The police reports are all inside. You can talk to the police inspector, but I suspect he won't be able to tell you anything more than what's already in here."

Biren took the file reluctantly. "So how do you suggest I go about this?" he asked, feeling suddenly inadequate.

Griffiths shrugged. "I haven't the slightest clue. Be creative. This is your chance to play detective. Get on the inside and see what is going on. You have advantages we do not have. If you solve this problem, you will be Thomson's blue-eyed boy and he will do anything for you."

Biren flipped listlessly through the file. It was full of carbon-stained copies of reports with scribbled notations. He thought to himself if he had only known the petty nature of this job he might have declined Thompson's offer. But maybe it was too early to tell.

Griffiths cracked his knuckles. "Cheer up, old chap. There are nice perks in this job. Like trips to Calcutta and stays at the Imperial Hotel. The ladies of Calcutta are quite lovely. You'll have a very good time, I assure you."

"Well, thank you," said Biren. "I have to earn my feather first." He walked to the doorway, turned and waved the file. "I'll take a look at this."

"Oh, Roy!" Griffiths called. "Tell my peon the name of those leaves for prickly heat, will you? I want to take some home and get my bearer to make the paste. I think I will pack up early today. I am totally wasted. It was club night yesterday. I must have gone to bed at 3:00 a.m."

CHAPTER 41

Biren found himself in a peculiar predicament. His high-profile job as a government officer set him apart from the Indian community. None of the other Indians had moved above their *babu* clerical status. He was the only one who lived in the European section of town and rode a horse, all of which garnered a great deal of unwanted attention. The Sylhetis at first gloated to see one of their own moved up the ranks. Everybody claimed to be a "cousin" or "uncle." But when they found he would not do them any favors, the tables quickly turned against him and Biren was viewed as a snob.

"Who does he thinks he is?" they grumbled. "With his fancy mustache, riding a horse and wearing big-big boots. He acts like he is a *belayti*. Why, he is just a Bengali village boy and he should have more respect for his elders. When I go back to Sylhet I am going to complain about him to his uncle."

Biren finally understood why the challenges of the job had overwhelmed Griffiths. It was enough to overwhelm anybody, not just a foreigner. There were several ethnic groups living in close proximity to one another, with their own religious and cultural differences, caste issues and language barriers. One had to be an insider to grasp what was really going on. To win the trust of the different communities he would have to be careful not to take sides—especially that of his own people.

He gave his peon boy strict instructions. "I don't want to see anybody in the office. No uncle, no cousin, not even my own father or mother, understand? If somebody wants to see me, ask him to leave a note. Tell them I am busy."

"These people are too *faltu* to be your relatives, sir," scoffed the peon boy, who had started cultivating some high and mighty airs of his own. "Only this morning a poor fisherman with one eye came here asking to see you. He said he was your brother. I told the scoundrel to get lost. Otherwise, I would beat him with a stick."

Biren, who was absently flipping through a file, sat up. "One-eyed fisherman? Where did he go?"

"He went back to the river," said the peon boy, startled at Biren's reaction.

Biren sighed. He had been to the river several times looking for Kanai. The other boatmen knew of Kanai but said he never stayed in one place for long. He moved from village to village, ferrying people and cargo. Sometimes he was spotted far north, fifty miles from town.

"If the one-eyed fisherman comes again you must tell me," said Biren, adding, "Of course, that's highly unlikely now that you chased him off with your stick, but keep an eye out for him. I need to talk to him urgently."

The peon, imagining his boss to be of charitable nature, piped up, "There is also a man with only one leg who stands outside the…"

Biren cut him short. "No, no, nobody else. Only this one-eyed fisherman," he said, waving him away.

It was just as well Kanai had not taken off on one of his sojourns, because Biren found him a few hours later sitting alone in the riverside tea shop. Kanai was now a wisp of man, hunched and beaten with none of the youthful cockiness Biren remembered so well.

Biren cantered up on his horse and called out his name. Kanai looked up with fear and dread. There was no recognition in his eyes and Biren realized, only too late, riding a horse and dressed in Western clothes, he must have looked like an officer of the law. Even after he identified himself, Kanai cowered and acted as if Biren was about to strike him for something he had not done.

"Will you take me for a ride in your boat, Kanai?" Biren pleaded. "It will be like old times. If you wait for me here, I will return this horse and come back."

Half an hour later, dressed in an inconspicuous *lungi* and shirt, Biren walked down to the river to meet Kanai's boat. It felt comforting to blend in. As a local, you could observe life much more closely.

They drifted out on the river. Under the open sky and with the familiar oar in his hands, Kanai finally relaxed.

They rowed past a cluster of waterfront villages pungent with the smell of drying fish. Naked children with ebony skin splashed in the water, and women sat on their haunches scrubbing clothes on slabs of river rock. Then the villages became fewer and farther between, and they passed a giant bog with dead tree branches sticking out like petrified hands. In the far distance gray spirals of smoke twisted above the treetops from the cremation grounds.

Bit by bit Kanai told Biren his tragic story. He had lost all the members of his family in the floods and the cholera epidemic: his parents, his young wife and two children. His village was full of ghosts, he said, and he could no longer bear to live there. He had abandoned the house where his family had lived for three generations, packed his meager belongings in his small boat and taken to the open water. He had been at the mercy of the river tides ever since.

As Kanai related his story, his single eye welled with tears that coursed down one side of his face. Biren could feel his sorrow, the endless drifting with no shore to call his own. He understood for the first time the true heartbreak behind the Bhatiyali boatman's songs. Wandering the open waters alone, the boatman was constantly reminded about the fragility of life. His song was a call for God's mercy.

"Why did death spare me?" Kanai wept. "What good am I to anyone?"

"You are plenty good to me," Biren said gently. "Kanai, you are the only person who knows the real me. All people see is my fancy clothes, my horse and my *belayti* job. But you knew me when I was a village lad. You took me fishing to the backwaters. I sat with you under the old flame tree and listened to your stories. You told me about river ghosts and devil's mud that swallowed a water buffalo whole, do you remember?"

Kanai gave a wry smile. "Yes, *mia*, I remember."

"I, too, am alone, Kanai," Biren said softly. "I don't belong anywhere. You are the only person from my past. You connect me to myself and I need you."

"If you say so, *mia*."

They came to a fork in the river. Kanai pointed to the left. "That is the Damaru River. It separates the living from the dead. We boatmen avoid that stretch. All the outcasts—Doms, *tantriks*, water gypsies, lepers—live on that side."

They passed the gypsy settlement of moored boats and threadbare tents pegged in the river mud. Two bare-bodied men sat on logs prying open oysters, surrounded by clamorous crows. One of the men looked like a dreamlike creature from a water world—a merman, if there ever was one. His long hair hung down his bronze back like river kelp. A muscle in his upper arm flexed as he twisted open each oyster before he tossed it into a pile. He looked up as their boat passed, his eyes the color of wild honey.

"These people are the *bedes*. The river is in their blood," Kanai said. "They dive for seed pearls and sell them in town. Some of them get quite rich but they are still considered outcasts."

Biren remembered the file sitting on his office desk.

"I heard there was some trouble with the *bedes* in the weavers' village and the police were called out."

"Oh, that!" Kanai shrugged. "The police are called when somebody wants to get somebody else into trouble. The villagers are trying to get the *bedes* evicted from these waters, so they just go and file a *faltu* complaint."

"See! This is exactly the kind of information I need," exclaimed Biren. "I can't trust anyone else to give me a true picture of what is really going on."

Kanai narrowed his eye and gave Biren a critical look. "Why should people trust you if you go riding around on your big horse wearing a *belayti* suit-boot?" He slapped his forehead and broke into a cackle. "*Hai Khuddah*, when I first saw you I thought you had come to take me to jail! Wait till I tell Chickpea, Dadu and the rest. They will fall down laughing!"

Biren grinned to see the old Kanai he remembered so well. For a brief moment, Kanai had forgotten that his old tea shop friends at Momati Ghat were all dead and gone.

A local fisherman is a government officer's best ally. Biren kept a tab on village activities through Kanai. Kanai brought news of any unrest before it brewed into trouble. Biren took to visiting the villages by boat rather than on horseback and chatted with the locals in tea shops. Often he was able to sort out petty grievances without involving the authorities. In most cases, an impartial mediator was all that was needed.

One sunset evening on the boat ride back from the villages Biren saw a floating flower. Or was it a dream?

She passed in a swish of oar barely six feet from his boat. Perhaps it was the fragrance of her passing that made him look up. Biren was staring at the water, lost in the hypnotic pattern of swirls and the clumps of water hyacinths as they floated past. Later, in retrospect, he wondered what it was that shifted his gaze up to the passing boat. He would never know.

She sat gracefully on the rush mat, chin in hands. Her dark silken braid twisted with jasmine hung to one side. As she passed, Biren got a fleeting glimpse of her delicate oval face, her finely arched eyebrows and the dark lashes resting softly on her cheek. The long tail end of her orange-red sari fanned gently in the river breeze as she passed.

He peered around the side of the boat but all he could see was the back of the boatman growing smaller against the slanted evening sun.

The image of her played on his mind: her jolting beauty, the delicate jasmine in her hair, the iridescent flame of her sari ignited by the setting sun as she floated by.

CHAPTER 42

The following week there was a note from Thompson asking Biren to submit an estimate for building his house. *His own house!* Biren had been so caught up with day-to-day affairs, he had not given the matter any thought. To his frustration he had not been able to talk to Thompson about the school project, either, as most of the time his boss was either in a foul mood or out of the office.

Designing a house tickled Biren's fancy. It was one dream he could see turned into a tangible reality for a change. To build a house he first had to find a plot of land. He kept his eyes open and stumbled upon the perfect location on one of his jaunts. It was a stretch of vacant land between the fish market and the river. Although relatively close to the center of town, there was no access road leading to it. Later he discovered he could ride his horse through a patch of dense scrub and thicket to get to the mile-wide vacant lot. It had rice fields and bamboo groves on one side and the tall embankments of the river on the other. Across the river was a fishermen's village.

Biren halted his horse to gaze at the open sky and waving green paddy and he knew in his heart that this would be the very spot on which he would build his house. Looking at the vast expanse of nature lifted his spirits and made the petty world of office politics fade away.

He found his way back to town through a residential neighborhood with rows of pukka houses made of brick and mortar with tin roofs. Many had neatly fenced yards, potted marigold plants decorating the front walk and latched gates with hand-painted signs of fanciful house names: Bono Kusum, Flower Garden; Ananda Niketan, Joyful Abode; Asha Nibash, Hope Dwelling. Middle-class Bengalis lived in houses like these, office *babus*, schoolteachers, postal and shipping clerks.

Biren was passing under a leafy plum tree when a small green plum whizzed past his ear, followed by another that bounced off the horse's flank, causing it to shy. He jerked his head around in time to see a flash of brown leg and a crimson skirt disappear into the tree's upper branches. Cowering among the leaves was a small girl, who looked down from the safety of her perch with big brazen eyes. She stuck a pink tongue out at him. Biren wagged an admonishing finger at her and rode off smiling to himself.

He made inquiries about the land and found it did not belong to anyone. It was a no-man's-land that separated the Muslim and Hindu sections of town. The two communities lived in clearly demarcated areas, and the land between them was used as a grazing ground for cattle.

The challenges of constructing a house in such a location were many. It involved clearing out dense vegetation, constructing an access road, and there would be no neighbors to speak of. All this to Biren's romantically inclined mind was beginning to sound quite appealing. His one concern was the budget. Surely the cost would be prohibitive? Thompson had told him he had an open budget at his disposal, and Biren wondered if asking for an access road leading up to his residence would be stretching it too far. But when he submitted the written proposal, the budget was quickly approved and he was given the go-ahead.

Two elephants were commissioned to do the bulky work of clearing the land, and Biren rode out whenever he could to watch them work. Meanwhile he worked feverishly on a floor plan. It morphed from a romantic jumble in his head to a concept of increasing complexity that kept him awake at nights. He made countless sketches, changing them frequently, only to scrap everything and start over again. Silchar had no architects to speak of, and he was at the mercy of Chinese *mistris*. They were skilled, diligent house builders who could construct anything to specification from even a rough sketch. Their specialty, however, was the faux-English-style bungalow with big formal rooms and long connecting passages. Biren had a radically different idea in mind. He knew what he wanted in his head but found it impossible to translate it into a sketch for the *mistris* to follow.

He finally enlisted the help of Ren Yamasaki, the famed Japanese architect and Haiku master whom Biren had met at the College Street Coffeehouse in Calcutta. Biren wrote to him explaining the project, and was overjoyed when he accepted his invitation to visit Silchar. Biren took him out to see the plot, and back at the guesthouse Yamasaki sat at the dining table and deftly drew a detailed sketch on a roll of rice paper with his beautiful calligraphic pens and black squid ink. It was a remarkable floor plan, stunning in its simplicity. The house had a wide-skirted veranda, sloping roofs and a clean skyline opening out to a vista of the river. The rooms flowed easily into one another with no dark, narrow passages. Yamasaki specified natural building materials—thatch, cane and bamboo—all cheap and abundantly available in Assam. The materials integrated the house seamlessly with its surroundings and gave it a very natural feel. He also agreed to send a Chinese master carpenter to oversee the project. The detailed plan with the handwritten notes was an exquisite work of art in itself, and Biren went to great lengths to get a woodblock print of the original made in Calcutta to send to Estelle. He was excited to share it with her. Estelle was the only person he knew who would appreciate the beauty of the design. She was a free-spirited country girl, after all, who embraced bold ideas and dreamed as freely as he did.

He waited impatiently to hear back from her.

I would have excepted nothing less from you, dear Biren, she wrote. *The house is as extraordinary and as original as you are. I can clearly picture the green rice fields, the big river and open sky just as you described them. Your idea of planting an avenue of shade trees leading up to your house is nothing short of magnificent. The only thing left to complete this picture is, of course, a beautiful Indian girl with jasmine in her hair sitting on your veranda! Don't mind me, dear friend, but you have put me in a dreamy mood with your beautiful descriptions.*

The image of the girl on the boat immediately flashed through Biren's mind. It was uncanny, almost as if Estelle had described her. He recalled the girl's poetic beauty, the pensive look on her face as she floated past. Which lucky man was she was dreaming of? he wondered. A man waiting for her on some distant riverbank, silhouetted against the setting sun. His eyes would light up to see her boat. He would rush up to hold her hand as she stepped delicately on the shore. She would lift her lovely eyes up to meet his and smile…

Biren sat up with a jolt and shook his head. Had he really succumbed to such imaginings? It was all Estelle's fault. Her dreamy mood was contagious. He snatched his pen and wrote with a furious scrawl.

Forgive me, dear Estelle, but I suspect your romantic notions are a reflection of your own state of mind. In your last letter there was a fleeting mention of a certain gentleman by the name of Luke Adler. I daresay I caught a suspicious whiff of coyness in your words. The Estelle Lovelace I know is by no means coy. Perhaps you would care to explain?

Selfish as it sounds, I am building this house for my own personal pleasure to enjoy in peace and solitude. I remain a confirmed bachelor to date.

Calcutta
18th March 1895

Dear Dada,
You will be pleased to know I got the posting as the assistant medical officer of Chandanagore Hospital I had applied for two months ago. As an added bonus I will be given staff quarters inside the hospital compound. I have one month's leave before I join and I am leaving for Sylhet tomorrow to get Bela and Ma.

I have convinced Ma to move to Chandanagore. I cannot leave her alone in the basha *without Bela. She is now almost completely blind and very dependent on Bela to take care of her. Ma, as you can imagine, does not want to leave the old* basha *because she will miss Apumashi.*

Chandanagore is a much smaller and quieter town even though it's only thirty kilometers from Calcutta. I hope on your next visit to Calcutta you will come to visit us in Chandanagore.

Your brother,
Nitin

Biren returned from a month-long trip to Calcutta to find the construction site of his house abandoned. Not an inch of progress had been made in his absence. The foundation had filled up with rainwater and the Chinese *mistris* were absconding. He later learned they had taken off to work on some other project in town.

Back at his office, he was greeted by a towering pile of paperwork and a curt note from Thompson sternly reprimanding him for failing to submit certain judicial council documents by the due date. Biren frowned. Surely this had to be a mistake? There were no such documents that he was even remotely aware of.

He slumped down in his chair, feeling utterly exhausted. This was not how he had envisioned his life. All he seemed to do was government paperwork, manage local squabbles, ferry documents up and down to the high court in Calcutta and build a house that was becoming unmanageable. These activities were taking up all his time, and he was losing sight of his dreams.

The last meeting with Samaresh and the group at the coffeehouse had turned out to be deeply frustrating. To Biren it had sounded as if their proposal was gathering dust in the education department and it was unlikely George McCauley had even glanced at the file. The group, meanwhile, had talked animatedly about starting another completely unrelated project. Listening to their intellectual arguments, Biren had became irritable and restless. He'd left the coffeehouse and wandered around the secondhand bookstalls of College Street with their precarious towers of mildewed books, all the while wondering what was going on with his life.

On the riverboat back to Silchar, it had suddenly struck Biren he was falling into the same trap as his father. His father had been a diligent, hardworking man, and the British had used him to their advantage only to further their own interests. Now he was being used in exactly the same way.

Reginald Thompson had dangled the carrot and fed Biren's dreams, but he had done nothing to further the school project. It was impossible to discuss anything constructive with him; he was always in such a murderous mood. Thompson's intentions were no doubt honorable, but unless one demanded fairness, one was likely to be sidelined. *They need me more than I need them*, Biren thought. *I can do without this job, but I am not going to give up my life's purpose.* Biren made up his mind to confront Thompson—bad mood or no—and hold him to his word. If Thompson ignored him, he would quit his job.

He was pondering this serious question when the peon boy rushed in with a letter marked URGENT & CONFIDENTIAL. It was from Ganesh Pain, the sweetshop owner, demanding "immediate punitive action" against the same "nuisance-making" neighbor, Nimai Das. The complaint was so ridiculous Biren furiously balled up the letter and flung it straight at the dustbin across the room, narrowly missing Griffiths, who had just walked in through the door. Griffiths nimbly dodged the paper missile as it whizzed past his ear.

"God almighty!" cried Griffiths, throwing up his hands.

His eyes darted from the balled-up papers on the floor back to Biren. "Is that a temper tantrum I see, Roy boy?"

Biren sank into his chair and glowered.

"Come on, old chap, tell Uncle Griffy what is wrong."

"Everything," said Biren wearily, squeezing his forehead with his fingers. "My whole life."

"I think we need to talk, old man," said Griffiths in a soothing voice.

Without giving Biren a chance to answer, he pointed his thumb toward the door and jerked his head. "Come on, off we go to the polo club. Social hour. You take everything too seriously, old chap. For God's sake, shake out those feathers once in while, will you? Learn to live a little."

At the polo club, Griffiths snapped his fingers at the bearer and pointed to Biren. "*Burra-peg* whiskey for sahib," he ordered.

"No!" protested Biren.

"Yes!" Griffiths insisted.

And from there onward it was all downhill.

Things took a sinister turn that day, and alcohol had plenty to do with it. It was one day Biren wished he could blot from his life, and it was just as well he remembered so little. Neither did Griffiths. When they compared notes the next day at Griffiths's bungalow, their recollections were different. They both remembered walking down to the river singing, "Here we go 'round the mulberry bush," with their jackets slung over their shoulders. At one point Biren vaguely remembered Griffiths removing his fine leather shoes and tossing them into the river, which was probably true because Griffiths's feet were shoeless and blistered the next morning.

They both recalled getting into a boat. The boatman's face was only half-visible behind the deep cowl of his reddish-brown shawl. He had red-stained teeth and the cunning eyes of a rodent.

"You swallowed a coin," said Biren. "And you insisted I do the same."

"Did I?" said Griffiths in a faint voice. He looked a wreck, lying in bed, his feet bandaged by the bungalow bearer. The room smelled strongly of disinfectant. To add to his woes, Griffiths had a terrible attack of dysentery and had to hobble to the bathroom every ten minutes.

"Oh, now I remember," he added weakly. "That boatman looked exactly like Charon, the ferryman of Hades. Awful-looking fellow." He sighed, sitting up. "I have to go to the bathroom. Give me a hand, will you?"

Biren shuddered at the memories of the evening before. It came back to him in snatches: the dark moonless night, the thick churning river. The lantern on the prow of the boat that swayed and creaked, throwing a glow on the dark water, turning it to blood.

"I hope you realize we had a narrow escape," said Griffiths, emerging from the bathroom. "A very narrow escape. We could have passed into oblivion by now."

Biren nodded grimly. "I feel responsible," he said quietly. "I put your life in danger."

"Nonsense," said Griffiths, waving him off. "You got drawn to my dark side. I encouraged it." He sat on the edge of the bed and waggled his feet. "I think I am going to be a cripple. I can't believe I threw my shoes into the river. At least you were not that foolish."

"Foolish enough," said Biren. "I don't even know what to say about yesterday."

"Do you think I should have some tea? Or will it upset my stomach more?"

Biren got up. "Tea is all right. Stick to tea and toast. No butter. I'll tell the bearer to get us some tea."

When he got back, Griffiths's face was buried under a pillow.

"Are you feeling rough again?" Biren said, peering at him. "Maybe the doctor should take another look at you."

Griffiths ignored him. "That place, Roy… That cremation ground was something else. All that fire, the drums, the dancing—who were those awful banshee women harassing us?"

"I don't know," said Biren miserably. His stomach churned remembering the putrid stench of a woman in a coarse sari and scaly hands. "I don't even know what happened."

"We smoked something. Out of a clay pipe," said Griffiths. "You were screaming your head off."

"I?" Biren said, sitting up. "Screaming my head off? I don't believe it!"

"Yes," said Griffiths soberly. "And not only that. You wanted to throw yourself into the fire like some Hindu widow doing suttee. I had the hardest time holding you back. I had to slap your head to bring you to your senses. Then you started bawling like a baby."

Biren did not remember a thing. The blackout was terrifying, and made his stomach tighten with panic. He wondered what else he had done. Maybe it was better not knowing.

"And all those burning human bodies, crackling and spluttering like pork rind." Griffiths groaned. He covered his face with his pillow. "I think I am going to throw up," he said in a muffled voice.

Biren felt very close to throwing up himself. Snatches of

what happened came back. They had strayed into the forbidden part of the Damaru River and landed up at the cremation grounds. He remembered the *tantriks* with their bloodshot eyes and ashen bodies, the fire spitting ashes like dead moths into the sky. He remembered faceless lepers, hideous women with no noses and rotting teeth. Naked children playing with bones. After that his mind was a blank.

Who had brought him home? He had woken up around midday in the veranda of his house, his new jacket purchased recently in Calcutta gone, his shirt torn, buttons missing. The bile had risen in his throat because everything—his hair, his clothes, his skin—had smelled of burning human flesh. The stench was lodged deep in his pores. His first thought when he'd woken had been, *Where is Griffiths?* He'd cleaned up hurriedly and rushed to Griffiths's bungalow to find him tucked in bed like a baby, his feet bandaged in soft white cotton. How? Who had gotten him there? Griffiths had no recollection, either.

"That's it!" said Griffiths, flinging his pillow against the wall. "I'm going back to Calcutta and I'm getting married. A man can't trust himself. Every man needs a wife to keep him out of trouble." He quickly added, "You better find yourself one, Roy."

Biren paced up and down the room. He ran his hands through his hair, stopped and sniffed his fingers. "I am going to the barber to shave off my hair," he said. "I am going to do penance and I will never get married. If I can't keep myself out of trouble, nobody can."

With that, he walked out of the room.

Finding Thompson in a rare mellow mood the following day, Biren broached the subject of the school.

Thompson, for all his ferocious bark, was a shrewd and canny man. He saw the steely determination in Biren's eyes and quickly realized he could lose a valuable employee if he did not take him seriously. Roy was the most unusual young man—he did not care for the prestige of his job; he did not care about the perks; he was polite but not intimidated by authority. He seemed to be an idealist and a visionary, a trailblazer in many ways. Roy reminded Thompson of another Bengali gentleman he had heard about whose name was Jatin Nandi.

"Have you met this gentleman Jatin Nandi?" Thompson asked Biren. "He is from your Bengali community. The *babus* in the office first told me about him. He is an excellent teacher, I am told. I had half a mind to meet him at one time. Nandi started an English girls' school in town. I don't know if it is still running. Perhaps you can find out? I will ask our senior *babu* to give you the details."

"Does that mean we will not be submitting a separate proposal to McCauley?" Biren said tersely. He had not meant it to sound like a veiled threat, but it probably came across as one.

"No, no, Roy, don't get me wrong." Thompson sighed, rubbing his eyes wearily. "I am not trying to shunt you off. I am only suggesting you meet this gentleman because it might be interesting for you both to exchange ideas. Jatin Nandi already has the support of the Bengali community. He is very well respected, I understand. Whether you choose to work with him or not, rest assured, we will still present your proposal to the education department. I know George McCauley well, so I do not envision a problem getting it approved."

Hearing that, Biren relaxed.

"Meanwhile, to give you more time to concentrate on

this venture," continued Thompson, "I will cut back your office duties. We will still count on you to manage community affairs and you will have to attend high court hearings in Calcutta as and when they come up, but I will take all other office paperwork off your hands. How does that sound to you?"

Biren could hardly believe what he was hearing. "Th-that sounds very good, sir," he stammered. "Thank you."

"Very well, then," said Thompson. He stood up and gave Biren's hand a surprisingly warm shake. "I'll count on you to work out a plan, and let's see where we can take this."

For the first time in many months, Biren's chest felt lighter. Now he could finally breathe.

CHAPTER 43

Jatin Nandi's school was a small hut set deep in the folds of a shaded mango grove full of chattering parrots. The classroom was empty and the door unlocked. Biren peeped through the cracked windowpane. Inside were two rows of benches, a small blackboard and a potbellied water pitcher in the corner with a brass tumbler covering the top. He walked around to the caretaker's hut at the back of the building. A woman sat on the mud stoop cleaning rice. She jerked a U-shaped bamboo tray and flipped the rice in a graceful arc without spilling a single grain. A fat brown hen pecked at her feet surrounded by a brood of newly hatched chicks that cheeped and tumbled over one another like cotton balls. The woman looked up as Biren approached.

"I am looking for Jatin Nandi, the schoolmaster," said Biren.

"Jatinbabu is not here today," said the woman. "He broke

his arm. He slipped and fell in the fish market yesterday. He is at home."

"Where does he live?" asked Biren.

The woman pointed to a bamboo grove. "On the other side of the *bamboobari*. Channa, my boy, can take you to his house if you like."

Without waiting for Biren to answer, she turned toward the house and shouted, "Channa! Aye, Channa!"

A small boy peeped out from behind the door, winding a string around a wooden top.

"Take this gentleman to Jatinbabu's house," she said. "And come right back. I don't want you playing in the rice fields."

The boy jumped off the stoop and took off around the schoolhouse, running into the *bamboobari*. His mother yelled after him, "Channa, don't run! Wait for the gentleman!" but he was gone.

Following his erratic path was like following the flight of a bumblebee. The boy climbed over a fence, squeezed through a hole in a hibiscus hedge, wobbled across a log straddling a muddy ditch and arrived in somebody's backyard, where he jumped over jars of mango pickle drying in the sun. A caged mynah with a yellow beak cocked its head and called after them in a cracked voice, "Hey, mister! Hey, mister!"

Biren was beginning to regret the idea of following the boy when he suddenly found himself in the same road he took as a shortcut to get to his plot. The small girl who had thrown a plum at his horse was playing under the tree. She came running up to him.

"It's you again!" she cried. "Where is your horse?" She tugged him by the hand. "Do you want to see a mynah egg?"

"No, no," said Biren, disengaging her hands. "I have to go somewhere."

He looked around for the small boy but there was no sign of him.

"Did you see a small boy?" he asked the girl. "I was following him to someone's house."

The girl shrugged and rolled her eyes.

"Mitra! Where are you?" a female voice called from inside the house. A young woman appeared in the doorway, casually twisting her hair back into a bun. She wore an orange cotton sari with a green embroidered border against which her skin glowed a warm honey brown. She leaned a slender shoulder against the door frame and stood there idly looking at her fingernails. When she looked up, she gave a gasp to see Biren. Her hand crept to her mouth and then slid to the hollow in her throat.

Biren stared her, transfixed. He was immediately transported back to the sunset river. He saw again the lovely woman with her flower-braided hair flowing past in the delicate strokes of a painter's brush. It was the woman in the boat! She was even lovelier than he remembered her.

"Excuse me," she said in a soft, husky voice. For a second her eyes were curious before a veil of politeness dropped over them.

Biren cleared his throat, still feeling a little disoriented. "I am trying to find someone's house," he said, looking around him. "But I seem to have lost my young guide."

The woman's eyes strayed to the bottom of his trousers.

He followed her eyes and saw his trouser legs spotted with spiny cockleburs.

"I arrived here via a rather adventurous shortcut." He laughed, bending down to pluck off the burs. They made small ripping sounds as they pulled away from the fabric.

"Whose house are you looking for?" the young woman

asked. A delicate frown wavered on her lovely brow—a crease in a rose petal. *What is it about her eyes?* Biren wondered. *There is something different about her eyes.*

"I..." Biren fumbled, trying to remember the schoolteacher's name.

The woman watched him, smiling faintly. He was acutely aware he was coming across as a numskull. Who else would rush around looking for the house of a person with no name?

"I just can't remember his name," said Biren lamely. "He's a schoolteacher..."

Her face brightened. "Is it Jatin Nandi?" she asked.

Biren gave a nervous laugh. "Yes, yes, that's right! Jatin Nandi, the schoolteacher."

"Won't you please come in," she said, stepping aside in the doorway.

"Oh, no, no," said Biren. "Thank you very much, but I must be on my way. Perhaps you can tell me the way to Jatin Nandi's house?"

The woman's eyes danced with amusement. "But you are here," she said. "This is Jatin Nandi's house. He is my father."

Biren felt slightly dizzy. "Your father?" he repeated faintly.

Little Mitra pulled him by the arm and jabbered excitedly. "You know Baba fell down in the fish market and broke his arm? He went to buy *magur* fish for my *dida*, who has stomach pain."

"Please come in, this way," the young woman said. "Baba is in his study."

She led the way inside the house, past the kitchen and the smell of frying eggplant fritters. Biren followed her graceful back, mesmerized by the spool of her shiny hair twisted into a low bun at the nape of her neck. As she walked, her hair began to slip, inch by inch, unfurling on its weight, and mere seconds before it cascaded down in a waterfall she twisted it back with a natural movement of her long, delicate fingers.

She tapped outside a door and waited, listening. "Baba?" she called softly. "Maybe he fell asleep," she whispered. She pushed the door ajar and little Mitra barreled into the room.

"Baba! Baba! Wake up! A very important man has come to see you!" she said.

"Who?" a groggy, sleep-laden voice answered.

"A man who rides on a horse. But today he came walking."

The woman turned to look at Biren, her eyes dancing. "I will leave it to my sister Mitra to complete the introductions," she said. They were standing close together, and when Biren looked at her eyes he finally understood why they were different. They were an unusual gray-green color with tiny flecks of gold.

An old memory stirred within him. He had dwelt in those eyes, perhaps in another lifetime. He saw again the waters of the estuary, gray-green, blending earth and sky, with soft pockets of golden sand.

Little Mitra appeared at the door and pulled Biren by the hand. "Come in, come in," she said eagerly. "He's awake."

"I'll get some tea," said the young woman in that soft, husky voice of hers. As she walked away Biren watched her receding back, that beautiful silken hair slipping out of its hold, surrendering to the gravitational force of its own beauty.

Jatin Nandi sat by the window, his feet propped on a cane ottoman. He was a scholarly man, with a high forehead and large ears with prominent earlobes. His right hand, encased in a sling, rested on a mustard seed pillow on the armrest of his easy chair. His eyes had spidery red veins and small tufts of hair stood up on the crown of his head like a half-plucked bird. He appeared to have fallen asleep with a book on his lap. When Biren entered the room he struggled to sit up and groped for his glasses on the side table.

"Here, here," said Mitra. She grabbed the glasses and pushed them down firmly on her father's nose, where they sat slightly askew.

As Biren introduced himself, he was surprised to find Jatin Nandi knew all about him.

"Oh, the brilliant Cambridge barrister from Sylhet with the coveted government job. Who has not heard about you?" Jatin Nandi smiled.

"The coveted job!" Biren laughed. "I wish. I am not exactly in an enviable position, to tell you the truth."

"Most Indians would think otherwise. You are an asset to the government. Why else would they hire you as the assistant to the deputy commissioner himself?"

"Because nobody wants to get involved with the local politics, that's why," Biren replied.

"I stay away from local politics. You can get your tail caught in a bamboo crack if you are not careful. Better to concentrate on the work that needs to be done."

"Indeed," agreed Biren. "Mr. Thompson, my boss, first told me about you. I dropped by your school on my way here to your house. I don't know if you are aware of this but the British government has several grants set aside for education. I can get you more information—that is, if you are interested, of course."

"That depends what they want from me in return. I am always suspicious of free money."

"Well, nothing, really," said Biren. "This is all a part of the new educational program sponsored by the government. There are two criteria, however. The funds have to be used primarily for female education, and the medium of instruction must be English. I think you qualify on both counts."

"Baba is a very poor man, you know," piped up Mitra from behind her father's chair.

Jatin Nandi smiled. "And what did I tell you, *maiyya*?" he asked gently.

"That you are only as rich as your mind."

"Exactly," said her father. "Now, if you will please ask Buri Kaki to make us some tea, it will make your old father very happy."

"All right," said Mitra loudly. She got up and scampered down the hallway.

Jatin Nandi sighed. "That one will never grow up," he said. "She is the opposite of her sister. Maya was born an old soul. She started reading when she was three and writing poetry when she was seven. Mitra, on the other hand, wants to play and climb trees all day." He laughed, suddenly appearing younger.

As Jatin Nandi talked, Biren learned he was a widower who lived in the house with his aged mother and his two daughters. They had an old housekeeper who ran the household.

"My wife died ten years ago after giving birth to Mitra. It is Maya who brought up her younger sister. Thanks to her tender care, Mitra has never felt the loss of a mother."

Maya. What a lovely name. Biren ran it over in his mind. It had a graceful sweep to its sound. It was impossible to say Maya too fast or too loud. It unfurled on its own beauty. Like her hair.

"I wish for my daughters, and all daughters, to have equal opportunity in our society. Education has given freedom and opportunity to men. Why should it be any different for girls?"

Biren's heart responded to his words with the vibrating energy of a tuning fork. How refreshing it was to meet somebody whose thoughts so closely matched his own.

"That is why female education is so critical," Biren said passionately. "Something has to be done."

There was a tinkle of teacups in the hallway and Biren's heart skipped a beat. He turned, expecting to see Maya, but he was disappointed to see a bent old crone enter with the tea.

"In our society, money, horoscope and family name are the only things that define a girl's worth," Jatin Nandi lamented. "Her own accomplishments mean nothing."

"Beauty is an asset," Biren said absently. He gazed outside the window. The evening sun filtered through the splayed leaves of the papaya tree, making the tubular stalks glow a translucent green.

"Beauty!" exclaimed Jatin Nandi. "Yes, beauty as defined by society. A typical Bengali beauty must have a betel-leaf-shaped face, almond-shaped eyes and wide child-bearing hips. Pedigree and dowry still outweigh beauty at the end. It offends me to see the way marriageable girls are examined like livestock at the market. I have vowed never to put my daughters through such humiliation."

Biren thought of Maya, her slender waist and her gray-green eyes faceted with gold. She was no typical Bengali beauty, and he was thankful for that.

He leaned forward eagerly, elbows on his knees. "I completely agree girls should be given a fair education. I came here to ask your advice on a proposal I am putting together for a free English-medium school exclusively for girls. I have heard you have an excellent curriculum. I would like to know more about it."

"I am actually following a model set up by Elizabeth Benson. Have you heard of this remarkable lady?"

Biren thought for a moment and shook his head. "Her name does not ring a bell. Who is she?"

"Elizabeth Benson is a Christian lady who started a free school for girls in Dhaka. It is called the New Horizon Academy. Hers is the only Christian school where the teenage girls are allowed to wear their saris instead of Western-style skirts. As you can imagine, many Indian families don't like their girls wearing skirts because it looks immodest."

"Are the teachers nuns?" Biren asked.

"No, the New Horizon Academy is a secular institution. The teachers are all Anglo-Indians. Miss Paulson, the Anglo-Indian teacher in my school, has been trained at the Benson Teachers' Institute, which Elizabeth Benson also founded. My dream is to send Mitra, my younger daughter, to Dhaka to study at the New Horizon Academy. The boarding school is excellent, but it is difficult to get admission. I applied for Mitra four years ago and I am still on the waiting list."

"And what about Maya? Did she study at the New Horizon Academy, as well?" Biren asked, trying to sound casual. He could not help his interest drifting back to Maya.

"Maya was privately tutored by an English governess at home. She completed her matriculation two years ago and now teaches at my school twice a week."

Biren did a rough calculation. That would make Maya eighteen or nineteen—a very marriageable age. She was so mature and self-possessed, she appeared older. He wondered how he could find out more about her without appearing too forward. Luckily Jatin Nandi came to the rescue.

"Maya also works at the weavers' village," he said conversationally. "She must have gone there today. She is helping the weavers to start a co-op. The weavers are very poor. There is no sanitation in the village, no clean drinking water. Most of the children die of disease or starvation. These are the traditional silk weavers of Bengal. Their weaving skills have been passed down for generations, but now with the commercial English textiles flooding the market they are in grave danger of becoming extinct."

"So what does Maya do for them?"

"Maya negotiates a fair deal for the weavers with the wholesalers. An agent of a wholesale sari dealer comes to the village every second Tuesday of the month to purchase saris and put in orders. Previously the agent used to take advantage of the poor weavers and pay them a pittance. Now he cannot cheat them because Maya is there. In her quiet way Maya is quite tough."

Biren was surprised to hear that. She seemed so delicate and soft-spoken. He remembered her soft, husky voice that made even a casual conversation sound so deliciously intimate. It was very charming, and yet clearly there was an invisible toughness to her that he had yet to encounter.

Biren left the house feeling soul laden. It was the surprise of finding something precious and rare he had not even known to exist. Stunned by the providential nature of their meeting, he wanted to dwell on the miracle and at the same time understand the unrest he felt inside.

He walked toward the river in a daze, feeling slightly intoxicated, and noted that the water was low and drawn back over a ribbed stretch of sand, ruffled with kelp. Biren sat on an upturned boat and contemplated the water. He thought of Maya's eyes, of the emotions that dimmed and darkened in their depths, the flecks of gold that floated, so constant and pure. He breathed in the balmy air, his mind empty of coherent thought. Taking a stick, he scratched the letters in the sand, watching the shapes dip and curve to form her name. He contemplated it, seeing past the gouge mark into the grains of sand and the entire universe within. Something compelled his hand to move, unbidden, of its own accord. Next to *Maya* he wrote with firm deliberate strokes *Roy*.

Maya Roy.

And there it was. The name of his future wife. Strangely, once having written it, he felt at peace.

CHAPTER 44

Life could be perverse and cruel, Biren concluded. Just when he wished to stay in Silchar, he was sent on multiple trips to Calcutta. It seemed as if all the high court cases of the world had been dumped on his head. How ironic—only a few weeks ago he was complaining about his dreary life in Silchar. Back then trips to Calcutta were few and far between. Now he was forced to spend several weeks at a stretch in Calcutta when all he wanted to do was visit Jatin Nandi's house or float up and down the river looking for Maya.

Four months went by and he never stopped thinking about her. When he finally returned, the flame trees were in the madness of bloom. Everywhere they blazed a heart-stopping red. They singed the sun and washed out the sky. Biren felt the same madness in his heart.

Over the next few weeks he visited Jatin Nandi's house several times. Each time he walked past the clatter of pots, the sizzles and smells of the kitchen, on his way to the study. All the while his heart tiptoed in the hope of seeing Maya, but she was never there. Even Mitra, whose chirpy presence filled the house, was hardly around. Each time it was on the tip of his tongue to ask where Maya was, but he was too self-conscious. Day after day the toothless old crone came and served them tea. Once the white-haired grandmother showed herself and was introduced. Each time Biren left with leaden feet, dispirited.

In desperation he walked to the school. A class was in session, and through the open doorway Biren caught a glimpse of a stout Anglo-Indian teacher with bobbed hair wearing a navy blue dress with white-cuffed sleeves. He walked around to the back of the schoolhouse, hoping perhaps to learn from the caretaker's wife which days Maya taught in the school, but the hut was empty, the bamboo tray leaning against the wall. There was nothing much to do but walk toward the river. It was unimaginable how a single meeting with Maya had shifted the pivot of his entire universe. He watched a boat idle along the water's edge. Kanai was perched on the prow. His slackened oar cut a thin knife line in the water.

Kanai raised his hand in greeting. "*Mia!* Care for a boat ride?"

Biren was about to decline when it occurred to him it was the second Tuesday of the month.

"Can you take me to the weavers' village?"

"Yes, *mia*."

Kanai turned the boat toward the bank, but Biren had already removed his shoes and rolled up his knife-creased trousers. He waded into the river and climbed in.

"What takes you the weavers' village today, *mia*?" Kanai

asked. He pushed back from the mud bank, catching the swirl of the midcurrent.

"My heart," replied Biren impulsively.

"Ah, you are but young. You still follow your inner tide."

He broke into a song. Biren listened, his bare foot trailing in the water. It was a haunting song from the great beyond, sung to the rhythmic chop of a falling oar. As the song dissolved into a hum, all that remained was the splash of wood on water.

He disembarked on the shore, feet bare, shoes in hand. The cracked river mud felt cold and the broken shells cut into the soles of his feet like shards of broken glass, but Biren did not notice the discomfort.

It was a flood-hazard area, Biren thought as he walked across the flat, cracked earth devoid of vegetation toward one of the meandering pathways leading into the village. The ground was covered with rows of saris in dazzling colors, stretched on bamboo frames. Twisted yarns of freshly dyed silk were drying looped on bamboo poles. For Biren it felt like walking through a rainbow.

The mud huts of the village were built on elevated slabs. A loud rhythmic *clack-clack* noise that sounded like a freight train grew louder as he drew near. He passed open sheds with women sitting in front of wooden looms operated by foot pedals as they pulled on shuttles of yarn threading the weft to create a woven fabric. He paused to watch them work, but his presence elicited curious stares that broke the rhythm of the weavers' work, so he moved on.

Soon he came to an emerald-green pond with lush banana plantations all around and what appeared to be the only pukka brick house in the entire village. It looked fairly new and prosperous, with lime-washed walls and marigolds planted in terra-cotta pots lined outside the front door. A small cluster of slippers crowded the veranda, indicating people were inside. Biren looked in through the doorway. He wasn't expecting to see Maya, and when he did he thought for a moment she was a mirage of some sort, so he stood looking at her, not daring to believe she was real. But she was. So engrossed was she in her work, she did not notice him as she sat cross-legged on a bamboo floor mat with her head tilted and the unsharpened end of a pencil dimpled into her cheek. Her hair, braided in a loose side plait, tumbled in a lazy coil to the floor, where a pile of saris lay in a massive heap. Two men sat across from her, their backs turned toward the doorway. Many of the saris were opened out of their ironed folds to display the inside patterning and intricate designs of the end piece. Next to Maya, a sultry young girl with liquid eyes was deftly folding the saris back into neat envelope-like folds and placing them into separate piles. The girl looked up and noticed Biren at the doorway. She cupped her hand and whispered something into Maya's ear. When Maya saw him, she didn't even look surprised. She tilted her head in a gesture that invited him inside.

Biren placed his shoes outside the door and entered the room. The two men turned around to glance briefly at him. They were dressed identically in starched white dhotis and embroidered kurtas the pale color of buttermilk.

He sat leaning against the back wall, feeling vaguely guilty. Maya glanced at him once or twice and went back to listening to the two men. One of the gentlemen fingered the edge of a sari and said something about thread count, border designs and motif placement. He could see Maya making neat diagrams in a notebook on her lap with a steady hand. She said something to the young girl beside her, who appeared to be her assistant. The girl went to the back room and came back with another pile of saris, which she started opening up and laying out on the floor.

Biren watched Maya as she sat beautifully in a lotus pose, her spine tall and erect, accentuating her long lovely neck. The light from the open window cast a glow around her and made her hair shine. He tried to sit quietly, all the while wishing he could swat the mosquitoes that were making a meal of his toes. He wriggled his toes constantly without appearing to do so.

One of the men counted out a wad of cash and handed it to Maya, who recounted it and jotted something in her notebook. She put the money inside a small metal box with a latch. The men got to their feet and Maya and the young girl accompanied them to the door.

When they were gone, Biren walked over to her. "Maya," he said, suddenly shy, wondering how he would explain what he was doing in the weavers' village. But she seemed to have arrived at her own conclusions.

"I am so happy you came to visit the weavers' village," she said. She was putting away her notebook and pencil inside a cloth bag embroidered with mirror work. "Did you come by boat?"

"Yes," he said, still feeling tongue-tied. She turned to the young girl who had reentered the room.

"This is Chaya," she said by way of introduction, "my assistant."

"Do you always have an assistant with a rhyming name?" Biren quipped. She made him feel gleeful and young, maybe because she was so composed and serious herself.

Maya laughed. "Chaya is the head *tanthi*'s daughter. She is a gifted weaver herself. Her family have been weavers for… how many generations now, Chaya?"

"I am the fifth generation," the girl said, smiling shyly and covering her mouth with the end of her sari.

"Five generations!" Maya said, turning to Biren. "All that collective expertise, know-how and patterning go into each exquisite sari. The temple-style weave is the signature pattern of this particular village. Not many weavers can accomplish this complicated design." She handed the girl a sheet of paper. "Here is the order list for next month. Make sure Yosef sees the special instructions."

"Yes, *didi*," said the girl, addressing Maya as her older sister.

Maya lifted the hem of her sari and slipped her shapely feet into a pair of leather slippers with red tassels. Biren sat on the stoop to put on his shoes and she sat beside him. Her silky braid brushed his arm softly like a caress.

She did not comment on his filthy feet, and he was glad he did not have to explain. How could he tell her he had been walking barefoot all over the village, shoes in hand, if not for the madness of looking for her?

"Do you have a boat?" she asked.

"I sent it back," said Biren lamely.

"Then, how will you get back? No boat will go toward town now. They are all returning to the villages this time of the day."

Biren felt a little foolish. All he had wanted was a one-way boat ride to Maya, and he did not care if he ever got back.

"My boatman is waiting," she said. "You can come with me if you like."

Biren smiled. "It will be my pleasure."

They walked toward the riverbank. She carried the embroidered tote easily on her shoulder and walked with quick, light steps. The sun caught the sparkle of a gold floret in her earlobe, and a single bangle with a clasp fashioned in the shape of two elephant heads sat easily on her slender wrist. She was almost too beautiful to be real.

When they reached the boat, he climbed in and held out his hand, feeling the thrill of her fingers grasping his own. Once in the boat they sat like strangers at opposite ends, too far to talk, but Biren did not mind. He was content to just watch her.

A gigantic sun dipped into the curve of the horizon. The oar broke the water into lilac ribbons. The boatman sang an old Bhatiyali song.

"Oh, friend of my heart, you leave me afloat on a shoreless sea."

Maya's face was turned toward the shore, her profile etched in the dying sun. *Every feature on her face is perfect*, marveled Biren. What made her so serene and self-assured? he wondered idly. It had to be the security of being deeply loved and cherished. It hit him with a sickening jolt. Of course, it was another man. The thought was just too painful to entertain.

CHAPTER 45

It slowly dawned on Biren that courting Maya was going to be complicated. First there was the protocol. When he visited her house, he rarely got to speak to her alone. Jatin Nandi was broad-minded, but it was the old granny who set the rules. Granny had firm views on how respectable girls should conduct themselves. Loafing around and going for boat rides with a young man was out of the question. That was what common people did. Boys from good families looked for a chaste bride, not some gadabout they could have a good time with.

Maya was allowed to go to the weavers' village, but only with a trusted boatman known to the family. It was just as well nobody had seen Biren in the boat with her the other day; otherwise, Maya would have some explaining to do.

All this put Biren in a bind. His only resort was to mentally keep tabs on Maya's whereabouts and pretend to accidentally bump into her, so that he could legitimately walk a short distance with her and slip into a conversation. But the occasions were few, and each situation had to be strategically planned to make it all look natural. This caused Biren a great deal of frustration, and he felt increasingly irritable with the Indian community's narrow-mindedness. His brother, Nitin, had been lucky. Calcutta was a big city and it was easy to remain anonymous. Also, Nitin had had an accomplice. Who did Biren have? He was lumped with the European community, where he did not belong, nor was he a part of the Indian community. There was nobody who could remotely act as a liaison between him and Maya.

The only thing left for him to do was to meet Maya at the weavers' village. The village was far from town and nobody knew him there. But that was only once a month. *Once a month!* If something at work came up that coincided with the second Tuesday of the month, Biren had to rack his brains for elaborate excuses. He was past caring if it raised suspicions at work. All he cared about was that it gave him four hours of uninterrupted time with Maya.

When the day came and he visited the village, he observed her as she went about her work. The weavers came to accept him as her relative—a distant cousin, perhaps. Maya visited the different sheds, talked to the weavers, checked samples with her young helper, Chaya, always in tow, keenly observing and learning. She obviously hero-worshipped Maya. Biren learned a lot about the weaving and selling of handloom saris on those days, and some things came as a shock. For one, it seemed that the practices of the British government were aimed at wiping out the weaver community.

"It's true," Maya asserted. "Earlier the British government used to send merchants from Calcutta to act as middlemen who paid the weavers very poorly. The weavers were forced to match the prices of mass-produced factory textiles imported from Britain. How could they? As a result they were starving to death."

She held up a delicate mauve sari with an inlay of intricate thread patterning in a subtle duotone. "Look at this exquisite weave," she said passionately. "Centuries and centuries of craftsmanship passed down from one generation to the next have gone into this. All that history in a single piece of cloth. How can we lose this heritage?"

As Biren felt the fineness of the cloth, their fingers touched.

She smoothed out the sari before creasing it back into its folds, and patted it reassuringly.

"I do what I can. I find buyers who will give them a fair price. I am always thinking of ways I can help them."

They walked back toward a small tea stall on the riverbank. She was beautiful both inside and out, Biren thought. She was quietly committed to doing good, without ever feeling the need to boast or even talk about it. She let her actions speak for her. Maya was so perfect she almost did not seem real.

"Do you sometimes think of me?" Biren asked suddenly. He stopped walking and looked at her wistfully. "Maya, tell me. Please."

She averted her face but she was smiling.

"I want to marry you," he said simply.

She looked at him, her eyes clear and steady, but she did not say anything.

"Will you?" he asked, his voice breaking a little. "Will you marry me, Maya?'

"Yes," she answered without hesitation.

Her candid answer stunned him. The river, the sand, the sky blurred before his eyes. He found it difficult to breathe.

They reached the tea stall and sat facing each other across a wooden table.

"Two cups of tea," Biren called to the tea shop owner. He felt like singing or breaking into a dance. Maybe both. "And make it extra special."

He turned to look at her, his eyes shining. "It's all settled, then. I will come to your house tomorrow and ask your father for your hand." He reached across the table and caressed the delicate pink nail of her little finger.

She did not pull her hand away. "It is not my father but my grandmother you must ask," she said in her soft, husky voice. "She is the one who will give the permission. The elders of your family must give the proposal on your behalf. You should not come yourself. It is not proper."

Biren drew a shaky puff of his cigarette. He knew nothing about these formalities. There appeared to be some social protocol he was expected to follow. He would have to consult Nitin and his mother about it. As luck would have it, just when he needed to talk to his mother and brother in person, there did not appear to be a single trip to Calcutta on his horizon. It would all have to be communicated through letters.

CHAPTER 46

Chandanagore
19th May 1896

Dear Dada,
Ma is overjoyed to hear about Maya. I think she had secretly given up hopes of you ever getting married. She is familiar with the Nandi family. They are a well-known family of the Shomapalli village of Sylhet. We have discussed the matter of your proposal in great depth. Normally it would be the duty of our uncle as the seniormost member of Baba's family to represent you. But uncle is now completely incapable. He looks like a beggar and wanders around the fish market in a daze. The opium has finished him.

Ma wrote to our father's first cousin in the Tamarind Tree Village. His name is Johor Kaka. You may not remember him. His son Bapi studied in medical school with me, which is why I am in touch with the family. Johor Kaka has agreed to represent our side of the family for your proposal. There is a great deal of formality in these matters, especially since the grandmother of the girl, who is the head of her family, will give the consent, and from what you tell me she is very traditional.

Since I myself did not have a proper Bengali wedding, I know little about these matters. But here is what I have gathered:

Johor Kaka will come to Silchar to meet with Maya's family and give the proposal. Typically a group of senior male members from the boy's family approaches the girl's side, and the first meeting is between the male members of both families—the prospective bride and groom are not included in this meeting. Maya's family will ask questions about our clan's origin, lineage, caste, etc. Even I don't know much about all this but Johor Kaka will have all the details. They will also want to know about your job and financial standing. They already have a good idea about this, I would imagine. My feeling is you are probably the most eligible bachelor in Silchar right now.

The only gray area is the matter of matching horoscopes. Maya's grandmother—I get the feeling—will insist on consulting their family astrologer, as most traditional families do. I must warn you, Dada, many marriage proposals fall through if the horoscopes do not match. You should be aware of this risk if you agree to allow the astrologer to be consulted by her family.

Johor Kaka may be too shy to tell you this, but it is customary for you to present him with a new set of silk dhoti-pajama to wear for the occasion. As he is representing the boy's side he is also expected to carry gifts for the girl's family, usually boxes of sweets, some fruit and a good-size freshly caught rohu *fish.*

But more about these details when we meet in Calcutta

next. Ma is eagerly awaiting your arrival to learn more about her future daughter-in-law. You must not forget to bring a photo.

Your loving brother,
Nitin

Biren folded Nitin's letter and looked at the dark clouds moving swiftly across the evening sky. He had a pounding headache. What he had imagined to be a simple formality of asking Jatin Nandi for his daughter's hand was turning out to be a song and dance. If only he could speak to Jatin Nandi man-to-man and express his intentions, which were honorable in every respect, Biren was confident he could make a winning proposal, but to leave it up to an unknown uncle he had never met to propose on his behalf—how did that even make sense?

It was disturbing to see his society still bound by such conservative customs. It was the business about matching the horoscopes that irked Biren most of all. It was one thing disclosing the family history, lineage, et cetera, but to be accepted or rejected based on which house the planets were lurking in at the time of his birth was both demeaning and insulting. It dismissed his education, his accolades and everything he had fought to achieve in his life as inconsequential. What was the point of his fine debate arguments and his grand vision for women's reform when he himself was perpetuating the same rigid traditions he was fighting against?

Jatin Nandi was an educated, forward-thinking man, and Biren could not imagine him consulting an astrologer for his daughter's marriage, but he was also traditional in many respects and he would bow to his mother's wishes.

What if the horoscopes were incompatible? Biren would

lose all chance of marrying Maya. Now that he was desperate to marry her, the very thought filled him with terror.

The monsoons would break in a day or two, Biren thought. The river would rise and boats would cease to ply. Work at the weavers' village would come to a standstill as it usually did during the rains. The looms in the open shed would get covered and all the yarn stored away.

The question that tortured Biren's mind was, how could he continue to see Maya? He wanted to share with her his worry about the horoscope and he needed to be comforted and reassured that everything would be all right. Now the monsoons were going to disrupt everything. A great big chasm was coming between them. Suddenly it felt as if they were standing on opposite banks of the river with no boat to row them across.

At long last, an official trip came up for Calcutta. Biren spent endless hours discussing the proposal with Shibani, Nitin and other family members and returned home more confused than ever. In his suitcase he carried the rolled-up parchment of his Vedic birth chart. The complicated diagrams and Sanskrit squiggles made little sense, but it could make or break his future. He learned for the first time that Maya had a "given" name. Her name on paper was Mandakini, and it was customary henceforth to refer to her by her formal name. The name Maya held an easy familiarity that in his new formal role as her suitor he was not entitled to call her by. In referring to Maya as Mandakini, half the time Biren had to remind himself whom they were talking about. It was finally decided that three senior male relatives from his father's side would meet with Maya's family. His uncle Johor Kaka would write the first formal letter of introduction to express their interest on Biren's behalf and propose a date for the first meeting. All three relatives would have to be housed, clothed and armed with sweets and gifts. After the initial meeting, the family astrologer would be consulted to match horoscopes. Until then, the possibility of marrying Maya floated in limbo.

CHAPTER 47

The office was quiet. Deathly quiet. The *babus'* hall, usually noisy with the clatter of typewriters, was deserted. Biren climbed the stairs trying to remember what date it was. Was it a public holiday? A roof leak in the passage outside Thompson's office had resulted in an alarming water bulge on the burlap ceiling, which hung down like a distended belly and threatened to unleash a deluge. The water had started to drip down with a tuneful *pip-pip* sound into a bucket. The two Manipuri guards were not outside the door, which meant Thompson was not in the building. Only Griffiths was in his office, rocking against the wall reading a comic book.

"Roy!" he cried, flinging the comic on his desk. "When did you get back, old chap?"

"This morning," said Biren. "Where is everyone? What's going on? Today's not a public holiday, is it?"

"I wish," grumbled Griffiths. "Thompson is out on an emergency call. I am holding the fort."

"Where are the *babus*?"

"Oh, somebody just died. You know how the *babus* are. They use any old excuse to shirk work. It is either a *puja* or some relative dying. And since the whole town is related one way or the other, they have all taken off. So it's just me in this cruddy old office." He twirled a pencil around his middle finger. "Have a seat. How was Calcutta? I hear it's all flooded."

"It was bad this year," said Biren. He picked up the files from the chair and set them on the desk. The covers were curling with the humidity.

"So tell me, what's new and exciting in the big city?"

"I didn't get to do too much," Biren said, sitting down. "Mostly high court and family. So who died? Must be somebody important. Is it a religious leader?"

"An old lady, some schoolteacher's mother. He runs an English girls' school. I guess they are an old respected family in this town—hang on now, where are you running off to?"

Biren was already halfway out of the door.

"I know the family," he yelled back. "I have to go and offer my condolences. I will see you tomorrow."

A month passed and the dry winds of September lifted some of the humidity from the air. The neem trees started to send out feathery new shoots and leaves. One day the peon boy walked in with a handwritten note for Biren. It was from Jatin Nandi, who wanted to see him.

Jatin Nandi had shaved his head after his mother's death to mark his mourning. Without his shock of gray hair and only a thin gray fuzz he looked bony and old, barely recognizable. He also appeared awkward and nervous.

"A marriage proposal has come on your behalf from your

uncle in Agartala. This actually puts me in a very awkward position."

Biren's heart went plummeting down. He waited to be told that the horoscopes had been compared and found to be incompatible and that therefore marriage was out of the question.

"As you know, my mother, Maya's grandmother, passed away a month ago, and as a result our family is forbidden to celebrate any occasion for a whole year."

"I understand," said Biren, still waiting for the ax to fall.

"So unfortunately, your marriage to Mandakini will have to wait. For a year."

It took Biren a moment to realize he was talking about Maya. His heart was beginning to make itself heard. "So, if I understand correctly," he said slowly, and paused, almost too afraid to ask, "after a year Maya, I mean, Mandakini and I can get married?"

"Yes." Jatin Nandi nodded solemnly. "Mandakini is disappointed as well, but she understands. I have written back to your family explaining why we have to delay the wedding. I hope it won't be too much of an issue."

"I don't think it will," said Biren, still blinded by his luck. The papaya tree outside the window seemed to glow with blessing. The birds were chirping, too.

"I have also written back to your uncle and mentioned that there is no need to take the trouble to come and propose formally to our family. If my mother were still alive, it would have been a different matter. But my mother is no more and I, as the current head of the family, have no need for such formalities. Also, the matter of consulting horoscopes is out of the question. I abhor such things, as you well know. All I care about is my daughter's happiness."

Biren was so relieved he had the sudden urge to embrace Jatin Nandi, but the house was still in mourning, so all he could do was give a somber nod. A large garlanded picture of the granny stared down at him severely from the wall.

"So I give you my blessings to marry Mandakini. We will have a small engagement ceremony, just for the family if that's all right, to formalize the matter. Then I'll break the news to the community. But I have one request of you. For the sake of propriety I ask that both of you not be seen alone in public. Tongues wag easily in this town, and especially since you are still regarded as rather unorthodox—with your British job and Western ways—I would rather keep things low-key until you get married. I am not asking that Mandakini be chaperoned at all times, just that you take a third person along when you are out together." He smiled. "You will find an eager, if not overenthusiastic, accomplice in our Mitra."

"I will certainly keep that in mind," said Biren.

He had not seen Maya in so many months his heart ached. He longed to speak to her. He felt bolder, more entitled now.

"I am keen to hear what Mandakini has to say," he said. "Perhaps I can have a word with her?"

"But of course," said Jatin Nandi. "She is waiting to talk to you. We were also hoping you could stay and have dinner with us tonight. We still don't know your food preferences, but next time we will prepare the dishes of your choice."

"Please don't worry. I am not a fussy eater," said Biren quickly. *Food! Who cared about food?* All he cared for was Maya—rather, Mandakini. He would have to remember to call her by her proper name in public. After they were married, of course, she would become his Maya.

★★★

By the third dinner, to Biren's relief, Mandakini had once again become Maya. Also, by the third dinner he was comfortable enough to arrive at the Nandi house with a fork and spoon in his pocket. He figured if dinner was going to be daily affair, which it was turning out to be, they might as well get used to his idiosyncrasies. It was not that Biren could not eat rice with his fingers; rather, he preferred to use a fork and spoon—a habit he had picked up in boarding school that had stayed with him. The Nandi family barely registered surprise, but Mitra was mightily impressed. She watched him keenly as he dissected a piece of fish, picking out the fine bones with the tip of his fork.

"I also have to eat with a fork and spoon," she declared. "I cannot eat with my hands."

"Here, take mine," offered Biren. "Or we can each use one if you like. What do you prefer, the fork or the spoon?"

Mitra eyed both. "The fork," she said.

Biren handed it across the table and continued to eat with the spoon.

Mitra poked at her fish only to find the fork less friendly than she had imagined. She gave it back to Biren. "You can have it," she said.

"Thank you," Biren replied solemnly. "If you need to use it at any time just let me know." He looked up and caught Maya's eyes. They were dancing with laughter.

He got to know the old crone who ran the household. Everybody called her Buri Kaki. Buri Kaki cleaned fish and beheaded chickens with shocking savagery. She also made mustard-chili paste on a grinding slab with a pillow-shaped rock, and muttered to herself as she swept around the yard. She became coy and coquettish around Biren after she learned he was engaged to Maya. She addressed him as "Jamai-babu"—the son-in-law of the house.

Biren pandered to her. "Buri Kaki, you make the best tea in the world," he said, lifting his cup to her in a toast. She gave him a gummy smile and almost swooned when he winked at her.

"She is besotted with you," said Maya. Dusk was falling as they sat on the stoop outside the house, drinking tea.

"And what about you?" he asked softly, his finger stroking her wrist.

"Same," she whispered, curling her little finger around his.

CHAPTER 48

January arrived with gray-green dawns, the color of Maya's eyes, and melted into mornings of pure gold. He saw her everywhere, even in the bare branches of the flame trees; the seedpods rattled her name with every passing breeze. He had ample time to be with her, but it was never enough. Most days he had dinner at the Nandis'. The better parts of the evenings was spent discussing building plans for the new school with his future father-in-law, or teaching Mitra arithmetic by amusing her with rocks, shells and a pile of peanuts, which she could eat to subtract one sum from another. Then there were moments with Maya. They went for boat rides and river walks where Little Miss Big Ears stuck like a cocklebur between them, walked toe to toe and listened to every word, acting as if it was her birthright to be part of this jolly threesome.

Biren took them both to see his new house. Maya was surprised at the location.

"It's in the middle of nowhere, I know," he apologized. "One day this road will be lined with gorgeous flame trees, just for you, my darling wife."

Maya smiled. "I did not know the British had built such an impressive road in this part of the town," she marveled. "Why, it's almost a highway. Is it going to connect to some place important eventually?"

"To my house," said Biren, adding, "for now."

Maya was incredulous.

"I am the person who commissioned this road," Biren said. "I can name it whatever I want. I was thinking of Maya—no, wait—Mandakini Avenue? Sounds impressive, yes?"

He opened the front gate and invited them in. "Welcome to your future home."

Mitra skipped up the garden path. Maya wandered from room to room, empty of furniture, filled only with books and light.

"Do you like it?" he asked anxiously. "It feels a little empty, I know. It needs a woman's touch. I haven't really had time to do anything."

"It's sheer poetry," she said softly. "I would not change a thing. This house is beautiful, unadorned, in its simplicity."

"You just described yourself," said Biren happily. "That's exactly how I see *you*."

Maya just gazed out at the river and smiled.

CHAPTER 49

Biren had escaped the formalities of the wedding proposal, but there was no escaping a full-fledged Bengali wedding with all its terrifying chaos. The wedding had little to do with him and Maya; it was the marriage of two villages, several communities and a medley of assorted people. Besides the entire population of the bride's and groom's ancestral villages, there were fishermen, potters and weavers, Bengali *babus* from the jute mill and Silchar offices, Nitin's college friends from Calcutta, a sprinkling of pink-faced *belaytis*, random relatives and wedding crashers. Everybody felt rightfully entitled to celebrate Biren and Maya's wedding.

Thankfully, five days of feasting and ceremonies came to an end, and a convoy of boats set sail for Silchar to a conch-blowing, ululating crowd who trampled the river mud to a squelchy mess. The bride and groom, seated on a decorated ferry, were accompanied by boisterous young men, Nitin and his college friends among them, while the women, children and elders followed in separate boats. During the past five days Biren and Maya had not had a chance to exchange a single private word. Now, seated among the joking and teasing men, they were brain-dead, exhausted.

The boat wound its way down the river to the big fork, where, to Biren's surprise, it veered toward the estuary instead of the main waterway leading to Silchar.

"This is the wrong direction," Biren called out to the boatman. "We have to turn around."

"Oh, Dada, I forgot to tell you," Nitin apologized. "My Calcutta friends want to do a little sightseeing. There's another boat waiting for them at the estuary." His face wore a strange expression. One of his friends—Bela's brother—winked back at him. "Oh, there it is, can you see the boat?"

Sure enough, there was a boat moored on the shore. And a fine boat it was, too, decorated with tuberose garlands, silk bolsters, and filled with fragrant lilies!

Nitin laughed and clapped his hands. "It's for you! Are you surprised, Dada? This is your private boat and will take you and *boudi* to Silchar. You don't want to be on this boat with my hoodlum friends. There won't be a moment of peace and quiet, I can tell you, because look—" he pointed to a jute bag stuffed with bottles of hooch under the boat bench "—they have made party plans of their own."

Biren looked at his brother with joy and relief. "Thank you," he said, embracing him.

"I can't take credit for the idea," confessed Nitin. "It was Ma's. She told me after Baba and she got married, Baba took her on a romantic boat ride and filled it with lilies. She wanted to do the same for you."

The boatman reached out to help Maya into the boat, and Biren stepped in after her.

"Take all the time you want to get home, Dada!" yelled Nitin as the ferry pushed off. "We will tell everybody you both got kidnapped by the water gypsies!"

His friends wolf-whistled and waved; their voices faded as their boat turned the bend in the river.

Biren turned to look at Maya. She looked like a goddess sitting in her flame-red sari surrounded by fragrant white lilies. Her gossamer bridal veil fluttered in the breeze. Surely this had to be a dream? Maya smiled; her eyes were warm.

"Which way should I take you, *mia*?" the boatman asked as he pushed out from the shore.

"The longest way," said Biren, settling down in the bolsters beside Maya. "Take us by the slowest, most scenic route you know. We are in no hurry to get home."

CHAPTER 50

Maya's peaceful entry into Biren's life was heralded by the arrival of a creature of mammoth proportions. Biren watched mystified from the veranda of his house as a bullock cart lumbered up to the gate carrying what looked like an elephant sewn up in burlap.

"What the dickens..." he muttered, sitting up in the plantation chair.

"Oh," said Maya, looking a little flustered. "I forgot to tell you. That's Baba's gift for me. He ordered a dressing table. I had to accept it. Otherwise, Baba's feelings would be hurt, you know. It looks very big, doesn't it?"

"I imagine you will need a very large dressing table." Biren grinned. "Where else will you put all your potions and powder puffs?" Maya's beauty tools consisted of an ivory comb and a bottle of sandalwood lotion, but Biren loved the idea of the dressing table. It was a purely feminine addition to their home and reinforced Maya's presence in his life.

He slipped into his clogs and ambled down the garden path to talk to the bullock-cart man.

The bandy-legged bullock-cart man was standing under the shade of the mango tree wiping his face with a dirty rag. "Jatin-babu told me to wait here," he said. "He is sending two coolies to unload this thing. I don't know what it is, *babu*, but it weighs like a small house."

The coolies arrived and the dressing table was maneuvered with some difficulty into the master bedroom, where it was placed facing the window with a leafy neem tree outside. Once unveiled, it turned out to be a monstrosity with three angled mirrors of curlicue patterns of etched glass, exaggerated moldings and enormous claw feet. Set against the Spartan simplicity of the room, the dressing table was a shocking assault to the senses.

For the next few days both Biren and Maya could only stare at it and burst out laughing. After a while Biren got used to its ponderous presence and even began to regard it with a certain fondness. Ostentatious and cumbersome, the only purpose the dressing table served was to remind Maya of her father's overwhelming love and gratitude—emotions too large and unwieldy to express in words.

Often Biren would lie in bed and watch Maya comb out her hair with her ivory comb. In the three-way angled mirrors every subtle aspect of her beauty was reflected back to him, manifold.

Silchar
16th May 1897

How quietly she slipped into my life. Like spring slips into summer. Her lovely presence is all around me—delicate, whisper soft and almost invisible. I find her in the hairpin tucked inside the pages of a book, the sandalwood scent on my pillow, the jingle of the silver key chain hooked in the waistband of her sari.

I think back to the time we first met. We had a soul connect even before we set eyes on each other, in another lifetime perhaps. There is an old knowing, a place of comfort and familiarity, that transcends time. I have never felt this way about anyone. Sometimes in the quiet evening when the throb of a busy day stills, we dwell on the wonder of how we found each other.

Two years passed, and the pages of Biren's diary remained empty. He felt no desire to record the bounty of his life. Pen, paper and words were inadequate to capture the magnitude and delicacy of his days with Maya, and any attempts to record it had the danger of sounding ornate, flowery and ultimately redundant—like Maya's dressing table.

It was not that they spent all their time together. They both had their work. Biren's travels took him away from home, but Maya was so deeply embedded in his being that he never felt they were apart. Initially he had misgivings about leaving Maya alone for long periods, but it turned out she was immersed in her own interests. She did not try to manipulate his attention or make him feel guilty for not spending time with her. She was the most self-contained person he knew.

In another six months the old century would be ushering in the new. There was something momentous about the turning of a century. If years could be compared to pages, decades to chapters, a century was like an entire history book. There was the nostalgia of closure, and at the same time the anticipation of new beginnings.

"Imagine, beloved," said Biren. "This is the only turn of

the century we will ever witness in our lifetime. I wonder what the twentieth century holds in store for us, don't you?"

They were lying in bed, fingers entwined. The moonlight filtered through the neem tree scattered like delicate lace on the bed. Maya pulled his hand and laid it wordlessly on her belly. She did not have to say it in words, but Biren knew. He imagined he felt an imperceptible tremor of the life they had created together. His tears of joy wet her breast, and when he reached out to touch Maya's face he felt her smile curl around his fingertips.

CHAPTER 51

Estelle was trimming back the rosebushes in Daddy's garden. She had pulled on a waterproof canvas jacket and a pair of gardening gloves a size too large, which made handling the pruning shears rather awkward.

After his heart attack Daddy tired easily. The rose garden, his pride and joy, had fallen into disrepair, although the hollyhocks along the garden wall bloomed carefree and tall with no attention.

Estelle used the garden shears to lop off all the dead wood and crossing branches, then deployed a pair of sharp secateurs to make angled cuts above the outward-facing buds. Her father's garden tools were always honed and sharp, as he insisted it was important to keep the cuts clean, because a frayed cut would leave the rosebushes open to pests and fungus.

She could feel a head cold coming on, the sniffles just starting. She reached into the pocket of her woolen skirt for her hanky and came across the letter she had received from James a few days ago. It had been folded and unfolded so many times the creases had become soft and tired, and now she felt compelled to read it again. She rested the tools on the upturned wheelbarrow and went into the kitchen.

Estelle filled the teakettle and put it on the stove. On the small kitchen table was the gift tea caddy that James had sent from India. It was fashioned out of polished wood with an exquisite enamel inlay of lotus motifs. Estelle ran her fingers over the design, admiring the beautiful workmanship. Inside the brass-hinged box was a foil-wrapped packet of tea. She found an empty canister in the kitchen cabinet and emptied the tea into it. A heady smell filled the air, and she stood there with her eyes closed, inhaling deeply.

While she waited for the water to boil, Estelle pulled out the letter, smoothed it on the kitchen table and began to read.

Calcutta
17th March 1900

Dear Sis,
I hope you enjoy the Assam tea. This is second-flush orthodox, a top-quality tea from our company's gardens in Assam. Jardine Henley, our company, owns nineteen tea estates in the Assam Valley. Recently I had the pleasure of visiting the Chulsa Tea Estate in the Mariani district, where I picked up this tea. I look forward to my garden visits. That is the most rewarding part of my job, although I can't say life in Calcutta is ever dull.

Bridgette is growing up quickly. She will turn two in another month. I wish you could see her, sister. She has red hair and quite a little temper. Aha! I wonder who she reminds me of?

I did make inquiries about Biren Roy, since you asked. He

is married and has a child. From what I hear, he is very well respected. Biren has established the first all-girls school with government funding in Silchar. Many of the townspeople are against it and they keep trying to shut it down. But he is a force to contend with, I would imagine.

I am grateful to you for looking after Mother and Father, and I sometimes feel guilty for leaving you with the responsibility. Hopefully I can make it all up to you.

Your brother,
James

Estelle folded the letter back into its well-worn creases and slipped it into her skirt pocket. She smiled, remembering how adamant Biren had been about not getting married. It must have taken an exceptional woman to get him to change his mind. She imagined his child to have dark eyes and curly hair just like him.

They had lost touch around six years ago after she volunteered as a nurse for the Red Cross and left for South Africa. She was gone for a year and half and returned when she got the news Daddy had suffered a heart attack. Now she lived at home and took care of him and led the quiet life of a writer. Estelle often wondered about Biren, which had prompted her to ask James to find out about him. Now knowing he was married and settled, she would not attempt to renew contact with him. It looked as though they had both found their own paths in life after all.

CHAPTER 52

Moni was a delicate child with a poor digestion. She cried often and refused to go to bed unless she could hold a fistful of Maya's hair, which she played with and pressed against her tiny cheek. Only then would her eyelids flutter like tiny butterflies as she drifted off to sleep.

She liked to go down to the river. On summer evenings when a strong river breeze drifted through the house, she would get restless. "Wa!" she would demand, and point in the direction of the river.

Biren put her on his shoulders and took her down to the water's edge. He sat on his haunches and pointed out to her the stealthy blue-gray heron hiding among the clumps of vegetation looking like a piece of driftwood.

"Shh, look!" he whispered as the heron's long neck darted out and its javelin-like beak speared a large frog. The heron threw back its neck and swallowed the frog with jerky movements, the lump pulsing its way down its throat.

Moni looked at him with big puzzled eyes. “Oh?” she asked.

He showed her the small silver fish caught in tidal pools, and stood around as she poked sticks in the mud and drummed her little feet, creating small splashes that seemed to amuse and delight her.

One day a solitary figure approached them. It was a tantric holy man, his bare body covered in ash, his dreadlocks gathered into an enormous pile at the top of his head. He walked as if he was in a trance. His bloodshot eyes, fierce and staring, were fixated at a point just above the horizon.

As he passed, he lifted his hand. “Take heed, brother,” he said in a low, throaty voice. “Keep that child away from water. It is waiting to claim her.”

Biren quickly snatched Moni into his arms.

The man walked by like a shadow. Even the river breezes stilled as he passed. He became a shimmering haze swallowed up by the sky. Moni screamed and struggled. When he set her down, the first thing she did was to grab a handful of filthy river mud and stuff it into her mouth.

“Moni. No!” Biren cried, grabbing her hand. She broke into a wail and struggled as he tried to clean her mouth out with the end of his shirt. He carried her screaming all the way home.

Maya was sitting on the plantation chair on the veranda reading. She stood up when she heard the screams coming from down the road.

“What happened?” she called. “Did she hurt herself?”

Moni was twisting and writhing in Biren’s arms. Her head hung down and she kicked her legs against his stomach, emitting an awful scream.

“I’ll take her,” said Maya. “Shh, baby,” she said softly, wiping Moni’s eyes with the end of her sari and pushing back her damp hair. “Shh. Everything is all right. Shh.”

Moni lay limp in her arms. Her screams subsided into hiccupping sobs. She leaned over and tried to grab the end of Maya's long braid. Maya gave it to her, and she rested her cheek against Maya's scented hair and closed her eyes. Maya took her inside.

Later Biren walked into the bedroom to find his wife and child asleep, side by side, Maya with a book open beside her. He touched Maya's shoulder and she opened her beautiful eyes, smiled and gently pried her hair out of the baby's fingers. They both tiptoed out of the room, closing the door behind them.

"At last," she whispered. "Peace and quiet."

They drank their tea sitting on the veranda, Biren with his feet propped up on the railing, Maya with her legs folded like a lotus. On soft dusky evenings like these Biren's heart was so laden with thankfulness that he did not have much to say.

Maya tried to detangle her hair with her fingers. "Eesh," she said. "The end of my braid is all ratty. I tried giving her my Kashmiri shawl instead, the black one with the long tassels, but she would not have it."

Biren stroked her cheek with the back of his finger. "I wish I could help," he murmured. "I would grow my hair if I could. I would do anything for you, Maya."

"Then you'd look like a holy man." She laughed. "And I would have to do *puja* to you."

Biren remembered the *tantrik*. He sat up and debated whether to tell Maya about the strange encounter. Perhaps there was no need. It would unnecessarily worry her. There was something eerie about how the man had appeared out of nowhere, said his ominous words and vanished like a mirage. Biren quickly dismissed it from his mind.

Maya twisted her hair into a bun, the bangles on her wrist jingling softly.

"I don't know what to do about the weavers," she said. "If I don't go to the village, everything comes to a standstill. If I take Moni with me she is a distraction. She runs around everywhere, touches everything, and it's impossible to get any work done."

"Can't you leave her with Buri Kaki here at home?"

Maya shook her head. "I am gone for four to five hours. She won't stay with Buri Kaki so long." She sighed. "I will just have to take her along, I suppose. I worry about her on the long boat ride, too. You have to really keep a close watch on her. She wants to lean over the edge and play with the water."

Biren remembered the chilling words of the *tantrik*: *Keep that child away from water. It is waiting to claim her.*

He sat up quickly and turned toward her. "Maya, please promise you won't take the child on the boat," he beseeched. "Promise me, please."

She looked at him, startled. "Why?" She laughed. "Don't you trust me to keep an eye on her?" She threaded her fingers through his and leaned her soft cheek against his hand. "Don't worry," she reassured him. "I am very careful."

Biren reached for his cigarettes. The clock in the hallway chimed eight o'clock. He rolled the tobacco in the cigarette paper, struck a match and smoked quietly, thinking. He would have to find a way to dissuade Maya from taking Moni on the boat.

"Can't the weavers come to the house?" he said finally. "You work mostly with Chaya and the head weaver, Yosef, right? Ask the two of them to come here instead." He leaned forward. "I think it's a brilliant idea. I wonder why we never thought of it before. Tell them to bring the Calcutta buyers with them. You can use the empty guest room to store the saris, samples or whatever. Make the guest room into your workspace. What do you think?"

"It is rather a good idea," admitted Maya. "Let me see if they agree. I will send word through the boatman to the weavers' village and ask Yosef to come and meet me. I don't know if Chaya will be allowed out of the village on her own. Her father is the head *tanthi*. He is very strict with her. Did you ever meet him?"

Biren stubbed out his cigarette. "No, I don't think so."

"He's a hard man. There is a certain cruelty about him, which I find disturbing. I see Chaya's mother with bruises on her face and arms. I think he beats her. Of course, she denies it when I ask her. Chaya's father wants Chaya to get married to a *tanthi*'s son of the same caste from another village. I don't even know if he suspects Chaya is in love with Yosef."

"Is she in love with him?"

Maya laughed softly. "Have you ever seen them together? That man can't keep his eyes off her. She admitted she has feelings for him, as well. She swore me to secrecy. Her father would kill her if he found out."

"I don't understand why they can't get married. Maybe her father will come around," said Biren.

Maya shook her head. "There is no hope of that," she said. "Yosef is Muslim and Chaya is Hindu—it's as simple as that."

"'And ne'er the twain shall meet,'" added Biren. "Even though they are both weavers and live in the same village. They probably played together as children. Such a shame, really."

"What would you have done if I were Muslim?" she joked, giving him a playful nudge.

He lifted her hand to his lips. "I would have married you,

Maya, no matter what. I would have even converted to Islam, Christianity—anything—if I had to. Religion means very little to me. I think organized religion is a perversion in God's name. It evolves out of fear and greed and makes people inhuman and mindless.

"Conversion is easy," he continued. "I was more worried our horoscopes would not match. There was not a thing I could have done about that, and that would have been it. I hate to say this, but your granny's death got that last hurdle out of the way. I don't know how else we could have gotten married."

"Did you not think I had a mind of my own?" she asked softly. "Did you think I would have accepted it without saying a word?"

"It sounded as if your granny had the last say in the matter," said Biren. "She was quite formidable. Even your father could not stand up to her."

"You don't have much faith in me, do you?"

"All right, then, you tell me. What would you have done if the marriage proposal was called off because our horoscopes didn't match?"

"I would have defied Granny and married you. There are no two ways about it. Surely you know that? I have gone against my granny's wishes many times. She did not want me to work in the weavers' village, but I did. She did not want me to raise Mitra, but I did..."

Biren marveled at her: so soft-spoken and gentle, yet so strong and wise. And to think she had been ready to go against her family to marry him, and he had done all that worrying for nothing!

"See, I have told you my secrets. Now you have to tell me some of yours," she said.

There were so many things he had not told her because

she had never asked. She did not know about the hardship of his days in England, nor of Estelle. How much was even necessary for him to share? But Biren knew that every secret is a cell of darkness. They became the shadows of the heart where no love can enter. A man can become his own prisoner and never be able to give truly of himself. And Biren longed to be free.

"How much do you want to know?" he asked.

"As much as you care to tell me," she said.

Just then Buri Kaki came to announce dinner was ready.

"Leave it covered on the dining table, Buri Kaki, and go to sleep," said Maya. She smiled at Biren. "Dinner can never be more important than matters of the heart. It can wait. So tell me."

They sat on the sofa because he needed to hold her close.

"There was this English girl, Estelle." He waited for her to stiffen but she sat quietly, her head against his shoulder, waiting for him to continue.

And deep into the night he talked. Biren told her everything in his heart that day, and from the trusting way her fingers entwined in his own, he knew she would understand. When he finished, he wondered if she had fallen asleep, but the soft flutter of her eyelash against his arm told him she was listening. His heart was clear except for one cell of darkness. For some reason he could not bring himself to talk about the *tantrik* he had met that day, and that patch of darkness remained in his heart, hidden to all, even to himself.

CHAPTER 53

Silchar
3rd May 1903

Dear brother Nitin,
I am happy to hear Ma is recovering from her pneumonia. It is a great comfort for me to know that she is with her doctor son and can avail of the best medical attention. Imagine if she was back in Sylhet? We would both be so worried.

The foundation for the new school building is coming along, but there is still paperwork and legalities to complete, a charter to be drawn up. The British government will match all foreign donations, so my trips abroad have been well worthwhile.

My only regret is being gone from home for such long stretches of time. Every time I return I find Moni has grown a few inches and has learned a new word or two. I wish I had been there the moment she first uttered them. I love to see the surprise on her face when she finds her tongue can twist itself into a word her brain is trying to say. She repeats the new word constantly and is filled with wonder. These are the moments I cherish. Right now her favorite English word is peppa *(paper), which she demands constantly and seems to take great pleasure in tearing to pieces. I tried to give her an old newspaper but she stamps her tiny feet and points to my desk and demands a fresh sheet. I held her hand and tried to make her write but she banged my fountain pen, and now the nib of my prized Parker I had since my college days is bent. Maya says I am trying to make her write before she can talk. Which I suspect is true. Most of all I want Moni to love books, like her mother does.*

Biren paused in his writing to look through the open door of his study, where he could see Maya reading at the dining table. She was bathed in a pool of light from the hurricane lamp, chin in hand, her head fallen on one arm, her hair shimmering to the side. She was wearing a sky-blue kimono patterned with pink cherry blossoms that Biren had picked up for her on his trip to Japan. The soft fabric draped over her shoulders and hugged the gentle curve of her breasts. He felt a rush of desire imagining her naked body beneath the silk, then sighed knowing this moment was not his to claim. She was lost in the pages of *Pride and Prejudice*, a beautiful emerald-green volume with a gold patterned spine and grainy cream-colored pages. So impatient was she with the story that her finger was already stroking the top of the next page to be turned. Just watching her excited him, but he would wait. Unlike Maya, he was a morning person and he usually retired to bed well before she did. Most days Maya read late into the night, always sitting at the dining table, a habit she'd had since she was a child. When she came to bed, she was satiated with words but bold with desire. She would slip into bed and tempt him awake with her warm sandalwood-scented skin, and he loved her for it. The very anticipation of loving her gave him a thrill.

He turned back to finish Nitin's letter.

I received word from the Imperial Bookstore on College Street that the book of Emily Dickinson love poems I ordered for Maya has arrived and has been kept on hold. Would you be so kind as to pick it up for me and keep it with you? It has already been paid for. My worry is that by the time I next go to Calcutta, the book will be lost in the jumble of the store. This has happened once or twice before.

I may have mentioned to you in my last letter that Jatin Nandi, my father-in-law, has decided to move back to his ancestral home in Sylhet. At long last Mitra's admission to the New Horizon Academy in Dhaka has come through, and she will study in one of the finest English academies of India. The wonderful thing about this revolutionary school is the education is directed at fostering independence and self-reliance in the girls. The schools in Silchar are still very rudimentary, and Mitra is growing up to be a bright, intelligent young girl and she is ready to be more academically challenged.

Maya, as you can imagine, is very sad her family is moving away from us but she understands it is for the best. Her father's health is frail and he suffered another fall from a blackout recently. In his old age he wants to live in his village basha *and be cared for by the members of his joint family.*

It has been decided Buri Kaki will come and live with us. She is too old to move anywhere, and besides, her son and his family live here. Her son is a good-for-nothing with a bad gambling habit and sponges off his old mother, but she is blind to his faults. Well, I am happy she will stay with us because she will be a comfort to Maya, who she raised since the day she was born.

He smiled, remembering something Maya had once told him. As soon as she was born, Buri Kaki had taken over her care with a bossy ferociousness that overruled any feeble ideas of child rearing Maya's own mother might have had. Maya had only been days old when she was laid across Buri Kaki's knees and her body kneaded with a small ball of wheat dough and turmeric dipped in almond oil. Around and around the ball traveled over her tiny body. This was followed by a brisk session of baby gymnastics where her tiny limbs were flexed energetically, left and right, up and down. Finally she was bathed with big whooshes of water and rocked to sleep on a patchwork quilt of old saris to *"Dol-dol-doloni,"* a village nursery rhyme sung by Buri Kaki in a loud cracked voice.

As a result of Buri Kaki's loving care, Maya grew up with naturally creamy skin and lustrous hair that no beauty product could ever match. Thanks to all the buffing and polishing with the wheat dough ball, her body was almost completely hairless, her limbs supple and strong.

"Did she do the same for Mitra?" Biren had asked, burying his nose in her arm and inhaling the scent he so adored.

Maya had shaken her head. "Ma died soon after Mitra was born and we were all too distraught to do anything. When Buri Kaki was finally ready to *malish-palish* Mitra, she was too old and she managed to slip out of her grasp and run away, and poor Buri Kaki was too old to chase behind her."

Biren ended the letter, sealed the envelope and wrote the address. Before he retired to bed he sat back to gaze one last time at his lovely Maya. And there she sat, his beautiful wife, draped in soft silk, bathed in golden lamplight, floating on the wings of a story.

CHAPTER 54

There is definitely some hanky-panky going on between those two, Biren decided. He was home early from work, and through the window of his study he had a clear view of Chaya and the head weaver, Yosef, as they waited on the veranda for Maya. Maya had gone to her father's house to help him with some last-minute packing and she was expected home soon.

Chaya and Yosef had their backs turned toward him as they leaned against the veranda railing looking out toward the river. Biren could not help but notice the way their bodies tilted toward each other like tented cards. Yosef turned to say something to Chaya, and even from his profile, Biren could see the unfiltered longing, while Chaya looked askance with a certain coyness that belied her delight at his attention. When he tilted his head toward her, Biren noticed a pearl stud glowing in the lobe of his left ear. Yosef was a virile young man with seductive eyes, well aware of the power he had over Chaya. He whispered something in her ear at which she gave a kittenish flutter and tried to move away, but he pulled her to him by the waist. With a look of mock exasperation, she disengaged his arm, but she did not move away and they remained, side by side, hips touching. Her coquettish rebuff looked more like a covert invitation.

Biren watched them, amused. Whenever he saw them in public, they always acted indifferent toward each other. Yosef even sometimes behaved in a callous manner and talked to Chaya with certain brusqueness.

Obviously they did not suspect anyone was watching them; Biren was usually at work during this time of the day after all. He wondered how far their relationship had developed. From their body language, he could tell they had been intimate. Having learned now that Chaya's father had arranged her marriage elsewhere, he knew they were treading on risky ground.

Biren decided to announce his presence. He slipped out of the study door, walked lightly to the kitchen and called out loudly to Buri Kaki for tea, then made his way noisily down the passage, looking as if he was coming from the direction of the bedroom. When he emerged on the veranda he found Yosef waiting at the bottom of the stairs, arms folded, looking out at the river, and Chaya standing at the far end of the veranda gazing at her fingernails. They looked like two perfect strangers, waiting, who had little to do with each other.

"Is *didi* still not back?" Biren inquired pleasantly. "Have you both been waiting long?"

Yosef acted startled. He folded his hands together respectfully in greeting. "I just got here five minutes ago, Dada," he said. "As for this one—" he tipped his head in a disdainful manner toward Chaya "—I don't know when she came."

"Have you had tea?" Biren asked. "Ask Buri Kaki to make you some. I am going out but wait here. Your *didi* will be home any moment now."

As he left them, he suppressed a smile. *The little crooks. They are fine actors, for sure.* But how long could their combustible passion be kept under wraps? They had come dangerously close to getting caught.

"Did you know this?" Biren asked Maya when they were alone later that evening. He had just finished telling her what he had witnessed between Chaya and Yosef.

"I suspected something," she said slowly. "But from what you are telling me, it sounds as if this has gone quite far. She will be in a lot of trouble if her father finds out."

"He is *bound* to find out," said Biren. "I don't think they can help themselves. They won't be able to keep this a secret for long."

Maya looked at him. "Do you have any idea what that means? Chaya is the head *tanti*'s daughter. She comes from a proud line of weavers who marry strictly within their community. Yosef is only hired help—a *karigar.* Besides, he is a Muslim and belongs to a lower class of people. If she has anything to do with him she will disgrace her family and the entire community."

"Maybe you can talk to her father when the time comes. Explain things nicely to him. They are, after all, two young people in love, and they should be allowed to get married."

Maya's gold bangles jingled as she lifted her arms to twist her unwinding hair back into a bun. He glimpsed her bare midriff and the half-moon sweat stains in the armpits of her red sari blouse, all of which Biren found devastatingly sensual.

"It's not so simple," she said. "There is nothing I can do

or say that will make her father think differently. Besides, I am a woman. It's all right for me to help the weavers sell their saris, but I can't expect to talk to Chaya's father about matters concerning his family. He'd be outraged! Why, if I were in that position, the first thing I'd tell him is to stop beating his wife. He's a very arrogant man. Everybody in the village fears him."

"Well, if it's a question of someone talking to him man-to-man, then maybe I can talk to him. I will tell him the times are changing and that his daughter should be allowed to choose the man she wants to marry."

Maya stared at him in disbelief. "Did you just hear what you said? You want to talk to him man-to-man. You want to tell him times are changing..." She stood up abruptly and tucked the end of her sari into her waistband. The jeweled key chain with the silver bells jingled furiously. She spoke quietly, fiercely. Gone was the husky sweetness. "Do you know why I asked you to stop coming to the village?"

"Why?" said Biren, taken aback. "I thought it was because I was getting in your way and you wanted to focus on your work. Was that not the reason?"

She shook her head so vehemently that her hair came tumbling down. "No, no, of course not! The reason was because Chaya told me her father did not like you to come."

Biren sat up. "Now what did I do? Why, I don't even know the man!"

"You may not know him, but he knows you," said Maya. "Everybody knows you. You work for the British government. You are not just a *babu* in an office following orders of a white man—you are giving orders, making decisions, changing certain laws that affect the community. Don't you see this? They see you as an outsider—a traitor. The British are flooding the Indian market with factory-made cloth, as you know—from Manchester, from Lancashire. This material is so cheap traditional weavers cannot compete with the factory prices. As a result they are losing their livelihood, and the entire community is in a danger of being wiped out. Weaving is the only skill they have ever known. It's the only way they have ever earned their living for generations, so you can imagine how threatened they feel. Thankfully, we have found new markets to sell their saris in Calcutta. Chaya's father has no qualms about using me to further the interests of their community, but when we got married and you came into the picture, it became complicated. So…" She paused, looking exhausted. "Do you see where I am going with this conversation?"

"What you are saying is I am not the right person to talk to Chaya's father, because he has already made up his mind I am a traitor. What about the fact that I am trying to establish a free school for girls like his daughter, so that they can get an education, become financially independent and hopefully lead useful lives, *and*—" he wagged a finger at her "—in the case of Chaya, be empowered to marry the man of her choice. What about that?"

"That makes it even worse!" exclaimed Maya. "Don't you see? You now become the foreign influence that is tearing Indian society apart. That makes you doubly dangerous."

Biren threw up his hands. "I give up, then," he said. "I refuse to deal with such moronic donkey people."

Maya laughed, her eyes dancing. "The best thing we can hope for, for both their sakes, is this is a youthful infatuation and it will pass. Maybe once Chaya gets married and moves away to another village, she will forget about Yosef."

Biren remembered the slant-eyed coquettish look Chaya

had given Yosef, the intimate way their bodies had touched. Yosef was unmistakably her lover.

"I don't think so," he said quietly. "Something tells me they have gone too far. I don't think there is any turning back."

CHAPTER 55

Silchar
30th September 1904

Dear brother Nitin,
Thank you for collecting the books from the Imperial Bookstore and leaving them with Samaresh. I am sorry we did not get to meet this time. I had to rush back to Silchar, as there are pressing matters I have to attend to at the office. Griffiths is being transferred to Calcutta and we are still waiting for his replacement.

My trip to Russia was exhausting, to say the least. I try to avoid the cold weather for travel to that part of the world, but the cultural summit where I was presenting my paper happened to be at this time of the year. I must say the cold of Moscow is horrific. Boris Ivanov, my dear friend, lent me a long wool coat, large enough to contain two of me. You remember what a big man he is, don't you? Still, I was very thankful for it.

Moni is growing up quickly. I got her a set of traditional Russian Matryoshka *dolls—five dolls, each nesting inside the other. She quickly dismantled them all and now the mother doll is missing her head. We searched high and low to no avail, so I am using the bottom half of the doll here on my desk to hold my paper pins while we look for the top.*

Now an update on the weavers' program. Maya has written to Bela, I believe, in detail about it. I think it will work out very well if Bela can handle the marketing and sales in Calcutta. Her family owned a sari business, after all, and Bela will have the right connections. The middlemen who come to the weavers' village are actually selling the saris to the same wholesale merchants in Calcutta. If we cut out the middlemen, the extra profits can go directly back to the weavers. Maya now conducts the entire operation from the house. Her assistant and the head weaver come there every week and it is far more efficient this way. I must end for now.

My love to you all.

Affectionately yours,
Dada

Biren woke one early October morning to find the coral jasmine tree had shed its blossoms in the night. They lay on the ground like a white carpet, the petals curled and wet with dew. He went back inside and picked up two-year-old Moni, still curled in sleep next to her mother, bundled her up in a shawl and took her outside.

"Look at all the flowers, Moni," he said, picking up a white blossom and twirling the pinwheel shape by its orange stem. "Do you see? They are called *shiuli* flowers. Can you say *shiuli*, Moni? See, so many flowers on the ground."

Moni reached out a tiny hand to take the flower. With

her face half-buried in his shoulder she looked at it with one eye and tried to twirl it like he did. The orange stem stained her fingers. She flung the flower to the ground and showed her stained fingers to Biren.

"Chee-chee," she said.

He kissed her open palm and rubbed it against his unshaven chin. "Do you know, Moni, Durga Puja will soon be here? The drums will beat *dhaka-dak*, and Durga-ma will come riding a big lion and we will all get new clothes, sweets, toys." He pushed the hair back from her eyes and bounced her on his shoulder. "It will be fun-fun-fun."

The word *toys* and *fun* seemed to wake Moni up. She took her thumb out of her mouth and stretched her hand toward the blossoms, opening and closing her palm.

"Doh?" she said in a sleepy, cracked voice.

"Yes, excellent idea," said Biren. He squatted down and formed the folds of his shawl into a small hammock. "Let's pick some *shiuli* flowers for your ma, shall we? When she wakes up she will be so happy to see all the flowers on her pillow."

They gathered the shawl full of flowers and went back inside the house. In the dim light of the bedroom Maya was still asleep, her breathing soft and peaceful. They spread the delicate blossoms on her pillow around her hair. The fresh, dewy scent made her stir, but before she could open her eyes, they tiptoed out of the room. Outside the door, unable to contain her excitement, Moni let out a loud squeal.

The flowering of the coral jasmine was indeed the beginning of the festive season. The starry white flowers bloomed at dusk and scented the cool night, and by dawn the fragrant blossoms lay like a fluffy carpet on the ground.

Something happened to the air this time of the year: it became charged with Durga Puja fever. The very anticipation of five days of nonstop festivities made people walk on lighter feet, greet one another with smiles and small children wake up in the morning with shining eyes and jump up and down on their beds.

A large bamboo structure—the *pandal*—was being erected in a football field in the middle of town. Domed like a giant beehive, it had a raised platform to display the magnificent goddess Durga. Every day villagers arrived in boats to help with the construction. The weavers worked tirelessly to create a gorgeous multihued fabric backdrop that was pleated and fanned out like a peacock's tail. Skilled artisans worked late into the night to carve and press elaborate molded forms of *sholapith*, a white spongy cork-like material, into elaborate shapes. Every day the hubbub at the *pandal* attracted a jostling crowd: office shirkers, nameless gawkers, bright-eyed tots, beggars and cows descended to check on the progress, while chai and chickpea sellers walked around calling out their wares in singsong voices.

The feverish excitement of Durga Puja was so catching it even permeated the somber offices of the British government. The *belayti* bosses loosened their shirt collars and ambled off to the polo club for long gin lunches, after which they rarely came back to work, which left the *babus* to chat animatedly all day long without doing a spot of work.

The day following the waxing of the moon, the goddess Durga arrived in all her splendid glory to the sound of earsplitting drums. Made of molded clay and festooned in red and gold, she had blazing eyes and streaming black hair that cascaded down to her ankles. Seated atop a fearsome lion, she towered over four lesser deities, and in each of her ten hands she held a different weapon of war. Her long trident was plunged into the side of a monstrous buffalo, from whose body emerged an ugly demon. The goddess Durga symbolized the powerful force of good defeating evil. The magnitude of her beauty evoked in all who gazed upon her a feeling of awe and primal love. Even though Durga Puja was a Hindu festival, the entire population of the town—Hindu, Muslim and Christian—were agog with excitement.

The Bengali Puja Association hosted a free lunch for the entire community on all five days. Maya, fresh from her bath, wearing a crisp new sari with jasmine garlands in her hair, left the house early to help with the floral decorations at the *pandal*. The holy food, which was cooked in large vats by Brahmins, was offered first to the gods, and then ladled out on banana leaves to the masses.

All morning, Biren lazed around the house in his pajamas drinking tea. At noon he bathed and changed into a traditional pleated dhoti and kurta of raw silk, while Buri Kaki dressed Moni in one of her fancy new frocks and fussed with the ribbons in her hair before they headed out to the *puja pandal*. The sound of the *dhaak* was earsplitting, to which was added the mournful lowing of conch horns interspersed with the melodious Vedic chant of the priest. Biren lifted Moni up on his shoulders so she could watch the *dhanachi* dancers, who twirled like dervishes holding earthen pots of burning camphor and coconut husk in trails of thick, scented smoke.

A pathway was cleared for Reginald Thompson as he arrived to see the festivities. He was accompanied by his tall, pale wife—coincidentally called Regina—their two little daughters and their ayah. The older girl, Enid, wore colorful Indian bangles on both her hands, which she admired from time to time by moving them up and down her wrists.

Reginald Thomson almost did not recognize Biren in his Indian clothes. His face softened to see little Moni perched on Biren's shoulders.

"Hello, little one," he said kindly.

"What a pretty dress," said Regina, touching Moni's cheek lightly. Moni shrank back and stared with big round eyes from one pink face to other.

Behind the *puja pandal*, a village fair was in full swing. Festoons, balloons, toys and cotton candy left children breathless and the adults glassy-eyed. Moni ate pink cotton candy and rode a creaky Ferris wheel with Biren, while Maya, unwilling to be drawn into such foolishness, waited. All the frolicking ended when Moni gushed up fluorescent pink vomit all over her pretty dress. Maya rushed her off to a tea stall to find water for an emergency cleanup while Biren waited and smoked a cigarette. He saw a familiar face in the crowd. It was Chaya from the weavers' village wearing a leaf-green sari with a garland of marigold around her hair. She was with Yosef, who pulled her by the hand. She lurched along laughing and they disappeared into the crowd.

"I saw Chaya," he told Maya when she returned. "She was with that Yosef."

Maya frowned. "That is taking a big risk," she said. "She should not be seen in public with him. Somebody from their village might report them to her father."

"Hopefully nobody will see them," said Biren. "There are thousands of people here." He looked at Moni, whose dress was completely drenched. Her teeth chattered. "Did you bring something warm for her, a shawl or something?"

"I did not think of it," Maya said. "It was so hot during the day."

"I think we should go home. Otherwise, she will catch a cold."

On the rickshaw ride back home Moni nodded off on Biren's lap, clutching a twirling paper turbine in her hand. They passed a dark patch with the fireflies winking in the bamboo grove. He slipped his arm around Maya's shoulders and kissed her cheek. How sweet it was to feel the softness of her skin, to smell the smoke and incense in her hair. He was so lucky. He thought of Chaya and her young lover. It would be cruel if fate were to deny them a life together.

CHAPTER 56

On the final day of Durga Puja, a big noisy procession passed by Biren's house on their way to the river for the immersion ceremony. First came the four *dhaakis* beating their barrel-shaped drums, followed by the dancing crowds, then the goddess herself carried aloft on long bamboo poles on the shoulders of a dozen swarthy men.

Biren picked up Moni and followed them to the river. One by one the devotees touched the feet of the deity, and many were tearful as they bid the beautiful goddess farewell. Moni struggled and kicked to be set down. Finally the goddess was lowered gently into the river, where she submerged bit by bit with all her finery, until only her lovely face with the big staring eyes remained. Then even that disappeared as she sank slowly under the water. A great pall of gloom descended on the crowd as they watched the marigold garlands and flowers swirl away with the river current. Biren turned to pick up Moni and didn't see her. He felt a stab of panic, but thank God, there she was a short distance away, bending down to touch a small green coconut.

He rushed over, swooped her up in his arms and shook her. "Don't ever leave Baba's side, do you hear me?" he shouted.

The roughness of his voice surprised her and her face began to pucker. Moni looked flushed, her eyes feverish. Biren felt her forehead; it was unnaturally warm.

He rushed her back to the house and was surprised to find Maya lying in bed.

"What's wrong?" he asked. "Don't you feel well?"

"I think I caught a cold," she said. Her voice sounded clogged and stuffy.

"This *maiyya* has one, too," he said, setting Moni down on the bed. She crawled under her mother's blanket. "She has been coughing since you hosed her down at the fair yesterday."

Maya pushed back Moni's hair and kissed her forehead.

"I think we all need rest," she said. "Five days of nonstop excitement is just too much."

"The whole town will be ill now." Biren sighed. "The post–Durga Puja collapse. This happens every year. None of the *babus* will come to work tomorrow, just you see."

"Please eat your dinner. I don't want any," Maya said. She looked at Moni fast asleep beside her and gently pried her thumb from her mouth. "I don't think she will eat anything, either."

Biren leaned over and felt Maya's forehead. "I hope you are not running a fever," he said anxiously, looking into her eyes. He felt her feet. "Why are your feet so cold? Shall I put on my socks for you?"

"No, no, I am all right, please. I just need to rest," she said.

He smoothed back her hair. "Yes, you must rest," he said, "because we leave for Calcutta a month from now. You and Moni must be fit for the journey." He tucked an extra shawl around them both. "I will be in my study. Call me if you need anything," he said. He went out and closed the door softly behind him.

A few days later Moni recovered, but Maya was still running a low fever. She lost her appetite, had the night chills, tossed and turned and woke up looking gray and tired. Her skin lost its luster and her hair hung lank and stringy. Alarmed at her rapid deterioration, Biren called the doctor.

Dr. Ghosh was an old friend of Jatin Nandi's. A kindly man given to pleasantries, he had seen Maya since she was a little girl. He said the fever was a virus, which would run its natural course. He pulled down Maya's eyelids, declared her anemic and prescribed a diet of ripe mashed banana, almonds soaked in milk and beetroot juice in small quantities, several times a day.

"Egg yolk, liver and spinach are all iron-rich foods," he added.

"But she is not eating at all," Biren complained, looking at Maya sitting up in bed. Her tea on the side table had turned cold.

"I will prescribe a tonic," said Dr. Ghosh, folding his stethoscope and placing it inside his medical valise. "It will help her regain her appetite."

Biren walked the doctor to the gate. "Will she be well enough to travel?" he asked. "I have steamer tickets booked for Calcutta a month from today."

"With plenty of rest and her new diet she should be fine," said the doctor. "Please pick up the medicine from my clinic this evening. My compounder *babu* will have it ready for you. She should take it three times a day before her meals. Rest assured, she will be well."

Biren monitored Maya's diet diligently. He cajoled her to eat raw egg yolk mixed with honey, and small pieces of toast with the liver pâté that Regina Thompson had sent after hearing about Maya's anemia. Nothing seemed to work. Some days she looked better, but it was always followed by a relapse. There was just one week left before their journey and Maya still had not recovered.

Biren was in a quandary. He had a critical meeting with the executive council of the governor-general to present his final proposal for the education program. It had been set up a whole year in advance, and Reginald Thompson had used all his connections and pulled the right strings to get Biren this appointment. The plan was for Moni and Maya to spend a few days in Chandanagore with Nitin's family while Biren took care of business in Calcutta, after which they would all enjoy the Christmas lights in the city before returning home.

Maya was certainly not fit to travel, and he worried about leaving her in Silchar. When he voiced his concerns, she was adamant.

"No!" she cried, clutching his hand. "You must go. This opportunity may never come again. Reginald Thompson went through a lot of trouble to secure this meeting with McCauley for you."

"But how can I leave you in this state, Maya?" Biren spoke in a choked voice. He took her hand in his own. How limp it felt, her fingers so cold. He rubbed her hand between his own, wishing he could pass some of his strength on to her. Maya was a shadow of her former self. Her gray-green eyes looked enormous in her small face. "Let's give it till the end of the week, then we can decide," he said.

"You must go to Calcutta," she said firmly, pulling her hand away. "I won't have it any other way. You are not going to cancel your trip because of me." Some of that old fire was back in her eyes. She struggled to sit up. Biren adjusted the pillow behind her back and helped her.

"How can I leave you here with Buri Kaki? She is getting very old and forgetful. I cannot rely on her to give you your medicine. If your father were still in Silchar, it would have been different. You could have stayed with him. I don't care what you say but I am not comfortable leaving you alone here with the child. I would be worried all the time."

"Tell me," she said, clutching his arm, "how long have you waited for this meeting? Years and years, yes? All those trips to Calcutta, all those preliminary meetings. And now you want to cancel the final meeting just because I have a little fever? It's a virus. It will pass. Now, if I promise to eat that raw egg, liver paste and whatever else Dr. Ghosh has asked me to eat, will you go?"

Biren did not answer. He got up and paced around the room.

"All right," Maya continued, "let's add dates to my menu. *I will eat dates!* Are you listening? You know how I hate dates, but yes, I will eat them, if you agree to go. Oh…" She sank back, closing her eyes, exhausted. "What is the use of talking to you? I don't think you are even listening."

"I am listening, Maya, I am listening."

"Do you know something?" she said suddenly. "You are being very unfair to me."

"Unfair to *you*?" Biren said, startled. "How?"

"Because if you miss this once-in-a-lifetime opportunity, I will have the guilt sitting on *my* head for the rest of my life.

I will blame myself for dashing your dreams. And it's not just your dreams. What about the dreams of all the young girls waiting to go to school? How can you do this to them? You are putting a heavy burden on me, really, you are. This is not fair."

"What is not fair is that you are emotionally blackmailing," said Biren. "And who is to say this opportunity won't come again? The meeting will just have to be rescheduled. I will send a telegram to McCauley saying my wife is serious..."

"Serious?" Maya's voice rose an octave. "Dr. Ghosh himself said the fever is just a virus. The virus has to run its course. Some viruses take a little more time than others."

"It has already been three weeks, Maya. I have not seen any signs of improvement. I cannot leave you in this condition. There are no neighbors nearby. If the doctor has to be called in the night, who will go? Please be sensible. I don't want any arguments about this."

Maya closed her eyes and turned her head wearily to the side. She was silent but he could tell her brain was ticking.

"Listen to me," she said suddenly. Her face brightened. "I just got an idea. Why don't you drop us both off at Baba's village in Sylhet? I have not seen my cousins in a long time." She grew animated. "Yes! Yes! I can manage the boat ride to Sylhet, no problem. At Baba's house we will be well cared for. We have such a big joint family. There are aunts, uncles, cousins, nephews and nieces. Moni will enjoy herself. Also, that way you won't be worried about us." She tugged his hand. "It is a grand idea, don't you agree?"

Biren remained silent, still reluctant to entertain the thought of going to Calcutta without Maya. There was so much that he had wanted to show her: the bookstores, Chowringhee dazzling with Christmas lights, the green expanse of

Fort William, the seaside at Digha. He pictured little Moni playing in the sand, collecting seashells, and Maya with the sea breeze whipping through her hair.

"What do you think? Tell me," Maya insisted. "I want to go and see how Baba is doing. It's been six months. He is getting old. I was so busy with the weavers I did not have time to go to Sylhet to see him. I don't want Moni to forget her grandfather. Also, also…" She tugged his hand urgently. "Mitra is coming home from Dhaka for her school holidays. She has been longing to see Moni."

"Let me give it some thought," said Biren reluctantly. "If you don't improve in the next few days, I don't think you should do the boat journey to Sylhet."

"I *will* improve," she said. She grabbed his hand and placed it on her forehead. "See, feel my head. No fever. Gone! Really, I feel so much better already. I'll tell you what—I will even eat that horrible English liver paste that Regina Thompson sent, if you like." She made a funny face, hoping to make him smile, but Biren turned and walked out of the room with a leaden heart.

The following Tuesday they took the boat to Sylhet. Dawn was just breaking and Kanai rowed them across the flat gray river over which a pale fog hung in folds like a shroud. The shrubs along the banks were soft and blurred, looking like hunched widows in mourning. Kanai sang a soulful Bhatiyali dirge of a broken-winged crane trapped in a fishing net. The crane's mate circled the sky crying for help, and finally plucked out his feathers one by one to make a wreath for his mate as she lay dying.

CHAPTER 57

Calcutta was bedecked for the holiday season. Colorful buntings and crepe streamers decorated Chowringhee, and the horses pulling the tongas wore festive plumes and jingled with Christmas bells. Every fortnight the big ocean liners brought shiploads of visitors from the cold shores of foreign lands, a majority of them eligible women, on the lookout for a husband. Pale and seasick, they sailed up the forked mouth of the Bay of Bengal and followed the mighty Hoogly River that led to the port city of Calcutta. They gasped to see the gargantuan Howrah Bridge that straddled the river like an iron centipede and the gleaming imperial city beyond with its temples and churches, its white domed buildings and tall minarets. Perhaps just as jaw-dropping was the unlikely sight of hundreds of loincloth-clad bathers who crowded the wide steps of the bathing ghats, while dozens of others ducked their heads in the turgid water, scrubbing themselves with shivering frenzy, deeply preoccupied with their morning ablutions.

This was the party season, with back-to-back galas at the Imperial Hotel, Fort William and the exclusive European clubs that dotted the city. Rankin and Company on Lindsay Street, dressmakers to the elite, were burdened with orders to create the latest Western-style dresses with an Indian twist using rich brocades and shot-spun silks that shimmered like liquid gemstones.

The colonial world of Calcutta was exotic and just a wee bit naughty. Bending a few rules was, after all, the norm. It was with this quickening of pulse and heightened sense of anticipation that the foreign visitors entered the city.

Biren Roy had learned a long time ago that it took a good set of clothes and the right English accent to gain acceptance into British social circles. Lineage counted, too, but thankfully the colonial bosses were still confused about the vagaries of Indian royalty. Chances were if you dressed right and talked right, your family was probably rich and of noble descent. Educated Indian men had soft hands and indolent ways. They reclined on silk tasseled bolsters and spoke English with the right public-school accent. Biren not only spoke the Queen's English, he had the oratorical delivery to match, and that cut ice with the people in high places.

George McCauley, the secretary of education, had invited Biren to lunch at the Royal Bengal Club. Never was there a more snobbish institution in colonial India than the Royal Bengal Club. It ranked in exclusivity among the top gentlemen's clubs of London: the Athenaeum and the Reform Club.

This was a critical meeting and Biren was not taking any chances. All formal paperwork had been reviewed, cleared of red tape and approved at various levels of government, and the lunch was going to be the final handshake.

Biren made an appointment with the gentlemen's barber for a proper shave and haircut. As he reclined in the red padded leather chair and closed his eyes for a luxurious lathering, he remembered the old village barber who'd sat on the street corner of the fish market with his rock-hard bar of shaving soap and cutthroat razors laid out on a rag. For the cost of a shave the barber had thrown in a haircut for an extra anna. The haircut had been finished off with a vigorous finger-drum head massage that made one want to yelp and swoon at the same time. The gentleman barbers of Calcutta who tended to the delicate pink scalps of foreigners were, of course, more humane.

Next, Biren took a tonga to Cuthbarton and Fink. He had an appointment to be fitted for a new set of clothes: an iron-gray morning coat in the latest cutaway style, with a waistcoat to match, and contrasting pin-striped trousers with turned-up cuffs. Next door at Allan Davis and Company he bought a pair of patent leather shoes and, after some deliberation, a slim ivory-handled cane.

It felt marvelous to walk down Chowringhee Road in his fine new clothes breathing the scent of his professionally twirled, sweet-smelling moustache. There was a new swagger in his step, and he already felt a sense of accomplishment. His only wish was that Maya could be beside him. He imagined her dressed in one of her beautiful Tanchoi silks, a fresh gardenia in her hair.

The crowds parted for him, and an armless, legless beggar, lumped inside his broken cart, let out a raucous wail as he walked by. At the entrance of Hogg Market, he stepped aside for two European ladies and they walked past giving

Biren slanted looks. He felt a pang, remembering his beautiful Maya. There was no woman in Calcutta who could even remotely compare to her. He made up his mind that as soon as his business was done in the city, he would catch the first steamer back home. No matter what time he reached Silchar, he planned to drop off his luggage and take a boat to Sylhet, and hopefully he would be with his precious Maya and Moni that very same evening.

George McCauley looked at his watch. He had another half an hour before his lunch meeting with Biren Roy—enough time to grab a couple of gin and tonics. What a morning! The two-hour meeting with the executive committee had wrung him dry. Every proposal he had put up for consideration had been shot down. The education department that he headed was the most neglected orphan child among government departments. Literacy for the Indian masses was hardly a priority in colonial India, where the main thrust was on trade and business.

There was one proposal, however, that had miraculously been given the green signal. The paperwork for the Female Literacy and Upliftment Project had sat on McCauley's desk for years, and it had taken the bullying presence of Reginald Thompson, the district commissioner of Silchar, to bring it to his attention and push it through the executive committee. The project was elaborate and the funds requested raised quite a few eyebrows among committee members.

More disconcerting was the fact that Thompson had appointed a young Indian named Biren Roy to spearhead the project. McCauley knew from experience that most proposals looked grand on paper, but getting the bullock cart to its destination was the main challenge in India. Also, to hand a plum position reserved exclusively for Europeans to an Indian—Oxbridge educated or no—was unprecedented in government circles.

Yet Roy came highly recommended, and McCauley was curious to meet the young man before he gave his final stamp of approval. There was also a slightly crafty motive for inviting him to lunch at the Royal Bengal Club. McCauley wanted to see how the young Indian would fare in the rarified European ambience of the Royal Bengal Club, with its insider etiquette, formal dress code and fine dining. Hopefully, it would send a message to the young upstart to stay on his side of the turf. A bit of intimidation was not necessarily a bad thing.

McCauley was just finishing his second drink when the bearer arrived with a chit to say Biren Roy was waiting for him at the reception.

At first McCauley didn't see him, or perhaps he was expecting someone a little different.

"Mr. McCauley, sir?" said a tall, handsome young man holding out his hand. His grip was firm, his eyes steady.

"Ah, Biren Roy, how do you do," said McCauley, appraising him. The fellow was a dapper dresser. McCauley was suddenly conscious of a spot of egg yolk on his tie from breakfast that morning. He had been running late for the committee meeting and not had time to change.

He led the way toward the tall-ceilinged dining hall, where they were seated at a corner table. McCauley observed the young man closely during lunch. Biren Roy had the most impeccable manners. What he had envisioned as a short business lunch turned into the most enlightening afternoon. Roy was well versed in both Indian and Western ways, and he was a persuasive talker. His vision was clear and he had carefully planned out the steps toward achieving the goals.

By the time they retired for coffee to the smoking room, McCauley was firmly convinced Thompson had picked the right man for the job.

"Your funds have been sanctioned for the next three years for both the Teachers' Training Institute and the flagship school," McCauley said, filling his pipe. "You have the full cooperation of my department and, if you need to, please feel free to contact me directly."

"Perhaps you would care to visit Silchar sometime to see how the project is progressing?" said Biren. "It will be my pleasure to show you around, sir."

"Yes, I would like that," said McCauley. "I have always wanted to visit the Silchar Polo Club. It's the first polo club in the world, I believe. Talking of which, would you like to be my guest at the races tomorrow? It's the Viceroy Cup challenge at the Royal Calcutta Turf Club."

"Thank you, but I must catch the steamer back to Silchar this evening. My wife is not very well, sir."

"Then, I should not detain you any further," said McCauley. He stood up and held out his hand. "I hope your wife gets better. It was indeed a pleasure meeting you, Roy, and good luck!"

CHAPTER 58

Biren arrived home in Silchar to find Buri Kaki hobbling up and down the veranda, muttering to herself. She tailed him into the study, wringing her hands. At first he thought she was worked up about Maya and Moni. With him being gone as well, she must have been lonely in the big, empty house. However, he quickly gathered that something had happened to agitate her. According to Buri Kaki, three rough-looking men had come twice to the house looking for him.

"Rough looking? What do you mean rough looking?" he asked.

Buri Kaki said they had red-red eyes and looked like ugly demons. *Asuras.*

Biren frowned. "What did they want?" he asked.

"They did not say, Jamai-babu," said Buri Kaki. "They just wanted to know when you would come back."

Biren was puzzled. What would three "ugly demons" want with him?

"What did you tell them?" he said.

"I chased them out of the gate with my broom. Then they came again the next day and I said, 'I will put a curse on you if you come to this house.' People are very afraid of my curses, as you know."

Biren smiled. Buri Kaki, bent double at three feet ten inches, was gnarled and knobby. She had a beaked nose, three elongated teeth and a chin that sprouted a crop of springy hairs. What she lacked in size she compensated for with a cackle that sent every hen in the neighborhood scurrying. Buri Kaki's reports tended to be dubious, like her story of the *petni* who lived in the fig tree and the "stinky spit" it cast on people passing below. It ultimately turned out to be fruit bats and bat guano.

Biren was about to dismiss her story about the three ugly demons in the same vein when she piped up, "When I said I would put a curse on those ugly demons, do you know what one of them said?"

"What?" said Biren, absently sifting through his mail. He turned over an envelope with a Russian stamp. It was a letter from Boris Ivanov.

"He said, 'Save your curses, you ugly witch. My shameless daughter has cursed me already. She has run off with a low-class Muslim. I wish she was dead.'"

Biren stopped slitting the envelope and looked at her. "Did he mention the girl's name? Was it Chaya?"

"I don't know, Jamai-babu, but the man said it was all your fault. You encouraged their immoral relationship and let them meet secretly in this house. That is why she ran away."

Biren looked at her, startled. "He blamed *me* for Chaya running away?"

"They were very bad men, Jamai-babu, that's all I know. I hope they never come to this house again," Buri Kaki muttered as she hobbled away.

No ugly demons or runaway daughters were going to stand in Biren's way, so impatient was he to see Maya and Moni. He consoled Buri Kaki as best as he could and immediately took the next available boat to his father-in-law's village, Shomapalli Ghat. The boat landing was just a rickety bamboo jetty with not even a tea shop. Several paths forked out leading to small hamlets. Biren remembered Maya telling him to take the one with the three date trees with all the vultures sitting on top.

"There's a madman who lives under those date trees," she said. "You will see a ragged tent strung across. You can't miss him. He's a permanent fixture."

His name was Bhola Pagol and he was the village idiot. Bhola looked like a giant catfish with small eyes set too far apart in his oversize head. His fat, blubbery lips stretched from ear to ear in a grotesque clown grin. He sat cross-legged in the shade surrounded by neat little piles of dates. All day long he swayed back and forth and counted his dates, moving them from one pile to the other.

Seeing Biren walk down the crooked path, Bhola gave a scream and waddled toward him. He wore burlap shorts with faded factory markings and a filthy vest with potato-size holes.

"Gurudev!" he greeted him, smiling with his blubbery lips. He offered Biren a handful of dates.

"No, thank you," said Biren. He smiled, remembering

Maya's story about the dates. Prior to her recent fever, Maya had insisted she would never touch another date in her life, thanks to Bhola. As young girl she had felt sorry for him and eaten the dates he offered her. They were rather tasteless with a funny texture, she said. She had not given it further thought until she made an appalling discovery—all the dates under Bhola's tree had passed through vultures' stomachs and popped out of the wrong end! No wonder the villagers never ate them. Just recalling the incident had made Maya gag.

Biren often teased her about it. When they were newly married, Regina Thompson invited them to the bungalow for high tea. She had baked a date loaf and Maya had politely declined, saying she was allergic to dates. She'd had a hard time keeping a straight face and had avoided looking at Biren the whole time they were there.

In Maya's father's house a group of small children played hopscotch in the front yard on chalk-drawn squares with pieces of broken tile. They were between the ages of four and eight, but Biren could not tell one from the other because all of them were completely bald. Seeing him approach, they stopped playing and ran up to meet him. To his shock he realized the littlest one was Moni.

"My goodness!" he cried. "What happened to everyone's hair?"

Moni touched her head and looked bashful. Then her face crumpled up to cry.

"No, no, don't cry," said Biren hastily. He set down his suitcase and held out his arms. But Moni just ran away and hid behind the eldest girl.

"We got lice," explained the girl. Biren recognized her as the daughter of Maya's first cousin, whose wife was a religious fanatic. “Ma put ant powder on our heads and covered our heads with old cotton vests. But the lice did not go away so the barber came and shaved all our heads.”

Biren listened, running his hand over Moni’s head. It was smooth as a boiled egg. He had no idea what to make of it. Then Moni smacked his hand away.

“What’s the matter?” he asked. “Don’t you love your Baba anymore?”

She shook her head so hard it became a blur.

“She also eats mud,” said another small girl, who was missing a tooth.

Moni again shook her head vigorously in denial. The girl wagged a finger under her nose.

“Liar! Liar!”

Moni’s eyes brimmed with tears and her chin started to wobble.

“Shush, now,” Biren admonished the girl. “Don’t call her a liar. You are not a liar, are you now, Moni, *maiyya*?” He stood up. “Where is her mother?”

“Inside,” said the little girl. “She’s sleeping.”

He went inside the house. The whole house was sleeping. When winter temperatures dropped, people in the village liked to stay in bed under their quilts. No wonder most village babies were born during the fall.

All the rooms were dark and shuttered. Biren could make out lumps and bumps on several beds and snores and wheezes came from under the covers. Defeated, he went back outside.

“Which room is she in?” he asked, and held his hand out to Moni. “Come, let’s go and find your mother.” But Moni just shook her bald head into another blur and hid behind the older child.

He sighed. “Can someone please take me to her mother?”

he begged, feeling irritable. He had been looking forward to seeing them, and had expected Moni to fly into his arms with shrieks of "Baba!" Now she was bald as an egg and showing signs of hostility toward her own father.

"I'll take you," said the one missing a tooth.

She led him past the mud-floored kitchen, where a cat was cleaning its paws in the doorway, past the prayer room, to a small bedchamber with a slanted roof. The room smelled of something strong and bitter, like turpentine, Biren thought. The girl pointed to a small figure curled up under the quilt.

"There," she said. "She's sleeping."

Biren sat on the side of the bed. "Maya," he whispered, and touched her gently on the shoulder. "Maya. I'm home."

She opened her eyes. "It's you," she said softly, stretching out her hand. "When did you get here?"

Biren turned to the girl, who was standing at the foot of the bed fingering the quilt, watching them. "Thank you," he said. "You can go outside and play."

She left the room reluctantly. When he was sure she was gone, he bent down and touched his cheek against Maya's. "Oh, Maya," he said, his voice breaking, "I missed you so much." He looked anxiously at her face and pushed back her hair. "How are you? I can't see your face. Can I open these shutters?"

"Do that," she said. "Come to think of it, I have never opened the shutters all the time I have been here."

"Why not?" he said, getting up. "How can you stay in a dark room like this? Isn't it depressing? Don't you want to see the outside world?"

"There's not much of a view from this window," she said. "Open it and you'll see."

He cracked open the shutters and saw she was right. All

he could see was a mildewed brick wall, a broken chair and rusted tin cans tumbled about in the corner.

He turned to look at Maya and stifled a cry. Maya's eyes were dull and sunken in her face, her skin had turned a pasty gray and her hair…her hair… Most of it had fallen out and what remained was braided into a thin rattail.

"Oh, Maya," he said in a strangled voice, blinking back his tears. "What happened to you?"

She touched her face. "What? I look that terrible, do I? I haven't seen a mirror for a long time."

He composed himself. "You've lost a lot of weight," he said quickly. Several medicine bottles lay by her bedside. "What is all this medicine? What did the doctor say was wrong with you?"

She ignored his question. "Look at you! You look so handsome," she said in a caressing voice. "I had forgotten how handsome you are, my husband." A touch of the old Maya, sensual and warm, returned to her eyes.

Her tenderness was almost too much to bear. A lump rose in Biren's throat. He pretended to study the labels of the bottles, blinking back his tears. What was all this? Pepsin, bismuth, creosote, sulphocarbonate of soda, bromides and several bottles of tonic. It looked as if she was being treated for some kind of stomach ailment.

"Who is this doctor?" he said. "I hope he is not some village quack."

"No, no." Maya laughed. Even her teeth had turned yellow. Biren felt the pain ripping through his heart. He found it difficult to breathe. "There have been three or four doctors. One of them is a specialist from the Dhaka Medical College, a friend of Ranen—you know, my first cousin, the one with the holy wife, Sabitri…"

"She is the one who put ant powder on the girls and made them shave off their hair! What did this doctor—this specialist—say? What kind of specialist is he, anyway?"

"He is doing his research in malaria. No, wait, wait…" She raised her hand, seeing Biren's look of exasperation. "He is doing research in malaria but he is very brilliant—first class—from Dhaka Medical School."

Biren wanted to scream, but instead he grew very quiet. "And what did he say?"

"And he is familiar with my symptoms—the anemia, stomach ailments and the rest. It's a common illness going around. Baba will know the name of the illness. He wrote it down. Is Baba still sleeping? Does he know you are here?"

He put his hands on her shoulders, his voice shaking. "I am taking you home, Maya. Today. Right now. I don't know what is going on. All I know is I should have never left you here. I should have never gone to Calcutta. That was a terrible, terrible mistake."

She tugged his hand, her eyes eager. "You never told me… how did the meeting go? Did you get the sanctions for the school?"

"Yes, it was very successful. I got everything we had hoped for and more. But it doesn't matter. Nothing matters anymore, except you getting well."

She sank back in the bed, smiling, her eyes closed. "Oh, thank God your trip was successful."

"I don't know," he said miserably, covering his eyes. His tears leaked out. He could no longer help himself. "I don't know, Maya. I expected to come back here and find you well. All I want to do now is to take you home."

CHAPTER 59

That night Maya caught pneumonia, which quickly spiraled out of control. In the early dawn hours her teeth began chattering, followed by convulsions and long, tortured wheezing that sounded like a broken harmonium. Biren remained by her bedside throughout the first night and the next, applying a cold compress to her forehead and smoothing her sparse hair from her face. She drifted in and out of consciousness, often crying out for her mother, talking animatedly in gibberish. Biren was greatly alarmed. She sounded nothing like his soft-spoken Maya. Then all of a sudden a perfect calm washed over her. There was a new clarity in her eyes, peacefulness in her breath. She looked at Biren and smiled, the old Maya smile—deep, calm and brave. After having stayed up for two nights without sleep, he could not believe what he was witnessing. *She is going to be well, she is going to be well,* his heart sang over and over again. He saw Maya's lips were parted; was she trying to say something?

"Tell me," he said eagerly, her face inches from his own.

"I want to go." She barely whispered the words.

"Yes, yes, of course," Biren reassured her. "We will leave first thing in the morning."

She shook her head slightly as if he had misunderstood and sank back, exhausted. Then she tried again, speaking more clearly this time.

"Please..." She beseeched him with her eyes, her beautiful gray-green eyes with their swimming depths of gold. "Please, I beg you to let me go."

"What are you saying, Maya?" he said in a stricken voice.

She nodded and closed her eyes.

It came to him with a sickening jolt that Maya was going to die. She was asking him—begging him—for his permission to let her go, and there was nothing in his power and no power in the world that could hold her back. Her eyes were closed but not all the way, a white luster visible between the lids. He gave a strangled cry and fell upon her chest, his body racked with sobs.

Maya, no, no, no, his mind screamed.

With great effort she lifted her hand to touch his hair. Through the thin covering of her nightclothes he could hear her tortured heart, her breath ragged and uneven. A staccato rattling came from the back of her throat.

She was slipping out of his grasp, drifting away to that place between land and water, between earth and sky, that opened to the great beyond. Yet a part of her held back. She waited for his permission. She would not go without it.

When he looked at her face, the question was still burning in her eyes.

Biren knew he had to set her free. He smoothed back her hair, laid his cheek against hers and closed her beautiful eyes gently with his fingertips.

"Go, my beloved Maya," he whispered. "Go in peace."

He lay there holding her, his head against her heart. Her breathing slowed in ebbs and stilled as the last crested wave stretched to the shore. She lay there, her small hands curled like fallen birds by her side.

Biren kissed her palms and placed her hands on her chest. He noticed the safety pin on her blouse was open. With great tenderness he pushed the sharp end back into the safety clasp so that it would not hurt her.

The professional mourners arrived almost instantaneously. It was almost as if they had been waiting outside the door expecting their summons. Dressed in motley rags, with tangled hair and ash-covered bodies, they took over the wailing and breast-beating to alert the entire village. Next came a bewildering swarm of holy men, astrologers, nameless relatives and village gawkers. Added to that was a brood of bald-headed children who were everywhere, staring at everything, getting in the way.

There was not a shred of dignity for the dead. The soul had left the body to be reincarnated elsewhere, and all that remained were ceremonies and rituals—clamorous, confusing, tedious and oddly festive, in a macabre sort of way, accompanied as they were with flowers, incense, Vedic chants and bell ringing.

Maya's body, bathed and dressed like a new bride in a ceremonial red, was laid on a bamboo palanquin in the entranceway, with her head facing south. Her skin had turned a silvery gray like the underbelly of a fish. Her thumbs and toes were tied together, and there were sandalwood lines drawn on her forehead. To stop her jaw falling open, a piece of white cloth was passed under her chin and secured at the top of her head, making her look vaguely mannish. She was so far removed from any living thing Biren had ever known that he was completely stripped of feeling and could only look on listlessly.

His mind had become a hard, shiny surface. Impenetrable. It absorbed nothing and reflected everything back. There was not a crack of sadness, not a shard of pain. At one point, he vaguely wondered who had died. When he came to his senses he grew frantic as he remembered he had a daughter. *Where was Moni?* He went looking for her and was told all the children had been sent off to a neighbor's house. It reminded him of the day his own father had died and how Nitin and he had been sent to Apu's house. The horror and confusion of the moment was identical to what he had felt when he was eight years old.

Finally Maya's body was borne aloft and taken amid chanting to the cremation ground. Biren walked behind the pallbearers with the men of the village, nauseated by the cloying smell of cheap incense the dead body left in its wake. He remembered very little of the cremation. Maya's eldest nephew, dressed in a single piece of white cloth, had his head shaved by the priest before he completed the funeral rites. Ghee was poured on the body and the pyre set alight. The wood crackled, and black and ugly smoke smelling of ghee and charred flesh drifted over them. The men sat around jiggling their feet, drinking tea and smoking. To Biren's utter disbelief, one of them pulled out a pack of cards and started a game; another group discussed politics—and all the while Maya crackled and burned. It was completely surreal. Biren's head began to swim, and bitter bile lurched around in his stomach and rose to his throat. He staggered over to an old banyan tree, leaned against the trunk and vomited until his throat felt ragged and sore. The tree had sooty leaves, and there was a torn red kite stuck in the branches. When his head cleared he saw an old billy goat staring at him with hard yellow eyes, munching on a marigold garland.

Three days passed, and Biren was still unable to feel anything. The house was always crowded with people he didn't know. Jatin Nandi collapsed with grief. He lay in bed, his face turned toward the wall, saying and eating little. As for Moni, she started acting strange and eating all kinds of things: mud, brick and lime paint off the wall. She refused to go to Biren and she did not cry for her mother. Disturbingly for Biren, she seemed to have become attached to the religious aunt, Sabitri. One day Biren found Moni wearing a *tabiz* amulet tied by a holy red thread around her arm. He was furious. Maya would have never allowed this. He grabbed Moni and tried to take the *tabiz* off, but it was tied with complicated knots. Moni screamed and clawed and acted as if he was torturing her while the bald-headed children stood around watching silently. Finally, his head pounding, Biren marched to the *puja* room, pulling Moni along, shrieking. Sabitri, the holy aunt, her hair dripping wet and sandalwood paste on her forehead, was ringing a small bell and sprinkling holy water with a mango leaf on the deities.

"What is this?" Biren shouted, yanking up Moni's arm. "How dare you put this kind of rubbish on my daughter? You would not have dared to do this if her mother was alive."

She looked at him with the cold flat eyes of a lizard. "Excuse me, I am doing my *puja*," she said in a deadpan voice.

Moni screamed and stretched her arms piteously toward Sabitri. In utter disgust, Biren let her go and watched, sickened, as she collapsed sobbing into the woman's arms. What had happened to his daughter?

When he saw the hostility on Sabitri's face he suddenly knew.

"What have you been telling my daughter about me?" Biren demanded coldly. "Why does she not come to me anymore? She was not like this before."

He paced outside the door of the *puja* room trying to quell his rising anger. Other family members had gathered behind him. Small bald heads peeped from behind the adults.

"I am only doing what I think is for her own good," Sabitri said. Her voice dripped like sugarplum molasses. "Do you know what the astrologer said? He said an evil spirit possessed Maya and, when she died, she would come back and take a loved one with her. This *tabiz* is to protect Moni from her mother's evil spirit."

The veins swelled on Biren's forehead. He was so angry he wanted to slap her. "And you believed the astrologer," he said acidly. "And you think it is right to impose your superstitions on a child who is too young to understand? Who is in no position to make up her own mind? Don't you have a conscience, Sabitri? What is the matter with you?"

Sabitri's eyes widened, then turned flat and cold. "I have more of a conscience than you, brother." All the honey in her voice was gone. She sounded almost diabolical. "I do not discard our traditional ways to follow a white man. You led Maya astray and now you are trying to do the same with your daughter." Biren watched with choking disbelief as Moni reached for Sabitri's wet hair and held a strand against her cheek. She stared unblinkingly at her father, her eyes full of hatred.

It was more than Biren could bear. "You—you are a very evil woman," he whispered before he could help himself. With a hurtful cry he turned around, pushed past the people and stormed out of the house, forgetting his slippers.

He heard someone say, "Let him go. He is just upset about his wife. Give him time, he will calm down."

He didn't know where he was going. Rocks and cocklebursr pierced the soles of his feet. Everything was a blur. Feelings of anger, despair, helplessness and loss ratcheted around his head, and the sound that escaped from his mouth was anguished, tortured, like a gutted pig. He wanted to feel the pain, to obliterate himself.

Through the thunder in his head, he heard a shriek.

"Gurudev!" Bhola Pagol ran out from behind the date trees. Startled vultures flapped and flew out, shaking the heavy palm fronds. Bhola ran up to the path, but Biren shoved him aside and continued to walk furiously toward the river. He halted abruptly at the steep mud bank and debated whether to throw himself in. Below him the brown water hissed and swirled.

He did not know how long he stood there, arms tightly crossed, rocking back and forth. There was a sharp clanging in his brain, like rocks hitting brass. The din was so unbearable he wanted to tear his hair out.

Moni's face swam into view. He had a daughter and she was alone. He remembered how crushed and small she'd looked, the way her eyes had darted with terror. With Maya gone, he was all she had left in the world.

He would have to go back for her. He would have to take her home.

CHAPTER 60

Even though Moni was only four, her rejection of her father was complete and final, almost adultlike in its cruelty. She acted as if she had never known him. At first this frustrated Biren; when he failed to gain even an inch of her affections, despite his best efforts, he was filled with bewilderment and panic. She was turning into a strange child. With her peanut-shaped head and hard elfin features, she was by no means a pretty girl. There was nothing childlike about her behavior, either. Moni didn't play like other children, laugh or cry. Nor did she crave anyone's affection, and endeared herself to none. On the other hand, she showed an unhealthy dependence on Sabitri. It was Sabitri who bathed her, fed her and carried her around straddled on her hip. What came as the ultimate shock to Biren was Moni's growing obsession with *puja* rituals. She was powerfully drawn to the *puja* room, where she sat for hours with sandalwood paste on her forehead, her lips moving, her eyes closed in prayer. Just watching her made Biren feel sick. Surely there was something abnormal and unhealthy about a four-year-old child behaving in this manner? Nobody else in the family seemed to think so. They may have even encouraged it to some extent. After all, people in the village believed a strong religious bent in early childhood was an indication of approaching sainthood.

Biren deeply regretted his ugly outburst in front of his in-laws, especially after he saw the fear and shrinking in his daughter's eyes. It had been improper of him, the son-in-law of the house, to behave that way. Deeply ashamed, he apologized to the family, but they remained cautious and treated him with exaggerated care.

The only sensible person Biren could talk to was Jatin Nandi, but there was one thing Biren learned about his father-in-law: for all his noble ideas and good intentions, Jatin Nandi was a mild man, spineless almost, and staunchly nonconfrontational. After Maya died, he sank into a depression and only wanted to be left alone.

Biren decided the most stable environment to raise Moni would be with Nitin's family in Chandanagore. But he would have to win her trust to take her there. He tried every means to reach out to her, at first cajoling, and finally in desperation he even contemplated whether he should take her by force with him back to Silchar. But what if she got further traumatized? Everything in their house would remind her of her mother. And who would care for her?

All of that was inconsequential because Moni would not even come to him. He tried to take her for a simple walk with disastrous consequences. Moni fought like a wildcat and screamed and kicked all the way. She was so exhausted by the time she came home, she collapsed and ran a high fever for days. Biren was beside himself with anguish. Only when Sabitri sprinkled Moni with holy water did she come around. Baffled and terrified, Biren did not know what to make of it all. After two more weeks of cajoling, tantrums and defeat, Biren was forced to return to Silchar alone.

For two weeks he slept on the veranda, wrapped in Maya's shawl. Every morning he woke at the dot of 3:11 a.m.—the exact time of Maya's death. At that mysterious hour when the world was still struggling to be born, he felt for the first time the brutal rawness of his pain. Losing Maya was like losing himself, and now it seemed Moni was slipping away. Everything in his life was slipping away.

One day his eye caught a movement by the wall, flickering in the long shadow of the jasmine trellis. As it moved he saw it was a monstrous snake, about twelve feet long; it was the biggest snake he had ever seen. The serpent slid across the stone with a dry rustling sound and came toward him. From the pale yellow chevron stripes on its neck, Biren recognized it as the deadly king cobra. Biren remained motionless as the snake paused by his wooden clogs, reared up and swayed back and forth, flicking its black, forked tongue just inches from his toe. He could see clearly the sinister smiley face marking on the cobra's hood. Biren's breath choked in his throat.

Then an insane thought entered his mind: this was his chance to end it all. A single bite from this venomous serpent was known to take down an elephant. All he had to do was make a quick movement and the cobra would surely strike. It would soon be over. He would die the same way as his father had died.

He was determined to do it.

Without further thought, he struck out at the cobra, hitting it across the hood. It felt like slapping a strong, muscular arm. The snake whipped around with a raspy hiss and reared up to a full four feet. The hood flared open, and its jaw dropped to display a pair of curved pointed fangs. It emitted a low, throaty growl and Biren could feel its whooshing breath on the soles of his feet.

He kicked the snake again and then again. The snake swayed from side to side, dodging his foot. "Kill me! Kill me, you bastard!" Biren muttered through clenched teeth.

To his surprise the cobra froze and retracted its hood. Then with a swift sinuous motion it slid across the veranda floor, tumbled down the stairs in heavy folds and disappeared into the dark garden.

Biren drew his knees up to his chest, feeling oddly defeated. He had offered himself to Death and Death had turned him down. A primal rage seared through his body in fiery waves. It cindered every cell and burned every emotion down to silent ash. A vast stillness came over him. As he slowly became aware of his surroundings, he saw a piercing light—so sharp was its intensity he had to shield his eyes with the back of his hand. A new day was breaking across the river.

CHAPTER 61

Buri Kaki hobbled in with Biren's morning tea, slopping it over the saucer as she set it down.

"Jamai-babu, you are up early *again*," she cackled, clueless to the fact that Biren had not gone to bed at all. "Wait, wait, I will complain to *didi* when she gets home. Too much work, work, work." She shook a long bony finger at him and clicked her tongue disapprovingly.

Biren had not told Buri Kaki about Maya's death. What good would it do? She was too old for such sorrow. Buri Kaki lived in her own senile little world, and nothing she did or said made much sense anymore. Once or twice she had asked Biren with a childlike eagerness when Moni and Maya were coming home, to which Biren replied, "Not right now." The answer to her was satisfactory. She muddled up the past with the present and talked as if dead people were still alive. She told Biren that Maya's mother had just gone to market, and Jatin Nandi's mother-in-law had made the fish curry. Biren just replied, "I see," or, "Good, good," to everything, and she was happy.

"Mia!" A shout came from the front gate.

Kanai was running toward the house. He looked very agitated. Biren set aside his cup and rose hurriedly, the shawl slipping to the floor.

"You must come at once," Kanai panted, wide-eyed with panic. "There has been a murder! Yosef is dead. They found his body in the estuary."

"What?" Biren shook him by the shoulders. "What are you saying?"

"The villagers killed him. They took him by boat to the estuary. They tortured him and left him to die there."

Biren felt nauseous with fear. "And Chaya?" he cried. "Where is Chaya?"

"They have taken her back to the village. I think they are going to kill her, too."

Biren did not wait to hear more.

"Wait here," he ordered Kanai as he charged back inside the house. "I have to get the police. You must take us to the weavers' village," he shouted over his shoulder.

Bit by bit he learned what had happened. Yosef and Chaya had escaped with the water gypsies. The gypsies were hard to trace. They moved like the silent undertow, carrying goods, people and currency from place to place.

Chaya's father had gone from village to village looking for the couple. He'd warned the villagers against the water gypsies. They were charlatans, thieves and sorcerers. Vagrants with no morals, no roots. They had kidnapped his virtuous daughter and turned her into a prostitute to earn money for them. He had to find her at any cost.

He had been relentless. He'd hired thugs from out of town and bribed boatmen with opium. Nobody knew who had actually turned the couple in, but they had been found hundreds of miles away in tiger country in the big river delta. And there in the forest of flame trees they had been captured. As for the gruesome way Yosef had been tortured and killed, it was beyond horror. He was practically unidentifiable: mutilated, dismembered, his genitals cut; his blood mixed with the crimson petals of the flame tree spilled everywhere on the ground.

Biren had to identify Yosef from the pearl earring on the man's left ear. Then he went to the police station and filed a detailed and comprehensive police report.

Securing the help of the police inspector, Biren set out with armed policemen in two boats to the weavers' village. The village was deathly quiet. They approached in a single file, and Biren could sense they were being watched from behind closed doors. Armed police storming a village was not common. Someone must have warned the villagers of their approach, because the weaving sheds looked as if they had been abandoned in a hurry, the spindles lying helter-skelter on the floor. Young children who were always seen on the stoop of the mud houses playing with sticks and stones were nowhere in sight. Not even a single chicken pecked in the yard.

The emerald-green pond where women washed their clothes was deserted. So was the community well. It looked like people had left in haste, judging by the half-filled bucket of water and the two pitchers abandoned beside it.

They came to Chaya's house. The doors and windows

were shuttered. Biren walked up and rapped sharply on the door. When nobody answered, he rattled the windows and yelled, "Open! Police!"

There was a long silence. A curtain lifted, then dropped, and the front door unlatched. A thin woman in her midforties, her head covered with the end of her sari, peered through the crack with frightened eyes. Biren guessed she was Chaya's mother from the striking resemblance in their features.

"I am here to see Chaya's father," said Biren.

"He is not home," said the woman. "He has gone to town."

From her shifty eyes, Biren could tell she was lying. "Tell him to come out," he demanded grimly. "Otherwise, the police are going to enter and check this house."

The woman looked over her shoulder. "He had to go to town," she repeated in a monotone. "He is not here."

"Where is Chaya?" said Biren. "Bring her out. I want to speak to her."

The woman's eyes dropped. She looked terrified. "I…I don't know where she is," she stuttered.

"What do mean, you don't know?" Biren shouted. "She's your daughter, isn't she? Where is she? She was brought back to the village. Your husband and some men dragged her home by her hair. They murdered Yosef. We know everything. Now go bring her out!"

"She is not here," repeated the woman. Her lips trembled as she blinked back frightened tears. "I don't know where she is. They took her away." Her voice was cracked from dryness.

"Who took her away?"

The woman began to weep. "They threw acid on her face and they took her away." She fell to the ground with a shriek.

Biren turned to the police. "Two of you search this house," he said. "The rest of you go and bang on every door in the village. I want every villager rounded up and assembled in this compound in five minutes. Hurry!"

The woman wailed inconsolably.

"You saw them do it?" Biren asked in a shaky voice. "You saw them throw acid on Chaya's face?"

"Yes," the woman sobbed. "They called her a *maagi*—a Muslim's whore. They kicked her and told her she can now go and screw for her living. Then they dragged her away."

Biren felt nauseated. "Didn't anybody try to stop them? You are her mother!"

"What can I do?" the woman cried. "They would kill me, too, if I tried to stop them. The whole village watched them kick her. It happened right outside this house. I just cleaned up all the blood. Her father wanted to finish her off but the men said she should be allowed to live as a lesson to others."

"Who were the other men? Are they people from this village?"

"They were local *goondas* from town. Her father paid them to find and kill Yosef."

"Sir?"

Biren turned around. It was the policeman.

"The villagers are all here, sir."

About thirty people were gathered outside. Not a single person looked him in the eye as he stepped forward to address them.

"All of you stood and watched today as a young girl was beaten by *goondas*. You watched her own father throw acid on her face to disfigure her. You watched the men drag her away by her hair. And not one of you did anything." He looked the people standing before him. They were all looking down.

"This girl could have been your own wife or daughter," Biren said slowly. "Someday, if this should happen to them, they will all stand around and watch like you did. This is not a matter of religion or morality. This is a matter of humanity. If there is no fairness and justice for this girl, there will be no fairness and justice for you. You will always be puppets in the hands of a bully, power won by corruption, by money.

"Your *didi*," he continued, and paused, choking with emotion, "my wife, Maya, tried to help you, did she not? She encouraged you to be self-reliant. She wanted you to be free. Free to make your own choice. And now...and now your *didi* and my wife is gone. She's dead."

Some of the women started crying.

"Some of you have daughters like I have a daughter. What happened to Chaya must never happen to them. I know you have been told I am a traitor because I work for the British. But remember the mighty power of the British rule can be used for our good, as well. I am an insider and I represent you. I was born in a small riverside village like you. I fished in ponds. I walked barefoot to school. I did not even own a pencil to write with. Just because I wear trousers and ride a horse does not make me a *belayti*."

He looked at the faces around him, and as he did so, he had a flash of being back in the Cambridge union debate presenting his argument. Only this was real life.

"I have taken a vow," he said, "for my mother, my dead wife, my young daughter and for all Indian women that they will never again be without a voice. I will be their voice and I will use the laws of our foreign rulers to bring about change. These changes cannot happen from the outside, by force or by anarchy. The machinery has to be manipulated from within the administration, which is why I work for the government. This is why I am a lawyer. Please understand I am not going against their policy. I am making their policy work for you. There is something much greater beneath appearances—beneath the garb of religion, politics and social status. And that is our common humanity and it unites us all. Today I want to remind you of that. Today I need you to help me."

Exhausted, he leaned against the wall of the house, crossed his arms and studied the faces before him. A small child crawled toward Biren and touched his shoe.

He picked her up and handed her to the young woman who came forward. His heart filled with grief when he thought of Moni. "Some of you have seen my little daughter, Moni—yes?" he said softly, choking with emotion. "Perhaps during the Durga Puja, or by the river where I sometimes used to take her. I am doing this for her and for all our daughters. I will not rest until all the men who have been involved in this atrocity are brought to justice. They will all go to jail. You may criticize our foreign rulers, but I can attest to one thing. They have established one of the finest judicial systems in the world, where all men rich or poor can be brought to trial. Did you know there are cases where even Englishmen have been tried and sentenced in this country? That is what I mean by justice. All of you have access to the same rights as anyone in this land. But I will need your help to identify the men. I will need to get signed statements from you as witnesses. In return you will be given full police protection. Our most critical need at this moment is to find Chaya. We don't know if she is dead or alive. How can you forget her? She is one of your own. She was born here. So many of you have seen her grow up from a little girl. What a fine young woman she turned out to be. You must help me to find her. I cannot do this without your help. Please."

One of the men cleared his throat and shuffled to his feet. He spoke to the others in a low voice. His back was turned and Biren saw him gesture, pointing this way and that, then the men dispersed in different directions.

"We will find her, *dada*," the man said, turning back to Biren.

Dada. Brother. He had addressed Biren as one of their own.

She was discovered the following day, barely alive outside a temple, ten miles away in another village. A bullock-cart man had brought her there after he had found her abandoned by the side of the road. At first he had thought she was a pile of dirty rags until she'd moved. He'd taken her to the next village where nobody knew who she was.

Biren brought her back to Silchar by boat. With Reginald Thomson's help, he admitted Chaya to the military hospital, where she lingered between life and death for eleven days. Chaya was four months pregnant and had suffered a miscarriage, the doctor said. She would live, although the acid burn would forever disfigure her face.

When she was released from hospital, Chaya had nowhere to go. Branded as a Muslim's whore, she was an outcast, so Biren brought her home. Buri Kaki took over Chaya's care with bristling energy. She nursed and bathed her, wrapped her in old worn quilts and fed her little bits of rice, and cooed words of encouragement when Chaya found it difficult to swallow. When Chaya wept at night, Biren heard soft shushing sounds and the crooning of a child's lullaby in Buri Kaki's cracked old voice.

Silchar
2nd February 1905

I remember, on my first steamer journey to Calcutta with Willis Duff, I spent long hours with a young deckhand learning to tie different marine knots. Looking back, I suspect Willis probably hoped this challenging activity would take my mind off missing home, and he was right. Sometimes Willis and I would have a competition to see who could tie the knots the fastest. I still remember the names of the knots and how to tie them: Sailor's Hitch, Stevedore Knot, Rosendahl Bend. This knowledge has served me well.

When we were newly married, I tried to impress Maya with my knot tying by demonstrating on her hair. The knots in her hair kept slipping out, but I still made a royal mess and she spent a long time sitting at her dressing table combing the tangles out. I relive these tender moments now that she is gone.

The knots in my life are more complicated now and not so easy to untangle. You could say I am caught in a Rosendahl Bend—an interlocking knot that pulls both ways. Sometimes I feel stretched to the breaking point.

The two priorities in my life are Moni and the criminal court case I am now involved in. The case has turned out to be more complicated than I ever imagined. It takes up months of my time because I have to be in Calcutta for all the hearings and to file the paperwork. When I return to Assam I try to spend as much time as I can with Moni.

I still have not been able to bring her back to Silchar with me. I have tried everything. I took back her old toys, I showed her Maya's photograph, Maya's shawl, comb and other items, hoping to trigger memories and reestablish the connection between us, but Moni is a blank wall. She has withdrawn into a tight hard shell. She does not connect to me as her father. For that matter, she does not connect to anybody, not even Sabitri anymore.

On one of my recent trips to Calcutta, I discussed Moni's condition with Ram. Ram is now a leading researcher in the newly emerging field of mental illness. He said Moni's case sounded as if she was suffering from a serious mental disorder, with a possible genetic link. This led me to ask around Maya's family and I was shocked to learn about the history of mental illness on her mother's side. Maya's aunt—her mother's own sister—suffered from depression and ultimately committed suicide. One of her uncles—her mother's first cousin—was pathologically insane and kept locked up for most of his life. There are other cases of minor aberrations among family members. Moni's symptoms are not identical, but I am convinced her disorder is genetic.

What frustrates me is nobody in Jatin Nandi's family seems to think so. Moni's solitary nature and God obsession leads them to believe she is on the verge of sainthood. They even encourage her delusional behavior. It is abhorrent and completely unacceptable. It is obvious to me the child is seriously disturbed but I am at a loss to pinpoint what exactly is wrong with her or know what to do about it.

She is growing up in front of my eyes, and each time I see her she has drifted a little farther away. I can't seem to reach her anymore or connect with her in any way. Except for the first few fleeting years of her life, I don't believe she was ever mine.

Calcutta
2nd June 1912

Precious Mitra,
Your accomplishments I wear like a rose in my heart. Your didi *I am sure is looking down today to see her little sister, the brightest star in the family, as you graduate with honors with your teaching certificate. The whole world is at your feet, and a great destiny awaits you. My blessings and love are always with you.*

I have been gone for long stretches to Calcutta. The complicated criminal case I am involved in has been dragging on and keeps getting moved from one court to the other, but I will not rest until all the culprits have been punished for their heinous crime. The supreme court's final hearing date has been set for four months from now. We have gathered affidavits from several witnesses and collected a strong body of evidence, which will work in our favor. I have full faith in our judicial process and I expect a fair trial. I will not rest until all eleven accused have been sent to jail.

Chaya, the victim, who you met on your last visit, is now fully recovered, physically at least. As for the wounds inside, only time will tell. She has taken over the running of my household, now that Buri Kaki has been safely retired to her village where she can boss over her great- and great-great-grandchildren. She is the grand matriarch of three generations, and commands over her clan with vim and vigor. Hats off to the old lady! I owe Buri Kaki my gratitude in more ways than one. She hand raised my Maya and she has seen me through my most difficult days.

I am grateful to you for keeping me in touch with Moni. My biggest regret is I have seen so little of her in the past few years, as I was in Calcutta most of the time. I have spared no effort in reaching out to her in every way possible, and to my sorrow, my only child will have nothing to do with me. Why the change came about, I may never know. I blamed myself initially, then I wondered if it was the trauma of her mother's death or maybe the environment she was put in, but I suspect more than a minor aberration and that she may be seriously and pathologically impaired.

A religious inclination is one thing, but the compulsive behavior she exhibits is deeply disturbing, as are her peculiar dietary habits. The last time I went to see her, she remained in the puja *room for five hours and then emerged dazed and incommunicado. We did not exchange a single word, which in effect made my trip to see her rather pointless. But I will not give up. I will try till my dying day to win her trust and love. I once saw in her child eyes her love for me, her Baba. How can I ever forget the way she used to hold out her hands to me? Those are the memories that keep me going. Perhaps one day she will know of the love I have always held in my heart for her. She is not only my child, but she is the one link I have to my Maya and I cannot let that go.*

Maya's memory is ever stirring in my soul. I have never told this to anyone, Mitra, but I will share this with you. The first time I saw your sister was when she passed by me on a boat, floating, delicate as the petal of a flame tree flower. I will always remember the pensive look on her face. I wondered with some jealousy back then if she was thinking about another man. I had not yet won her heart—for that matter we had not even met—but from the moment I set eyes on her I longed for her. But she was never mine to keep, and my Moni may not be, either. I can only love them with all my heart and let them go. All true love belongs to a greater universe. I am simply grateful they passed through my world and enhanced it for me.

To you, my little sister-in-law, who threw a plum at my horse and walked between my Maya and me for a little while, I send my deepest affection and love.

Yours,
Dada (Biren Roy)

Silchar
12th May 1915

It's a miracle!

The top half of the Russian Matryoshka *doll that was lost for thirteen years has been found! Chaya discovered the doll inside Maya's sari trunk when she cleaned out our old bedroom yesterday. The bedroom has remained unoccupied since the day my Maya died. I cannot bear to go in there. Her memory is still too strong.*

Chaya went into the room on her own. The memory of her didi *is something she likes to dwell on and pay homage to. She treats the old bedroom like a shrine. Chaya opened the windows, dusted and aired it out. She took all Maya's saris from her cupboard and the items from the dressing table and packed them inside the old trunk.*

The trunk came with Maya the day she entered this house as my new bride. It contained her trousseau of beautiful heirloom silks, most of which she never wore, preferring instead the ordinary hand-loom cottons from the weavers' village. The fresh cotton saris made her look like a spring leaf, a flower petal or a newly emerged pearl according to the color she selected. She was simple as she was beautiful, my Maya.

How that Russian doll got inside her old sari trunk I will never know. I suspect it was our little Moni's doing. She was an inquisitive little squirrel, our daughter. She took things from here and there and hid them in unexpected places. I once found a foot of my English dress socks pushed into a marigold pot out in the garden.

How on earth had that small child opened the heavy trunk and put the doll inside? I shudder to think what would have happened if the lid had fallen on her tiny fingers. She was only three after all. A bold and curious child she was, unafraid of the world back then.

I remember the day I returned home from Russia and gave her the doll. Each time I opened up one doll to reveal another inside, Moni gave a squeal and clapped her hands. To add to the drama, I made a small "whooshing" sound. When we got to the very last doll—the tiny baby one—she looked at me with mournful eyes, and held up her empty hands and said, "Nai, nai!" *No more. I put the dolls back, nesting them one inside the other, but as soon as I was done, she took all the dolls apart and threw a minor tantrum till I repeated the whole act complete with the sound effects. When she insisted on doing the same thing, over and over, it got very tiresome, so I hid the doll away. The next time I opened the doll I found the mother doll was missing her head.*

I used the bottom half of the mother doll to store the paper pins on my desk. After a while I forgot all about it. All the dolls eventually got dismantled or lost except the bottom half of the mother doll that remained on my desk. Here we are, thirteen years later, and Chaya finds the matching half. And voilà! The two pieces fit perfectly and now we now have a complete mother doll.

But Maya and Moni are both gone.

Looking at the doll made me feel very emotional. I thought of all the mismatched and lost pieces of my life that can never come together again. The doll triggered memories of happier times. Suddenly I felt the need to write down my feelings for Moni. I sat and wrote her a letter. I told her of the times we would go down to the river, where she would pick strings of river kelp and chase behind herons with her small pattering feet. I told her of the shiuli *flowers we gathered around Durga Puja time to place around her mother's hair. Of the duck feathers she brought home that Buri Kaki stuck into a ball of wheat dough and shaped into a bird for her. They were mostly small everyday memories. Because I had held her for such a short time, those memories are very intense and sweet. I relived them one by one and I thanked her for them. I folded the letter into an origami paper crane like I used to make for her when she was small and put the letter inside the mother doll. I will give this to her. It does not matter if she reads my letter or not. The important thing is I have bared my soul and said what I needed to say to my child.*

Silchar
16th May 1915

I went to see Moni yesterday. She did not smile or even appear to listen when I told her the story of the doll. She is fifteen years old now, almost a woman, but she is thin, underdeveloped and pale. Her eyes are a hard green like bottle glass and devoid of any expression. I have concluded there is nothing basically wrong with her intelligence; in some ways I would say she is above average. She still spends most of her time in religious rituals but now her interests include political thought, and she has been reading a lot of communist literature lately. I was relieved to see her interests have expanded beyond religion. It does not really matter if I agree with her political views or not, I simply see this as another avenue to communicate with her.

I was a little concerned when I learned she has joined a communist group and attends their meetings. My biggest worry is that she is young and mentally unsound and somebody could take advantage of her.

When I asked her about the group she lashed out and accused me of being a spy for the British government—I don't know where she got that idea. She claimed her group members were true patriots fighting for the freedom of our country, unlike her own father, who pandered to our foreign leaders. Then she got up and stormed out of the room, leaving me wounded and close to tears. As I got up to leave, I noticed she had taken the Russian doll that was lying on the table beside her.

Dhaka
12th November 1915

Dear Dada,
I don't know how to reach you. Chaya was uncertain about the date of your return from Calcutta. I write to you with disturbing news. Moni has run away.

Nobody knows where she is and nobody dares to find out. She ran away with Anirban Das, her tutor. I don't know if you've met the man. He is at least twenty years older than Moni and the member of a secret militant group. The key members of this group are on the government watch list. They meet in secret and sometimes there are surprise police raids on their meetings. The villagers are sympathetic to their cause and warn them of approaching police by blowing conch horns from house to house in identifiable patterns. The members disband and throw their weapons into the courtyard of houses and the village women hide the guns under their saris till the coast is clear.

This group is wanted for several crimes against the British. I just found out they were behind the recent steamer hijacking on the river delta. The steamer loaded with tea and other cargo was looted and burned on its way to Calcutta. I am told the steamer belonged to the family of Samir Deb, your friend from Cambridge.

This was also the same group behind the killing of British officers at the recent jute mill massacre. I was deeply saddened to hear Willis Duff, the jute mill manager, was murdered. What a tragic irony to think he was the same young Scot who befriended you on your first journey to boarding school. You told me of Willis Duff when you taught me the card game Fish at our Silchar house—do you remember? You and didi *were still not married back then.*

I wondered if Moni knew about your association with Samir Deb and Willis Duff, but I have since concluded the two incidents and their links to you are purely coincidental. The agenda of this militant group is to attack anything and everything related to the British. The group members live in a commune and they smuggle arms illegally across the Burmese border. Their main plan is to organize an armed uprising against the British and overthrow the government by force.

Whether or not Moni is romantically involved with her tutor, I do not know. She was always secretive and I don't think anybody knows what really went on in her head. Her tutor strongly influenced her political views, that much I am certain. I learned Moni had been going to the secret meetings for quite some time. People at Baba's basha *probably suspected this, and my religious cousin, Sabitri, might have even encouraged her involvement to some extent. Anirban Das is Sabitri's first cousin.*

You should not go looking for Moni, Dada. To do so would put her life in danger. The government has many spies and it would not surprise me if they are keeping a close watch on you. They know you are her father and you go frequently to meet her at Baba's basha, *so please be very careful.*

It grieves me deeply to give you all this distressing news. If my gentle didi *were alive today, she would weep to see what has become of her daughter and how Moni continues to hurt you despite your ceaseless efforts to win her heart.*

With my respect and affections to you,
Mitra

CHAPTER 62

Moni's militant group disappeared into the shadowy underworld. It was rumored they lived in the jungles, traveled with the water gypsies and moved from village to village, never staying in one place for long. Overnight a gypsy settlement would sprout like a clump of ragged mushrooms on a riverbank and just as abruptly they would be gone, leaving mysterious symbols on the sand and crabs to scuttle into the empty peg holes of their tents. Biren got sporadic news of their movements through the boatmen's network.

Then, just as suddenly, there was no trace of them. Several months passed and there was still no news. Biren had almost given up his daughter for dead when Kanai brought news that Moni had been spotted in a village, deep down south in the Chittagong river delta.

She was married and lived under a different name: Behula Palit. Biren had not seen her for fourteen years. Moni would be twenty-nine years old now. Upon learning she was alive, he was determined to go and find her.

Biren grew a beard and dressed like a fisherman, and it was with great secrecy he made the boat journey alone to her village in the dead of night. At dawn, he disembarked at a small landing and took a rickshaw to the address given to him by Kanai.

He was appalled to see the abject state of her neighborhood. Biren's village in Sylhet was poor but clean. You could see the pride of ownership in the freshly swept courtyards, the holy basil thriving by the stoop and a plump chicken or two pecking in the yard. In this village there was a sense of vagrancy and desperation in the scummy ponds, broken-down wells and cows with bony hips that walked crookedly down the riverbed. Even dressed in a simple *lungi* and white tunic, Biren felt conspicuously rich among the emaciated, gaunt-eyed people he passed. His heart filled with sorrow to think his beloved Moni lived in such abject poverty when he was ready to give her the world.

He arrived at the address to find a small thatched hut with a crooked tree with pelican-beak-shaped flowers. The door and windows were shuttered. Biren knocked several times but nobody answered. He walked around to the mud courtyard at the back of the house. There was a clump of banana trees in one corner and behind that a small lily pond. On a tired-looking clothesline strung between two sugar palms, a faded green blouse, white sari petticoats and small items belonging to a child were drying. The clothes were still damp, indicating somebody had pegged them recently, but there were no other signs of life.

It had to be the wrong house, Biren concluded. He saw a small tea shop across the road and walked over to it. Two men wearing *lungis* and dirty vests sat on the bench outside chatting. The tea shop man eyed Biren warily. Biren ordered a tumbler of tea and a bidi.

"Does Behula Palit live here?" he asked casually. "A girl with green eyes?"

The tea shop man looked at him suspiciously. "Are you from the police?" he asked.

Biren laughed. "Do I look like the police?" He lit his bidi from the smoldering rope and took a puff. "No, I am from her grandfather's village in Barisal. I was passing by. Her aunt asked me to give her some money."

The tea shop man relaxed. "Yes, she lives here," he said.

"I knocked on the door several times but I don't think she is home."

"She has gone to the temple," said one of the other men. "Behula is a little cracked in the head. The religious type."

"Does her husband live with her?"

"Oh, he is hardly around," said the tea shop man. "He comes to the village once in a while. He is fond of the child. He takes her for a walk to the river."

"Behula…has a child?" Biren could hardly contain his surprise.

"Yes, a little girl, around three years old. Her father brings her to the tea shop when he is here. Her name is Layla."

Biren's hands trembled as he smoked his bidi. Overcome with joy at being a grandfather, he was simultaneously deeply worried. *A small child inside a shuttered house with a mentally unbalanced mother.* A great feeling of helplessness overwhelmed him.

He glanced around the tea shop. The walls were plastered with pictures of Hindu gods, and a stick of incense burned on a small altar. The tea shop owner seemed like a god-fearing man. Hopefully he could be trusted with the money.

"Her aunt Sabitri has sent her some money," he said, taking some notes out from his kurta pocket. "Can you please give it to her? Tell her it is for the child."

It was the only way he could get Moni to accept the money, Biren figured. He did not care as long as he could help her and her child in some way. His heart ached when he recalled the desolate courtyard and the shabby clothes hanging on the clothesline.

He had a granddaughter! Her name was Layla. Would he ever get to see her? It was a delicate situation. He could jeopardize his relationship with Moni even further if he was not careful, and God only knew what she might do. But at least she was alive and well. Biren decided he would send money periodically through Kanai and ask him to leave it with the tea shop man and say it was from Sabitri. That is the only way he could reach out to her for now.

CHAPTER 63

Biren was unable to sleep for weeks. Finding Moni had churned up memories of the past and forced him to examine buried regrets. When he looked back, he saw life had set him on a carefully plotted course, and in all the years he had given to the service of others, he had sacrificed his own loved ones along the way: Estelle, Maya, Moni—all were gone. Now, when he was ready to give of himself, there was nobody to give to.

Only Shibani remained. Shibani, now totally blind, still lived with Nitin in Chandanagore. Lately she talked about retiring to an ashram to live out her last days.

The criminal case that dragged on for eleven years finally came to an end. Chaya's father and three other men were sentenced to forty years in jail, and the eight men who had acted as their accomplices received varying sentences.

Had it all been worthwhile? There was no clear answer.

Given his driving need at that time, he was not sure he could have done anything differently. Yet when he looked back, all his achievements felt diminished given what he had lost.

Biren never saw Moni again.

A month after his visit to her village she drowned herself in the lily pond behind her house. Biren was in Europe on a lecture tour and difficult to trace. Mitra's letter followed him from Austria to France and reached him three months later in Leipzig, Germany. He was sitting in a coffeehouse when he opened Mitra's letter. The news made his hands shake uncontrollably, and his cup of coffee fell with a clatter, soiling the white tablecloth.

"Oh, was ist denn hier passiert?" cried the German waitress.

She ran up to clean the mess. When she glanced at the Indian man she was shocked to see the tears streaming down his handsome face. By the time she returned with fresh coffee, he had left the money on the table and gone.

Biren cut his lecture tour short and returned to India.

He pieced together the information from different sources to learn what happened. It was raining that day, the tea shop man said, when he was alerted by a child's screams. He went behind the house and found three-year-old Layla, dressed in a red sari and veil, tied to a banana tree, and Moni floating facedown in the lily pond.

In the weeks leading up to her death a holy sadhu had visited Moni's house several times. The sadhu, who was a garrulous type, often stopped by the tea shop. He told the tea shop man that Moni was beside herself with anxiety and had pulled all her hair out. Her husband had been arrested and she was worried about her daughter, Layla, who had been born under the unlucky astrological sign of *Manglik*. Layla's horoscope portended bad luck, and Moni's aunt, who was a holy and good woman, had sent her money to do *puja* for the child. The sadhu advised Moni to marry her daughter to a banana tree in a religious ceremony. It was the only way to cross out the bad luck, he said.

It was just as well the tea shop man had had all this information. He was aware of the day the ritual was going to be performed. He saw the sadhu arrive in his ceremonial dress with his *puja* items. The sadhu spent a long time at Moni's house. The tea shop man could hear the chanting and ringing of bells from across the road. When the ceremony was over the sadhu stopped by the tea shop for a cup of tea and mentioned the *puja* had gone well. Then he left. For a few hours all was quiet in the house. Then the tea shop man heard the sound of the child crying. It was a ceaseless wail and sounded a little odd. He went to investigate and found three-year old Layla tied to the banana tree and her mother drowned in the lily pond.

Mitra had arrived from Dhaka and taken Layla home with her.

After hearing the story, Biren recalled how a mysterious old *tantrik* on the riverbank had prophesized Moni would be claimed by water. Now, twenty-six years later, that prophecy had come true.

CHAPTER 64

Biren's heart almost stopped the first time he saw Layla. She was four years old and living with Mitra, who was now married and a schoolteacher in Dhaka with a daughter of her own. Moon, her daughter, was exactly six months older than Layla.

Biren's granddaughter stared at him solemnly with big gray-green eyes the color of river fog. Something ancient and familiar stirred deep within him. They were Maya's eyes looking back at him. Layla's resemblance to Maya was eerie, from her straight shining hair down to her delicate arched feet. When she brushed her hand across her forehead Biren noticed her hairline met at the center of her forehead in a widow's peak, exactly like his late wife's.

His first impulse had been to embrace her, but Layla shied away, her eyes becoming anxious.

"Give her time," Mitra consoled him. "She only opened

up to me after weeks. I just let her and Moon play together. If anybody can draw her out of her shell, it's Moon."

The girls were building a tower with used matchboxes. Moon, the bossy one, did all the building while Layla stood watching with somber eyes.

"I am still shocked at her uncanny resemblance to Maya," Biren said.

"I would never have thought that the first day I saw her, Dada," Mitra said. She covered her eyes and shook her head slowly. "I could hardly bear to look at her. Her hair was all knotted, her skin lumpy and red with ant bites. I shudder to think how long she had been left out in the rain. Every night she would wake up screaming. Only recently it has stopped. After Moni's cremation I did not want to leave Layla in Baba's *basha* so I brought her back with me to Dhaka."

"I wish I was there, Mitra. You should never have had to go through this alone."

"We tried our best to trace you. We sent a telegram to you in Calcutta, but I suppose you had already left for Europe." Mitra was silent for a little while. "I dread to think how much Layla saw of her mother's suicide. I cannot imagine how traumatic is must be for a child to see her mother drown in front of her eyes and not be able to go to her because she is tied to a tree. No child should have to go through what Layla has been through."

Biren covered his eyes, his heart lacerated with pain. "The poor child, the poor child," he cried in a strangled voice.

"Don't feel bad, Dada," Mitra said, putting her hand on Biren shoulder. "It could have been worse. We could have lost Layla, as well. I am greatly encouraged by her improvement. Every day she seems to get better. I have to thank Moon for that. I try not to mollycoddle Layla. I don't even reprimand Moon when she acts bossy with her. I let them work it out between themselves. It is an odd friendship. They are complete opposites. Moon is a rascal and Layla is soulful and sage-like. The wisdom of the universe is in Layla's eyes."

Biren remembered Maya's peaceful eyes when she'd woken in the morning, and the luxurious way she'd raised her supple arms in a feline stretch. He had loved this soft, unhurried quality about her.

"Dadamoshai!" shouted little Moon. She skip-hopped up to Biren, her black curls bouncing, and tugged him by the hand. "Come and play."

Layla stayed where she was. She watched them and twirled a strand of hair around her finger. Biren's heart again skipped a beat. Maya had had exactly the same habit.

He got up from the chair and walked over to the matchboxes. "Shall we play a counting game?" he said. "Who is going to line up the matchboxes? All right, I will go first." He pointed to the first matchbox. "One. Who's next?"

"Two," said Moon. She sat on her haunches and bounced her bottom.

"Next?" said Biren, looking at Layla. Moon gave her a little prod.

"Three," whispered Layla, her voice barely audible.

"My turn. Four," said Biren.

"Five!" shouted Moon, clapping her hands.

"Six," whispered Layla.

And they went all the way up to stop at eleven, where the matchboxes ended.

"Game over," said Biren.

"Again-again-again!" cried Moon.

Biren got to his feet and dusted his hands. "Now you two play," he said, and walked back to his chair.

"You are good with children." Mitra chuckled. "Remember how you taught me sums using peanuts?"

Biren grew sad thinking of all years he had missed out on with his own daughter.

"I never had the opportunity to watch Moni grow," he said softly. "She slipped through my fingers."

Mitra was thoughtful. "Now you have these two," she said. "Maybe you can give them what you could not give her."

"I don't know if Layla will ever accept me as her grandfather. She is so painfully shy."

"Give her time, Dada. She sees how Moon adores you. She follows Moon around and imitates everything she does."

"I want to spend more time with the girls," said Biren. "It will give me the opportunity to get to know Layla."

"I have an idea," said Mitra. "When school closes for the summer I'll bring them to Silchar and we will spend the summer months with you. The change will do me good and the girls will love your big house. You can show them your school and teach them things."

Their visit could not come soon enough.

That summer Biren studied Layla carefully. She was painfully shy. Often the girls wandered into his study. Moon, incapable of sitting still, ran around like a hurricane and then ran out, but Layla lingered. She ran her fingers along Biren's desk and sometimes touched his books. Once she picked up Charulata's bookmark lying next to his diary and stared at it for the longest time, running her finger over the bumpy pattern. She held the bookmark a few inches from her face, her tiny brow furrowed in puzzlement.

"B," she whispered to herself. Biren could hardly believe

his ears. She had deciphered the first hidden alphabet symbol of his name!

There was something about her furtive curiosity that reminded Biren of the young fox he had befriended in the Grantham meadows. If he acted busy and preoccupied, Layla crept closer. Sometimes she stood so close he could feel the warmth of her small body against his arm. But she still did not speak.

One day she pushed a small hard object in his hand.

"What is it?" Biren muttered absently. He looked out of the corner of his eye and his heart took a tumble. It was Moni's Russian doll!

A lump rose in his throat as he fought back the sting of tears. Afraid to trust his voice, he took the doll and turned it around, pretending to examine it. Something rattled inside.

"Is there something inside?" he asked nonchalantly.

Layla nodded vigorously. Her silky hair shimmered like a scarf. Biren smiled at her enthusiasm.

"You can open it," she said, pushing against his arm.

Biren unscrewed the top half of the doll. Inside the hollowed chamber were several shiny oblong seeds.

Biren spread a few seeds on his palm.

"What are these?" he asked, separating the seeds with his forefinger.

"Seeds," Layla said. Her eyes widened and she spread out her thin arms. "From a big-big tree."

Biren thrilled to hear her voice. It was solemn and sweet, just like her eyes.

"Oh," Biren said, feigning casualness. "I wonder what kind of tree it is." He had learned by now if he directed a question at her, she would not answer. To trick her into a conversation he had to sound as if he was talking to himself.

"A big red tree," she said eagerly, leaning into his arm.

He knew he had to proceed delicately. An inch in the wrong direction and she would curl back into herself like a sleeping fern.

"I used to have a doll like this once upon a time," he said slowly to himself. "I wonder who gave Layla the doll."

"My Moni-ma," said Layla, clear as day. "Moni-ma told me to keep this doll because she was going away."

Moni-ma. So that's what she called her mother. Biren eyes welled up; he had to look away.

Layla picked up the seeds one by one from Biren's open palm and put them back inside the doll. She capped the top half and offered the doll to him.

"Take this," she said solemnly.

"No, it's yours," Biren replied quickly. "Your Moni-ma gave it to you. You must keep it."

"*You* keep it *for* me," she pleaded, and pushed the doll into his hand. "Because—" she paused to look furtively over her shoulder "—Moon will break it."

Biren smiled. He took the doll and rattled the seeds.

"I'll tell you what," he said. "I'll keep it with me, and when you come again we will plant the seeds together, all right?"

Layla nodded. She turned and skipped out of the room.

They planted the seeds in mud pots the following summer. The girls watered them every day, and soon twenty-nine flame tree seedlings unfurled their feathery leaves to the sun. After the big rains in June the seedlings turned into healthy saplings with sturdy stems, and by the end of that summer they had all been planted at thirty-foot intervals along the road leading to Biren Roy's house.

Today it is a shimmering avenue of flame trees: twenty-nine in all that meet in a glorious canopy overhead and provide a dappled shade to walkers below. It struck Biren only recently that Maya was twenty-nine years old when she died. There is one tree for every glorious year of her life. It comforted him to know the avenue of flame trees would be there to shower down blessings on future generations long after he was gone.

2nd April 1950

Mitra maiyya,
I write to you from beautiful Falmouth in Cornwall. Spring arrives here earlier than the rest of the UK and right now the Enys Gardens is resplendent with bluebells.

Estelle lives close to Gyllyngvase Beach. This is the perfect weather for long walks, plenty of good reading, pots of tea and cozy evenings.

We are both in our eighties now, although, if you count my actual birthdays on the leap years, it makes me nineteen years old. This was my age when I met Estelle. So in effect I am taking up from where I left off. Estelle tells me I have become rather juvenile in my old age. I was an old man in my youth, which surely entitles me to youth in my old age, don't you think? Estelle, on the other hand, has mellowed like a rather fine wine. She is doing serious writing while I dabble in children's stories. Right now I am writing the story of two ants, Elo and Jhelo, and their adventures on a boat, complete with pen and ink illustrations done by Nitin. Nitin—who inspired the book—is eager to get a copy for his granddaughter. He is retired and settled in Chandanagore and has made quite a name for himself as the cartoonist for the local paper.

My school in Silchar is running effortlessly. Estelle's niece,

Bridgette Olson—James's daughter—has taken a keen interest. Our teachers' training institute is one of the best in the country. We have a fine hostel and provide free accommodation to single women, mostly Hindu widows and spinsters who have enrolled in our teaching program.

Estelle and I plan to return to India in early fall. We will spend the Christmas season in the tea plantations of Aynakhal with Layla.

I am pleased to know you will visit Silchar to see the new vocation center. Chaya will take good care of you all. This is a splendid time of year when the flame trees are in full bloom. There are many dreams I have realized in my life, maiyya, *but planting the flame trees have given me the greatest joy of all.*

Yours,
Dada

*****

A Note to Readers

I believe it is the land that shapes its people. My ancestors migrated from Sylhet in East Bengal—now Bangladesh—to Assam several generations ago. The Bengal and Assam settings for *Flame Tree Road* are entirely fictitious, constructed mostly from imagination and stories I have heard. I used the vast riverine delta of East Bengal with its ever-changing waterways, its monsoons, floods and famine to set the mood for this novel. The unpredictability of life in these parts creates a certain restlessness and a sense of fatality in the mind-set of the people. This is echoed in the lonely, haunting songs of the river boatman. As a child I learned these folk songs from my father. He hummed them in the morning as he laced his canvas boots getting ready for *kamjari*—field supervision—in the tea plantations where he worked as a manager. I have carried these river songs in my heart to distant worlds; they are embedded in my blood.

It was a deliberate decision on my part not to revisit the places I was writing about. New sensory experiences have a way of overriding imagination, sometimes to its detriment. As a result the elusive dream-like quality I wanted to capture in my storytelling would have been lost.

I am often asked if the character of Biren Roy—Dadamoshai in *Teatime for the Firefly*—was inspired by a real person. The answer is no. Biren Roy is an amalgamation of several enlightened thinkers of India. I constructed his character drawing from the lives and teachings of Rabindranath Tagore, Gandhi, Vivekananda, Ramakrishna and Sri Aurobindo, among others. Doing my research, I was deeply humbled by the immense spiritual wealth our great teachers have bestowed on us. Surely in this treasure trove of wisdom are the keys to a peaceful, more unified world.

Shona Patel
Fountain Hills, Arizona
October 2014

Acknowledgments

As usual my debts are substantial.

Thanks to all my readers who loved *Teatime for the Firefly* and encouraged me to write another novel. This book is for you. My heartfelt appreciation goes to Barbara Peters of Poisoned Pen Bookstore, for being my passionate champion and holding *Teatime* up to the world.

Special thanks to Emily Ohanjanians, my talented editor at MIRA Books, who was quick to grasp the essence of the story in all my incoherent ramblings and coax it out with sensitivity, insight and intelligence.

To April Eberhardt, literary agent extraordinaire, my deepest gratitude. She pulled me out of the weeds and kept me buoyed with endless doses of optimism and unconditional faith. She is my secret ally and a dear friend.

To Mimi Dutt and Mithoo (Mothy) Wadia, my love. They were with me from the very beginning and I counted on their honest, unfiltered feedback every step of the way. They know me better than I know myself and I would be completely lost without them.

I was halfway through my first draft when I met the delightfully quirky and quintessentially English Paul Tucker, who has more stories, trivia and knowledge in his head than several bookshelves. I am grateful to him for his openhearted sharing. Also to Roisin Hannon for her research and story details for the Cambridge Union Society section. To Priscilla Myers, Rae Iverson, Davey Lamont and Dr. Mickey Wadia for their thoughtful inputs on early drafts.

With all my love to Vinoo Patel, who handles my thrills, throes and constant woes with characteristic aplomb. I can never adequately express my gratitude for his sweet, caring presence in my life. Thank you!

FLAME TREE ROAD

SHONA PATEL

Reader's Guide

What was the inspiration for this story?

The initial prompt for telling Biren Roy's story came from my readers. After the publication of Teatime for the Firefly, *many readers wrote to say how much they loved the character of Layla's grandfather, Dadamoshai—Biren Roy in this book—and wished they could learn more about him. I had not written* Teatime *intending to write a prequel, but luckily for me, there were several open leads I could use to recreate Biren Roy's backstory. It was a formidable task to delve into the past of a fictitious character and imagine the life events that might have shaped his inner journey. I based the story on the belief that some people arrive at their inner peace and wisdom only by transcending great personal tragedy. As Shamol says in* Flame Tree Road, *sometimes one has to lose everything to renew and bloom again. I imagined Biren Roy to be that kind of person.*

The story explores many different themes. Was there a particular theme that was close to your heart, that you enjoyed exploring most?

I am fascinated by the role of human conscience in a moral or ethical dilemma. I want to understand why a person makes a certain choice and how the consequences affect his life and ultimately reshape his character.

I am also deeply interested in social and political issues that collectively affect the mind-set of a society. It becomes impossible to judge a race or religion when viewed in the context of its cultural history. Nothing is simple, or black-and-white. I like to understand the issues from different sides.

Is there a character in the story that you identify with? Or a favorite character among the varied cast?

I am deeply invested in all my characters, both major and minor, and I don't really have a favorite. I create specific characters to act as foils to my main character or to further my story. It is crucial for me to have a firm grip on my characters. I must intimately "know" them and see them clearly to be able to write about them. Without my characters I don't have a story.

What kind of research went into writing *Flame Tree Road*?

In a nutshell: extensive, involved and far, far more than what you ultimately see in the novel. I am not comfortable unless I am sitting on a huge bedrock of research to even begin to write. I find too little research makes my writing flat. Only when I have enough matter to play with can I paint with finer strokes and greater control. Besides written material, I rely on visual and auditory sources: movies of the period, videos, photos, paintings, music, even actual objects. To write about a striking cobra I have to watch a video to see how high it rears up and hear the actual "growl" in its throat. To write about death I have to hear the actual death rattle of a dying person—yes, it's all on YouTube; very disturbing and not recommended. Even to describe a caterpillar crawling on a windowsill, I research to make sure it is the right species of caterpillar that eats the leaves of the Bramley apple trees. You have no idea how obsessive I am!

What was the most challenging part of writing this book? What was the most enjoyable?

The most challenging—and terrifying—part of writing this book was the idea of writing a second book in the first place! I had written my first book at my own pace and own time and I had no idea what a writer's life really entailed. Suddenly there were interviews, public appearances, deadlines, self-imposed expectations, acute self-doubt and fear of judgment and failure. I had no clue what the story of the second book would be. Even after working out some kind of outline I was all over place. There were false starts, dead ends, bouts of howling—just ask my husband!—and a frozen shoulder that most likely resulted from a frozen brain. I finally had to calm down and get centered so I could write the novel, and voilà! Here I am!

I really enjoy the revision process because I love problem solving. I like to understand where the holes are in the story and figure out ways to fix them. Seeing a book evolve to its final form in the editing process is very thrilling for me.

What do you hope your readers will take away from this novel?

I hope this novel gives my readers new insights into a foreign culture. Many Westerners—I hate to say—have a very simplistic understanding of Indian society. The caste system, arranged marriages, joint families, superstition, religion and rituals, no matter how seemingly backward and barbaric, have all evolved for societal reasons. To understand why they prevail one must understand the history and culture of the people. I hope my novel prompts open discussion. If my story brings my reader to a new place of empathy and understanding, I will have done my job as a writer.

Can you describe your writing process? Do you tend to outline first or dive right in and figure out the details as you go along?

My writing process is chaotic and messy and I would not recommend it to any writer. Typically I don't begin with an outline, and even if I do, I almost never know which way my story will go once I start writing. On the other hand I usually have a clear idea for my main character. Besides character, I must also have a clear idea for the setting of my story, which is usually a place of geographical and historical interest, preferably one I am familiar with. The plot and the minor characters all unfold in the writing process itself. My first draft is the sacrificial goat—a pathetic animal that makes sad bleating noises. This is hacked to pieces amid much hair tearing and breast-beating. My near and dear ones all flee during this period. When the dust settles and if I am very, very lucky, a few threads of the story begin to emerge. After that it is all work. I am ruthless with my revisions and have no qualms about throwing massive chunks of the novel out if it does not fit the story. I am never happy with the end result and the danger is I can nitpick a story to its demise. Thank God for deadlines as this forces me to give up the manuscript.

Can you tell us anything about what you're working on right now?

Writing the third novel is an intimidating thought. The old terror creeps up, but I think I am getting more savvy, more blasé or wise—call it what you will. I am toying with the idea of going back to the tea plantations of Assam as the setting for my third novel. There is an old comfort in writing about what I know. I may explore the Jimmy O'Connor story. He was the oddball Irish tea planter in Teatime for the Firefly, *a very interesting multidimensional character. Again there will be social and cultural themes embedded in the story. But I will need to take a break and clear my head before I jump in.*

1. Shamol Roy is a decent, gentle man and a loving husband and father. Biren seems to have a lot of the same traits when he grows up, marries and has a family of his own. What are the similarities between them, and what are the differences? Do you think this is a result of nature or nurture?

2. Sammy Deb is a spoiled rich boy who gets every last thing handed to him. In the end, he is happy and content to be a husband and father. What do you make of his character and his journey?

3. Biren spends his whole life fighting for women, and yet he suffers the loss of almost every woman he loves. Why do you think the author made this choice, and what significance does it seem to have to the story?

4. Shibani, Estelle and Maya are the most important influences on Biren's life and ambitions for female equality. But they are not the only characters who influence him. Who are some of the minor characters who play a significant role?

5. What are the differences between Estelle and Maya? What are the differences between the relationships Biren has with each? Who is better suited to him and why?

6. Biren describes Estelle as reminding him of his mother when his father was still alive. What are the similarities between the characters of Estelle and Shibani? What are the differences? Do you think these affected Biren's feelings toward Estelle?

7. When Biren meets the potter, the old man says, "Without the blessings of your ancestors and the roots of your community, a man can lose himself." Do you agree? What do you think of this statement in relation to Biren's journey to find himself?

8. The title and the story make much of the flame tree. What is the significance of this motif for you as a reader?

9. Nitin cares for Shibani in her old age; Mitra adopts Layla; Samaresh and Sammy have secure jobs when they return home from England. On the other hand, Shamol's brother shirks work and deprives his younger sibling of an education, and Maya and Moni do not receive individual care when crowded together with other relatives in their village home. What are the pros and cons of the joint family system?

10. Biren is a practical man who likes to work with his hands and see tangible results. What makes him different from the Calcutta/Cambridge armchair intellectuals?

11. Why is the widow's hand-painted bookmark significant to the story?

12. At Maya's insistence Biren goes to Calcutta to fulfill his dream. Was that a wise decision? Did Biren's ambition override his concern for Maya?